The Second Ruth Rendell Omnibus

RUTH RENDELL is crime fiction at its very best. Her first novel, *From Doon With Death*, appeared in 1964, and since then her reputation and readership have grown steadily with each new book. She has received ten major awards for her work: three Edgars from the Mystery Writers of America; the Crime Writers' Gold Dagger Award for 1976's best crime novel for *A Demon In My View*; the Arts Council National Book Award for Genre Fiction in 1981 for *Lake of Darkness*; the Crime Writers' Gold Dagger Award for 1986's best crime novel for *Live Flesh*; in 1987 the Crime Writers' Gold Dagger Award for *A Fatal Inversion* and in 1991 the same award for *King Solomon's Carpet*, both written under the name of Barbara Vine; the *Sunday Times* Literary Award in 1990; and in 1991 the Crime Writers' Cartier Diamond Award for outstanding contribution to the genre. Her books are translated into 21 languages.

Ruth Rendell bestsellers
from Arrow Books

INSPECTOR WEXFORD STORIES

The Best Man to Die
From Doon with Death
A Guilty Thing Surprised
Kissing the Gunner's Daughter
Means of Evil and Other Stories
Murder Being Once Done
A New Lease of Death
No More Dying Then
Put on by Cunning
The Ruth Rendell Mysteries
Shake Hands Forever

A Sleeping Life
Some Lie and Some Die
The Speaker of Mandarin
An Unkindness of Ravens
The Veiled One
Wolf to the Slaughter.
The Second Wexford Omnibus
The Third Wexford Omnibus
The Fourth Wexford Omnibus
Wexford: An Omnibus

OTHER NOVELS AND SHORT STORIES

Collected Short Stories
The Ruth Rendell Omnibus
The Bridesmaid
The Copper Peacock
The Crocodile Bird
A Demon in My View
The Face of Trespass
The Fallen Curtain
  and Other Stories
The Fever Tree
  and Other Stories
Going Wrong
Heartstones
A Judgement in Stone

The Lake of Darkness
Live Flesh
Make Death Love Me
Master of the Moor
The New Girlfriend
  and Other Stories
One Across, Two Down
The Secret House of Death
Talking to Strange Men
To Fear a Painted Devil
The Tree of Hands
Vanity Dies Hard
The Killing Doll

The Second
RUTH
RENDELL
Omnibus

TO FEAR A PAINTED DEVIL
VANITY DIES HARD
THE SECRET HOUSE OF DEATH

Ruth Rendell

ARROW

Published by Arrow Books in 1994

1 3 5 7 9 10 8 6 4 2

© Kingsmarkham Enterprises Ltd. 1993

Ruth Rendell has asserted her right under the Copyright,
Designs and Patents Act, 1988 to be identified as the
author of this work

This omnibus first published in the United Kingdom
by Hutchinson, 1993

To Fear a Painted Devil
First published in 1965 by John Lang

Vanity Dies Hard
First published in 1966
by Hutchinson & Co. (Publishers) Ltd

The Secret House of Death
First published in 1968
by Hutchinson & Co. (Publishers) Ltd

Arrow Books Limited
Random House, 20 Vauxhall Bridge Road, London, SW1V 2SA

Random House Australia (Pty) Limited
20 Alfred Street, Milsons Point, Sydney,
New South Wales 2061, Australia

Random House New Zealand Limited
18 Poland Road, Glenfield
Auckland 10, New Zealand

Random House South Africa (Pty) Limited
PO Box 337, Bergvlei, South Africa

Random House UK Limited Reg. No. 954009

ISBN 0 09 936301 1

Printed and bound in Great Britain by
The Guernsey Press Co. Ltd, Guernsey, Channel Islands

Contents

TO FEAR A
PAINTED DEVIL

**For
Margaret and Cyril Rabs
with love**

Prologue

He was nine. It was his first morning in England and he began to wonder if all English houses were like this one, large yet with small rooms, full of things that no-one could use: armless statues, vases with lids to them, curtains as immoveably draped as one of his mother's evening gowns.

They had arrived the night before and he had passed through the hall wrapped in a blanket and carried in his father's arms. He remembered only the great front door, a heavy wooden door with a picture of a tree on it in coloured glass. They had left him to sleep as long as he would and someone had brought breakfast for him on a tray. Now as he descended the stairs, crossing the half-landing which a bronze soldier guarded with his lance, he saw the hall below him and his steps faltered.

It was a fine morning but the room looked as rooms do at twilight, dim and still. Instead of being papered the walls were hung with embroideries stretched on frames, and between them curtains that covered – what? Windows? Doors? It seemed to him that they covered things people were not supposed to see. There was a single mirror with a wooden frame and this frame, of carved and polished red wood, looked as if it had grown branches of its own, for strips of wood shaped into leaves and twigs twined across the glass.

Within this mirror he could see not himself but an open door reflected and beyond it the beginning of the garden. The door stood wide and he went through it, seeking the garden where he knew the sun must be shining. Then he saw the picture. He stood quite still and he stared at it.

It was a painting of a lady in an old-fashioned dress of striped silk, bright blue and gold, with a little gold cap on her head. She was holding a silver plate and in the plate was the head of a man.

He knew it must be a very good painting because the

artist had made it look so real. Nothing was left out, not even the blood in the plate and the white tube things in the man's neck where it had been cut from his body.

The lady wasn't looking at the thing in the plate but at him. She was smiling and there was a strange expression on her face, dreamy, triumphant, replete. He had never seen such a look in anyone's eyes before but suddenly he knew with an intuition that had in it something of an *a priori* knowledge, that grown-ups sometimes looked at each other like that and that they did so out of the sight of children.

He tore his eyes from the picture and put his hand up to his mouth to stop them hearing his scream. Then he rushed blindly away, making for the glass place that separated this room from the garden.

He stumbled at the step and put out his hand to save himself. It touched something cool and soft – but only for a moment. The coolness and softness were succeeded by a terrible burning pain that seemed to smite him exactly like the shock he had had from his mother's electric iron.

Away in the garden someone laughed. He screamed and screamed and screamed until he heard doors banging, feet flying, the women coming to him from the kitchen.

PART ONE

1

'Prussic acid?' The chemist was startled. He had been a member of the Pharmaceutical Society for ten years and this was the first time anyone had made such a request to him. Not that he would grant it. He was a responsible citizen, almost – in his own estimation – a doctor. 'Cyanide of Potassium?' He looked severely at the small man in the suit that was too dark and too thick for a hot day. 'What d'you want that for?'

Edward Carnaby, for his part, was affronted. Mr. Waller was only a chemist, a pharmacist really, not a proper chemist who worked in a laboratory. Everyone knew that doctors poked their noses into one's affairs, trying to find out things that were no business of theirs, but not chemists. You asked for what you wanted – razor blades or shaving cream or a camera film – and the chemist gave it to you. He wrapped it up and you paid for it. When all was said and done Waller was only a shopkeeper.

'I want it for killing wasps. I've got a wasp nest on the wall of my house under the roof.'

He fidgeted uneasily under Waller's accusing gaze. The fan on the ceiling, instead of cooling the shop, was only blowing the hot air about.

'May I have your name, please?'

'What for? I don't have to have a prescription for it, do I?'

Waller ignored the sarcasm. Responsible professional men must not allow themselves to be ruffled by cheap cracks.

'What gave you the idea of cyanide?' As he spoke the curtain of coloured plastic strips that hung across the entrance to the dispensary parted and Linda Gaveston came out in her pink overall. Her appearance angered Edward, partly because she looked so cool, partly because he felt that a girl whose parents lived on Linchester had no business to be working as an assistant in a chemist's shop. She smiled at him vaguely. Edward snapped:

'If you must know, I read about it in a gardening book.'

Plausible, Waller thought.

'Rather an old-fashioned book, surely? These days we get rid of wasps by using a reliable vespicide.' He paused, allowing the unfamiliar word to sink in. 'One that is harmless to warm-blooded . . .'

'All right,' Edward interrupted him. He wasn't going to make a scene in front of one of those snooty Gavestons. 'Why didn't you say so before? I'll take it. What's it called?'

'Vesprid.' Waller shot him a last baleful look and turned round, but the girl – showing off, Edward thought – was already holding the tin towards him. 'Two and eleven.'

'Thanks,' Edward said shortly, taking the penny change.

'The instructions are enclosed.'

Linda Gaveston lifted her shoulders slightly and slipped between the waving strips in the way she had seen a night club girl insinuate herself through a bead curtain on television.

'There goes a nut,' she said to Waller when Edward had gone. 'He lives near us.'

'Really?' Like all the shopkeepers in Chantflower village Waller had a great respect for Linchester. Money flowed from it as from a spring of sweet water. 'Not quite what one has been led to expect.' He watched Edward get into his salesman's car, its back seat full of cardboard boxes. 'It takes all sorts,' he said.

On that hot afternoon Freda Carnaby was the only Linchester housewife who was really working and she was not a wife at all. She was cleaning the windows in the single living room of Edward's chalet partly because she was houseproud and partly because it was a good excuse for watching the cars coming round The Circle. Linchester business men kept short hours and the man she was looking for might be early. He would wave, even perhaps stop and renew his promise to see her later, and he would notice afresh how efficient she was, how womanly. Moreover he would see that she could look smart and pretty not only in the evenings but also with a wash leather in her hand.

Considering who she was looking for it was ironic that the first car to appear was Tamsin Selby's. Even if you didn't see the number plate (SIN 1A) you would know it was Tamsin's Mini because, although it was new, its black body and white roof were already marked with raindrops and with dust, and the back seat was full of leaves and twigs, rubbish from the fields. Freda pursed her lips in happy disapproval. If you had money and you bought nice things (what that monogram of a number plate must have cost!) you ought to take care of them.

Dr. Greenleaf's car followed fast on her tail. It was time, Freda considered, that he bought a new one. A doctor, she had read in one of her magazines, was nowadays the most respected member of a community, and therefore had appearances to keep up. She smiled and bobbed her head. She thought the doctor's kindly grin meant he was grateful to her for being so healthy and not taking up his surgery time.

By the time Joan Smith-King arrived with her shooting brake full of the Linchester children she had fetched from school, Freda had finished the window.

'All delivered in plain vans,' Joan said cheerfully. 'Den says I ought to have a C licence.'

'Can I go to tea with Peter?' Cheryl called. 'Can I, Auntie Free? Please.'

'If you're sure she's no trouble,' Freda said. Cheryl might be only a salesman's daughter, but she had nice manners. She, Freda, had seen to that. But going out to tea was a nuisance. Now Cheryl would come rushing in at seven just when Freda wanted to be relaxed and ready with coffee cups on the best traycloth, paper napkins and sherry in a decanter.

'Ghastly these wasps.' Joan looked up at the chalet roof where the wasps were dribbling out from under the eaves. 'Tamsin said Patrick got a nasty sting on his hand.'

'Did he?' Freda took her eyes from Joan's face and stared innocently at the hedge. 'Don't be late,' she said to Cheryl. Joan moved off, one hand on the wheel, the other pulling Jeremy off Peter, shoving her daughter Susan into Cheryl's lap. The baby in its carry-cot on the front seat began to cry. Freda went round the back and into the spotless kitchen.

She was re-doing her face from the little *cache* of cosmetics she kept in a drawer when she heard Edward's car draw up on the drive. The front door slammed.

'Free?'

She bustled into the lounge. Edward was already at the record-player, starting up The Hall of the Mountain King.

'You might have shut the gates,' she said from the window, but she didn't press the point. A wife could expect small services, not a sister. A sister was only a housekeeper, a nanny to Edward's motherless daughter. Still . . . she cheered up. A couple of years and she might have a child of her own.

'How long till tea?'

'Five thirty sharp,' said Freda. 'I'm sure I never keep you waiting for your meals, Ted.'

'Only it's car maintenance at seven.'

Edward went to a different class each night. French on Mondays and Thursdays, accountancy on Tuesdays, carpentry on Wednesdays, car maintenance on Fridays. Freda approved his industry. It was a way, she supposed, of forgetting the wife who had lived just long enough to put the curtains up in the new house and who had died before the first instalment was due on the mortgage.

'What are you going to do?'

She shrugged. He was her brother, but he was also her twin and as jealous of her time as a husband might be.

'Sometimes,' he said, 'I wonder if you haven't got a secret boy-friend who pops in when I'm out of the way.'

Had there been talk, gossip? Well, why not? Only a few days now and everyone would know. Edward would know. Funny, but it made her shiver to think of it.

He turned the record over and straightened up. Solveig's Song, music for a cold climate, soared into the stuffy room. The pure voice pleased Freda, reminding her of large uncluttered rooms she had so far seen only from the outside as she passed with her shopping baskets. On the whole, she thought, she would like to live there. She wouldn't be squeamish. He loves me, she thought, not thinking of Edward. A long shudder of pain and anxious happiness travelled down from her shoulders and along her thighs to her feet in their tight pointed shoes.

'I wouldn't like that, Free,' he said. 'You're best off here with me.'

'We shall have to see what time brings forth, shan't we?' she said, staring through the diamond panes at Linchester, at ten more houses that encircled a green plot. How nice, how stimulating it would be next year to see it all from a different angle. When she turned round Edward was beside her, flicking his fingers in front of her face to break up the myopic stare.

'Don't,' she said. Hurt, he sat down and opened his homework book, *An Outline of Monetary Economics*. Freda went upstairs to lacquer her hair, straighten her stocking seams and spray a little more Fresh Mist under her arms.

Denholm Smith-King was used to performing small and, for that matter, large services for his wife. With five children he could hardly do otherwise. He was already at home when she arrived back, making what he called euphemistically 'a cup of tea'. In the Smith-King household this meant slicing and buttering a whole large loaf and carving up a couple of pound cakes.

'You're early,' she said.

'Not much doing.' He greeted Cheryl vaguely as if he was uncertain whether or not she was one of his own children. 'Things are a bit slack so I hied me to the bosom of my family.'

'Slack?' She found a tablecloth and spread it on what had once been a fine unblemished sheet of teak. 'I don't like the sound of that, Den. I'm always meaning to talk to you about the business. . . .'

'Did you find anyone to sit in with the mob tomorrow night?' he asked, adroitly changing the subject.

'Linda Gaveston said she'd come. I asked her when I was in Waller's.' Joan found the piece of pasteboard from the mêlée on the mantelpiece and read its message aloud: 'Tamsin and Patrick Selby At Home. Saturday, July 4th, eight p.m. Of course I know how affected Tamsin is, but At Home's going a bit far.'

'I reckon you can go as far as you like,' said Denholm, 'when you've got a private income and no kids.'

'It's only a birthday party. She's twenty-seven tomorrow.'

Denholm sat down heavily, a reluctant paterfamilias at the head of his table. 'Twenty-seven? I wouldn't have put her at a day over twenty.'

'Oh, don't be so silly, Den. They've been married for years.' She had been piqued by his admiration of another woman, but now she looked at him tenderly over their children's heads. 'Fancy being married for years to Patrick Selby!'

'I daresay it's all a matter of taste, old girl.'

'I don't know what it is,' Joan said, 'but he frightens me. I get the shivers every time I see him walking past here with that great German dog of his.' She wiped the baby's chin and sighed. 'It came in the garden again this morning. Tamsin was most apologetic. I'll grant her that. She's a nice enough girl in her way, only she always seems only half awake.'

'Pity they haven't got any kids,' Denholm said wistfully. Uncertain as to whether he was wishing children on to the Selbys from genuine regret for their childlessness or from motives of revenge, Joan gave him a sharp look.

'They're first cousins, you know.'

'Ah,' said Denholm, 'brought up together. One of those boy and girl things, was it?'

'I don't know,' said his wife. 'He's not likely to confide in anyone and she's far too much of the little girl lost.'

When tea was over the children drifted into the garden. Joan handed her husband a tea towel and began to wash up. Jeremy's scream made them both jump and before it had died away Denholm, who knew what it meant, was out on the lawn brandishing the stick he kept in the storm porch for this purpose.

Only Cheryl had not backed away. The other children clung to Denholm as he advanced between the swing and the sandpit.

'Get out of it, you great brute!'

The Weimaraner looked at him courteously but with a kind of mild disdain. There was nothing savage about her but nothing endearing either. She was too autocratic, too highly-bred for that. Haunch-deep in marigolds, she was standing in the middle of Denholm's herbaceous border and now, as he shouted at her again, she flicked out a raspberry pink tongue and delicately snapped off a larkspur blossom.

Cheryl caught at Denholm's hand. 'She's a nice dog, really she is. She often comes to our house.'

Her words meant nothing to Denholm but he dropped the stick. Insensitive as he was, he could hardly beat the dog in the presence of the woman who had appeared so suddenly and so silently on the lawn next door.

'Queenie often comes to our house,' Cheryl said again.

Tamsin Selby had heard. A spasm of pain crossed her smooth brown face and was gone.

'I'm so dreadfully sorry.' She smiled without showing her teeth. 'Please don't be cross, Denholm. She's very gentle.'

Denholm grinned foolishly. The Selbys, both of them, always made him feel a fool. It was the contrast, perhaps, between their immaculate garden and his own cluttered playground; their pale hand-stitched clothes and what he called his 'togs'; their affluence and his need.

'It puts the wind up the youngsters,' he said gruffly.

'Come on, Queenie!' The long brown arm rose languidly in an elegant parabola. At once the dog leaped, clearing the hedge with two inches to spare. 'I hope we'll see you tomorrow, Denholm?'

'You can count on us. Never miss a good booze-up.' He was embarrassed and he went in quickly. But Cheryl lingered, staring over the hedge with curious intelligent eyes and wondering why the lady who was so unlike Auntie Free had fallen to her knees under the willow tree and flung her arms round the dog's creamy sable neck.

2

Five years before when Nottinghamshire people talked about Linchester they meant the Manor and the park. If they were county they remembered garden parties, if not, coach trips to a Palladian house where you paid half-a-crown to look at a lot of valuable but boring china while the children rolled down the ha-ha. But all that came to an end when old Marvell died. One day, it seemed, the Manor was there, the next there were just the bulldozers Henry Glide brought over from the city and a great cloud of dust floating above the trees, grey and pancake-shaped, as if someone had exploded a small atom bomb.

Nobody would live there, they said, forgetting that commuting was the fashion even in the provinces. Henry himself had his doubts and he had put up three chalet bungalows before he realised he might be on to a better thing if he forgot all about retired farmers and concentrated on Nottingham company directors. Fortunately, but by the merest chance, the three mistakes were almost hidden by a screen of elms. He nearly lost his head and built big houses with small gardens all over the estate, but he had a cautious look at the Marvell contract and saw that there was an embargo on too much tree-felling. His wife thought he was getting senile when he said he was only going to put up eight more houses, eight beautiful architect-designed houses around a broad green plot with a pond in the middle.

And that was what people meant now when they talked about Linchester. They meant The Green with the pond where swans glided between lily leaves as big as dinner plates; The Circle which was a smart name for the road that ran around The Green; the Cotswold farmhouse and the mock-Tudor lodge, the Greenleafs' place that might have been prefabricated in Hampstead Garden Suburb and flown complete into Nottinghamshire, the Selbys' glass box and Glide's own suntrap bungalow. They pointed from the tops of buses on the Nottingham road at the Gavestons' pocket-sized grange, the Gages' Queen Anne and the Smith-King place that had started off as a house and now was just a breeding box. They criticised the chalets, those poor relations and their occupants, the Staxtons, the Macdonalds and the Carnabys.

The two men in the British Railways lorry lived in Newark and they had never been to Linchester before. Now, on the calmest, most beautiful evening of the summer, they saw it at its best. Yet it was not the loveliness of the place that impressed them, the elegant sweep of The

Circle, the stone pineapples on the pillars at the Manor gates, nor the trees, elms, oaks and sycamores, that gave each house its expensive privacy, but the houses themselves and their opulence.

Over-awed and at the same time suspicious, they drove between the pillars and into The Circle itself, looking for a house called Hallows.

The lorry rumbled along the road, making ruts in the melting tar and sending white spar chips flying, past the three mistakes, past Shalom, The Laurels, Linchester Lodge.

'That's the one I'd fancy,' said the driver, pointing to the Cotswold farmhouse with a hint of Swiss chalet in its jade-coloured balconies. 'If my pools come up.' His mate was silent, consumed with envy and with scorn.

'Keep your eyes open, Reg. It's gone knocking-off time.'

'Blimey,' said his mate, throwing his cigarette end into the Gavestons' rhododendrons, 'I haven't got X-ray eyes. It's half a mile up to them front doors, and what with the trees.'

'Now, I'd have them down. Keep out the light, they do. And I'd do something about that empty bit in the middle. You could put up a couple of nice bungalows where that pond is. Here we are. Hallows. I don't know what I brought you for. I could have done better on my tod.'

But he was glad of Reg's help when it came to unloading the parcel. It was heavy and, according to the label, fragile. Something like a door it was or a big mirror. He could just feel a frame thing through the corrugated cardboard.

They humped it up the drive between two rows of young willows until they came to the paved court in front of the house.

Hallows was beautiful – by most people's standards. Reg and the driver found it on the dull side compared with its ornate neighbours. This house was plain and rectangular, built of York stone and pale unpolished wood; there were no gables and no chimneys, no shutters and not a single pane of stained glass. The windows were huge, backed with white venetian blinds, and the front doors were swing affairs of glass set in steel.

'Are you looking for me?' The voice, delicate, vague,

unmistakeably upper-class, came from above their heads. The driver looked up to a long undecorated balcony and saw a woman leaning over the rails.

'British Railways, lady.'

'Too dreadful!' Tamsin Selby said. 'I'd forgotten all about it.'

It was true, she had. The delivery of this parcel had been planned in a sprightly, almost malicious mood, very different from her present one. But it had taken so long in coming, so much had happened. She disappeared through the balcony windows back into the bedroom.

'How the rich live,' Reg said to the driver. 'Forgotten, my foot!'

Tamsin came out to them breathlessly. At all costs it must be got in and, if possible, hidden, before Patrick came home. She tried to take it from them but the weight was too much for her. The men watched her efforts with a kind of triumph.

'Would you be terribly sweet,' Tamsin said, 'and carry it upstairs for me?'

'Now, look,' the driver began, 'it's heavy . . .'

She took two half-crowns from the bag she had snatched up in the hall.

'Can't leave it here, can we?' Reg was grinning reluctantly.

'So kind,' said Tamsin. She led the way and they followed her, carrying the parcel gingerly to avoid scraping the dove-grey hessian on the hall walls, the paint on the curled iron baluster rails.

'In here, I think.'

The room was too beautiful for them. Poverty, never admitted, scarcely felt before, scummed their hands with ineluctable dirt. They looked away from the velvet curtains, the dressing-table glass ringed with light bulbs, the half-open door that showed a glimpse of a shower cabinet and tiles hand-painted with fishes, and down at their own feet.

'Could you put it on one of the beds?'

They lowered it on to the nearer of the cream silk counterpanes, avoiding the bed by the window where the turned-back cover revealed a lemon lace nightgown folded between frilled nylon pillow and frilled nylon sheet.

'Thank you so much. It won't be in the way here.'

She didn't even bother to smooth the silk where a corner of the parcel had ruffled it, but signed her name quickly and hustled them out of the house. After they had gone she closed the spare bedroom door and sighed deeply. Patrick would be home any minute now and she had meant to use those spare moments checking on everything, making sure she looked her best.

She went into the bedroom with the balcony and looked at herself in the glass. That was all right, just the way Patrick liked her to look, the way he had liked her to look once . . . The sun – she had spent most of the day in the sun – had done wonders for her already brown skin and had faintly bleached her dark honey hair. No make-up. To have put on lipstick would have been to spoil the image she liked to create, the facsimile of a smooth teak-coloured mask, straight nose, carved lips, cheekbones that were arched polished planes.

Her hair hung quite straight on to her brown shoulders. Even for him she refused to cut it short and have it set. The dress – that was all right at any rate. Patrick hated bright colours and this one was black and white. Plain as it was, she knew there might be something too casual about it, too suggestive of a uniform for emancipated women. O God, she thought, making a face at her own image and wishing for the first time in her life that it could be transmuted into the reflection of a brisk blonde *hausfrau*.

Downstairs the table was already laid for dinner: two place mats of blue linen – he had made her give up using the big damask cloths – black Prinknash plates, a long basket of French bread, Riesling dewed from the refrigerator. Tamsin gasped aloud when she saw that she had forgotten to throw away the vaseful of grasses. She grabbed them, scattering brown seeds, and rushed to the kitchen. The dog now, had she fed the dog?

'Queenie!'

How many times in the past months had he scolded her for failing to feed the dog on the dot of five? How many times had he snapped at her for wasting her days dreaming in the garden and the fields, learning country lore from

Crispin Marvell, when she should have been at home keeping up with the Gages and the Gavestons.

But she must have done it and, in her panic, forgotten all about it. The plate of congealing horsemeat and biscuit meal was still on the floor, untouched by the dog. Flies buzzed over it and a single wasp crawled across a chunk of fat.

'Queenie!'

The bitch appeared silently from the garden door, sniffed at the food and looked enquiringly at Tamsin with mournful eyes. She is the only thing that we have together now, Tamsin thought, the only thing that we both love, Kreuznacht Konigin, that we both call Queenie. She dropped to her knees and in her loneliness she put her arms round Queenie's neck, feeling the suede-smooth skin against her own cheek. Queenie's tail flapped and she nuzzled against Tamsin's ear.

Of the two female creatures desirous of pleasing Patrick it was the dog who heard him first. She stiffened and the swinging lethargic tail began to wag excitedly, banging against the cooker door and making a noise like a gong.

'Master,' Tamsin said. 'Go, find him!'

The Weimaraner stretched her lean body, cocked her head and stood for a moment poised, much as her ancestors had done listening for the huntsman's command in the woods of Thuringia a century ago. The heavy garage door rumbled and fell with a faint clang. Queenie was away, across the patio, leaping for the iron gate that shut off the drive.

Tamsin followed, her heart pounding.

He came in slowly, not looking at her, silent, his attention given solely to the dog. When he had fondled Queenie, his hands drawing down the length of her body, he looked up and saw his wife.

Tamsin had so much to say, so many endearments remembered from the days when it was necessary to say nothing. No words came. She stood there, looking at him, her hands kneading the black and white stuff of her dress. Swinging the ignition key, Patrick pushed past her, shied at a wasp that dived against his face, and went into the house.

'She hasn't eaten her dinner,' were the first words that he spoke to her. He hated dirt, disorder, matter in the wrong place. 'It's all over flies.'

Tamsin picked up the plate and dropped the contents into the waste disposal unit. Meat juice rubbed off on to her fingers. Patrick looked pointedly at her hand, turned and went upstairs. She ran the tap, rinsed her fingers. It seemed an age since he had gone – the wine, would it get too warm? Ought she to put it back in the fridge? She waited, the sweat seeping into her dress. Presently she switched on the fan.

At last he came in wearing terylene slacks and a tee shirt of pale striped cotton, and he looked handsome if you admired men with ash-blond hair and freckles so dense that they looked like tan.

'I thought you'd like melon,' she said. 'It's canteloupe.'

Suspiciously Patrick skimmed away the melting golden sugar.

'Not honey, is it? You know I hate honey.'

'Of course it isn't.' She paused timidly. 'Darling,' she said.

He made his way silently through chicken salad, potato sticks, fruit salad (all good hygienic food from tins and packets and deep freezers), eating sparingly, absent-mindedly. The fan whirred and Queenie lay beneath it, paws spread, tongue extended.

'I've got everything in for the party,' Tamsin said.

'Party?'

'Tomorrow. It's my birthday. You hadn't forgotten?'

'No, it slipped my mind, that's all.'

Had it also slipped his mind to get her a present?

'There's heaps to do,' she said brightly. 'The lights to put up, and we've got to move the furniture in the –' Now it was more than ever important to pick the right word, '– the lounge in case it rains. And – Oh, Patrick, could you do something about the wasps? I'm sure there's a nest somewhere.' She remembered belatedly and reached for his hand. The fingers lay inert in hers, the big red swelling showing at the base of his thumb. 'Too frightful for you. How's it been today?'

'The sting? Oh, all right. It's going down.'

'Could you possible try to get rid of them? They'll ruin the party.'

He pushed away his plate and his half-finished glass of wine.

'Not tonight. I'm going out.'

She had begun to tremble and when she spoke her voice shook.

'There's so much to do. Please don't go, darling. I need you.'

Patrick laughed. She didn't look at him but sat staring at her plate, moving the viscous yellow juice about with her spoon.

'I *am* going out. I have to take the dog, don't I?'

'I'll take the dog.'

'Thank you very much,' he said icily. 'I can manage.' He touched the venetian blind and glanced at the faint patina of dust on his fingertips. 'If you're bored there are things here which could do with some attention.'

'Patrick.' Her face had paled and there were goose pimples on her arms. 'About what you said last night – you've got to change your mind. You've got to forget all about it' With a great effort she pushed three words from stiff lips: 'I love you.'

She might not have spoken. He walked into the kitchen and took the leash from the broom cupboard.

'Queenie!'

From deep sleep the Weimaraner galvanised into impassioned life. Patrick fastened the steel clip to her collar and led her out through the french windows.

Tamsin sat among the ruins of her meal. Presently she began to cry silently, the tears splashing into the wine glass she held in her cupped hands. Her mouth was dry and she drank. I am drinking my own sorrow, she thought. Five minutes, ten minutes passed. Then she went to the front door and out into the willow avenue. The sky was clear, azure above, violet and apricot on the horizon, thronged with wheeling swallows.

She stopped at the end of the drive and leaned on the gate. Patrick hadn't gone far. She could see him standing with his back to her on The Green staring down at the waters of the pond. The dog had tried, unsuccessfully as always, to intimidate the three white swans. Now she had given up and was following a squirrel trail, pausing at the foot of each tree and peering up into the branches. Patrick was waiting for something, whiling away his time. For what?

As she watched him, a pale green Ford swung into view from behind the elms. That funny little salesman fellow from the chalets, she thought, on his way to his evening class. She hoped he'd pass on with a wave but he didn't. He stopped. Few men passed Tamsin Selby without a second glance.

'Hot enough for you?'

'I like it,' Tamsin said. What was his name? Only one chalet dweller was known to her by name. 'I love the sun.'

'Ah well, it suits you. I can see that.'

Conversation would have to be made. She opened the gate and went over to the car. He mistook her action and opened the door.

'Can I give you a lift? I'm going to the village.'

'No. No, thanks.' Tamsin almost laughed. 'I'm not going out. Just enjoying the evening.'

His face fell.

'As a matter of fact,' he said, stalling, trying to keep her with him long enough for the neighbours to see him talking to the beautiful Mrs. Selby, 'as a matter of fact I'm playing truant. Supposed to be doing a little job exterminating pests.'

'Pests?'

'Wasps. We've got a nest.'

'Have you? So have we.' She looked up. Patrick was still there. 'My husband – we want to get rid of them but we don't know how.'

'I've got some stuff. It's called Vesprid. I tell you what. When I've done mine I'll bring the tin round. There's bags of it, enough to kill all the wasps in Nottinghamshire.'

'But how kind!'

'I'll bring it round in the morning, shall I?'

Tamsin sighed. Now she would have to have this wretched man in the way while she was preparing for the party.

'Look, why don't you come to a little do I'm having, a few friends in for drinks at about eight?' He looked at her adoringly and his eyes reminded her of Queenie's. 'If you could come early we could do the wasps then. Bring a friend if you like.'

A party at Hallows! A party at the biggest house on Linchester! Putting on his maudlin widower's voice, he said: 'I haven't been to a party since I lost my wife.'

'Really?' A chord had been struck. 'His wife's dead,' Patrick had said, 'and that's why . . .' What had she done? 'I'm sorry but I don't think I know your name.'

'Carnaby. Edward Carnaby.'

He looked at her, smiling. She took her hand from the car door and pressed it against her breastbone, breathing like one who has run up a steep hill.

Trust Tamsin Selby to be talking to a man, Joan thought, as she came out of her gate, holding Cheryl by the hand.

'Wave to your Daddy.'

The child was more interested in the man and the dog on The Green. Telling herself that she had meant to go that way in any case, Joan followed her reluctantly.

Patrick had never been one to waste words on the weather or other people's health. His eyes, which had been fixed with a kind of calculating disgust on Edward Carnaby, now turned upon Joan, taking in the details of her limp cotton dress, her sunburned arms and the brown roots of her hair where the rinse was growing out.

'Isn't it *hot*?' She was uncomfortable in his presence and felt the remark had been foolish. In fact, it was no longer particularly hot. A faint breeze was stirring the waters of the pond, ruffling it to match the mackerel sky.

'I don't know why English people make a cult of grumbling about the weather,' he said. He looked very Teutonic as he spoke and she remembered someone had told her he had spent his childhood in Germany and America. She laughed awkwardly and made a grab for Cheryl's hand. He had made it so clear he didn't want to talk to her that she jumped and blushed when he called her back.

'How's business?'

'Business?' Of course he meant Denholm's business, the factory. 'All right, I suppose,' she said, and then because ever since before tea there had been a vague, half-formed worry nagging at her mind, 'Den says things have been a bit slack lately.'

'We can't all get Harwell contracts.' He touched the trunk of a great oak and with a small smile looked up into its branches. 'They don't grow on trees. It's a matter of work, my dear Joan, work and single-mindedness. Denholm will have to watch his step or I'll be taking him over one of these days.'

She said nothing. Malice quirked the corners of his thin mouth. She looked away from him and at the dog. Then she saw that he, too, was staring in the same direction.

'Expansion is life,' he said. 'Give it a few months and then we'll make things hum.'

Shivering a little, she drew back from him, feeling a sudden chill that seemed to come not from the scurrying wind but from the man himself.

'We're late, Cheryl. It's past your bedtime.'

'She can come with me,' said Patrick, his curious smile broadening. 'I'm going that way.'

The green Ford had moved away from the Hallows gate but Tamsin was still there, watching. As the man and child walked off towards the chalets, Joan suddenly thought she would go and speak to Tamsin, demand the explanation she knew Patrick would never give to her. But Tamsin, she saw, was in no mood for talking. Something or someone had upset her and she was retreating up the willow drive, her head bent and her hands clenched beneath her chin. Joan went home and put the children to bed. When she came downstairs Denholm was asleep. He looked so like Jeremy, his eyes lightly closed, his cheek pink and smooth against the bunched-up cushion, that she hadn't the heart to wake him.

Edward Carnaby kept on turning back and waving all the way down to the Manor gates. Tamsin stared after him, unable to smile in return. Her knees felt weak and she was afraid she might faint. When she reached the house she heard Queenie bark, a single staccato bark followed by a howl. The howls went on for a few seconds; then they stopped and all was silent. Tasmin knew what the howls meant. Patrick had tied up the dog to go into someone's house.

She went upstairs and into the balcony room. In the faint bloom on the dressing-table Patrick had written with a precise finger: Dust this. She fell on the bed and lay face-downwards.

Half an hour had passed when she heard the footsteps and at first she thought they were Patrick's. But whoever it was was coming alone. There was no accompanying tip-tap of dog's claws on stone. O God, she thought, I shall have to tell him. Otherwise Patrick might, there in front of everyone at the party.

The doors were unlocked. There was nothing to stop him coming in, but he didn't. He knocked with the prearranged signal. What would he do when he knew it all? There was still a chance she could persuade Patrick. She put her fingers in her ears, willing him to go. He knocked again and it seemed to her that he must hear through glass and wood, stone walls and thick carpets, the beating of her heart.

At last he went away.

'Damnation!' she heard him say from beneath her as if he were looking through the lounge window. The footsteps hurried away down the avenue and out through the footpath on to the Nottingham road. The gate swung, failed to catch and flapped against the post, bang, swing, bang. Tamsin went into the room where the men had put the parcel. She broke her nails untying the string but she was crying too much to notice.

3

There are perhaps few things more galling to one's *amour propre* than to act in a covert, clandestine way when no such discretion is necessary. Oliver Gage was a proud man and now, creeping round the Hallows paths, tapping signals on the glass doors, he felt that someone had made a fool of him.

'Damnation!' he said, this time under his breath.

She had obviously gone out with *him*. Pressure had been put on her. Well, so much the better if that meant she had been preparing the ground. He would make his intentions clear at the party.

He went out into The Circle and made the humiliating detour necessary before he could find his car that he had parked on the ride off the main road. When he entered Linchester for the second time that night it was by the Manor gates and he drove into his own garage drive with a sense of disgruntled virtue and the shame he always felt when he returned to his house. Oliver lived in one of the largest houses on Linchester but it was too small for him. He hated it already. Every Friday night when he came up from his four days in London the sight of the house, magnified perhaps in his mind during his absence, sickened him and reminded him afresh of his misfortunes. For, as Oliver grew older, the sizes of his houses diminished. This was not due to a reversal in his financial life. One of the executives of a national daily, his income now topped the seven thousand mark, but only about a third of this found its way into Oliver's pocket. The rest, never seen by him yet never forgotten, streamed away via an army of solicitors and bank managers and accountants into the laps of his two discarded wives.

When he had married Nancy – pretty, witty Nancy! – and built this, the smallest of his houses to date, he had forgotten for a few months the other pressures on his income. Was not love a Hercules, still climbing trees in the Hesperides? Now, a year later, he reflected that the gods were just and of his pleasant vices had made instruments to plague him.

He unlocked the door and dropped his keys on to the hall table between the Flamenco doll and the cherry heering bottle that Nancy by the addition of a shade stuck all over with hotel labels had converted into a lamp. In all his matrimonial career Oliver had never before given houseroom to such an object. He hated it but he felt that, in ensuring it was the first thing his eye fell on when he entered his home, Providence was meting out to him a stern exquisite justice.

Nancy's sewing machine could be heard faintly from the lounge. The querulous whine of the motor fanned his ill-temper into rage. He pushed open the reeded glass door and went in. The room was tightly sealed and stifling, the windows all closed and the curtains drawn back in the way he loathed, carelessly, with no attention to the proper arrangement of their folds. Those curtains had cost him thirty pounds.

His wife – to himself and to one other Oliver occasionally referred to her as his present wife – lifted her foot from the pedal which controlled the motor and pushed damp hair back from a face on which sweat shone. Shreds of cotton and pieces of coloured fluff clung to her dress and littered the floor. There was even a piece of cotton dangling from her bracelet.

'My Christ, it's like an oven in here!' Oliver flung back the french windows and scowled at Bernice Greenleaf who was walking coolly about the garden next-door, snipping the dead blossoms off an opulent Zephirine Drouhin. When she waved to him he changed the scowl into a rigid smirk 'What in God's name are you doing?' he asked his wife.

She pulled a cobbled strip of black and red silk from under the needle. 'I'm making a dress for Tamsin's party.'

Oliver sat down heavily, catching his foot in one of the Numdah rugs. ('If we have wood block flooring and rugs, darling,' Nancy had said, 'we'll save pounds on carpeting.')

'This I cannot understand,' Oliver said. 'Did I or did I not give you a cheque for twenty pounds last Tuesday with express instructions to buy yourself a dress?'

'Well . . .'

'Did I or did I not? That's all I ask. It's a perfectly simple question.'

Nancy's babyish, *gamine* face puckered. A curly face, he had called it once, tenderly, lovingly, touching with a teasing finger the tip-tilted nose, the bunchy cheeks, the fluffy fair eyebrows.

'Well, darling, I had to have shoes, you see, and stockings. And there was the milk bill . . .' Her voice faltered. 'I

saw this remnant and this pattern . . .' She held an
envelope towards him diffidently. Oliver glowered at the
coloured picture of three improbably tall women in cylin-
drical cotton frocks. 'It'll be all right, won't it?'

'It will be quite ghastly,' Oliver said coldly. 'I shall be
covered with shame. I shall be mortified. Tamsin always
looks wonderful.'

As soon as the words were out he regretted them. Now
was not the time. Nancy was going to cry. Her face swelled
as if the skin itself was allergic to his anger.

'Tamsin has a private income.' The tears spouted. 'I only
wanted to save you money. That's all I think about, saving
your money.'

'Oh, don't cry! I'm sorry, Nancy.' She almost fell from
her chair into his lap and he put his arms round her with
the distaste that was part of his marital experience, the
distaste that always came as love ebbed. Every bit of her
was damp and clinging and unbearably hot.

'I do want to economise, darling. I keep thinking of all
that money going out month after month to Jean and
Shirley. And what with both the boys at Bembridge . . . '
Oliver frowned. He disliked the reminder that he had been
unable to afford to send the sons of his first marriage to
Marlborough. 'And Shirley always so greedy, insisting on
sending Jennifer to a private school when state education
is so good these days.'

'You know nothing at all about state education,' Oliver
said.

'Oh, darling, why did you have to marry such unattractive women? Any other women would have got married
again. Two such disastrous – well, tragic marriages. I lie
awake at night thinking about the inroads on our income.'

She was off on a well-worn track, the Friday night special. Oliver let her talk, reaching to the mantelpiece for a
cigarette from the box.

'And I haven't got anything exciting for your dinner,' she
finished on a note of near-triumph.

'We'll go out to eat, then.'

'You know we can't afford it. Besides I've got to finish
this filthy dress.' She struggled from his lap back to the
sewing machine.

'This,' said Oliver, 'is the end.' Nancy, already involved once more in fitting a huge sleeve into a tiny armhole, ignored him. She was not to know that it was with these words that Oliver had terminated each of his previous marriages. For him, too, they sounded dreadfully like the mere echoes of happy finalities. Must Nancy be his till death parted them? More securely than any devout Catholic, any puritan idealist, he had thought himself until recently, bound to his wife. Hercules had climbed his last tree. Unless – unless things would work out and he could get a wife with money of her own, a beautiful, well-dowered wife . . .

He stepped across the rugs, those small and far from luxuriant oases in the big desert of polished floor, and poured himself a carefully-measured drink. Then he sat down and gazed at their reflections, his and Nancy's, in the glass on the opposite wall. Her remarks as to the unattractiveness of his former wives had seemed to denigrate his own taste and perhaps even his own personal appearance. But now, as he looked at himself, he felt their injustice. Anyone coming in, any stranger would, he thought bitterly, have taken Nancy for the cleaning woman doing a bit of overtime sewing, her hair separated into rough hanks, her face greasy with heat and effort. But as for him, with his smooth dark head, the sharply cut yet sensitive features, the long hands that held the blood-red glass . . . the truth of it was that he was wasted in these provincial, incongruous surroundings.

Nancy got up, shook her hair, and began to pull her dress over her head. She was simply going to try on the limp half-finished thing but Oliver was no fool and he could tell from the way she moved, slowly, coquettishly, that there was also intention to tempt him.

'If you must strip in the living room you might pull the curtains,' he said.

He got up and put his hand to the cords that worked the pulley, first the french windows, then at the long Georgian sashes at the front of the house. The silk folds moved to meet each other but not before, through the strip of narrowing glass, he had seen walking past the gate, a tall fair man who rested a freckled hand on a dog's head, a man who was strolling home to a beautiful well-dowered wife . . .

With this glimpse there came into his mind a sudden passionate wish that this time things might for once go smoothly and to the advantage of Oliver Gage. He stood for a moment, thinking and planning, and then he realised that he had no wish to be here like this in the darkness with his wife, and he reached quickly for the light switch.

It was fully dark, outside as well as in, when Denholm awoke. He blinked, passed his hands across his face and stretched.

'Ah, well,' he said to his wife, 'up the wooden hill.'

She had meant to save it all for the morning, but the hours of sitting silently beside the sleeping man had told on her nerves. His expression became incredulous as she began to tell him of the meeting on The Green.

'He was pulling your leg,' he said.

'No, he wasn't. I wouldn't have believed him only I know you've been worried lately. You have been worried, haven't you?'

'Well, if you must know, things have been a bit dicey.' She listened as the bantering tone left his voice. 'Somebody's been building up a big stake in the company.' Only when he was talking business could Denholm shed facetiousness and become a man instead of a clown. 'It's been done through a nominee and we don't know who it is.'

'But, Den,' she cried, 'that must be Patrick!'

'He wouldn't be interested in us. Selbys are glass, nothing but glass and we're chemicals.'

'He would. I tell you, he is. He's got that contract and he means to expand, to take you over. And it does rest with him. The others are just – what do you call it? – sleeping partners.'

She would have to say it, put into words the grotesque fear that had been churning her thoughts the entire evening.

'D'you know what I think? I think it's all malice, just because you once hit that dog.'

The shot had gone home, but still he hesitated, the jovial man, the confident provider.

'You're a proper old worry-guts, aren't you?' His hand reached for hers and the fingers were cold and not quite steady. 'You don't understand business. Business men don't carry on that way.'

Did they? he wondered. Would they? His own holding in the firm had decreased precariously as his family had increased. How far could he trust the loyalty of those Smith-King uncles and cousins? Would they sell if they were sufficiently tempted?

'I understand people,' Joan said, 'and I understand you. You're not well, Den. The strain's too much for you. I wish you'd see Dr. Greenleaf.'

'I will,' Denholm promised. As he spoke he felt again the vague indefinable pains he had been experiencing lately, the continual malaise. 'I'll have a quiet natter to him tomorrow at the party.'

'I don't want to go.'

Denholm did. Even if it was cold and there wasn't enough to drink, even if they made him dance, it would be wonderful just to get away for one evening from baby-feeding at ten, from Susan who had to have a story and from Jeremy who never slept at all until eleven.

'But we've got a sitter,' he said and he sighed as from above he heard his son's voice calling for a drink of water.

Joan went to the door. 'You'll have to talk to Patrick. Oh, I wish we didn't have to go.' She went upstairs with the glass and came down again with the baby in her arms.

Trying to console her, Denholm said weakly, 'Cheer up, old girl. It'll be all right on the night.'

4

When he had been married to Jean, when indeed he had been married to Shirley, he had always been able to pay a man to clean the car. Now he had to do it himself, to stand on the gravel like any twenty-five pound a week commuter, squelching a Woolworth sponge over a car that he was ashamed to be seen driving into the office underground car park. There was, however, one thing about this morning slopping to be thankful for. Since he was outside he had been able to catch the postman and take the letters himself. With a damp hand he felt the letter in his pocket, the letter that had just come from his second wife. There was no reason why Nancy should see it and have cause to moan at him because of its contents. Those begging letters were a continual thorn in his flesh. Why should his daughter go on holiday to Majorca when he could only manage Worthing? Such a wonderful chance for her, Oliver, but of course she, Shirley, couldn't afford the air fare or equip Jennifer with a suitable wardrobe for a seven-year-old in the Balearics. Fifty pounds or perhaps seventy would help. After all, Jennifer was his daughter as well as hers and she was his affectionately, Shirley.

He dropped the sponge into the bucket and bent down to polish the windscreen. Over the hedge he saw that his neighbour was opening his own garage doors, but although he liked the doctor he was in no mood for conversation that morning. Resentment caught at his throat like heartburn. Greenleaf was wearing another new suit! Gossip had it that the doctor was awaiting delivery of another new car. Oliver could hardly bear it when he compared what he thought of as the doctor's miserable continental medical degree with his own Double First.

'Good morning.'

Greenleaf's car drew level with his own and Oliver was forced to look up into his neighbour's brown, aquiline face. It was a very un-English face, almost Oriental, with dark, close-set eyes, a large intelligent mouth and thick hair, crinkly like that of some ancient Assyrian.

'Oh, hallo,' Oliver said ungraciously. He stood up, making an effort to say something neighbourly, when Nancy came running down the path from the kitchen door. She stopped as she saw the doctor and smiled winningly.

'Off on your rounds? What a pity to have to work on a Saturday! I always tell Oliver he doesn't know his luck, having all these long week-ends.'

Oliver coughed. His other wives had learned that his coughs were pregnant with significance. In Nancy's case there had hardly been time to teach her, and now . . .

'I hope I'll see you tonight,' said the doctor as he began to move off.

'Oh, yes, tonight . . .' Nancy's face had taken on its former lines of displeasure. When Greenleaf was out of earshot she turned sharply to her husband. 'I thought you said you left Tamsin's present on the sideboard.'

Oliver had a nose for a scene. He picked up the bucket and started towards the house.

'I did.'

'You bought that for Tamsin?' She scuttled after him into the dining-room and picked up the scent bottle with its cut-glass stopper. 'Nuit de Beltane? I never heard of such extravagance!'

Oliver could see from the open magazine on the table that she had already been checking the price.

'There you are.' Her finger stabbed at a coloured photograph of a similar bottle. 'Thirty-seven and six!' She slammed the magazine shut and threw it on the floor. 'You must be mad.'

'You can't go to a birthday party empty-handed,' Oliver said weakly. If only he knew for certain. There might, after all, be no point in bothering to keep Nancy sweet. He watched her remove the stopper, sniff the scent and dab a spot on her wrist. While she waved her wrist in front of her nose, inhaling crossly, he washed his hands and closed the back door.

'A box of chocolates would have done.' Nancy said. She lugged the sewing machine up on its rubber mat. 'I mean, it's fantastic spending thirty-seven and six on scent for Tamsin when I haven't even got a decent dress to go in.'

'Oh my God!'

'You don't seem to have a sense of proportion where money's concerned.'

'Keep the scent for God's sake and I'll get some chocolates in the village.'

Immediately she was in his arms. Oliver crushed the letter down more firmly in his pocket.

'Can I really, darling? You are an angel. Only you won't be able to get anything nice in the village. You'll have to nip into Nottingham.'

Disengaging himself, Oliver reflected on his wife's economies. Now there would be the petrol into Nottingham, at least twelve and six for chocolates and he'd still spent nearly two pounds on Nuit de Beltane.

Nancy began to sew. The dress had begun to look passable. At least he wouldn't be utterly disgraced.

'Can I come in?'

The voice was Edith Gaveston's. Quick as a flash Nancy ripped the silk from the machine, rolled up the dress and crammed it under a sofa cushion.

'Come in, Edith.'

'I see you've got into our country way of leaving all your doors unlocked.'

Edith, hot and unwholesome-looking in an aertex shirt and a tweed skirt, dropped on to the sofa. From the depths of her shopping basket she produced a wicker handbag embroidered with flowers.

'Now, I want the opinion of someone young and "with it".' Oliver who was forty-two scowled at her, but Nancy, still in her twenties, smiled encouragingly. 'This purse . . .' It was an absurd word, but Edith was too county, too much of a gentlewoman, to talk of handbags unless she meant a small suitcase. 'This purse, will it do for Tamsin's present? It's never been used.' She hesitated in some confusion. 'I mean, of course, it's absolutely new. As a matter of fact I brought it back from Majorca last year. Now, tell me frankly, will it do?'

'Well, she can't very well sling it back at you,' Oliver said rudely. 'Not in front of everyone.' The mention of Majorca reminded him of his second wife's demands. 'Excuse me.' He went outside to get the car.

'I'm sure it'll do beautifully,' Nancy gushed. 'What did Linda say?'

'She said it was square,' Edith said shortly. Her children's failure in achieving the sort of status their parents had wanted for them hurt her bitterly. Linda – Linda who had been at Heathfield – working for Mr. Waller; Roger, coming down from Oxford after a year and going to agricultural college! She would feed them, give them beds in her house, but with other people she preferred to forget their existence.

Nancy said with tactless intuition: 'I thought you weren't terribly keen on the Selbys. Patrick, I mean . . .'

'I've no quarrel with Tamsin. I hope I'm not a vindictive woman.'

'No, but after what Patrick – after him influencing Roger the way he did, I'm surprised you – well, you know what I mean.'

Nancy floundered. The Gavestons weren't really county any more. Their house was no bigger than the Gages'. But still – you'd only got to look at Edith to know her brother lived at Chantflower Grange. I suppose she's only going to the party to have a chance to hob-nob with Crispin Marvell, she thought.

'Patrick Selby behaved very badly, very wrongly,' Edith said. 'And it was just wanton mischief. He's perfectly happy and successful in *his* job.'

'I never quite knew . . .'

'He set out to get at my children. Quite deliberately, my dear. Roger was blissfully happy at The House.' Nancy looked puzzled, thinking vaguely of the Palace of Westminister. 'Christ Church, you know. Patrick Selby got talking to him when he was out with that dog of theirs and the upshot of it was Roger said his father wanted him to go into the business but he wasn't keen. He wanted to be a farmer. As if a boy of nineteen knows what he wants. Patrick said he'd been forced into business when all he wanted was to teach or some absurd thing. He advised Roger to – well, follow his own inclinations. Never mind about us, never mind about poor Paul with no-one to take over the reins at Gavestons, no heir.'

Nancy, greedy for gossip, made sympathetic noises.

'Then, of course, Roger had to say his sister wanted to earn her own living. Made up some stupid tale about our keeping her at home. The next thing was that impossible interfering man suggested she should work in a shop till she was old enough to take up nursing. I don't know why he did it, unless it was because he likes upsetting people. Paul had a great deal to say about it, I assure you. He had quite a stormy interview with Patrick.'

'But it was no good?'

'They do what they like these days.' She sighed and added despondently, 'But as to going tonight, one has one's neighbourhood, one cannot pick and choose these days.'

'Who else is coming?'

'The usual people. The Linchester crowd and Crispin of course. I think it's splendid of him to come so often considering how bitter he must feel.' Edith's sensible, pink-rimmed glasses bobbed on her nose. 'There was a clause in the Marvell contract, you know. No tree feeling. Everyone's respected it except Patrick Selby. I know for a fact there were twenty exquisite ancient trees on that plot, and he's had them all down and planted nasty little willows.'

It was just like Oliver, Nancy thought, to come in and spoil it all.

'If you're looking for your cheque book,' she said innocently, 'it's on the record player. While you're about it you might collect my sandals.'

'Oh, are you going to the village?' Edith got up pointedly.

'I'm going into Nottingham.'

'Into *town*? How perfectly splendid. You can give me a lift.'

She picked up the wicker basket and they departed together.

Two fields and a remnant of woodland away Crispin Marvell was sitting in his living room drinking rhubarb wine and writing his history of Chantefleur Abbey. Some days it was easy to concentrate. This was one of the others. He had spent the early part of the morning washing his china and ever since he had replaced the cups in the cabinet and the plates on the walls, he had been unable to keep his eyes from wandering to the glossy surfaces and the warm rich colours. It was almost annoying to reflect what he had been missing in delaying this particular bit of spring-cleaning, the months during which the glaze had been dimmed by winter bloom.

For a moment he mused over the twin olive-coloured plates, one decorated with a life-size apple in relief, the other with a peach; over the Chelsea clock with its tiny dial and opulent figurines of the sultan and his concubine. Marvell kept his correspondence behind this clock and it disturbed him to see the corner of Henry Glide's letter sticking out. He got up and pushed the envelope out of sight between the wall and the Circassian's gold-starred trousers. Then he dipped his pen in the ink-well and returned to Chantefleur.

'The original building had a clerestory of round-headed windows with matching windows in the aisle bays. Only by looking at the Cistercian abbeys now standing in France can we appreciate the effect of the . . .'

He stopped and sighed. Carried away by his own domestic art, he had almost written 'of the glaze on the apple'. It was hardly important. Tomorrow it might rain. He had already spent two years on the history of Chantefleur. Another few months scarcely mattered. In a way, on a wonderful morning like this one, nothing mattered. He gave the plate a last look, running his fingers across the cheek of the apple – the artist had been so faithful he had even pressed in a bruise, there on the underside – and went into the garden.

Marvell lived in an almshouse, or rather four almshouses all joined together in a terrace and converted by him into a long low bungalow. The walls were partly of white plaster, partly of rose-coloured brick, and the roof was of pantiles, old now and uneven but made by the hand of a craftsman.

He strolled round the back. Thanks to the bees that lived in three white hives in the orchard the fruit was forming well; they hadn't swarmed this year and he was keeping his fingers crossed. The day spent in carefully cutting out the queen cells had been well worth the sacrifice of half a chapter of Chantefleur. He sat down on the bench. Beyond the hedge in the meadows below Linchester they were cutting the hay. He could hear the baler, that and the sound of the bees. Otherwise all was still.

'All right for some people.'

Marvell turned his head and grinned. Max Greenleaf often came up about this time after his morning calls.

'Come and sit down.'

'It's good to get away from the wasps.' Greenleaf looked at the lichen on the bench, then down at his dark suit. He sat down gingerly.

'There were always a lot of wasps on Linchester,' Marvell said. 'I remember them in the old days. Thousands of damned wasps whenever Mamma gave a garden party.' Greenleaf looked at him suspiciously. An Austrian Jew, he could never escape his conviction that the English landed gentry and the Carinthian aristocracy came out of the same mould. Marvell called it his serfs to the wolves syndrome. 'The wasps are conservative, you see. They haven't got used to the idea that the old house has been gone five years and a lot of company directors' Georgian gone up in its place. They're still on the hunt for Mamma's brandy snaps. Come inside and have a drink.' He smiled at Greenleaf and said in a teasing voice, 'I opened a bottle of mead this morning.'

'I'd rather have a whisky and soda.'

Greenleaf followed him to the house, knocking his head as he always did on the plaque above the front door that said: 1722. Andreas Quercus Fecit. Marvell's reasons for living there were beyond his understanding. The countryside, the flowers, horticulture, agriculture, Marvell's own brand of viticulture, meant nothing to him. He had come to the village to share his brother-in-law's prosperous practice. If you asked him why he lived in Linchester he would answer that it was for the air or that he was obliged to live within a mile or two of his surgery. Modern conveniences, a house that differed inside not at all from a town house, diluted and almost banished those drawbacks. To invite those disadvantages, positively to court them in the form of cesspools, muddy lanes and insectivora as his host did, made Marvell a curio, an object of psychological speculation.

These mysteries of country life reminded him afresh of the cloud on his morning.

'I've just lost a patient,' he said. Marvell, pouring whisky, heard the Austrian accent coming through, a sign that the doctor was disturbed. 'Not my fault, but still . . .'

'What happened?' Marvell drew the curtains, excluding all but a narrow shaft of sunlight that ran across the black oak floor and up Andreas Quercus's squat wall.

'One of the men from Coffley mine. A wasp got on his sandwich and he ate the thing. So what does he do? He goes back to work and the next thing I'm called out because he's choking to death. Asphyxiated before I got there.'

'Could you have done anything?'

'If I'd got there soon enough. The throat closes with the swelling, you see.' Changing the subject, he said: 'You've been writing. How's it coming on?'

'Not so bad. I did my china this morning and it distracted me.' He unhooked the apple plate from the wall and handed it to the doctor. 'Nice?'

Greenleaf took it wonderingly in short thick fingers. 'What's the good of a thing like this? You can't put food on it, can you?' Without aesthetic sense, he probed everything for its use, its material function. This plate was quite useless. Distastefully he imagined eating from it the food he liked best, chopped herring, cucumbers in brine, cabbage salad with caraway seeds. Bits would get wedged under the apple leaves.

'It's purpose is purely decorative,' Marvel laughed. 'Which reminds me, will you be at Tamsin's party?'

'If I don't get called out.'

'She sent me a card. Rather grand. Tamsin always does these things well.' Marvell stretched himself full-length in the armchair. The movement was youthful and the light dim. Greenleaf was seldom deceived about people's ages. He put Marvell's at between forty-seven and fifty-two, but the fine lines which the sun showed up were no longer apparent, and the sprinkling of white hairs was lost in the fair. Probably still attractive to women, he reflected.

'One party after another,' he said, 'Must come expensive.'

'Tamsin has her own income, you know, from her grandmother. She and Patrick are first cousins so she was his grandmother too.'

'But she was the favourite?'

'I don't know about that. He had already inherited his father's business so I daresay old Mrs. Selby thought he didn't need any more.'

'You seem to know a lot about them.'

'I suppose I do. In a way I've been a sort of father confessor to Tamsin. Before they came here they had a flat in Nottingham. Tamsin was lost in the country. When I gave that talk to the Linchester Residents' Association she bombarded me with questions and since then – well, I've become a kind of adopted uncle, Mrs. Beeton and antiquarian rolled into one.'

Greenleaf laughed. Marvell was the only man he knew who could do women's work without becoming old-womanish.

'You know, I don't think she ever really wanted that house. Tamsin loves old houses and old furniture. But Patrick insists on what are called, I believe, uncluttered lines.'

'Tell me, don't you *mind* coming to Linchester?' Always fascinated by other people's emotions, Greenleaf had sometimes wondered about Marvell's reactions to the new houses that had sprung up on his father's estate.

Marvell smiled and shrugged.

'Not really. I'm devoutly thankful I don't have to keep the old place up. Besides it amuses me when I go to parties. I play a sort of mental game trying to fix just where I am in relation to our house.' When Greenleaf looked puzzled he went on, 'What I mean is, when I'm at Tamsin's I always think to myself, the ha-ha came down here and here were the kitchen gardens.' Keeping a straight face he said, 'The Gages' house now, that's where the stables were. I'm not saying it's appropriate, mind.'

'You're scaring me. Makes me wonder about my own place.'

'Oh, you're all right. Father's library and a bit of the big staircase.'

'I don't believe a word of it,' the doctor said and added a little shyly, 'I'm glad you can make a game of the whole thing.'

'You mustn't think,' said Marvell, 'that every time I set foot on Linchester I'm wallowing in a kind of maudlin *recherche du temps perdu*.'

Greenleaf was not entirely convinced. He finished his whisky and remembered belatedly his excuse for the visit.

'And now,' he said, at ease on his own home ground, 'how's the hay fever?'

If the doctor had not perfectly understood Marvell's Proustian reference, he had at least an inkling of its meaning. On Edward Carnaby it would have been utterly lost. His French was still at an elementary stage.

Jo-jo monte. Il est fatigué. Bonne nuit, Jo-jo. Dors bien!

He looked up towards the ceiling and translated the passage into English. Funny stuff for a grown man, wasn't it? All about a kid of five having a bath and going to bed. Still, it was French. At this rate he'd be reading Simenon within the year.

Bonjour, Jo-jo. Quel beau matin! Regarde le ciel. Le soleil brille.

Edward thumbed through the dictionary, looking for *briller*.

'Ted!'

'What is it, dear?' It was funny, but lately he'd got into the habit of calling her dear. She had taken the place of his wife in all ways but one. Sex was lacking but freedom and security took its place. Life was freer with Free, he thought, pleased with his pun.

'If you and Cheryl want your lunch on time you'll have to do something about these wasps, Ted.' She marched in, brisk, neat, womanly, in a cotton frock and frilled apron. He noted with pleasure that she had said lunch and not dinner. Linchester was educating Freda.

'I'll do it right now. Get it over.' He closed the dictionary. *Briller*. To shine, to glow, emit a radiance. The verb perfectly expressed his own mental state. He was glowing with satisfaction and anticipation. *Edouard brille*, he said to himself, chuckling aloud. 'I've promised to pass the stuff on to some people.'

'What people?'

'The gorgeous Mrs. Selby, if you must know. I met her last night and she was all over me. Insisted I go to her party tonight.' Now you couldn't say things like that to a wife. 'She wouldn't take No for an answer,' he said.

Freda sat down.

'You're kidding. You don't know Tamsin.'

'Tamsin! That's all right, that is. Since when have you and her been so pally?'

'And what about me? Where do I come in?'

'Now, look, Free, I'm counting on you to sit in with Cheryl.'

The tears welled into her eyes. After all that had happened, all the love, the promises, the wonderful evenings. Of course it wasn't *his* fault. It was Tamsin's party. But to ask Edward!

'There's no need to get into a tiz. She said I could bring a friend. I don't know about Cheryl, though.'

'Mrs. Staxton'll sit,' Freda said eagerly. 'She's always offering.' Seeing his face still doubtful, his eyes already returning to the French primer, she burst out miserably, 'Ted, I want to go to the party! I've got a right. I've got more right than you.'

Hysteria in Freda was something new. He closed the book.

'What are you talking about?' She was his twin and he could feel the pull of her mind, almost read her thoughts. A terrible unease visited him and he thought of the previous night, the woman's eyes staring past him towards the pond, her sudden unexplained coldness when he had said who he was.

'Freda!'

It all came out then and Edward listened, angry and afraid. The happy mood had gone sour on him.

5

Strings of little coloured bulbs festooned the willow trees. As soon as it grew dusk they would be switched on to glow red, orange, green and cold blue against the dark foliage of the oaks in the Millers' garden next door.

Tamsin had shut the food and drink in the dining room away from the wasps. Although she had only seen two throughout the whole day she closed the double windows to be on the safe side. The room was tidy, and apart from the food, bare. Functional, Patrick called it. Now, cleaned by him while Tamsin hovered helplessly in the background, it met even his exacting requirements.

'It is, after all, a *dining* room, not a glory hole,' he had remarked in a chill voice to the vacuum cleaner. To his wife he said nothing, but his look meant Please don't interfere with my arrangements. When the tools were put away and the dusters carefully washed, he had taken the dog to Sherwood Forest, smug, silent with his private joy.

It was too late now to bother with a show of loving obedience. Tamsin dressed, wishing she had something bright and gay, but all her clothes were subdued – to please Patrick. Then she went into the dining room and helped herself to whisky, pouring it straight into a tumbler almost as if it was the last drink she would ever have. Nobody had wished her a happy birthday yet but she had had plenty of cards. Defiantly she took them from the sideboard drawer and arranged them on top of the radiator. There were about a dozen of them, facetious ones showing dishevelled housewives amid piles of crocks; conventional ones (a family of Dartmoor ponies); one whose picture held a secret significance, whose message meant something special to her and to its sender. It was unsigned but Tamsin knew who had sent it. She screwed it up quickly for the sight of it with its cool presumption only deepened her misery.

'Many happy returns of the day, Tamsin,' she said shakily, raising her glass. She sighed and the cards fluttered. Somehow she would have liked to break the glass, hurl it absurdly against Patrick's white wall, because she had come to an end. A new life was beginning. The drink was a symbol of the old life and so was the dress she wore, silver-grey, clinging, expensive. She put the glass down carefully (her old habits died hard), looked at the cards and blinked to stop herself crying. For there should have been one more, bigger than the others, an austere costly card that said To My Wife.

Patrick was never late. He came back on the dot of seven in time to bath and shave and leave the bathroom tidy, and by then she had washed her glass, returning it to its place in the sideboard. She heard the bathroom door close and the key turn in the lock. Patrick was careful about propriety.

Tamsin remained in the dining room for some minutes, feeling an almost suicidal despair. In an hour or so her guests would begin to arrive and they would expect her to be gay because she was young and rich and beautiful and because it was her birthday. If she could get out of the house for a few minutes she might feel better. With Queenie at her heels she took her trug and went down to where the currants grew in what had been the Manor kitchen gardens. The dog lay down in the sun and Tamsin began stripping the bushes of their ripe white fruit.

'I will try to be gay,' she said to herself, or perhaps to the dog, 'for a little while.'

Edward and Freda came up to the front doors of Hallows at a quarter to eight and it was Edward who rang the bell. Freda, whose only reading matter was her weekly women's magazine, had sometimes encountered the cliché 'rooted to the spot' and that was how she felt standing on the swept white stones, immobile, stiff with terror, a sick bile stirring between her stomach and her throat.

No-one came to the door. Freda watched her brother enviously. Not for him the problem of what to do with one's sticky and suddenly over-large hands that twitched and fretted as if seeking some resting place; he had the Vesprid in its brown paper bag to hold.

'Better go round the back,' he said truculently.

It was monastically quiet. The creak of the wrought iron gate made Freda jump as Edward pushed it open. They walked round the side of the house and stopped when they came to the patio. The garden lay before them, waiting, expectant, but not as for a party. It was rather as if it had been prepared for the arrival of some photographer whose carefully angled shots would provide pictures for one of those very magazines. Freda had read a feature the previous week, *Ideal Homesteads in the New Britain*, and the illustrations had shown just such a garden, lawns ribbed in pale and dark green where the mower had crossed them, trees and shrubs whose leaves looked as if they had been individually dusted. At the other end of the patio someone had arranged tables and chairs, some of straw-coloured wicker, others of white-painted twisted metal. A small spark of pleasure and admiration broke across Freda's fear, only to be extinguished almost at once by the sound of water gurgling down a drainpipe behind her ankles. A sign of life, of habitation.

The garden, the house, looked, she thought, as if it hadn't been kept outside at all, as if it had been preserved up to this moment under glass. But she was unable to express this thought in words and instead said foolishly:

'There isn't anybody about. You must have got the wrong night.'

He scowled and she wondered again why he had come, what he was going to say or do. Was it simply kindness to her – for he was, as it were, her key to this house – Tamsin's fascination or something more?

'You won't say anything, will you? You won't say anything to show me up?'

'I told you,' he said. 'I want to see how the land lies, what sort of a mess you've got yourself into. I'm not promising anything, Free.'

Minutes passed, unchanging minutes in which the sleek garden swam before her eyes. Then something happened, something which caused the first crack to appear in Edward's insecure courage.

From behind the willows came a sound familiar to Freda, a long drawn-out bay. Queenie. Edward jerked convulsively and dropped the Vesprid with a clang – a clang like the crack of doom – as the dog bounded from a curtain of shrubs and stopped a yard from him. It was an ominous sound that came from her, a throb rather than an actual noise, and Edward seemed to grow smaller. He picked up the tin and held it in front of him, a ridiculous and wholly inadequate shield.

'Oh, Queenie!' Freda put out her hand. 'It's all right. It's me.'

The dog advanced, wriggling now, to lick the out-stretched fingers, when the gate opened and a tall fair man entered the garden. He was wearing a green shirt over slacks and Edward at once felt that his own sports jacket

(Harris tweed knocked down to eighty nine and eleven)
was unsuitable, an anachronism.

'How do you do?'

He was carrying something that looked like a bottle
wrapped in ancient yellowing newspaper, and a huge bunch
of roses. The roses were perfect, each bud closed yet about
to unfurl, and their stems had been shorn of thorns.

'I don't think we've met. My name's Marvell.'

'Pleased to meet you,' Edward said. He transferred the
Vesprid to his left arm and shook hands. 'This is my sister,
Miss Carnaby.'

'Where is everyone?'

'We don't know,' Freda said sullenly. 'Till you came we
thought we'd got the wrong night.'

'Oh, no, this is Tamsin's birthday.' He pushed Queenie
down, smiled suddenly and waved. 'There she is picking
my currants, bless her! Will you excuse me?'

'Well!' Freda said. 'If those are county manners you can
keep them.'

She watched him stride off down the path and then she
saw Patrick's wife. Tamsin got to her feet like a silvery
dryad arising from her natural habitat, ran up to Marvell
and kissed him on the cheek. They came back together,
Tamsin's face buried in roses.

'Josephine Bruce, that's the gorgeous dark red one,'
Freda heard her say. 'Virgo, snow-white; Super Star – Oh,
lovely, lovely vermilion! And the big peachy beauty – this
one – is Peace. You see, Crispin, I *am* learning.'

She stepped on to the greyish-gold stones of the patio
and dropped the roses on to a wicker table. The Weimaraner romped over to her and placed her paws on the
table's plaited rim.

'And look, lovely mead! You are sweet to me, Crispin.'

'You look like one of those plushy calendars,' Marvell
said laughing. 'The respectable kind you see in garages on
the Motorway. All girl and dog and flowers and liquor, the
good things of life.'

'*Wein, weib und gesang* as Patrick says.' Tamsin's voice
was low and her face clouded.

Edward coughed.

'Excuse me,' he said.

'O God, I'm so sorry.' Marvell was crestfallen. 'Tamsin dear, I'm keeping you from your guests.'

Afterwards, looking back, Freda thought Tamsin honestly hadn't known who they were. And after all Edward's stupid airs! Tamsin's face had grown dull and almost ugly; her eyes, large and tawny, seemed to blank out. She stood looking at them still holding a rose against her paintless lips. At last she said:

'I know! The man who goes to evening classes.'

Freda wanted to go then, to slink back against the stone wall, slither between the house and the wattle fence and then run and run until she came to the chalets behind the elms. But Edward was holding her arm. He yanked her forward, exposing her to their gaze like a dealer with his single slave.

'This is my sister. You said I could bring someone.'

Tamsin's face hardened. It was exactly like one of those African art masks, Freda thought, the beautiful goddess one in the saloon bar of that roadhouse on the Southwell road. Freda knew she wasn't going to shake hands.

'Well, now you're here you must have a drink. Masses of drink in the dining room. Where's Patrick?' She looked up to the open windows on the first floor. 'Patrick!'

Edward thrust the Vesprid at her.

'A present? How very sweet of you.'

She pulled the tin out of the bag and giggled. Freda thought she was hysterical – or drunk.

'It's not exactly a present,' Edward said desperately. 'You said to bring it. You said to come early. We could do the wasps.'

'The wasps? Oh, but I've only seen one or two today. We won't worry about wasps.' She flung back the doors and Patrick must have been standing just within. He stepped out poised, smiling, smelling of bath salts. 'Here's my husband. Do go and check the lights, darling.' And she linked her arm into his, smiling brightly.

Freda could feel herself beginning to tremble. She knew her face had paled, then filled with burning blood. Her hand fumbled its way into Patrick's, gaining life and strength as she felt the faint special pressure and the familiar cold touch of his ring. As it came to Edward's turn her

heart knocked, but the handshake passed off convention-
ally. Edward's spirit was broken and he gazed at Patrick
dumbly, half-hypnotised.

'What's this?'

Patrick picked up the Vesprid and looked at the label.

Freda couldn't help admiring his aplomb, the coldly
masterful way he shook off Tamsin's hand.

'Doesn't it look horrid on my birthday table?' Tamsin
bundled the tin back into the paper and pushed it into
Edward's arms. She took his fingers in her own and curled
them round the parcel. 'There. You look after it, sweetie,
or pop it in a safe place. We don't want it mingling with
the drinks, do we?'

Then Marvell rescued them and took them into the dining room.

By the time Greenleaf and Bernice got to Hallows everyone
had arrived. He had been called out to a man with renal
colic and it was eight before he got back. Fortunately
Bernice never nagged but waited for him patiently, smoking and playing patience in the morning room.

'I shall wear my alpaca packet,' Greenleaf said. 'So it
makes me look like a bowls player? What do I care? I'm
not a teenager.'

'No, darling,' said Bernice. 'You're a very handsome
mature man. Who wants to be a teenager?'

'Not me, unless you can be one too.'

Well-contented with each other, they set off in a happy
frame of mind. They took the short cut across The Green
and paused to watch the swans. Greenleaf held his wife's
hand.

'At last,' Denholm Smith-King said as they appeared in
the patio. 'I was just saying to Joan, is there a doctor in the
house?'

'Ha ha,' said Greenleaf mechanically. 'I hope no-one's
going to need one. I've come to enjoy myself.' He waved
to Tamsin who came from the record-player to greet him.
'Happy birthday. Nice of you to ask us.' He pointed to the
now loaded table. 'What's all this?'

'My lovely presents. Look, chocs from Oliver and Nancy,
this marvellous bag thing from Edith.' Tamsin held the

gifts up in turn, pouting at the bag as she praised it. 'Sweet delicious *marrons glacés* from Joan, and Crispin brought me – what d'you think? Wine and roses. Wasn't that lovely?'

Marvell smiled from behind her, looking boyish. 'Thy shadow, Cynara,' he said. 'The night is thine. . . .'

'So kind! And Bernice . . .' She unwrapped the tiny phial of scent Bernice had put into her hand. 'Nuit de Beltane! How gorgeous. And I've just been telling Nancy how lovely she smells. Imagine, she's wearing it herself. You're all so good to me.' She waved a long brown hand as if their munificence exhausted her, making her more languid than usual.

Greenleaf crammed himself into a small wicker armchair. From within the dining room the music had begun the Beguine.

'Your daughter not coming?' he said to Edith Gaveston. She sniffed. 'Much too square for Linda.'

'I suppose so.'

Tamsin had gone, swept away in the arms of Oliver Gage.

'If you've a minute,' said Denholm Smith-King,' I've been meaning to ask you for ages. It's about a lump I've got under my arm. . . .'

Greenleaf, preparing for a busman's holiday, took the drink Patrick held out to him, but Smith-King was temporarily diverted. He looked quickly about him as if to make sure that most of the others were dancing, and he touched Patrick's arm nervously.

'Oh, Pat old man. . . .'

'Not now, Denholm.' Patrick's smile was brief, mechanical, gone in a flash. 'I don't care to mix business with pleasure.'

'Later, then?'

Patrick glanced at the ashtray Smith-King was filling with stubs, opened the cigarette box insolently and let the lid fall almost instantly.

'I'm not surprised you've got a lump,' he said, 'but don't bore my guests, will you?'

'Funny chap,' Smith-King said and an uneasy flush seeped across his face. 'Doesn't care what he says.' The red faded as Patrick strolled away. 'Now about this said lump. . . .'

Greenleaf turned towards him and tried to look as if he was listening while keeping his thoughts and half an eye on the other guests.

Most of them were his patients except the Selbys and the Gavestons who were on Dr. Howard's private list, but he sized them up now from a psychological rather than a medical standpoint. As he sometimes said to Bernice, he had to know about human nature, it was part of his job.

The Carnabys now, they weren't enjoying themselves. They sat apart from the rest in a couple of deck chairs on the lawn and they weren't talking to each other. Freda had hidden her empty shandy glass under the seat; Carnaby, like a parent clutching his rejected child, sat dourly, holding what looked like a tin in one of Waller's paper wrappings.

Beyond them among the currant bushes Marvell was showing Joan and Nancy the ancient glories of the Manor kitchen gardens. Greenleaf knew little about women's fashions but Nancy's dress looked out of place to him, ill-fitting (she'll have to watch her weight, said the medical part of him, or her blood pressure will go soaring up in ten year's time). It contrasted badly with the expensive scent she wore, whiffs of which he had caught while they were standing together by Tamsin's birthday table. Why, incidentally, had Gage looked black as thunder when Bernice handed over their own phial of perfume?

He was dancing with Tamsin now and of the three couples on the floor they were the best matched. Clare and Walter Miller lumbered past him, resolutely fox-trotting out of time. Rather against her will Bernice had been coaxed into the stiff arms of old Paul Gaveston who, too conscious of the proprieties to hold her close, stared poker-faced over her shoulder, his embracing hand a good two inches from her back. Greenleaf smiled to himself. Gage was without such inhibitions. His smooth dusky cheek was pressed close to Tamsin's, his body fused with hers. They hardly moved but swayed slowly, almost indecently, on a square yard of floor. Well, well, thought Greenleaf. The music died away and broke suddenly into a mambo.

'The thing is,' Smith-King was saying, 'it's getting bigger. No getting away from it.'

'I'd better take a look at it,' Greenleaf said.

A fourth couple had joined the dancers. Greenleaf felt relieved. Patrick was a difficult fellow at the best of times but he could rise to an occasion. It was nice to see him rescuing the Carnaby girl and dancing with her as if he really wanted to.

'You will?' Smith-King half-rose. His movement seemed to sketch the shedding of garments.

'Not now,' Greenleaf said, alarmed. 'Come down to the surgery.'

The sun had quite gone now, even the last lingering rays, and dusk was coming to the garden. Tamsin had broken away from Gage and gone to switch on the fairy lights. But for the intervention of his wife who marched on to the patio exclaiming loudly about the gnats, Gage would have followed her.

'How I hate beastly insects,' Nancy grumbled. 'You'd think with all this D.D.T. and everything there just wouldn't be any more mosquitos.' She glared at Marvell. 'I feel itchy all over.'

As if at a signal Walter Miller and Edith Gaveston broke simultaneously into gnat-bite anecdotes. Joan Smith-King gravitated towards Greenleaf as people so often did with minor ailments even on social occasions, and stood in front of him scratching her arms. He got up at once to let her sit next to her husband but as he turned he saw that Denholm's chair was empty. Then he saw him standing in the now deserted dining room confronting Patrick. The indispensable cigarette was in his mouth. Greenleaf could not hear what he was saying, only Joan's heavy breathing loud and strained above the buzz of conversation. The cigarette trembled, adhering to Denholm's lip, and his hands moved in a gesture of hopelessness. Patrick laughed suddenly and turning away, strode into the garden as the lights came on.

Greenleaf, not sensitive to a so-called romantic atmosphere, was unmoved by the strings of coloured globes. But most of the women cried out automatically. Fairy lights were the thing; they indicated affluence, taste, organisation. With little yelps of delight Nancy ran up and down, pointing and exhorting the others to come and have a closer look.

'So glad you like them,' Tamsin said. 'We do.' Patrick coughed, dissociating himself. He was taking his duties to heart, Greenleaf thought, watching his hand enclose Freda Carnaby's in a tight grip.

'Now, have we all got drinks?' Tamsin reached for Marvell's empty glass. 'Crispin, your poor arms!'

'There are mosquitos at the bottom of your garden,' Marvell said, laughing. 'I meant to bring some citronella but I forgot.'

'Oh, but we've got some. I'll get it.'

'No, I'll go. You want to dance.'

Gage had already claimed her, his arm about her waist.

'I'll tell you where it is. It's in the spare bedroom bathroom. Top shelf of the cabinet.'

Joan Smith-King was giggling enviously.

'Oh, do you have two bathrooms? How grand!'

'Just through the spare room,' Tamsin said, ignoring her, 'You know the way.'

The expression in her eyes shocked Greenleaf. It was as if, he thought, she was playing some dangerous game.

'I'm being absurd,' he said to Bernice.

'Oh, no, darling, you're such a practical man. Why are you being absurd anyway?'

'Nothing,' Greenleaf said.

Marvell came back holding a bottle. He had already unstoppered it and was anointing his arms.

'Thank you so much,' he said to Tamsin, 'Madame Tussaud.'

Tamsin gabbled at him quickly.

'You found the stuff? Marvellous. No, sweetie, that isn't a pun. Come and dance.'

'I am for other than for dancing measures,' Marvell laughed. 'I've been in the chamber of horrors and I need a drink.' He helped himself from the sideboard. 'You might have warned me.'

'What *do* you mean, chamber of horrors?' Nancy was wide-eyed. The party was beginning to flag and she was eager for something to buoy it up and, if possible, prise Oliver away from Tamsin. 'Have you been seeing ghosts?'

'Something like that.'

'Tell, tell!'

Suddenly Tamsin whirled away from Oliver and throwing up her arms, seized Marvell to spin him away past the record player, past the birthday table, across the patio and out on to the lawn.

'Let's all go,' she cried. 'Come and see the skeleton in the cupboard!'

They began to file out into the hall, the women giggling expectantly. Marvell went first, his drink in his hand. Only Patrick hung back until Freda took his hand and whispered something to him. Even Smith-King, usually obtuse, noticed his unease.

'Lead on, Macduff!' he said.

6

If it had been earlier in the day or even if the lights had been on it would have looked very different. But as it was – day melting into night, the light half-gone and the air so still that nothing moved, not even the net curtains at the open windows – the effect was instant and, for a single foolish moment, shocking.

Marvell pulled a face. The other men stared, Paul Gaveston making a noise that sounded like a snort. Smith-King whistled, then broke into a hearty laugh.

The women expressed varying kinds of horror, squeals, hands clamped to mouths, but only Freda sounded genuinely distressed. She was standing close to Greenleaf. He heard her low gasp and felt her shudder.

'Definitely not my cup of tea,' Nancy said. 'Imagine forgetting it was there and then coming face to face with it in the night on your way to the loo!'

Greenleaf was suddenly sickened. Of all the people in the Selbys' spare room he was the only one who had ever seen an actual head that had been severed from an actual body. The first one he had encountered as a student, the second had been the subject of a post-mortem conducted on a man decapitated in a railway accident. Because of this and for other reasons connected with his psychological make-up, he was at the same time more and less affected by the picture than were the other guests.

It was a large picture, an oil painting in a frame of scratched gilt, and it stood propped on the floor against the watered silk wallpaper. Greenleaf knew nothing at all about painting and the view many people take that all life – or all death – is a fit subject for art would have appalled him. Of brushwork, of colour, he was ignorant, but he knew a good deal about anatomy and a fair amount about sexual perversion. Therefore he was able to admire the artist for his accuracy – the hewn neck on the silver platter showed the correct vertebra and the jugular in its proper place – and deplore a mentality which thought sadism a suitable subject for entertainment. Greenleaf hated cruelty; all the suffering of all his ancestors in the ghettos of Eastern Europe was strong within him. He stuck out his thick underlip, took off his glasses and began polishing them on his alpaca jacket.

Thus he was unable to see for a moment the face of the man who stood near him on the other side of Freda Carnaby, the man whose house this was. But he heard the intake of breath and the faint smothered cry.

'But just look at the awful way she's staring at that ghastly head,' Nancy cried, clutching Oliver's hand. 'I think I ought to understand what it means, but I don't.'

'Perhaps it's just as well,' her husband said crisply.

'What is it, Tamsin? What's it supposed to be?'

Tamsin had drawn her finger across the thick painted surface, letting a nail rest at the pool of blood.

'Salome and John the Baptist,' Marvell said. He was quickly bored by displays of naiveté and he had gone to the window. Now he turned round, smiling. 'Of course she wouldn't have been dressed like that. The artist put her in contemporary clothes. Who painted it, Tamsin?'

'I just wouldn't know,' Tamsin shrugged. 'It was my grandmother's. I lived with her, you see, and I grew up with it, so it doesn't affect me all that much any more. I used to love it when I was a little girl. Too dreadful of me!'

'You're never going to hang it on the wall?' Clare Miller asked.

'I might. I don't know yet. When my grandmother died two years ago she left all her furniture to a friend, a Mrs. Prynne. I happened to be visiting her a couple of months ago and of course I absolutely drooled over this thing. So she said she's send it to me for my birthday and here it is.'

'Rather you than I.'

Tamsin giggled.

'I might put it on the dining-room wall. D'you think it would go well with a grilled steak?'

They had all looked at the picture. Everyone had said something if only to exclaim with thrilled horror. Only Patrick had kept silent and Greenleaf, puzzled, turned now to look at him. Patrick's face was deathly white under the cloud of freckles. Somehow the freckles made him look worse, the pallor of his skin blotched with what looked like bruises. When at last he spoke his voice was loud and unsteady and the icy poise quite gone.

'All right,' he said, 'the joke's over. Excuse me.' He pushed at Edward Carnaby, shoving him aside with his shoulder and stripping the counterpane from one of the beds, flung it across the picture. But instead of catching on the topmost beading of the frame it slipped and fell to the floor. The effect of its falling, like the sweeping away of a curtain, exposed the picture with a sudden vividness. The gloating eyes, the parted lips and the plump bosom of Herod's niece arose before them in the gloom. She seemed to be watching with a dreadful satisfaction the slithering silk as it unveiled the trophy in the dish.

'You bitch!' Patrick said.

There was a shocked silence. Then Tamsin stepped forward and looped the counterpane up. Salome was veiled.

'Oh, really!' she said. 'It was just a joke, darling. You *are* rude.'

Smith-King moved uneasily.

'Getting late, Joanie,' he said. 'Beddy-byes.'

'It's not ten yet.' Tamsin caught Patrick's hand and leaning towards him, kissed him lightly on the cheek. He remained quite still, the colour returning to his face, but he didn't look at her. 'We haven't eaten yet. All that lovely food!'

'Ah, food.' Smith-King rubbed his hands together. It would be another story if a scene could be avoided and Patrick perhaps yet made amenable. 'Must keep body and soul together.'

'The wolf from the door?' Marvell said softly.

'That's the ticket.' He slapped Marvell on the back.

Patrick seemed to realise that his hand was still resting in Tamsin's. He snatched it away, marched out of the room and down the stairs, his dignity returning. With a defiant glance at Tamsin, Freda followed him.

'It's a lovely night,' Tamsin cried. 'Let's go into the garden and take the food with us.' Her eyes were very bright. She linked her arm into Oliver's and as an afterthought clasped Nancy's hand and swung it. 'Eat, drink and be merry for tomorrow we die!'

They went downstairs and Tamsin danced into the dining-room. Greenleaf thought they had seen the last of Patrick for that night, but he was on the patio, subdued, his face expressionless, arranging plates on the wicker tables. Freda Carnaby stood by him, sycophantic, adoring.

'Well!' said Nancy Gage. She pulled her chair up alongside Greenleaf's. 'I thought Patrick made an exhibition of himself, didn't you? Immature I call it, making all that fuss about a picture.'

'It is the eye of childhood that fears a painted devil.' Marvell passed her a plate of smoked salmon rolled up in brown bread.

'Juvenile,' Nancy said. 'I mean, it's not as if it was a film. I don't mind admitting I've seen some horror films that have absolutely terrified me. I've wakened in the night bathed in perspiration, haven't I, Oliver?' Oliver was too far away to hear. He sat on the stone wall in gloomy conference with Tamsin.

Nancy, beckoning to him, raised the salmon roll blindly to her mouth.

'Look out!' Greenleaf said quickly. He knocked the roll out of her hand. 'A wasp,' he explained as she jumped. 'You were going to eat it.'

'Oh, no!' Nancy leapt to her feet and shook her skirt. 'I hate them. I'm terrified of them.'

'It's all right. It's gone.'

'No, it hasn't. Look, there's another one.' Nancy flapped her arms as a wasp winged past her face, circled her head and alighted on a fruit flan. 'Oliver, there's one in my hair!'

'What on earth's the matter?' Tamsin got up reluctantly and came between the tables. 'Oh, wasps. Too maddening.' She was taller than Nancy and she blew lightly on to the fair curls. 'It's gone, anyway.'

'You shouldn't have brought the food out,' Patrick said. 'You would do it.' Since he had been the first to do so, this Greenleaf thought, was hardly fair. 'I hate this damned inefficiency. Look, dozens of them!'

Everyone had pushed back their chairs, leaving their food half-eaten. The striped insects descended upon the tables making first for fruit and cream. They seemed to drop from the skies and they came quite slowly, wheeling first above the food with a sluggish yet purposeful concentration like enemy aircraft engaged in a reconnaissance. Then, one by one, they dropped upon pastry and jelly, greedy for the sweet things. Their wings vibrated.

'Well, that's that,' Tamsin said. Her hand dived for a plate of petit fours but she withdrew it quickly with a little scream. 'Get off me, hateful wasp! Patrick, do something.' He was standing beside her but farther removed perhaps than he had ever been. Exasperated and bored, his hands in his pockets, he stared at the feasting insects. 'Get the food in!'

'It's a bit late for that,' Marvell said. 'They're all over the dining-room.' He looked roofwards. 'You've got a nest, you know.'

'That doesn't surprise me at all,' said Walter Miller who lived next door. 'I said to Clare only yesterday, you mark my words, I said, the Selbys have got a wasp nest in their roof.'

'What are we going to do about it?'

'Kill them.' Edward Carnaby had opened his mouth to no-one except his sister since, on their arrival, Tamsin had snubbed him. Now his hour had come. 'Exterminate them,' he said. He pulled the tin of Vesprid from its bag and dumped it in the middle of the table where Nancy, Marvell and Greenleaf had been sitting. 'You should have let me do it before,' he said to Tamsin.

'Do it? Do what?' Tamsin looked at the Vesprid. 'What do you do, spray it on them?'

Edward seemed to be about to embark on a long technical explanation. He took a deep breath.

Walter Miller said quickly: 'You'll want a ladder. There's one in my garage.'

'Right,' said Edward. 'The first thing is to locate the nest. I'll need someone to give me a hand.' Marvell got up.

'No, Crispin, Patrick will go.' Tamsin touched her husband's arm. 'Come on, darling. You can't let your guests do all the work.'

For a moment he looked as if he could. He glanced mulishly from Marvell to his wife. Then, without speaking to or even looking at Edward, he started to walk towards the gate.

'Blood sports, Tamsin,' Marvell said. 'Your parties are unique.'

When Patrick and Edward came back carrying Miller's ladder the others had moved out on to the lawn. By now the patio was clouded with wasps. Droves of them gathered on the tables. The less fortunate late-comers zoomed enviously a yard above their fellows, fire-flies in the radiance from the fairy lights.

Edward propped the ladder against the house wall. Making sure his heroics were witnessed, he thrust a hand among the cakes and grabbed one swiftly. Then he unscrewed the cap on the Vesprid tin and poured a little liquid on to the pastry.

'You'd better nip up to the spare bedroom,' he said to Patrick importantly. 'I reckon the nest's just above the bathroom window.'

'What for?' Patrick had paled and Greenleaf thought he knew why.

'I shall want some more light, shan't I?' Edward was enjoying himself. 'And someone'll have to hand this to me.' He made as if to thrust the poisoned cake into his host's hand.

'*I* am going up the ladder,' Patrick said icily.

Edward began to argue. He was the expert, wasn't he? Hadn't he just dealt efficiently with a nest of his own?

'Oh, for heaven's sake!' Tamsin said. 'This is supposed to be my birthday party.'

In the end Edward went rebelliously indoors carrying his bait. Marvell stood at the bottom of the ladder, steadying it, and when a light appeared at the bathroom window, Patrick began to climb. From the lawn they watched him peer along the eaves, his face white and tense in the patch of light. Then he called out with the only flash of humour he had permitted himself that evening:

'I've found it. Apparently there's no-one at home.'

'I reckon they've all gone to a party,' Edward called. Delighted because someone on the lawn had laughed, he licked his lips and pushed the cake towards Patrick. 'Supper,' he said.

Greenleaf found himself standing close by Oliver Gage and he turned to him to make some comment on the proceedings, but something in the other man's expression stopped him. He was staring at the figure on the ladder and his narrow red lips were wet. Greenleaf saw that he was clenching and unclenching his hands.

'Oh, look! What's happening?' Suddenly Nancy clutched Greenleaf's arm and startled he looked roofwards.

Patrick had started violently, arching his back away from the ladder. He shouted something. Then they saw him wince, hunch his shoulders and cover his face with his free arm.

'He's been stung,' Greenleaf heard Gage say flatly, 'and serve him bloody well right.' He didn't move but Greenleaf hurried forward to join the others who had gathered at the foot of the ladder. Three wasps were encircling Patrick's head, wheeling about him and making apparently for his closed eyes. They saw him for a moment, fighting, both arms flailing, his blind face twisted. Then Edward disappeared and the light went out. Now Patrick was just a silhouette against the clear turquoise sky and to Greenleaf he looked like a marionette of crumpled black paper whose convulsively beating arms seemed jerked by unseen strings.

'Come down!' Marvell shouted.

'O God!' Patrick gave a sort of groan and collapsed against the rungs, swaying precariously.

Someone shouted: 'He's going to fall,' but Patrick didn't fall. He began to slide down, prone against the ladder, and his shoes caught on each rung as he descended, tap, tap, flap, until he fell into Marvell's arms.

'Are you all right?' Marvell and Greenleaf asked together and Marvell shied at the wasp that came spiralling down towards Patrick's head. 'They've gone. Are you all right?'

Patrick said nothing but shuddered and put up his hand to cover his cheek. Behind him Greenleaf heard Freda Carnaby whimpering like a puppy, but nobody else made a sound. In the rainbow glimmer they stood silent and peering like a crowd at a bullfight who have seen a hated matador come to grief. The hostility was almost tangible and there was no sound but the steady buzz of the wasps.

'Come along.' Greenleaf heard his own voice pealing like a bell. 'Let's get him into the house.' But Patrick shook off his arm and blundered into the dining room.

They gathered round him in the lounge, all except Marvell who had gone to the kitchen to make coffee. Patrick crouched in an armchair holding his handkerchief against his face. He had been stung in several places, under the left eye, on the left wrist and forearm and on the right arm in what Greenleaf called the cubital fossa.

'Lucky it wasn't a good deal worse,' Edward said peevishly.

Patrick's eye was already beginning to swell and close. He scowled at Edward and said rudely:

'Get lost!'

'Please don't quarrel.' No-one knew how Freda had insinuated herself into her position on the footstool at Patrick's knees, nor exactly when she had taken his hand. 'It's bad enough as it is.'

'Oh, really,' Tamsin said. 'Such a fuss! Excuse me, will you? It might be a good idea for my husband to get some air.'

For the second time that night Denholm Smith-King looked first at his watch, then at his wife. 'Well, we'll be getting along. You won't want us.'

Marvell had come in with the coffee things but Tamsin didn't argue. She lifted her cheek impatiently for Joan to kiss.

'Coffee, Nancy? Oliver?' She by-passed the Carnabys exactly as if they were pieces of furniture. Oliver rejected the cup coldly, sitting on the edge of his chair.

'Perhaps we'd better go too.' Nancy looked hopelessly from angry face to angry face. 'Have you got any bi-carb? It's wonderful for wasp stings. I remember when my sister . . .'

'Come *along*, Nancy,' Oliver said. He took Nancy's arm and pulled her roughly. It looked as if he was going to leave without another word, but he stopped at the door and took Tamsin's hand. Their eyes met, Tamsin's wary, his, unless Greenleaf was imagining things, full of pleading disappointment. Then when Nancy kissed her, he followed suit, touching her cheek with the sexless peck that was common politeness on Linchester.

When they had gone, taking the Gavestons with them, and the Willises and the Millers had departed by the garden gate, Greenleaf went over to Patrick. He examined his eye and asked him how he felt.

'Lousy.'

Greenleaf poured him a cup of coffee.

'Had I better send for Dr. Howard, Max?' Tamsin didn't look anxious or excited or uneasy any more. She just looked annoyed.

'I don't think so.' Howard, he knew for a fact, wasn't on the week-end rota. A substitute would come and – who could tell? – that substitute might be himself. 'There's not much you can do. Perhaps an anti-histamine. I'll go over home and fetch something.'

Bernice and Marvell went with him, but he came back alone. The Carnabys were still there. Tamsin had left the front doors open for him and as he crossed the hall he heard no voices. They were all sitting in silence, each apparently nursing private resentment. Freda had moved a little way away from Patrick and had helped herself to coffee.

As if taking her cue from his arrival, Tamsin said sharply: 'Isn't it time you went?' She spoke to Edward but she was looking at Freda. 'When you've quite finished, of course.'

'I'm sure I didn't mean to be *de trop*.' Edward blushed but he brought out his painfully acquired French defiantly. Freda lingered woodenly. Then Patrick gave her a little push, a sharp sadistic push that left a red mark on her arm.

'Run along, there's a good girl,' he said and she rose obediently, pulling her skirt down over her knees.

' 'Night,' Patrick said abruptly. He pushed past Edward, ignoring the muttered 'We know when we're not wanted.' At the door he said to Greenleaf, 'You'll come up?' and the doctor nodded.

When he entered the balcony room behind Tamsin, Patrick was already in bed and he lay with his arms outside the sheets, the stings covered by blue pyjama sleeves.

By now his face was almost unrecognisable. The cheek had swollen and closed the eye. He looked, Greenleaf thought, rather as if he had mumps.

Queenie was stretched beside him, her feet at the foot of the bed, her jowls within the palm of his hand.

'You'll be too hot with him there,' the doctor said.

'It's not a him, it's a bitch.' Tamsin put her hand on Queenie's collar and for a moment Patrick's good eye blazed. 'Oh, all right, but I shan't sleep. I feel like hell.'

Greenleaf opened the windows to the balcony. The air felt cool, almost insolently fresh and invigorating after the hot evening. There were no curtains here to sway and alarm a sleeper, only the white hygienic blinds.

'Do you want something to make you sleep?' Prudently Greenleaf had brought his bag back with him. But Tamsin moved over to the dressing-table with its long built-in counter of black glass and creamy wood textured like watered silk. She opened one of the drawers and felt inside.

'He's got these,' she said. 'He had bad insomnia last year and Dr. Howard gave them to him.'

Greenleaf took the bottle from her. Inside were six blue capsules. Sodium amytal, two hundred milligrammes.

'He can have one.' He unscrewed the cap and rattled a capsule into the palm of his hand.

'One's no good,' Patrick said. He held his cheek to lessen the pain talking caused him, and Tamsin, white and fluttering against her own reflection in the black glass wardrobe doors, nodded earnestly. 'He always had to have two,' she said.

'One.' Greenleaf was taking no chances. He opened his bag and took out a phial. 'The anti-histamine will help you to sleep. You'll sleep like a log.'

Patrick took them all at once, drinking from the glass Tamsin held out to him. 'Thanks,' he said. Tamsin waited until the doctor had fastened his bag and replaced the capsules in the immaculately tidy drawer. Then she switched off the light and they went downstairs.

'Please don't say Thank you for a lovely party,' she said when she and Greenleaf were in the hall.

Greenleaf chuckled. 'I won't,' he said.

The swans had gone to bed long ago in the reeds on the edge of the pond. From the woods between Linchester and Marvell's house something cried out, a fox perhaps or just an owl. It could have been either for all Greenleaf knew. His short stocky body cast a long shadow in the moonlight as he crossed The Green to the house called Shalom. He was suddenly very tired.

Marvell, on the other hand, was wide awake. He walked home through the woods slowly, reaching out from time to time to touch the moist lichened tree trunks in the dark. There were sounds in the forest, strange crunching whispering sounds which would have alarmed the doctor. Marvell had known them since boyhood, the tread of the fox – this was only a few miles north of Quorn country – the soft movement of dry leaves as a grass snake shifted them. It was very dark but the darkness was not absolute. Each trunk was a grey signpost to him; leaves touched his face and although the air was sultry they were cold and clean against his cheek. As he came out into Long Lane he heard in the distance the cry of the nightjar and he sighed.

When he had let himself into the house he lit one of the oil lamps and went as he always did before going to bed from room to room to look at his treasures. The porcelain gleamed, catching up what little light there was. He held the lamp for a moment against the mezzotint of Rievaulx. It recalled to him his own work on another Cistercian abbey and, setting the lamp by the window, he sat down with his manuscript, not to write – it was too late for that – but to read what he had written that day.

Red and white by the window. The snowflake fronds of the Russian Vine and beside it hanging like drops of crimson wax, Berberidopsis, blood-red, absurdly named. The moonlight and the lamplight met and something seemed to pierce his heart.

Moths seeing the light, came at once to the lattice and a coal-black one – Marvell recognised it as The Chimney Sweeper's Boy – fluttered in at the open casement. It was followed by a larger, greyish-white one, its wings hung with filaments, swansdown in miniature. For a second Marvell watched them seek the lamp. Then, fearful lest they burn their wings, he gathered them up, making a loose cage of his hands, and thrust them out of the window.

They spiralled away from yellow into silvery light. He looked and looked again. There was someone in the garden. A shape, itself moth-like, was moving in the orchard. He brushed the black and white wing dust from his hands and leaned out to see who was paying him a visit at midnight.

7

On Sunday morning Greenleaf got up at eight, did some exercises which he told his patients confidently would reduce their waist measurements from thirty-four to twenty-nine, and had a bath. By nine he had looked at *The Observer* and taken a cup of coffee up to Bernice. Then he sat down to write to his two sons who were away at school.

It was unlikely that anyone would call him out today. He had done his Sunday stint on the Chantflower doctors' rota the previous week-end, and he intended to have a lazy day. Bernice appeared at about ten and they had a leisurely breakfast, talking about the boys and about the new car which ought to arrive in time to fetch them home for the holidays. After a while they took their coffee into the garden. They were near enough to the house to hear the phone but when it rang Greenleaf let Bernice answer it, knowing it wouldn't be for him.

But instead of settling down to a good gossip Bernice came back quickly, looking puzzled. This was odd, for Bernice seldom hurried.

'It's Tamsin, darling,' she said. 'She wants you.'

'Me?'

'She's in a state, but she wouldn't tell me anything. All she said was I want Max.'

Greenleaf took the call on the morning room phone.

'Max? It's Tamsin.' For almost the first time since he had met her Tamsin wasn't using her affected drawl. 'I know I shouldn't be ringing you about this but I can't get hold of Dr. Howard.' She paused and he heard her inhale as if on a cigarette. 'Max, I can't wake Patrick. He's awfully cold and I've shaken him but . . . he doesn't wake.'

'When was this?'

'Just now, this minute. I overslept and I've only just got up.'

'I'll be right over,' Greenleaf said.

She murmured, 'Too kind!' and he heard the receiver drop.

Taking up his bag, he went by the short cut, the diameter of The Circle across the grass. On the face of it it seemed obvious what had happened. In pain from his stings Patrick had taken an extra one of the capsules. I ought to have taken the damned things away with me, Greenleaf said to himself. But still, it wasn't for him to baby another man's patients. Howard had prescribed them, they were safe enough unless . . . Unless! Surely Patrick wouldn't have been fool enough to take *two* more? Greenleaf quickened his pace and broke into a trot. Patrick was a young man, apparently healthy, but still, three . . . And

the anti-histamine. Suppose he had taken the whole bot-
tleful?

She was waiting for him on the doorstep when he ran
up the Hallows drive and she hadn't bothered to dress.
Because she never made up her face and always wore her
hair straight she hadn't the bleak unkempt look of most of
the women who called him out in an emergency. She wore
a simple expensive dressing-gown of candy-striped cotton,
pink and white with a small spotless white bow at the neck,
and there were silver chain sandals on her feet. She looked
alarmed and because of her fear, very young.

'Oh, Max, I didn't know what to do.'

'Still asleep, is he?'

Greenleaf went upstairs quickly, talking to her over his
shoulder.

'He's so white and still and – and heavy somehow.'

'All right. Don't come up. Make some coffee. Make it
very strong and black.'

She went away to the kitchen and Greenleaf entered the
bedroom. Patrick was lying on his back, his head at an odd
angle. His face was still puffy and the arms which were
stretched over the counterpane, faintly swollen and white,
not red any more. Greenleaf knew that colour, the yellowish ivory of parchment, and that waxen texture.

He took one of the wrists and remembered what Tamsin
had said about the heavy feeling. Then, having slipped one
hand within the bedclothes, he lifted Patrick's eyelids and
closed them again. He sighed deeply. Feeling Patrick's
pulse and heart had been just a farce. He had known when
he came into the room. The dead look so very dead, as if
they have never been alive.

He went out to meet Tamsin. She was coming up the
stairs with the dog behind her.

'Tamsin, come in here.' He opened the door to the room
where last night they had looked at the picture. One of the
beds had been slept in and the covers were thrown back.
'Would you like to sit down?'

'Can't you wake him either?'

'I'm afraid . . .' He was a friend and he put his arm about
her shoulders. 'You must be prepared for a shock.' She
looked up at him. He had never noticed how large her eyes

were nor of what a curious shade of transparent amber.
'I'm very much afraid Patrick is dead.'

She neither cried nor cried out. There was no change of
colour in the smooth brown skin. Resting back against the
bed-head, she remained as still as if she too were dead. She
seemed to be thinking. It was as if, Greenleaf thought, all
her past life with Patrick was being re-lived momentarily
within her brain. At last she shuddered and bowed her
head.

'What was it?' He had to bend towards her to catch the
words. 'The cause, I mean. What did he die of?'

'I don't know.'

'The wasp stings?'

Greenleaf shook his head.

'I don't want to trouble you now,' he said gently, 'but
those capsules, the sodium amytal, where are they?'

Tamsin got up like a woman in a dream.

'In the drawer. I'll get them.'

He followed her back into the other bedroom. She
looked at Patrick, still without crying, and Greenleaf
expected her to kiss the pallid forehead. They usually did.
When instead she turned away and went to the dressing
table he drew the sheet up over Patrick's face.

'There are still five in the bottle,' she said, and held it
out to him. Greenleaf was very surprised. He felt a creeping
unease.

'I'll get on to Dr. Howard,' he said.

Howard was out playing golf. Mrs. Howard would ring
the club and her husband would come straight over. When
Greenleaf walked into the dining room Tamsin was kneeling on the floor with her arms round the neck of the
Weimaraner. She was crying.

'Oh, Queenie! Oh, Queenie!'

The room was untouched since the night before. The
drinks were still on the sideboard and out on the patio
some of the food still remained: heat-curled bread, melting
cream, a shrivelled sandwich on a doyley. On the birthday
table Marvell's roses lay among the other gifts, pearled with
Sunday's dew. Greenleaf poured some brandy into a glass
and handed it to Tamsin.

'How long has he been dead?' she asked.

'A good while,' Greenleaf said. 'Hours. Perhaps ten or twelve hours. Of course you looked in on him before you went to bed?'

She had stopped crying. 'Oh, yes,' she said.

'It doesn't matter. I don't want to upset you.'

'That's all right, Max. I'd like to talk about it.'

'You didn't sleep in the same room?'

'Not when one of us was ill,' Tamsin said quickly. 'I thought if he was restless it would be better for me to go in the back. Restless!' She passed her hand across her brow. 'Too dreadful, Max!' She went on rather as if she were giving evidence, using clipped sentences. 'I tried to clear up the mess in the garden but I was too tired. Then I looked in on Patrick. It must have been about midnight. He was sleeping then. I know he was, he was breathing. Well, then I went to bed. I was terribly tired, Max, and I didn't wake up till eleven. I rushed into Patrick because I couldn't hear a sound. Queenie had come up on my bed during the night.' Her hand fumbled for the dog's neck and she pushed her fingers into the plushy fur. 'I couldn't wake him so I phoned Dr. Howard. You know the rest.'

Patrick had died, Greenleaf thought, as he had lived, precisely, tidily, without dirt or disorder. Not for him the sloppy squalor that attended so many death-beds. From mild discomfort he had slipped into sleep, from sleep into death.

'Tamsin,' he said slowly and kindly, 'have you got any other sleeping pills in the house? Have you got any of your own?'

'Oh, no. No, I know we haven't. Patrick just had those six left and I never need anything to make me sleep.' She added unnecessarily: 'I sleep like a log.'

'Had he a weak heart? Did you ever hear of any heart trouble?'

'I don't think so. We'd been married for seven years, you know, but I've known Patrick since he was a little boy. I don't know if you knew we were cousins? His father and mine were brothers.'

'No serious illnesses?'

A petulant cloud crossed her face briefly. 'He was born in Germany,' she said. 'Then, when the war came, they lived in America. After they came back to this country they used to come and see us sometimes. Patrick was terribly spoiled, coddled really. They used to make him wrap up warm even in the summer and I had swimming lessons but they wouldn't let him. I always thought it was because they'd lived in California.' She paused, frowning. 'He was always all right when he was grown-up. The only time he went to Dr. Howard was when he couldn't sleep.'

'I think you will have to prepare yourself,' Greenleaf said, 'for the possibility of an inquest, or, at any rate, a post-mortem.'

She nodded earnestly.

'Oh, quite,' she said. 'I understand. That'll be absolutely all right.' She might have been agreeing to cancel an engagement, so matter-of-fact was her tone.

After that they sat in silence, waiting for Dr. Howard to come. The Weimaraner went upstairs and they heard her claws scraping, scraping at the closed door of the balcony room.

As things turned out, it never came to an inquest. Greenleaf stood in at the post-mortem because he was interested and because the Selbys had been friends of his. Patrick had died, like all the dead, of heart failure. The death certificate was signed and he was buried in Chantflower cemetery on the following Thursday.

Greenleaf and Bernice went to the funeral. They took Marvell with them in Bernice's car.

'Blessed are the dead,' said the Rector, a shade sardonically, 'which die in the Lord.' Since coming to Linchester Patrick had never been to church.

Patrick's parents were dead; Tamsin had been an orphan since she was four. They had both been only children. Consequently there were no relatives at the graveside. Apart from the Linchesterites, only three friends came to support the widow: the two other directors of Patrick's firm of glass manufacturers and old Mrs. Prynne.

Tamsin wore a black dress and a large hat of glossy black straw. Throughout the service she clung to Oliver Gage's arm. On her other side Nancy, sweating in the charcoal worsted she had bought for her February honeymoon, sat with a handkerchief ready. But she never had to hand it to Tamsin who sat rigid and dry-eyed.

It was only when the coffin was being lowered into the ground that a small disturbance occurred. Freda Carnaby tore herself from Mrs. Staxton's arm and, sobbing loudly, fell to her knees beside the dark cavity. As he said afterwards to Greenleaf, Marvell thought that like Hamlet she was going to leap into the grave. But nothing dramatic happened. Mrs. Staxton helped her to her feet and drew her away.

When it was all over Tamsin slung two suitcases into the back of the black and white Mini (SIN 1A) and with Queenie in the seat beside her, drove away to stay with Mrs. Prynne.

PART TWO

Two days later the weather broke with a noisy spectacular thunderstorm and a man died when a tree under which he was sheltering on Chantflower golf course was struck by lightning. The silly season had begun and this was national news. For the Linchester housewives kept indoors by continuous rain, it was for days the prime topic of conversation – until something more personal and sensational took over.

The young Macdonalds had taken their baby to Bournemouth; the Willises and the Millers, each couple finding in the other the perfect neighbours and friends, were cruising together in the Canaries. Tamsin was still away. With four empty houses on Linchester Nancy was bored to tears. When Oliver came home for the week-ends, tired and uneasy, he found his evening programmes mapped out for him.

Tonight the Greenleafs and Crispin Marvell were invited for coffee and drinks. Opening his sideboard, Oliver found that Nancy had laid in a stock of cheap Cyprus sherry and bottles of cocktails as variously coloured as the liquid that used to be displayed in the flagons of old-fashioned pharmacy windows. He cursed, clinging to the shreds of his pride and remembering the days that were gone.

The mantelpiece was decorated with postcards. Nancy had given pride of place to a peacock-blue panorama from Clare Miller, relegating two monochrome seascapes to a spot behind a vase. He read Sheila Macdonald's happy scrawl irascibly. Tamsin was at the seaside too, but Tamsin had sent nothing . . .

From where he stood, desultorily watching the rain, he could hear Nancy chattering to Linda Gaveston in the kitchen. Occasionally something clearly audible if not comprehensible arose above the twittering.

'I said it was dead grotty' or 'How about that, doll?' conflicted inharmoniously with Nancy's 'You are awful, Linda.'

Oliver grunted and lit a cigarette. These visits of Linda's, ostensibly made to deliver Nancy's order of tablets of soap or a packet of Kleenex, always put him in a bad temper. They invariably led to petulance on Nancy's part, to dissatisfaction and a carping envy. It amazed Oliver that a village chemist like Waller could stock such an immense and catholic variety of luxury goods, all of which at some time or another seemed so desirable to his wife and at the same time so conducive to the saving of money. The latest in Thermos flasks, automatic tea-makers, thermostatically-controlled electric blankets, shower cabinets, all these had in the year they had lived on Linchester, been recommended to Nancy and coveted by her.

'It would be such a saving in the long run,' she would say wistfully of some gimmick, using the suburban colloquialisms Oliver hated.

Moreover it was surprising that behind Waller's counter there stood concealed the most expensive ranges of cosmetics from Paris and New York, scent and creams which were apparently exclusive to him and not to be found in Nottingham or, for that matter, London. He was therefore pleasantly astonished when the door had closed on Linda to see Nancy come dancing into the room, contented, gay and in a strange way, gleeful.

'What's got into you?'

'Nothing.'

'For a poor house-bound, forsaken child bride,' he said, recalling earlier complaints, 'you're looking very gay.'

Indeed she appeared quite pretty again in the honeymoon skirt and a pink sweater, not a hand-knitted one for a change but a soft fluffy thing that drew Oliver's eyes and reminded him that his wife had, after all, an excellent figure. But his words, sharp and moody, had altered her expression from open calm to secretiveness.

'Linda told me something very peculiar.'

'Really?' he said. 'Surprise me.'

She pouted.

'Not if you're going to talk to me like that.' For a

moment, a transient moment, she looked just as she had when he had first seen her dancing with the man she had been engaged to. It had been such fun stealing her from him, especially piquant because the fiancé had also been Shirley's cousin. 'Nasty Oliver! I shall save it all up till the Greenleafs get here.'

'I can see,' said Oliver in his best co-respondent's voice, 'I can see I shall have to be very nice to you.'

'Very, very nice,' said Nancy. She sat on the sofa beside him and giggled. 'You are awful! It must be the country air.' But she didn't say anything after that and presently Oliver forgot all about Linda Gaveston.

When Marvell rang the door-bell she didn't bother to tidy her hair or put on fresh make-up. There was something of a bacchante about her, exhibitionistic, crudely female. Suddenly Oliver felt old. Her naiveté embarrassed him. He went to dispense drinks from his own stock, leaving the bright mean bottles in the sideboard.

Greenleaf and Bernice had barely sat down when she said brightly:

'Has anyone heard from Tamsin?'

Nobody had. Oliver fancied that Marvell was looking at him quizzically.

'I don't suppose she feels like writing.' Bernice was always kind and forbearing. 'It's not as if we were any of us close friends.'

'What would she have to write about?' Greenleaf asked. 'She's not on holiday.' And he began to talk about his own holiday, planned for September this year, and to ask about the Gages'.

Holidays were a sore point with Oliver who hoped to do without one altogether. He need not have worried. Nancy was obviously not going to let the subject go as easily as that.

'Poor Tamsin,' she said loudly, drowning the doctor's voice. 'Fancy being a widow when you're only twenty-seven.'

'Dreadful,' said Bernice.

'And in such – well, awkward circumstances.'

'Awkward circumstances?' said Greenleaf, drawn unwillingly from his dreams of the Riviera.

'I don't mean money-wise.' Oliver winced but Nancy went on: 'The whole thing was so funny, Patrick dying like that. I expect you'll all think I've got a very suspicious mind but I can't help thinking it was . . .' She paused for effect and sipped her gin. 'Well, it was fishy, wasn't it?'

Greenleaf looked at the floor. The legs of his chair had caught in one of the Numdah rugs. He bent down and straightened it.

'I don't know if I ought to say this,' Nancy went on. 'I don't suppose it's common knowledge, but Patrick's father . . .' She lowered her voice. 'Patrick's father committed suicide. Took his own life.'

'Oh, dear,' said Bernice comfortably.

'I really don't know who it was told me,' Nancy said. She picked up the plate of canapés and handed it to Marvell. To his shame Oliver saw that only half a cocktail onion topped the salmon mayonnaise on each of them. 'Do have a savoury, won't you?'

Marvell refused. The plate hovered.

'Somebody told me about it. Now who was it?'

'It was me,' Oliver said sharply.

'Of course it was. And Tamsin told you. I can't imagine why.'

All childish innocence, she looked archly from face to face.

Marvell said: 'I'm afraid I'm being obtuse, but I can't quite see what Patrick's father's suicide has to do with his son dying of heart failure.'

'Oh, absolutely nothing. Nothing at all. You mustn't think I was insinuating anything about Patrick. It's just that it's one of the funny circumstances. On its own it would be nothing.'

Oliver emptied his glass and stood up. He could cheerfully have slapped Nancy's face. 'I think we're boring our guests,' he said, bracketing himself with his wife and trying to make his voice sound easy. 'Another drink, Max? Bernice?' Marvell's glass was still full. 'What about you, darling?'

'Oh, really!' Nancy burst out laughing. 'You don't have to be so discreet. We're all friends. Nothing's going to go beyond these four walls.'

Oliver felt himself losing control. These people *were* discreet. Would it, after all, ruin his career, damn him as a social creature, if in front of them he were to bawl at Nancy, strike her, push her out of the room?

He stared at her, pouring sherry absently until it topped over the glass and spilled on the tray.

'Damnation!' he said.

'Oh, your table!' Bernice was beside him, mopping with a tiny handkerchief.

'Linda Gaveston was here today,' Nancy said. 'She told me something very peculiar. No, I won't shut up, Oliver. I'm only repeating it because I'd be very interested in having an opinion from a medical man. You know that funny little man who's a commercial traveller? The one who lives in the chalets?'

'Carnaby,' said Marvell.

'That's right. Carnaby. The one who was so difficult at the party. Well, the day before Patrick died he came into Waller's shop and what d'you think he tried to buy?' She waited for the guesses that never came. 'Cyanide! That's what he tried to buy.'

Greenleaf stuck out his lower lip. They had only been in the house half an hour but he began to wonder how soon he could suggest to Bernice that it was time to leave. His drink tasted thin. For the first time since he had given up smoking as an example to his patients he longed for a cigarette.

'Waller wouldn't sell anyone cyanide,' he said at last.

'Ah, no,' said Nancy triumphantly, 'he didn't. But that's not the point, is it? He wanted cyanide and maybe he managed to get it . . .' She drew breath. 'Elsewhere,' she said with sinister emphasis. 'Now why did he want it?'

'Probably for killing wasps,' said Marvell. 'It's an old remedy for getting rid of wasps.'

Nancy looked disappointed.

'Linda overheard the conversation,' she said, 'and that's just what this fellow Carnaby said. He said he wanted it for wasps. Linda thought it was pretty thin.'

Thumping his fist on the table, Oliver made them all jump.

'Linda Gaveston is a stupid little trouble-maker,' he said furiously.

'I suppose that goes for me too?'

'I didn't say so,' said Oliver, too angry to care. 'But if the cap fits . . . I hate all this under-hand gossip. If you're trying to say Carnaby gave Patrick cyanide you'd better come straight out with it.' He drank some whisky too quickly and choked. 'On the other hand, perhaps you'd better not. I don't want to pay out whacking damages for slander.'

'It won't go any further. Anyway, it's my duty as a citizen to say what I think. Everyone knows Edward Carnaby had a terrific motive for getting Patrick out of the way.'

There was an appalled silence. Nancy had grown red in the face and her plump breasts rose and fell under the clinging pink wool.

'You're all crazy about Tamsin. I know that. But Patrick wasn't. He didn't care for her a bit. He was having an affair with that awful little Freda. Night after night he was round there while her brother was out at evening classes. He used to tie that great dog of theirs up to the gate. It was just a horrid sordid little intrigue.'

As much as Oliver, Greenleaf wanted to stop her. He was immeasurably grateful for Bernice's rich cleansing laughter.

'If it was just a little intrigue,' Bernice said lightly, 'it can't have been important, can it?'

Nancy allowed her hand to rest for a moment beneath Bernice's. Then she snatched it away.

'They're twins, aren't they? It means a lot, being twins. He wouldn't want to lose her. Patrick might have gone off with her.'

But the tension was broken. Marvell, who had taken a book from the fireside shelves and studied it as if it were a first edition, now relaxed and smiled. Oliver had moved over to the record player and the red glaze had left his face.

'Well, what does Max think?' Nancy asked.

How wise Bernice had been, laughing easily, refusing to catch his eye! Greenleaf didn't really want to do a Smith-King and flee at the scent of trouble. Besides Oliver had some good records, Bartok and the wonderful Donizetti he wanted to hear again.

'You know,' he said in a quiet gentle voice, 'it's amazing the way people expect the worst when a young person dies suddenly. They always want to make a mystery.' He wondered if Bernice and, for that matter Marvell, noticed how dismay was evoking his guttural accent. 'Real life isn't so sensational.'

'Fiction stranger than truth,' Marvell murmured.

'I can assure you Patrick didn't die of cyanide. You see, of all the poisons commonly used in cases of homicide cyanide is the most easily detected. The smell, for one thing . . .'

'Bitter almonds,' Nancy interposed.

Greenleaf smiled a smile he didn't feel.

'That among other things. Believe me, it's fantastic to talk of cyanide.' His hands moved expressively. 'No, please,' he said.

'Well, what do you really think, then?'

'I think you're a very pretty girl with a vivid imagination and Linda Gaveston watches too much television. I wonder if I might have some more of your excellent whisky, Oliver?'

Oliver took the glass gratefully. He looked as if he would gladly have given Greenleaf the whole bottle.

'Music,' he said, handing records to the discerning Marvell.

'May we have the Handel?' Marvell asked politely. Nancy made a face and flung herself back among the cushions.

The sound of the rain falling steadily had formed throughout the conversation a monotonous background chorus. Now, as they became silent, the music of The Faithful Shepherd Suite filled the room. Greenleaf listened to the orchestra and noted the repetition of each phrase with the appreciation of the scientist: but Marvell, with the ear of the artist *manqué*, felt the absurd skimped room transformed about him and, sighing within himself for something irrevocably lost, saw a green grove as in a Constable landscape and beneath the leaves a lover with the Pipes of Pan.

9

The rain ceased as darkness fell and the sky cleared suddenly as if washed free of cloud. It was a night of bright white stars, so many stars that Greenleaf had to point out and admire – although he did not know their names – the strung lights of Charles's Wain and Jupiter riding in the south.

'Patines of bright gold,' said Marvell. 'Only they're not gold, they're platinum. Patines of bright platinum doesn't sound half so well, does it?'

'It's no good quoting at me,' said the doctor. 'You know I never read anything but the *B.M.J.*' He drew a deep breath, savouring the night air. 'Very nice,' he said inadequately. 'I'm glad I summoned up the energy to walk back with you.'

'It was a sticky evening, wasn't it?' Marvell went first, holding back brambles for Greenleaf to pass along the path.

'Silly little woman,' Greenleaf said, harshly for him. 'I hope Gage can stop her gossiping.'

'It could be awkward.' Marvell said no more until the path broadened and the doctor was walking abreast of him. Then suddenly, 'May I ask you something?' he said. 'I don't want to offend you.'

'You won't do that.'

'You're a doctor, but Patrick wasn't your patient.' Marvell spoke quietly. 'I asked you if I would offend you because I was thinking of medical etiquette. But – look, I'm not scandal-mongering like Nancy Gage – weren't you very surprised when Patrick died like that?'

Greenleaf said guardedly, 'I was surprised, yes.'

'Thunderstruck?'

'Like that poor fellow on the golf course? Well, no. You see a lot of strange things in my job. I thought at first Patrick had taken an overdose of sodium amytal. I'd given him an anti-histamine, two hundred milligrammes of Phenergan, and one would potentiate . . .' He stopped, loth to give these esoteric details to a layman. 'He had the sodium amytal and I advised him to take one.'

'You left the bottle with him?'

'Now, look.' Greenleaf had said he wouldn't be offended. 'Patrick wasn't a child. Howard had prescribed them. In any case, he didn't take any more. That was the first thing Glover looked for at the post-mortem.'

Marvell opened the orchard gate and Greenleaf stepped from the forest floor on to turf and the slippery leaves of wild daffodils. The petals of a wet rose brushed his face. In the darkness they felt like a woman's fingers drenched with scent.

'The first thing?' Marvell asked. 'You mean, you looked for other things? You suspected suicide or even murder?'

'No, no, no,' Greenleaf said impatiently. 'A man had died, a young, apparently healthy man. Glover had to find out what he died of. Patrick died of heart failure.'

'Everybody dies of heart failure.'

'Roughly, yes. But there were signs that the heart had been affected before. There was some slight damage.'

They had come to the back door. The kitchen smelt of herbs and wine. Greenleaf thought he could detect another less pleasant scent. Mildew. He had never seen mushrooms growing but Marvell's kitchen smelt like the plastic trays of mushrooms Bernice bought at the village store. Marvell groped for the lamp and lit it.

'Well, go on,' he said.

'If you must know,' Greenleaf said. 'Glover made some enquiries at Patrick's old school. Tamsin didn't know anything and Patrick's parents were dead. He'd never complained to Howard about feeling ill. Only went to him once.'

'May I ask if you got anything from the school?'

'I don't know if you may,' Greenleaf said severely. 'I don't know why you want to know. But if there's going to be a lot of talk . . . Glover wrote to the headmaster and he got a letter back saying Patrick had had to be let off some of the games because he'd had rheumatic fever.'

'I see. So you checked with the doctor Patrick had when he was a child.'

'We couldn't do that.' Greenleaf smiled a small, bitter and very personal smile. 'Patrick was born in Germany. His mother was German and he lived there till he was four. Glover talked to Tamsin's Mrs. Prynne. She's one of these old women with a good memory. She remembered Patrick had had rheumatic fever when he was three – very early to have it, incidentally – and that the name of his doctor had been Goldstein.'

Marvell was embarrassed.

'But Dr. Goldstein had disappeared. A lot of people of his persuasion disappeared in Germany between 1939 and 1945.'

'Stopping for a quick drink?' Marvell asked.

Five minutes passed before he said anything more about Patrick Selby. Greenleaf felt that he had been stiff and pompous, the very prototype of the uppish medical man. To restore Marvell's ease he accepted a glass of carrot wine.

The brilliance of the white globe had increased until now only the corners of the parlour remained in shadow. A small wind had arisen, stirring the curtains and moving the trailing violet and white leaves of the Tradescantia that stood in a majolica pot on the window sill. It was rather cold.

Then Marvell said: 'I was curious about Patrick.' He sat down and warmed his hands at the lamp. Greenleaf wondered if Bernice, at home in Shalom, had turned on the central heating. 'Perhaps I have a suspicious mind. Patrick had a good many enemies, you know. Quite a lot of people must be glad he's dead.'

'And I have a logical mind,' said Greenleaf briskly. 'Nancy Gage says Carnaby tried to buy cyanide. Patrick Selby dies suddenly. Therefore, she reasons, Patrick died of cyanide. But we *know* Patrick didn't die of cyanide. He died a natural death. Can't you see that once your original premise falls to the ground there's no longer any reason to doubt that? No matter how much Carnaby hated him – if he did, which I doubt – no matter if he succeeded in buying a ton of cyanide, he didn't kill Patrick with it because Patrick didn't die of cyanide. Now, just because one person appears to have a thin motive and access – possible access – to means *that were never used at all*, you start reasoning that he was in fact murdered, that half a dozen people had motives and that one of them succeeded.' He drank the carrot wine. It was really quite pleasant, like sweet Bristol Cream. 'You're not being logical,' he said.

Marvell didn't reply. He began to wind the clock delicately as if he was being careful not to disturb the sultan and his slave whose fingers rested eternally on the silent zither. When he had put the key down he blew away a money spider that was creeping across the sultan's gondola-shaped shoe. Then he said:

'Why wasn't there an inquest?'

Greenleaf answered him triumphantly. 'Because there wasn't any need. Haven't I been telling you? And that wasn't up to Glover and Howard. That's a matter for the coroner.'

'No doubt he knows his own business.'

'You don't have inquests on people who die naturally.' Greenleaf got up, stretching cold stiff legs, and changed the subject. 'How's the hay fever?'

'I've run out of tablets.'

'Come down to the surgery sometime and I'll let you have another prescription.'

But Marvell didn't come and Greenleaf saw nothing of him for several days. Greenleaf began to think that he would hear no more of Patrick's death – until surgery time on Wednesday morning.

The first patient to come into the consulting room through the green baize door was Denholm Smith-King. He was on his way to his Nottingham factory and at last he had summoned the courage to let Greenleaf examine him.

'It's nothing,' the doctor said as Smith-King sat up on the couch buttoning his shirt. 'Only a gland. It'll go down eventually.'

'Then I suppose I shall just have to lump it.' He laughed at his own joke and Greenleaf joined in politely.

'I see you've cut down on the smoking.'

He was startled and showed it, but his eyes followed the doctor's down to his own right forefinger and he grinned.

'Quite the detective in your own way, aren't you?' Green-leaf had only noticed that the sepia stains had paled to yellow and this remark reminded him of things he wanted to forget. 'Yes, I've cut it down,' Smith-King said and he gave the doctor a heavy, though friendly buffet on the back. 'You quacks, you don't know the strains a businessman has to contend with. You don't know you're born,' but his hearty laugh softened the words.

'Things going better, are they?'

'You bet,' said Smith-King.

He went off jauntily and Greenleaf rang the bell for the next patient. By ten he had seen a dozen people and he asked the last one, a woman with nettle rash, if there were any more to come.

'Just one, Doctor. A young lady.'

He put his finger on the buzzer but no-one came so he began to tidy up his desk. Evidently the young lady had got tired of waiting. Then, just as he was picking up his ignition key, the baize door was pushed feebly open and Freda Carnaby shuffled in wearily like an old woman.

He was shocked at the change in her. Impatience died as he offered her a chair and sat down himself. What had become of the bright bird-like creature with the practical starched cotton dresses and the impractical shoes? Even at the funeral she had still looked smart in trim shop-girl black. Now her hair looked as if it hadn't been washed for weeks, her eyes were bloodshot and puffy and there was a hysterical downward quirk at the corner of her mouth.

'What exactly is the trouble, Miss Carnaby?'

'I can't sleep. I haven't had a proper night's sleep since I don't know how long.' She felt in the pocket of the mocksuede jacket she wore over her crumpled print dress. The handkerchief she pulled out was crumpled too. She pressed it with pathetic gentility against her lips. 'You see, I've had a great personal loss.' The linen square brushed the corner of one eye. 'I was very fond of someone. A man.' She gulped. 'He died quite recently.'

'I'm sorry to hear that.' Greenleaf began to wonder what was coming.

'I don't know what to do.'

He had observed before that it is this particular phrase that triggers off the tears, the breakdown. It may be true, it may be felt, but it is only when it is actually uttered aloud that its full significance, the complete helpless disorientation it implies, brings home to the speaker the wretchedness of his or her plight.

'Now you mustn't say that,' he said, knowing his inadequacy. 'Time does heal, you know.' The healer passing the buck, he thought. 'I'll let you have something to make you sleep.' He drew out his prescription pad and began to write. 'Have you been away yet this year?'

'No and I'm not likely to.'

'I should try. Just a few days would help.'

'Help?' He had heard that hysterical note so often but not from her and he didn't like it. 'Help a – a broken heart? Oh, Doctor, I don't know what to do. I don't know what to do.' She dropped her head on to her folded arms and began to sob.

Greenleaf went to the sink and drew her a glass of water.

'I'd like to tell you about it.' She sipped and wiped her eyes. 'Can I tell you about it?'

He looked surreptitiously at his watch.

'If it would make you feel better.'

'It was Patrick Selby. You knew that, didn't you?' Greenleaf said nothing so she went on. 'I was very fond of him.' They never say 'love', he thought, always 'very fond of' or 'devoted to'. 'And he was very fond of me,' she said defiantly. He glanced momentarily at her tear-blotched face, the rough skin. When she said out of the blue, 'We were going to be married,' he jumped.

'I know what you're going to say. You're going to say he was already married. Tamsin didn't care for him. He was going to divorce her.'

'Miss Carnaby . . .'

But she rushed on, the words tumbling out.

'She was having an affair with that awful man Gage. Patrick knew all about it. She used to meet him in London during the week. Patrick knew. She said she was going to see some old friend of her grandmother's, but half the time she was with that man.'

Sympathy fought with and finally conquered Greenleaf's distaste. Keeping his expression a kindly blank, he began to fold up the prescription.

Misinterpreting his look, she said defensively:

'I know what you're thinking. But I wasn't carrying on with Patrick. It wasn't like that. We never did anything wrong. We were going to be married. And Nancy Gage is going about all over Linchester saying Edward killed Patrick because . . . because . . .' Her sobs broke out afresh. Greenleaf watched her in despair. How was he to turn this weeping hysterical woman out into the street? How stem the tide of appalling revelation?

'And the terrible thing is I know he was killed. That's why I can't sleep. And I know who killed him.'

This was too much. He shook her slightly, wiped her eyes himself and held the glass to her lips.

'Miss Carnaby, you must get a grip on yourself. Patrick died a perfectly natural death. This is certain. I know it. You'll only do your brother and yourself a lot of harm if you go about saying things you can't substantiate.'

'Substantiate?' She stumbled over the word. 'I can *prove* it. You remember what it was like at that awful party. Well, Oliver Gage went back by himself when it was all over. I saw him from my bedroom window. It was bright moonlight and he went over by the pond. He was carrying something, a white packet. I don't know what it was, but, Doctor, suppose – suppose it killed Patrick!'

Then he got her out of the surgery, bundled her into his own car and drove her back to Linchester.

Three letters plopped through the Gage letter box when the post came at ten. Nancy was so sure they weren't for her that it was all of half an hour before she bothered to come down from the bathroom. Instead, her hair rolled up in curlers, wet and evil-smelling with home-perm fluid, she sat on the edge of the bath waiting for the cooking timer to ping and brooding about what the letters might contain.

Two bills, she thought bitterly, and probably a begging letter from Jean or Shirley. A saturated curler dripped on to her nose. By this time the whole of the first floor of the house smelt of ammonia and rotten eggs. She would have to use masses of that air freshener stuff before Oliver came home. Still, that was a whole two days and goodness knew how many hours away. Surely Oliver would scarcely notice the smell when he saw how wonderful her hair looked, and all for twenty-five bob.

The timer rang and she began unrolling excitedly. When the handbasin was filled with a soggy mess of curlers and mushy paper she put a towel round her shoulders, a mauve one with Hers embroidered on it in white; His, the other half of the wedding present, was scrupulously kept for Oliver – and went downstairs.

The first letter she picked up was from Jean. Nancy knew that before she saw the handwriting. Oliver's first wife was their only correspondent who saved old envelopes and stuck new address labels on them. The second was almost certainly the telephone bill. It might be as well to lose that one. Now, who could be writing to her from London?

She opened the last envelope and saw the letter heading, Oliver's newspaper, Fleet Street. It was *from* Oliver. She looked again at the envelope and at the slanted stamp. To her that meant a kiss. Did it mean that to Oliver or had it occurred by chance?

'My darling . . .' That was nice. It was also unfamiliar and unexpected. She read on. 'I am wondering if you have forgiven me for my unkindness to you at the week-end. I was sharp with you, even verging on the brutal . . . ' How beautifully he wrote! But that was to be expected. It was, after all, his line. 'Can you understand, my sweet, that this was only because I hate to see you cheapening yourself ? I felt that you were making yourself the butt of those men's wit and this hurt me more bitterly than I can tell you. So for my sake, darling Nancy, watch your words. This is Tamsin's business and she is nothing to us . . .' Nancy could hardly believe a letter would make her so happy. '. . . She is nothing to us. We each possess one world. Each hath one and is one.' Hath, she decided, must be typing error, but the thought was there. 'The merest suggestion that I might be . . .' Then there was a bit blanked out with x's '. . . associated with a scandal of this kind has caused me considerable disquiet. We were not close friends of the Selbys . . .'

There was a great deal more in the same vein. Nancy skipped some of it, the boring parts, and lingered over the astonishing endearments at the end. She was so ecstatically happy that, although she caught sight of her elated face in the hall mirror, she hardly noticed that her hair was hanging in rats' tails, dripping and perfectly straight.

Marvell was determined to get Greenleaf interested in the circumstances of Patrick's death and he thought it would do no harm to confront him with a list of unusual poisons. To this end he had been to the public library and spent an instructive afternoon reading Taylor. He was so carried away that he was too late for afternoon surgery – his ostensible mission, he decided, would be to collect another prescription – so he picked a bunch of acanthus for Bernice and walked up to Shalom.

'Beautiful,' Bernice said. Her husband touched the brownish-pink flowers. 'What are they?' Diffidently he suggested: 'Lupins or something?'

'Acanthus,' said Marvell. 'The original model for the Corinthian capital.'

Bernice filled a white stone vase with water. 'You are a mine of information.'

'Let's say a disused quarry of rubble.' The words had a bitter sound but Marvell smiled as he watched her arrange the flowers. 'And the rubble, incidentally, is being shaken by explosions. I've been sneezing for the past three days and I've run out of those fascinating little blue pills.'

Bernice smiled. 'If this is going to turn into a consultation,' she said, 'you'd better go and have a drink with Max.'

She began on the washing up and Marvell followed Greenleaf into the sitting room. Greenleaf pushed open the glass doors to the garden and pulled up chairs in the path of the incoming cooler air. The sky directly above was a pure milky blue and in the west refulgent, brazen gold, but the long shadow of the cedar tree lapped the walls of the house. The room was a cool sanctuary.

'It might be worth finding out exactly what you're allergic to, have some tests done,' the doctor said. 'It need not be hay, you know. You can be allergic to practically anything.'

Marvell hadn't really wanted to talk about himself but now, as if to give colour to his excuse, a tickle began at the back of his nose and he was shaken by a vast sneeze. When he had recovered he said slyly:

'Well, I suppose it can't kill me.'

'It could lead to asthma,' Greenleaf said cheerfully. 'It does in sixty to eighty per cent of cases if it isn't checked.'

'I asked,' said Marvell, re-phrasing, 'if an allergy could kill you.'

'No, you didn't. And I know exactly what you're getting at, but Patrick wasn't allergic to wasp stings. He had one a few days before he died and the effect was just normal.'

'All right,' Marvell said and he blew his nose. 'You remember what we were talking about the other night?'

'What you were talking about.'

'What I was talking about, then. Don't be so stiff-necked, Max.'

They had known each other for two or three years now and at first it had been Dr. Greenleaf, Mr. Marvell. Then, as intimacy grew, the use of their styles had seemed too formal and Greenleaf who hadn't been to a public school baulked at the bare surname. This was the first time Marvell had called his friend by his first name and Greenleaf felt the strange warmth of heart, the sense of being accepted, this usage brings. It made him weak where he had intended to be strong.

'Suppose,' Marvell went on, 'there was some substance, perfectly harmless under normal circumstances, but lethal if anyone took it when he'd been stung by a wasp.'

Reluctantly Greenleaf recalled what Freda Carnaby had told him about the white package carried by Oliver Gage.

'Suppose, suppose. There isn't such a substance.'

'Sure?'

'As sure as anyone can be.'

'I'm bored with Chantefleur Abbey, Max, and I've a mind to do a spot of detecting – with your help. It obviously needs a doctor.'

'You're crazy,' said Greenleaf unhappily. 'I'm going to give you a drink and write out that prescription.'

'I don't want a drink. I want to talk about Patrick.'

'Well?'

'Well, since I last saw you I've been swotting up forensic medicine . . .'

'In between the sneezes, I imagine.'

'In between the sneezes, as you say. As a matter of fact I've been reading Taylor's *Medical Jurisprudence*.'

'Fascinating, isn't it?' Greenleaf said, in spite of himself. He added quickly: 'It won't tell you a thing about wasp stings or rheumatic fever.'

'No, but it tells me a hell of a lot about poisons. A positive Borgias' Bible. Brucine and thallium, lead and gold. Did you know there are some gold salts called Purple of Cassius? But of course you did. Purple of Cassius! There's a name to conjure death with.'

'It didn't conjure Patrick Selby's death.'

'How do you *know*? I'll bet Glover didn't test for it.'

'No, and he didn't test for arsenic or hyoscine or the botulinus bacillus, for the simple reason that there wasn't the slightest indication in Patrick's appearance or the state of the room to suggest that he might remotely have taken any of them.'

'I have heard,' Marvell said, 'that a man can die from having air injected into a vein. Now there's a very entertaining novel by Dorothy Sayers . . .'

'*Unnatural Death.*'

'So you do read detective stories!' Marvell pounced on his words.

'Only on holiday.' Greenleaf smiled. 'But Patrick hadn't any hypodermic marks.'

'Well, well,' Marvell mocked. 'Max, you're a hypocrite. How do you know Patrick hadn't any hypodermic marks unless you looked for them? And if you looked for them you must have suspected at the least suicide.'

For a few moments Greenleaf didn't answer him. What Marvell said was near the truth. He had looked and found – nothing. But had he been in possession of certain facts of which he was now cognisant, would he have acted as he had? Wouldn't he instead have tried to dissuade Howard and Glover from signing the death certificate? He had done nothing because Patrick had not been his patient, because it would have been unprofessional to poach on Howard's preserves, because, most of all, Patrick had seemed a reasonably happily married man leading a quiet normal life. Happily married? Now, of course, it sounded an absurd description of the mess he and Tamsin had made for themselves, but then . . . You had to make allowances for the uninhibited way people behaved at parties, Tamsin's close dancing with Gage, Patrick's flirtation with Freda Carnaby. The possibility of murder had never crossed his mind. Why, then, had he looked? Just to fill the time, he thought, almost convincing himself, just for something to do.

And yet, as he answered Marvell, he was fully aware that he was skirting round the question.

'I looked,' he said carefully, 'before Glover began his examination. At the time there seemed nothing to account for the death. It was afterwards that Glover found the heart damage. There were no punctures on Patrick's body apart from those made by wasps. And he didn't die from wasps' stings, unless you might say he had a certain amount of shock from the stings.'

'If by that you mean the shock affected his heart, wouldn't you have expected him to have a heart attack at once, even while he was on the ladder, not three or four hours later?'

The damage caused by the rheumatic fever had been slight. Patrick must have had it very mildly. But in the absence of Patrick's parents and Dr. Goldstein, who could tell? 'Yes, I would,' Greenleaf said unhappily.

'Max, you're coming round to my way of thinking. Look, leaving the cause of death for a moment, wasn't there something very – to use Nancy's word – fishy about that party?'

'You mean the picture?'

'I mean the picture. I went upstairs to get the citronella and there was the picture. Now, it wasn't covered up. It was in a room in Patrick's house. But he didn't know it was there. Did you see his face when he saw it?'

Greenleaf frowned. 'It was a horrible thing,' he said.

'Oh, come. A bit bloodthirsty. By a pupil of Thornhill, I should say, and those old boys didn't pull their punches. But the point is, Patrick was terrified. He couldn't have been more upset if it had been a real head in a real pool of blood.'

'Some people are very squeamish,' said Greenleaf who was always coming across them.

'About real wounds and real blood, yes. But this was only a picture. Now, I'll tell you something. A couple of weeks before he died Patrick was in my house with Tamsin and I showed them some Dali drawings I've got. They're only prints but they're much more horrifying than Salome, but Patrick didn't turn a hair.'

'So he didn't like the picture? What's it got to do with his death? He didn't die from having his head chopped off.'

'Pity,' Marvell said cheerfully. 'If he had we'd only have two-thirds of our present problem. No longer How? but simply Why? and Who?'

He got up as Bernice came in to take him on a tour of the garden.

'I need the advice of someone with green fingers.' She raised her eyebrows at their serious faces. 'Max, you're tired. Are you all right?'

'I'm fine.' He watched them go, Bernice questioning, her companion stooping towards the border plants, his head raised, listening courteously. Then Bernice went up to the fence and he saw that Nancy Gage had come into the garden next door. She evidently had some news to impart, for she was talking excitedly with a kind of feverish desire for the sound of her own voice that women have who are left too much alone. Greenleaf could only remember the last time she had looked like that, but today there was no Oliver to stop her.

His wife's voice floated back to him. 'Tamsin's home, Max.'

Was that all?

He had hardly reached the lawn and heard Bernice say, 'Should we go over?' when Nancy caught him.

'Don't look at my hair,' she said, attracting his attention to it by running her fingers through the strawy mass. 'Something went wrong with the works.'

'Did you say Tamsin was home?'

'We ought to go over, Max, and see if she's all right.'

'Oh, she's all right. Brown as a berry,' said Nancy, and she made a mock-gesture of self-reproach, protruding her teeth over her lower lip. 'There I go. Come back all I said.

Oliver says I mustn't talk about the Selbys to anyone, not anyone at all because of you-know-what.'

Marvell tried to catch Greenleaf's eye and when the doctor refused to co-operate, said, 'And what are we supposed to know?'

'Oliver says I mustn't go about saying Patrick didn't die naturally because it wouldn't do him any good.' She giggled. 'Oliver, I mean, not Patrick. He wrote it in a letter so it must be important.'

'Very prudent,' said Marvell.

Greenleaf opened his mouth to say something, he hardly knew what, and closed it again as the telephone rang. When he came back to the garden Nancy had gone.

'Little boy with a big headache,' he called to Bernice. 'Boys shouldn't have headaches. I'm going to see what it's all about and I'll look in on Tamsin on my way back.'

He went to get the car and nearly ran over Edith Gaveston's dog as he was backing it out. After he had apologised she picked up the Scottie and stuck her head through the car window.

'I like your new motor,' she said archaically. 'Only don't blood it on Fergus, will you?'

Fox-hunting metaphors were lost on the doctor. He made the engine rev faintly.

'I see the merry widow's back.' She pointed across The Green. At first Greenleaf saw only Henry Glide exercising his Boxer; then he noticed that the Hallows' windows had all been opened, flung wide in a way they never were when Patrick was alive. The Weimaraner was standing by the front doors, still as a statue carved from creamy marble.

'Poor girl,' he said.

'Tamsin? I thought you meant Queenie for a minute. Poor is hardly the word I'd choose. That house, the Selby business and a private income! In my opinion she's well rid of him.'

'Excuse me,' Greenleaf said. 'I must go. I have a call.' The car slid out on to the tarmac. The Scottie yapped and Edith bellowed:

'Let's hope she hasn't come back to another scandal. One's enough but two looks like . . .'

Her last words were lost in the sound of the engine but he thought she had said 'enemy action'. He had no idea what she was talking about but he didn't like it. I'm getting as bad as Marvell, he thought uneasily, compelling his eyes to the road. Then he made himself think about headaches and children and meningitis until he came to the house where the sick boy was.

10

The dog Queenie traversed the lawn of Hallows, re-acquainting herself by scent with the home she had returned to after a fortnight's absence. She assured herself that the squirrels' dray still remained in the elm by the gate, that the Smith-Kings' cat had on several occasions crossed the wattle fence and come to the back door, and that a multitude of birds had descended upon the currants, leaving behind them famine and evidence that only a dog could find.

When she had visited the locked garage and peered through the window, whining a little by now, she knew that the man she sought was not on Hallows land. She went back to the house, her tail quite still, and found the woman – her woman as he had been her man – sitting in a bedroom singing and combing her hair as she sang. The dog Queenie placed her head in the silk lap and took a little comfort from the combings that fell upon her like thistle-down.

At first Greenleaf thought that the singing came from the wireless. But then, as he came up to the front doors, he realised that this was no professional but a girl who sang for joy, vaguely, a little out of tune. He rang the bell and waited.

Tamsin was browner than he had ever seen her and he remembered someone saying that Mrs. Prynne lived at the seaside. She wore a bright pink dress of the shade his mother used to call a wicked pink and on her arms black and white bangles.

'I came,' he said, very much taken aback, 'to see if there was anything I could do.'

'You could come in and have a drink with me,' she said and he had the impression she was deliberately crushing the gaiety from her voice. She had put on weight and she looked well. The harsh colour suited her. 'Dear Max.' She took both his hands. 'Always so kind.'

'I saw you were back,' he said as they came into the lounge. 'I've been to see a patient in the village and I thought I'd look in. How are you?'

'I'm fine.' She seemed to realise this was wrong. 'Well, what is it you people say? As well as can be expected. You've had awful weather, haven't you? It was lovely where I was. Hours and hours of sun. I've been on the beach every day.' She stretched her arms high above her head. 'Oh, Max!'

Greenleaf didn't know what to say. He looked about him at the room which Bernice used to say was like a set-piece in a furniture store or a picture in *House Beautiful*. Now it was a mess. Tamsin could scarcely have been home more than two hours but there were clothes on the sofa and on the floor, magazines and newspapers on the hearthrug. She had covered the stark mantelpiece with shells, conches, winkles, razor shells, and there was a trail of sand on the parquet floor.

'How's everyone? How's Bernice? If you've been thinking I neglected you, I didn't send a single postcard to anyone. How's Oliver? And Nancy? What have you all been doing?'

Talking, he thought, about your husband. Aloud he said:

'We've all been going on in the same way. No news. Crispin Marvell's with Bernice now giving her some tips about gardening.'

'Oh, Crispin.' There was scorn in her voice. 'Don't you think he rather overdoes this country thing of his?' She caught his astonished eye. 'Oh, I'm being mean, I know. But I just don't care about anyone any more – not you and Bernice, Max – I mean the others. The first thing I'm going to do is sell this place and go far far away.'

'It's a nice house,' he said for something to say.

'Nice?' Her voice trembled. 'It's like a great hothouse without any flowers.' He had never thought her mercenary and he was surprised when she said, 'I ought to get eight or nine thousand for it. Then there's the Selby business.'

'What exactly . . . ?'

'Oh, glass,' she said vaguely. 'Test tubes and things like that. It never did terribly well until recently. But a couple of months ago they got a marvellous contract making stuff for Harwell. The money's rolling in. I don't know whether to stay or sell out to the other directors. Really, Max, I'm quite a rich woman.'

There were such a lot of things he longed to ask her but could not. Where, for instance, if the business hadn't been doing well, had the money come from to buy Hallows? Why had Patrick's father committed suicide? What of Oliver Gage? And why, most of all, was she, a widow of three weeks' standing, singing for joy when she returned to the house where Patrick had died? It struck him suddenly that in their conversation, so intimately concerned with him, resulting as it did, solely from his death, she had never once mentioned his name.

She took a shell from the mantelpiece and held it to her ear. 'The sound of the sea,' she said and shivered. 'The sound of freedom. I shall never marry again, Max, never.' Freedom, he thought, unaware he was quoting Madame Roland, what crimes are committed in your name!

'I must go,' he said.

'Just a minute, I've something to show you.'

She took his hand in her left one and he sensed at the back of his mind that there was an unfamiliar bareness something missing. But he forgot about it as they entered the dining room. The french windows were open and beyond them the wicker furniture on the patio was damp from many rains. This room, he remembered, had always been the most austere in the house, its walls painted white, its window hung with white blinds, so that it looked like a ward in a new hospital. But above the long sleek radiator there had once been a plaque of smoky blue pottery, a tiny island in an ocean of ice. It had been removed to lie rejected and dusty on the table, and in its place hung the picture that had frightened Patrick, dominating the room and emphasising its barrenness by contrast with its own crusted gilt, its blue and gold and bloody scarlet.

'The gardener was here when I got back,' Tamsin said. 'He helped me to hang it. Too absurd, but I thought he was going to be sick.' She smiled and stroked the mother-of-pearl conch. His gaze, withdrawn for a moment from Salome, followed the movement of her hand and he saw what he had sensed. Tamsin had discarded her wedding ring.

'She always seems to be looking at you,' Tamsin said, 'like the Mona Lisa.'

It was true. The painter had contrived that Salome's eyes should meet yours, no matter in what part of the room you were standing.

'Is it valuable?' he asked, thinking of the thousands rich men would pay for monstrosities.

'Oh, no. Mrs. Prynne said it's only worth about twenty pounds.'

She was still looking at the picture but with neither gloating nor horror. As he turned curiously to look at her he thought he saw in her eyes only the same pride of possession one of his sons might feel for a tape recorder or an electric guitar. One woman's meat, one man's poison . . .

'Patrick . . .' he tried to begin, but he could not speak the name aloud to her.

'What's the matter, darling? Not the little boy?'

'No, no, he'll be all right. I'm looking in again tomorrow.'

'You've been so long.'

Instead of sitting down Greenleaf began to pace the room. The circumstances of Patrick's death were beginning to worry him a lot. If in fact there were sufficient grounds to suspect homicide, wasn't it his duty as the first medical man to have seen Patrick's body, as one of those present at the post-mortem, to see justice done? And if he only suspected shouldn't he, as discreetly as possible, probe just enough to discover whether suspicion was well-founded? Some of the information he had was given in confidence and he couldn't tell Marvell about it. But there was one person he could tell, one from whom he had never felt it necessary to keep the secrets of the consulting room. He could tell his wife.

Bernice might well laugh away his fears and this, he had to confess, was what he wanted. She would tell him he was tired, that he needed his holiday.

The television was on, dancers in some grotesque ballet gyrating like demons. He touched the knob. 'D'you want this?' She shook her head. He switched it off and told her.

She didn't laugh but said thoughtfully:

'Tamsin and Oliver. Yes, I can believe that.'

'You can?'

'I couldn't help noticing the way they danced together at Tamsin's party. I never thought Tamsin and Patrick were very happy together. Except – except until a few days before he died. It was when I called on them collecting for the Cancer Campaign. Tamsin kept calling Patrick darling – she was very sweet to him. I remember thinking how odd it was.'

'But apparently Patrick was in love with Freda Carnaby. Freda Carnaby after Tamsin?'

Bernice lit a cigarette and said shrewdly, 'Did you ever notice how very teutonic Patrick was? The first four years of his life must have influenced him a lot. Of course, his mother was German. He was an awfully *kinder, küche, kirche* sort of person, house-proud, passionately neat and tidy. But Tamsin's a sloppy girl. Not in her appearance, she's vain about that, but about the house. You could see it narked Patrick.'

Greenleaf's mind went back half an hour. Again he saw the untidy rooms, the shells dribbling sand.

'Now, Freda Carnaby, she'd be different again. Very brisk and practical – or she used to be. All the time they've been here I've never seen her in slacks or without stockings, Max. Time and time again I've noticed it, women who wear those tight little pointed shoes are mad keen on polishing and turning out rooms. Patrick was cruel, too, you know, Max, but I don't think cruelty would get very far with Tamsin. She's too vague and self-sufficient. But Freda Carnaby! There's a masochist if ever I saw one.'

'You may be right,' Greenleaf said. 'But forget the Carnabys for a minute. What about Gage? I can imagine he might want to marry Tamsin.' He grinned faintly. 'He has marriages like other people have colds in the head. But apparently Patrick was going to divorce Tamsin anyway. Would Gage want to' – He almost baulked at the word – 'to *kill* him?'

Bernice said unexpectedly, 'He's rather a violent man.'

'Violent? Oliver Gage?'

'Nancy told me something when they first came here. I didn't repeat it because I know how you hate that kind of thing. She was proud of it.'

'So?'

'Well, when Oliver first met her she was engaged to some relative of his second wife's. Apparently Oliver just set out to get her. It's a strange way of conducting one's life, isn't it? Oliver and the fiancé were playing billiards in Oliver's house and Nancy came in. Anyway, the fiancé said something to her she didn't like and she told him she'd finished with him and that she was going to marry Oliver. Just like that. Oliver and the fiancé had a violent quarrel and the upshot of it was Oliver hit him over the head with a billiard cue.'

Greenleaf smiled incredulously.

'It isn't really funny, Max. He knocked the fellow out cold.'

'Hitting someone over the head is a long way from poisoning a man in cold blood. Freda Carnaby says she saw him carrying a packet. A packet of what? Glover was very thorough in his tests.' He sighed. 'I've never been interested in toxicology. When I was a student I didn't care much for medical jurisprudence. But I always come back to that in the end. If Patrick was killed, what was he killed with?'

'One of those insecticides?' Bernice asked vaguely. 'You know, you read about them in the papers. I thought they weren't supposed to leave any trace.'

'Not in the body maybe. But there would have been signs. He would have been very sick. The sheets on the bed, Bernice, they weren't clean sheets. I don't mean they were dirty – just not fresh on.'

'Observant of you,' said Bernice. She reached for the cigarettes, caught her husband's eye and let her hand drop.

'Besides, why would Gage want to do away with Patrick? There's always divorce. Unless he couldn't afford two divorces. He'd have to pay the costs of both of them, remember.'

'On the other hand, Tamsin has her private income.'

Greenleaf banged his fist on the chair arm.

'Wherever I go I keep hearing about that private income. What does it amount to, I'd like to know. Hundreds? Thousands? A couple of hundred a year wouldn't make any difference to a man in Oliver's position. Killing Patrick would secure his money too and that might pay for Nancy's divorce. And Tamsin . . .'

Bernice stared.

'You don't mean you think Tamsin . . . ? Would a woman murder her own husband?'

'They do, occasionally.'

She got up and stood before him. He took her hand and held it lightly.

'Don't worry,' he said. 'Maybe I do need that holiday.'

'Oh, darling, I don't want you to get into this. I'm scared, Max. This can't be happening, not here on Linchester.'

Reading her thoughts, he said gently, 'Whatever we have said no-one can hear us.'

'But we have said it.'

'Sit down,' he said. 'Listen. There's something we've got to realise. If someone did kill Patrick, Tamsin must be in it too. She was in the house. I left her and she says she went to bed. You're not going to tell me someone got into the house without her knowing?'

'You said she was happy?'

'Now? Yes, she's happy now. I think she's glad Patrick's dead. After I told her he was dead she didn't cry, but she cried later. She put her arms round the dog and she cried. Bernice, I think she was crying from relief.'

'What will you do?'

'I don't know,' he said. 'Maybe, nothing. I can't go about asking questions like a detective.' He stopped, listening. A key turned in the lock and he heard the boys come into the hall. And if those women talk, he thought, if Nancy goes about saying Carnaby killed Patrick with cyanide and Freda says Gage killed him with a mysterious white packet, I shall begin to lose my patients.

11

'One large jar of zinc and castor oil cream, half a dozen packets of disposable nappies, a dozen tins of strained food . . .' Mr. Waller reckoned up the purchases rapidly. 'Gone are the days of all that mashing and fiddling about with strainers, Mrs. Smith-King. I always say you young mothers don't know how lucky you are. A large tin of baby powder and the Virol.' He handed the things to Linda who wrapped each up efficiently and sealed it with sellotape. 'I'm afraid that comes to three pounds seven and tenpence. Say it quickly and it doesn't sound so bad, eh?'

Joan Smith-King gave him a new five pound note.

'It's terrible the way it goes,' she said. 'Still, you can't expect it to be cheap taking five children away on holiday.' She jerked Jeremy's hand from its exploration of Linda's carefully arranged display of bathing caps, each an improbably-coloured wig of nylon hair on a rubber scalp. 'I can't tell you how relieved I am to be going at all. My husband's had a very worrying time lately with the business but now everything's panned out well and he'll be able to take a rest.'

'There you are, Mrs. Smith-King. Three pounds, seven and ten, and two and two is ten, and ten and a pound is five pounds. Sure you can manage? What can we do for you, Mr. Marvell?'

'Just a packet of labels, please,' said Marvell who was next in the queue. 'I'm going to start extracting honey in a day or two.' He pocketed the envelope and they left the shop together. Outside Greenleaf's car was parked against the kerb and the doctor was emerging from the newsagent's with the local paper.

'Have you seen it?' Joan Smith-King asked him. 'On the property page. You have a look.'

Greenleaf did as he was told, struggling with the pages in the breeze. The display box among the agents' advertisements wasn't hard to find: Luxury, architect-designed modern house on the favoured Linchester estate at Chantflower in the heart of rural Notts. yet only ten miles from city centre. Large lounge, dining room with patio, superb kitchen, three bedrooms, two bathrooms.

'She doesn't let the grass grow under her feet,' said Joan. 'I'll be glad to see the back of that dog, that Queenie thing. My children are scared stiff of dogs.' Jeremy listened, learning terror at his mother's knee. 'You might not believe it but Patrick Selby was all set to ruin Den's business just because he once hit that dog. I mean, really! Imagine trying to take away someone's livelihood just because he took a stick to an animal.'

Marvell said softly:

'The dog recovered from the bite, the man it was that died.'

'Now look, I didn't mean . . .' A deep flush spread unbecomingly across her lantern jaws. She stepped back. 'I'm sorry I can't give you a lift. I've got a car full of kids.'

'Come on,' Greenleaf said. He tossed the paper into the back of the car. Marvell got in beside him.

'Sorry,' he said. 'I can see you don't like my detective methods. But it's funny, nobody loved him. His wife was bored with him, he got in the way of his wife's lover – Oh, I've found out about that – his girl friend's brother was afraid of him. Even I was annoyed with him because he cut down my father's trees. Edith disliked him because he played God with her children and now you have Smith-King. I wonder what he was up to there, Max. He told me he was trying to get a Stock Exchange quotation for his shares and expand a bit. Do you suppose he had his cold fishy eye on Smith-King's little lot?'

'I'm not listening.'

'Do you happen to know what Smith-King's line is?'

'Chemicals,' Greenleaf said.

'Drugs mainly. And you realise what that means. He must have access to all kinds of lethal stuff. Or there's

Linda. She works for Waller and I don't suppose she's above "borrowing" a nip of something for her mother. And what about that Vesprid stuff?'

Bernice had suggested insecticides. Doubt stirred until Greenleaf remembered how he had answered her. 'You'll have to stop all this, you know,' he said, 'Nobody could have got into the house because Tamsin was there.'

'Not all the time. After you'd gone she went out.'

'What?' Greenleaf signalled right and turned into Long Lane. 'How do you know?'

'Because she came to see me,' Marvell said.

Greenleaf had intended to drop Marvell at the almshouse and drive straight home. But Marvell's statement had suddenly put a different complexion on things. He slammed the car doors and they went up to the house.

'She came,' Marvell said, 'to bring me the currants. You remember the currants? She picked them before the party and put them in a trug.'

'A what?'

'Sorry. I keep forgetting you're not a countryman. It's a kind of wooden basket, a gardener's basket. In all the fuss I forgot them and Tamsin brought them up to me. It must have been all of midnight.'

Midnight, Greenleaf thought, and she walked through those woods alone. She came down here while Patrick – if not, as far as anyone then knew, dying – was at least ill and in pain. She came to bring a basket of currants! It was no good, he would never understand the habits of the English countryside. But Tamsin was accustomed to them. She had learnt in these two years as much from Marvell as she would have from a childhood spent among the fields and hedgerows.

'I was sitting at the window reading through my stuff and I saw her in the orchard.' Marvell knelt down to tie up a hollyhock that the wind had blown adrift from the porch wall. Greenleaf watched him smooth the stem and press back the torn green skin. 'She looked like a moth or a ghost in that dress. Patrick didn't like bright colours. She was carrying the trug and that straw handbag Edith Gaveston gave her for a birthday present. I was – well, somewhat surprised to see her.' He straightened up and stepped into the porch. Greenleaf fancied that he was embarrassed, for, as he lifted the can and began watering the pot plants that stood on the shelves, he kept his face turned away.

'She came all this way to give you some currants?'

Marvell didn't answer him. Instead he said:

'It means, of course, that anyone could have got into the house. Nobody around here bothers to lock their doors except you and Bernice. I walked back with her as far as her gate.' He stroked a long spear-shaped leaf and, wheeling round suddenly, said fiercely: 'My God, Max, don't you think I realise? If I'd gone in I might have been able to do something.'

'You couldn't know.'

'And Tamsin . . . ?'

'Thought he was asleep,' he said, voicing a confidence he didn't feel. 'Why did she really come?'

Marvell was touching with the tips of his fingers a dark green succulent plant on the borders of whose leaves tiny leaflets grew.

'The Pregnant Frau,' he said. 'You see, she grows her children all round the edges of her leaves and each one will grow into another plant. They remind me of the leaves in Jacobean embroidery. And this one . . .' He fingered the spear-shaped plant, '. . . is the Mother-in-law's Tongue. You see I keep a harem in my porch.'

'Why did she come?'

'That,' Marvell said, 'is something I can't really tell you.' Greenleaf looked at him, puzzled as to whether he meant he refused to tell him or was unable to do so. But Marvell said no more and presently the doctor left him.

He hadn't meant to go back to the village and into Waller's shop. He *meant* to turn off at the Manor gates, but something impelled him on down the hill, unease perhaps, or the knowledge that Tamsin had left Patrick alone on the night he died.

'I want a tin of Vesprid,' he said, cutting short Waller's obsequious greeting. Instead of calling for Linda, Waller got it down himself.

'I suppose I shall have to wear gloves and a mask,' Greenleaf said innocently.

'Absolutely harmless to warm-blooded . . .' Waller's voice trailed away. In this company, and only then, was his confidence shaken. A small voice within his heart told him that to Greenleaf, Howard and their partners, he could never be more than the village medicine man. 'At least . . . well, I don't have to tell *you*, Doctor.'

When he got home Greenleaf transferred some of the liquid into a small bottle and wrapped it up. It was far-fetched, incredibly far-fetched, to imagine Edward Carnaby going back to Hallows after the party, to wonder if Freda's story of Gage and the white packet was a cover-up for her brother's own trip with a tin of insecticide. Or was it? He went back to the car, drove to the post office and sent the package away to be analysed.

12

The Chantflower Rural Council dustmen hadn't bargained on the extra load of rubbish that awaited them outside the Hallows back door. They grumbled loudly, muttering about slipped discs and no overtime. Queenie stood on the steps and roared at them.

'Now, if you'll just take these over to Mrs. Greenleaf I'll give you a shilling,' said Tamsin to Peter Smith-King. He was only ten and he looked dubiously at the two suitcases. 'The money'll be useful for your holiday. Come on, they're not really heavy and you can make two journeys. Tell her they're for Oxfam.'

The little boy hesitated. Then he went home and fetched his box barrow. He trundled the cases across the Green, dawdling to throw a stone at the swans, and found Bernice on the lawn giving coffee to Nancy Gage and Edith Gaveston.

'Can we have a peep?' Nancy asked. Without waiting for permission she undid the clasps on the larger case. The lid fell back to reveal, on top of a pile of clothes, a straw handbag embroidered with raffia.

'Oh, dear!' Nancy said.

Edith blushed.

'Of course, I could see she didn't like it,' she said. 'She barely said two words to me when I gave it to her, but really!'

'There's such a thing as tact,' Nancy said happily.

Edith snatched the bag and opened it.

'She hasn't even bothered to take the tissue paper out.'

'Goodness,' Nancy giggled, 'I don't know what use she thinks a handbag is to a starving Asian.' And her eyes goggled as she imagined an emaciated peasant clutching Edith's present against her rags.

'The clothes will be useful though,' Bernice said pacifically.

Nancy stared in horrified wonder as the doctor's wife lifted from the case the slacks and tee-shirt Patrick had worn on the evening of his death. For all their careful laundering they suggested a shroud.

Nancy was on her knees now, unashamedly burrowing.

'Two suits, shoes, goodness knows how many shirts.' She unfastened the other case. 'All Patrick's clothes!'

'Now if it were Paul. . . .' Edith began to describe minutely exactly how she would dispose of her husband's effects in the event of his death. While she was talking Bernice quietly sealed the cases and re-filled the coffee pot.

Returning after a few moments, she was aware from Nancy's expression that the conversation had taken a different and more exciting turn. The two women under the cedar tree wore ghoulish lugubrious looks. As she approached she caught the words 'very unstable' and 'a most peculiar family altogether'.

How difficult it was to close one's ears to gossip, how impossible to reprimand friends! Bernice sat down again, listening but not participating.

'Of course I don't know the details,' Nancy was saying.

'Black, please, Bernice,' Edith said. 'Well, that Mrs. Selby – I mean Patrick's mother – it gets so confusing, doesn't it? That Mrs. Selby ran away with another man. We used to call it bolting when I was a girl.' She pronounced it 'gel', snapping her tongue wetly from the roof of her mouth. 'Apparently they'd always been most happily married, married for years. Patrick was grown up when she went off. She must have been all of fifty, my dear, and the man was older. Anyway, she persuaded Patrick's father to divorce her and he did, but . . .'

'Yes?' Nancy's forlorn, ghoulish face would have deceived no-one. Her mouth was turned down but her bright eyes flickered.

'But on the day she got her decree Patrick's father gassed himself!'

'No!'

'My dear, it was a terrible scandal. And that wasn't all. Old Mrs. Selby, the grandmother – Tamsin's grandmother, too. Dreadful this in-breeding. Look what it does to dogs! She made a terrible scene at the inquest and shouted that her son would still be alive but for the divorce.'

Bernice moved her chair into the shade. 'You're romancing, Edith. You can't possibly know all this.'

'On the contrary. I know it for certain.' Edith drew herself up, the lady of the manor making her morning calls. 'It so happens I read the account of the inquest in *The Times*. It stuck in my mind and when Nancy mentioned the suicide it all came back to me. Selby, a glass factory. There's no doubt about it being the same one.'

'It's all very sad.' Bernice looked so repressive that Nancy jumped up, scattering biscuit crumbs.

'I must love you and leave you. Oh, Bernice, I nearly forgot to ask you. Have you got the name of that man who put up your summer house?'

'I can't remember. Max would know.'

Nancy waited for her to ask why. When she didn't she said proudly:

'We're going to have that extension done at last, but Oliver says Henry Glide's a bit too pricey. A sun loggia. . . .' She paused. 'And a pram park!'

'Nancy, you're not. . . . ? How lovely!'

Nancy pulled in her waist and laughed.

'No, not yet,' she said, 'but Oliver says we can go in for a baby any time I like.'

Trying not to smile at the ludicrous phrase, Bernice found herself saying once more that it was lovely.

'He's been as nice as pie about it and he's all over me. He hasn't been so lovey-dovey for months. Aren't men the end?'

I really ought to thank Tamsin properly for the clothes, Bernice thought after they had both gone. But she felt reluctant to go. Hardly anyone had set eyes on Tamsin since her return. She had become like a sleeping beauty shut up in her glass castle, or like a lurking witch. Bernice couldn't make up her mind whether Tamsin was really bad or whether the gossip had created in her own fancy an unreal Tamsin, a false clever poisoner. Anyway, she must go and be polite.

As she hurried across The Green she encountered Peter sitting on his barrow.

'I went to collect my shilling,' he said, 'but I couldn't find *her*.' He picked up a flat stone and concentrated on sending it skimming across the water. 'The dog's there, though.'

He threw this piece of information out quite casually but Bernice remembered what Max had told her and detected a current of fear.

'I'm on my way over now,' she said. 'Come with me if you like.'

Queenie was indeed there so Tamsin must be too. As she put out her hand to the dog's soft mouth Bernice had a strange feeling that something ought to click. When Tamsin went out without the dog she always shut her in the kitchen. The Weimaraner had been bred as a sentinel as well as a hunter. What was it Max had said last night about Tamsin visiting Crispin Marvell? She stopped and pondered. Tamsin's voice from above broke into her reverie.

'Come on in. I was in the bath.'

Peter slunk past the dog.

'Go into the dining room. I won't be a minute.'

Bernice pushed open the double doors and Peter went in first. The dining room door was just ajar. Peter went obediently ahead but Bernice waited in the hall. The last thing she wanted was to stay and talk.

She expected Peter to sit down and wait for his wages but he didn't. He stopped and stared at something. She could see nothing inside the room but the child's figure in profile, still as a statue. Then he came out of the room again, backing from whatever it was like someone leaving the presence of royalty. He looked at her and she saw that his face was white but stoical.

'Ughugh,' he said.

At once she knew what he had seen. Surely nothing else Tamsin possessed could summon that squeamish pallor even in a child of ten. She closed the door firmly and turned round. A gasp escaped her before she could control it. Tamsin was behind her, awfully near, clean and gleaming as a wax doll in her pink and white dressing gown. Suddenly Bernice felt terribly frightened. Tamsin had come so silently, the child was silent and now all the doors were closed.

'What's the matter with him?'

If he had been her own child Bernice would have put her arms around him and pressed his grubby cheek against her face. But she could give him no physical comfort. He was too old to hug and too young for explanations.

She felt her voice quiver and jerk as she said, 'I think he saw that picture of yours'.

'Too uncanny,' said Tamsin. She looked at Peter as if she were seeing not him but another child staring out through his eyes. 'Patrick was just about your age when he first saw it, but he wasn't tough like you. He ran away and then *it* happened. The fuss and bother — you can't imagine.'

Bernice was just going to ask what had happened when Peter said sullenly, 'Can I have my shilling?'

'Oh, of course you can. It's there, all ready for you on the table.'

The moment of revelation had passed. Tamsin evidently thought Bernice had come to give Peter moral support, for she opened the door to show them both out.

'I only came to thank you for the things.'

'So glad they're useful. And now I must chase you both away. I've got people coming to look over the house.'

Edith was the first person on Linchester to find out that Hallows was sold and she got it from the gardener the

Gavestons shared with Tamsin. As soon as he had told her, over mid-morning tea in the utility room, she slipped out to pass the news on to Mrs. Glide. Henry, after all, ought to be pleased that his handiwork found favour in the sight of buyers. On her way back she met Marvell returning from the shops with his sparse groceries in a string bag.

'Only yesterday, it was,' she said, 'and they made an offer on the spot. These *noveaux riches*, they buy and sell houses like you or Paul might job in and out on the stock market.'

Marvell pursed his lips, listening gravely.

'Now when we were young a house *was* a house. One's grandfather had lived in it and in the fulness of time one's grandson would live in it too.' She ended with sublime insensitivity, 'It was *there*, like the Rock of Ages'.

He smiled, murmured something, his mind working furiously. So Tamsin was leaving soon, escaping . . . When Edith had left him he walked slowly across The Green towards Shalom. He tried the front door and the back. Both were locked. The Greenleafs were townspeople, fearful of burglars, cautious people who yet declared their absence with fastened bolts and conspicuously closed windows. Marvell scribbled a note on the grocer's chit and left it on the back doorstep weighted down with a stone.

Greenleaf found it when he came in at one.

'Can you drop in this afternoon?' he read. 'I've something to tell you. C.M.'

He suppressed a sigh. Tamsin would soon be gone and with her departure surely the rumours would cease. In a fortnight's time he would be off on holiday and when he came back Nancy would be too preoccupied with plans for the baby, Freda too tranquillised by drugs to bother about the vanished Selbys. And yet, he thought as he began to eat the cold lunch Bernice had left him, Marvell might want him for something quite different. In the past he had often been summoned to give an emergency injection of piriton when Marvell was almost numbed and blinded by hay fever. Without a telephone, Marvell was obliged to call or leave a note. It was even possible that he wanted to show the doctor his manuscript, perhaps finished at last. 'I've something to tell you . . .' Patrick. He could only mean

Patrick. Probably another undetectable poison theory. Well, it was a way of passing his free afternoon.

As he washed his plate and stuck it in the rack to drain, he thought with the small grain of superiority he allowed himself, that when people spoke of the rewards of a medical vocation they ignored this one: the pleasure of shooting the layman's theories down in flames.

On the wooden bench by the back door Marvell sat reading a recipe for ratafia. It was an old recipe, part of a collection his mother had made while still chatelaine of Linchester, and it had been handed down to her, mother to daughter, from a long line of forbears. Brandy, peach kernels, sugar, honey, orange flower water . . . He had no peaches, nor the money to buy them. The recipe said five hundred kernels and, basking in the warm soft sunlight, he imagined with some delight the preliminary labour to the making of ratafia: the consumption of those five hundred ripe peaches.

Presently he got up and began to walk around the house, touching the bricks, themselves peach-coloured. When he came to the side wall where Henry Glide had discovered the fissure, the terrible sign that the whole building was beginning to subside, he closed his eyes and saw only a red mist filled with whirling objects. Then, because he refused to deny facts and deceive himself, he forced his fingers to seek the crack as a man fearful of cancer yet resolute, compels his hand to probe the swelling in his body.

He jumped when Greenleaf coughed behind him.

'Penny for your thoughts.'

'They're worth more than that,' Marvell said lightly. 'To be precise, a thousand pounds.'

Greenleaf looked at him inquiringly.

'That,' said Marvell, 'is the price Glide is prepared to pay me for this land.'

'You're selling? But this place – I thought you were so fond of it.' Greenleaf described with splayed fingers a wide arc that embraced the squat yet elegant house, the shaven lawn, the orchard and the hawthorn hedge over which honeysuckle climbed, a parasite more lovely than its prey.

All this meant little to the doctor but by a terrific effort of empathy he had learned its value to his friend. Even he who could scarcely tell a lily from a rose, felt that here the air smelled more sweetly and the sun's heat was moderated to a mellow beneficence. 'The house. It's so old. It's quaint.' He added helplessly, 'People like that sort of thing. They'd want to buy it.'

Marvell shook his head. He was still holding the recipe book and slowly the thought formed in his mind: I will make some ratafia, just a very small quantity, to take away and to remind me. . . .

Aloud he said to Greenleaf: 'It's falling down. The council says it's not safe to live in. I've had Glide here to look at it and all he said was he'd give me a thousand for the land.'

'How long have you known?'

'Oh, about a month now. A thousand's good going, you know. When the Marvells had Andreas Quercus – he was really called Andrew Oakes or something – when they had him build this place for four old persons of the parish of Chantflower, they didn't care that you could only get to it down a muddy lane and the old persons were too grateful to care.'

With what he felt to be tremendous inadequacy, Greenleaf said: 'I'm sorry. Where will you live?' So many questions leapt to his mind, Have you any money? What will you live on? He couldn't dream of asking them. The proximity of Linchester made poverty a more than usually shameful thing.

'I suppose I can get a room somewhere. I can teach. I shall have my thousand pounds. You'd be surprised what a long time I can live on a thousand pounds.' He laughed dryly and Greenleaf, seeing him in the light of this new knowledge, noticed how gaunt he was. This, then, was why Marvell had sent for him, to unburden his soul. I wonder, he thought, if I could rake up a bit, just to tide him over and have the place made watertight. But Marvell's next words temporarily banished all thoughts of a loan.

'I saw Edith this morning,' he said, 'as I was coming back from the village. She said Tamsin had sold the house. Some people came and made her an offer.'

'Then she'll soon be gone,' said Greenleaf, relieved.

'And since perhaps neither of us will ever see her again I think I can tell you why she came to see me on the night Patrick died.'

He could see her now as she had come up through the orchard, swinging her basket, all pale in the moonlight with her mist-coloured dress, and paler still when she came within the radiance of his lamp. To his fanciful imagination the currants had seemed like beads of white jade veined with crimson. For all her affected speech, the superlatives that came from her lips so often that they lost their meaning and their force, her face had always been a mask, a shield deliberately maintained to hide intellectual cunning or perhaps a chance trick of nature concealing only vacuity.

'I think she is really very clever,' he said to Greenleaf.

He had put his head out of the window and called to her, then gone into the garden and asked after Patrick.

'Oh, Patrick – he spoiled my lovely party. Maddening creature.'

'You shouldn't have come all this way alone. I would have come up tomorrow.'

'Crispin darling, how should I know what you do here in your enchanted cottage? You might have wanted to make your wine tonight at some special witching hour.'

'I'll walk back with you.'

But she had unlatched the door already and pulled him after her into the little damp kitchen. The scent of the night came in with her and as for a moment she stood beside him, very close with her face uplifted, he could smell the richer perfume she wore, Nuit de Beltane, exotic, alien to an English garden. This essence with its hint of witchcraft enhanced the atmosphere of magic unreality.

'So we sat down,' he said, shaking his shoulders as if to shed a memory. 'We sat a long way from each other but the lamp was between us and you know what oil lamps are. They seem to enclose you in a little snug circle. For a while we talked the usual trivia. Then, quite suddenly, she began to talk about us.'

'You and herself?'

'Yes. She said what a lot we had in common, how we both loved country things. She said there had always been a kind of bond between us. Max, I felt very uneasy.'

'And then?'

'I want you to understand how curiously intimate the whole situation was, the darkness around us, the circle of light. After a while she got up and sat beside me on the footstool. She took my hand and said she supposed I realised she hadn't been happy with Patrick for a long time. She's got one of those thick skins that can't blush, but I felt the blush was there.'

'Everyone can blush,' said the doctor.

'Well, be that as it may, she went on to tell me she knew why I came to the house so often. I didn't say a word. It was horribly awkward. She kept hold of my hand and she said she'd only realised how I felt when I brought her the mead and the roses. Max, believe me, they were just presents for a pretty woman from a man who can't afford scent or jewellery.'

'I believe you.'

'Suddenly she said very abruptly: "Patrick's leaving me. He wants a divorce. In a year I'll be free, Crispin." It was a blunt proposal of marriage.' Marvell went on quickly: 'I don't want marriage. For one thing I can't afford it. Everybody thinks I'm comfortably off, but the fact is most of the money my father got for Linchester went in death duties. What was left was divided between my brother, my sister and myself and my share went on buying the almshouses. The family had sold them long ago. But I couldn't tell Tamsin all that. I felt she might offer me her own money.'

'That mysterious private income,' Greenleaf said.

'Not mysterious. It amounts to about fifty thousand pounds – the capital, that is – but Tamsin can't touch that. It's invested in oil or something and she has the income for life. I believe it would pass to her children, if she ever had any children. So, you see, I couldn't talk about money to her. Instead I said I was too old for her. I'm fifty, Max. She has a lot of natural dignity, but I thought she was going to cry. I don't mind telling you, it was the most embarrassing experience of my life. I suppose I was weak. I said quite truthfully that she was the most beautiful and the most exciting woman I knew. Then I said, "Wait till the year is up. I'll come and see if you've changed your mind." But she only laughed. She got up and stood outside the lamplight and said quite coolly, "Patrick will probably name Oliver Gage. I've been having an affair with him. Did you know?" I realised she was telling me I'd be taking Gage's leavings.'

'And that was all?'

'That was all, or nearly all. I tipped the currants into a bowl and walked back with her, carrying the empty trug. All the way back she was utterly silent and at the gate I left her.'

'Did you see anyone?'

'No-one. It was all so extraordinary, like a dream. But the most extraordinary thing was when I saw her the day after Patrick died, the next day. I didn't want to go, Max, but I felt I should. She was as cold as ice. Not miserable, you understand; the impression she gave me was of happiness and freedom. She might never have come to see me the night before. Then, when she came back, I met her out with Queenie in Long Lane. She waved to me and said hallo. I asked her how she was and she said fine. I'm selling up and leaving as soon as I can. It was as casual as if we'd never been more than acquaintances.'

'Peculiar,' Greenleaf said.

'I don't mind telling you,' Marvell said with a smile, 'it was a hell of a relief.'

PART THREE

13

Two days later Marvell began extracting honey. Greenleaf's jar would be ready for him in the afternoon, he told the doctor, if he cared to come along and collect it. But at half-past three Greenleaf was still sitting in his deck-chair under the shade of the cedar tree. Bernice had gone out and he was half-asleep. Each time he nodded off, snatches of dreams crept upon him, bright pictures rather than actual episodes. But they were not pleasant images and they mirrored a subconscious of which he had been unaware. Worst of all was the hideous cameo of Tamsin's painting that spiralled and enlarged, twisted and distorted until the head on the plate became Patrick's. He jolted out of sleep to a shrill insistent ringing. Consciousness, reality, came back as with the familiar feel of the canvas, the cool springy grass, he sought tranquillity. Almost in the past days he had found peace of mind. Was it all there still below the surface, a whirlpool of fear and doubt and indecision? The ringing continued and he was suddenly aware that this was not a sound within his head, but the peal of a real bell, the telephone bell.

Reminding himself that he was supposed to be on call, he hastened into the morning room. It was Edward Carnaby.

'I thought I wasn't going to get you,' he said reproachfully. 'It's my Cheryl, my daughter. A wasp got her on the lip, Doctor. Her and Freda, they were having a bit of a picnic on The Green and this wasp was on a piece of cake . . .'

'Her lip?' From Patrick, Greenleaf's thoughts travelled back to the dead miner. 'Not inside her mouth?'

'Well, sort of. Inside her lip. She's scared stiff. Mind you, Freda's had something to do with that. They're both sobbing their hearts out.'

'All right, I'll come.'

'I thought we'd seen the last of those wasps,' he said as he walked into the Carnaby lounge. Of course it was the only living room they had but it seemed strange to him to cover the entire centre of the carpet with what looked like a dismantled internal combustion engine spread on sheets of newspaper.

'You'll have to excuse the mess,' Carnaby said, blackening his fingers in his haste to remove obstacles from the doctor's path. 'I borrowed it from the class. I can't seem to . . .'

'Never mind all that!' Freda was on the sofa, squeezing the child in a vice-like hug against her fussy starched blouse. Greenleaf picked his way over to her, stepping gingerly across coils and wheels. He thought he had seldom seen anyone look so tense. Her mouth was set as if she was grinding her teeth and the tears poured down her cheeks. 'Tell me quickly, Doctor, is she going to die?'

Cheryl struggled and began to howl.

'Of course she isn't going to die,' Greenleaf said roughly while Carnaby fumbled at his feet with bits of metal.

'She is, she is! You're just saying that. You'll take her to the hospital and we'll never see her again.'

He was surprised at so much emotion for she had never seemed to care for the child. Patrick's death must have left a real wound into which a new-found maternal love might pour. Patrick, always back to Patrick . . . He looked quickly at Carnaby, wondering when the report would come from the analyst, before saying sharply to Freda:

'If you can't control yourself, Miss Carnaby, you'd better go outside.'

She gulped.

'Let's have a look at it, Cheryl.' He prised Freda off her and gently eased the handkerchief from her mouth. The lower lip was bulging into a grotesque hillock and it reminded the doctor of pictures he had seen of duck-billed women. He wiped her eyes. 'You're going to have a funny face for a day or two.'

The child tried to smile. She edged away from her aunt and pushed tendrils of hair from her big characterful eyes, eyes that she must surely have inherited from her mother.

'Mr. Selby had wasp stings,' she said and darted a precocious glance at Freda. 'I heard Daddy talking about it when they got back from that party. I was awake. I never sleep when I have a sitter.' Her lip wobbled. 'It was that Mrs. Staxton. She said wasps were ever so dangerous and she was scared of them, so Daddy said he'd got some stuff and she could take the tin. And she did, she took it home with her and a jolly good thing, because wasps *are* dangerous.' Greenleaf sighed with silent relief. The analyst's report could hardly matter now. Cheryl's voice rose into fresh panic. 'Mr. Selby *died*. Aunty Free said I might die.'

Greenleaf felt in his pocket for a sixpence.

'There's an ice-cream man by The Green,' he said. 'You'll catch him if you hurry. You get a lolly.' Carnaby looked at him, a foolish smile curling his mouth uneasily as if at some inconsequential joke. 'It'll be good for your lip.'

Freda watched her go with tragic eyes. She evidently thought Greenleaf had got rid of Cheryl in order to impart confidential information as to her probable fate. She looked affronted when he said instead:

'Patrick Selby did *not* die of wasp stings. I thought you had more sense, Miss Carnaby. To talk of dying to a child of eight! What's the matter with you?'

'Everybody knows Patrick didn't die of heart failure,' she said stubbornly.

Greenleaf let it pass. Her bosom quivered. The fallen tears had left round transparent blotches on the thin blouse through which frilly fussy straps and bits of underclothes showed.

'He must have died of the stings,' she insisted, 'and he only had four.'

'Five, but it doesn't matter. Cheryl . . .'

'He didn't. He only had four I was sitting with him and I could see.'

Greenleaf said impatiently:

'I should give that a rest, Miss Carnaby.'

Carnaby who had remained silent, ineffectually picking up things that might be ratchets or gaskets, suddenly said rather aggressively, 'Well, it's a matter of accuracy, isn't it, Doctor? It so happens Selby had four stings. I was in the bathroom and I saw the wasps get him. Unless you're counting the one he had a couple of days before.'

'One on his face,' Freda said, 'two on his left arm and one inside his right arm. I thought Cheryl – well, it might have taken her the same way, mightn't it?' The sob that caught her throat came out ludicrously like a hiccup. 'She's all I've got now,' she said. 'Patrick – I could have given him children. He wanted children. I'll never get married now, never, never!'

Carnaby hustled the doctor out into the hall, kicking the door shut behind him. Recalling what Bernice had said, Greenleaf wondered whether Freda's renewed cries were caused by true grief or the possible damage to the paint-work. Then, as he stood, murmuring assurances to Carnaby, the penny dropped. Not the whole penny, but a fraction of it, a farthing perhaps.

'She'll be all right,' he said mechanically. 'There's nothing to worry about.' The worry was all his now.

Then he went, almost running.

Back at Shalom his deck-chair awaited him. He sat down, conscious that on his way round The Circle he had passed Sheila Macdonald and Paul Gaveston without even a smile or a wave. They had been shadows compared with the reality of his thoughts. Before his eyes he could again see Patrick's body in the bed at Hallows that Sunday morning, the thin freckled arms spread across the sheet, sleeves pushed back for coolness. And on the yellowish mottled skin red swellings. One sting on the face, two on the left arm, one on the right arm in the cubital fossa – and a fifth. There *had* been a fifth, about six inches below. Not the old sting; that had been just a scar, a purplish lump with a scab where Patrick had scratched it. The Carnabys could be wrong. Both wrong? They couldn't both be mistaken. Why should they lie? He, Greenleaf hadn't bothered to count the stings on the previous night and when he had visited Patrick in bed the blue cotton sleeves had covered both arms down to the wrists. Tamsin had been uninterested, the others embarrassed. But Carnaby had watched the wasps attack, he had been there in the line of fire, staring from the bathroom window, and Freda had sat at Patrick's feet, holding his hand. Of all the guests at the party they were in the best position to know. But at the same time he knew he wasn't wrong. *Five* stings, one on the face, two on the left arm . . .

'Hot enough for you?' It was a high-pitched irritating voice and Greenleaf didn't have to look up to know it was Nancy Gage.

'Hallo.'

'Oh, don't get up,' she said as he began to rise. 'I'll excuse you. Much too hot to be polite. You men, I really pity you. Always having to bob up and down like jack-in-the-boxes.'

'I'm afraid Bernice has taken the boys into Nottingham.'

'Never mind. Actually I came to see you. Don't get me a chair. I'll sit on the grass.' She did so quite gracefully, spreading her pink cotton skirts about her like an open parasol. The renewal of love, strained and contrived though that renewal might be, was gradually restoring her beauty. It was as if she was a wilting pink and gold rose into whose leaves and stems nourishment was climbing by a slow capillarity. 'What I really came for was the name of that man who put up your summer house. We're rather spreading our wings – I don't know if Bernice told you – having an extension to our humble domain, and Mr. Glide – well, he is a bit steep, isn't he?'

'He's in the phone book. Swan's the name. J. B. Swan.'

'Lovely. What a wonderful memory! What do you think? As I was coming across The Green I met that funny little Carnaby girl with an enormous lump in her lip. I asked her what it was and she said a wasp sting. She was sucking one of those filthy lollies. I ask you, the last thing! I said, now you run straight home to Mummy – I forgot she hasn't got a Mummy, just an Auntie and what an Auntie! – and get her to put bi-carbonate of soda on it.'

'Not much use, I'm afraid.'

'Oh, you doctors and your anti-biotics. I'm a great believer in the old-fashioned remedies.' She spoke with a middle-aged complacency and Greenleaf thought he knew exactly what she would be like in fifteen years' time, stout, an encyclopaedia of outworn and inaccurate advice, the very prototype of an old wife spinning old wives' tales. 'If I've said it once I've said it a dozen times, Patrick would be alive today if Tamsin had only used bi-carb.' As an after-thought she exclaimed in an advertising catch phrase, 'And so reasonably priced!'

Momentarily Greenleaf closed his eyes. He opened them suddenly as she went on:

'As soon as we got back from that ghastly party I said to Oliver, you pop straight back to Hallows with some bi-carb. He hung it out a bit. Waiting for you to go, I'm afraid. Aren't we crafty? Anyway, he trotted across with his little packet . . .' It was an absurd description of the movement of that graceful, saturnine man, but Greenleaf was too interested to notice . '. . . but Tamsin must have gone to bed. She'd forgotten to lock the back door because he tried it, but that Queenie was shut up in the kitchen and she wouldn't let him in. He went round the back and all the food was still out there and Tamsin had left her presents on the birthday table, the chocolates and that bag and Crispin's flowers. She must have been terribly upset to leave it all like that. He hung about for five minutes and then he came home.'

'I expect she was tired,' Greenleaf said, his thoughts racing. So that was the answer to what he had been calling in his mind the Great White Packet Mystery. Simply Oliver Gage taking bi-carbonate of soda to his mistress's husband. And probably, he thought vulgarly, hoping for a little love on the side. No wonder he waited for me to go.

What Marvell had said about anyone being able to get into Hallows while Tamsin was out had now been shown to be manifestly false. The dog Queenie would guard her master against all comers – against all except one. The feeble motives of Edith Gaveston and Denholm Smith-King evaporated like puddles in the sun. But Tamsin had a motive, or rather many motives which crystallised into a gigantic single drive against Patrick's life. Tamsin was rich now and free. Not to marry Gage whom she had evidently sent about his business, but free to be herself in a glorious scented bright-coloured muddle.

'You're so silent,' Nancy said. 'Are you all right? I'll tell you what I'll do. I haven't got a thing on hand this after-noon. I'll nip indoors and make the poor grass widower a nice cup of tea.'

Greenleaf hated tea. He thanked her, rested his head against the canvas and closed his eyes.

14

Patrick had died too late. Greenleaf repeated the sentence to himself as he came up to the front door of Marvell's house. Patrick had died too late. Not from the point of view of Tamsin's happiness, but medically speaking. Marvell had suggested it at the time the rumours began and Greenleaf had shrugged it off. Now he realised that it was this fact which all the time had been nagging at his mind. Had he died soon after receiving the stings or even if he had had a heart attack on seeing the picture – for Greenleaf was beginning to believe that in Patrick's history it corresponded to the something nasty in the woodshed of Freudian psychology – there would have been no mystery. But Patrick had died hours later.

Why had there been a fifth sting? A wasp in the bedroom? It was possible. Patrick had been heavily sedated. You could probably have stuck a pin in him without waking him. But why should a fifth sting kill him when four had made him only uncomfortable? He banged on the alms-house door for the second time, but Marvell wasn't at home. At last he went round to the back and sat down on the bench.

He had come for his honey and, after much heart-search-ing, to offer his friend a loan. Talking it over with Bernice after she came back from Nottingham, he had thought he could raise a few hundreds, enough perhaps to have the house made habitable according to the standards of Chant-flower Rural Council. It was an awkward mission even though he intended to be quite pompous about it, insisting for the sake of Marvell's pride on the money being repayed at the normal rate of interest – Marvell would have to put his back into the history of Chantefleur Abbey. I am a peasant, he thought, and he is an aristocrat (the serfs to the wolves syndrome again). He might hit me. All alone in the garden, he chuckled faintly to himself. He didn't think Marvell would do that.

Presently he got up and walked about, for he was nervous. He hadn't counted on having to wait. Perhaps Marvell would be away for hours and he would have screwed up his courage in vain.

He passed the kitchen window and looking inside, saw that the table was laden with jars of honey, clear and golden, not the sugary waxen stuff you bought in the shops. There would be a pot for them and a pot for the Gages and the Gavestons. Poor though he was, Marvell was a generous man. Last year the harvest had been poor but there had been a jar on almost every Linchester table. Not Patrick's though. Patrick recoiled from honey as if it were poison.

Greenleaf turned away and began to follow the path towards the orchard. Under the trees he stopped and sat down on the stump of a withered ancient apple Marvell had felled in the winter. Apple, plum and pear leaves made a dappled pattern on the turf as the sunlight filtered through gnarled branches. All about him he could hear the muted yet ominous hum of the bees that had been robbed of their treasure. Marvell, he guessed, had reimbursed them, giving them – as he put it – silver for their gold. He had once shown the doctor the tacky grey candy he made for them from boiled sugar. But, just the same, bewilderment over their loss made them angry.

There were three hives made of white painted wood and this had surprised Greenleaf the first time he had seen them for he had expected the igloos of plaited straw you see in children's picture books. Beneath the entrance to each hive – a slit between the two lowest boards – was a wooden step or platform on to which the bees issued, trickling forth in a thin dark stream. There was a suggestion of liquid in their movement, measured yet turbulent, regular and purposeful. Marvell had told him something of their ordered social life, and because of this rather than from the interest of a naturalist, he approached the hive and knelt down before it.

At first the bees ignored him. He put his ear to the wall of the hive and listened. From inside there came the sound as of a busy city where thousand upon thousand of workers feed, love, breed and engage in industry. He could hear a soft roar, constant in volume, changing in pitch. There was warmth in it and richness and an immense controlled activity.

For a moment he had forgotten that these insects were not simply harvesters; they were armed. Then, as he eased himself into a sitting position, one of them appeared suddenly from a tree or perhaps from the roof of the hive. It skimmed his hair and sank on the windless air until it was in front of his eyes. He got up hastily and brushed at it and at the others which began to gather about it. How horrible, how treacherous Nature could be! You contemplated it with the eye of an aesthete or a sociologist, and just as you were beginning to see there might be something in it after all, it rose and struck you, attacked you . . . He gasped and ran, glad that there was no-one to see him. Two of the bees followed him, sailing on the hot fruit-scented air. He stripped off his jacket and flung it over his head. Panting with panic and with sudden revelation, he stumbled into Marvell's garden shed.

The bee-keeper's veiled hat and calico coat were suspended from the roof, taped gloves protruding from the sleeves. The clothes looked like a guy or a hanged man. When he had slammed the door between himself and his pursuers, he sat down on the garden roller, sweating. He knew now how Patrick Selby had died.

'But wouldn't he have swelled up?' Bernice asked. 'I thought the histamine made you swell up all over.'

'Yes, it does.' Greenleaf bent over the kitchen sink, washing tool-shed cobwebs from his hands. 'I gave him anti-histamine . . .'

'Why didn't it work, Max?'

'I expect it did, up to a point. Don't forget, Patrick wasn't allergic to wasp stings. But if he was allergic to *bee* stings, as I think he must have been, the histamine reaction would have been very strong. Two hundred milligrammes of anti-histamine wouldn't have gone anywhere. The only thing for people with that sort of allergy is an injection of adrenalin given as soon as possible. If they don't have it

they die very quickly.' She shivered and he went on:
'Patrick didn't have that injection. He was heavily sedated,
he couldn't call for help and if there was no-one near . . .'
He shrugged. 'There would have been a lot of swelling but
the swelling would gradually disappear. I didn't see him till
ten or eleven hours after he died. His face was a bit puffy
and I put it down to the wasp sting under the eye. By the
time Glover got to work on him – well!'

'An accident?'

'To much of a coincidence. Four wasp stings and then
you get stung by a bee in your own bedroom?'

'He must have known he was allergic to bee stings.'

'Not necessarily, although I think he did. He hated
honey. Remember? He knew about it all right and someone
else knew too.'

'You mean he told someone?'

'Bernice, I have to say this. At the moment I can only
say it to you, but I may have to tell the police. People with
this sort of allergy usually find out about it when they're
children. They get stung, have the adrenalin, and afterwards they're careful never to get another. But others know
about it, the people who were there at the time.' Turning
his back on the window behind which Nature seemed to
seethe, he looked at the manufactured, man-made things
in the modern kitchen, and at civilised, corseted, powdered
Bernice. 'Tamsin and Patrick weren't only husband and
wife; they were cousins. They'd known each other since
they were children. Even if he half-forgot it, never spoke
of it, she might remember.

'So simple, wasn't it? Patrick has the wasp stings and he
takes the sodium amytal to make him sleep heavily. When
he's asleep she goes to the only place where she can be sure
of getting hold of a bee, Marvell's orchard, and she takes
with her a *straw* handbag.'

'I see. Straw for ventilation, you mean. The bee wouldn't
suffocate. She found the bee before Crispin saw her. But
why stay there, why make love to him?'

'I don't know. So it was a good excuse for coming? I tell
you I don't know, Bernice. But when she got back Patrick
was under heavy sedation. You could have stuck a pin in
him.'

'Oh, Max, don't!'

'I'm going over to see her now.' He brushed away the warning hand Bernice rested on his arm. 'I have to,' he said.

She was loading cases into the big car, Patrick's car, when he came slowly between the silver-green crinolines of the willows. The car was standing in front of the double doors and Queenie was lying on the driving seat watching the flights of swifts that swooped across the garden, off-course from their hunting ground on The Green.

'I'm leaving tomorrow, Max,' she said. He took the biggest case from her and lifted it into the boot. 'Such a mad rush! I've sold my house and the solicitor's dealing with everything. Queenie and I – we don't know where we're going but we're going to drive and drive. All the furniture – they've bought that too. I shan't have anything but my clothes and the car – I've sold the Mini – and oh, Max! I shall have enough money to live on for the rest of my life.'

The mask had not slipped at all. Only her lips, russet against the egg-shell brown of her face, smiled and swelled the lineless cheeks.

'Leave Queenie,' she said, for Greenleaf, no lover of animals, was caressing the dog's neck to hide his embarrassment and his fear. 'She thinks she's a bird dog. Come into the house.'

He followed her into the dining-room. The picture had been taken down and was resting against the wall. Was she planning to take it with her or have it sent on? She must have seen him hesitate for she took his hand and drew him to a chair by the window. He sat down with his back to the painted thing.

'You don't like it, do you?'

Greenleaf, unable to smile, wrinkled his nose.

'Not much.'

'Patrick didn't like it either.' Her voice sounded like a little girl's, puzzled, naive. 'Really, too silly! He wasn't awfully mature, you know. I mean, people grow out of things like that, don't they? Like being frightened of the dark.'

'Not always.' In a moment he would have to begin questioning her. He had no idea how she would react. In films, in plays, they confessed and either grew violent or threw themselves upon your mercy. His mission nauseated him.

She went on dreamily, apparently suspecting nothing:

'That picture, it used to hang in a room in my grandmother's house in London. The garden room we called it because it opened into a sort of conservatory. Patrick made an awful fuss the first time he saw it – well, the only time really. My uncle and aunt had come home from America and they stayed a couple of nights with my grandmother. Patrick was terribly spoilt.' She swivelled round until her eyes seemed to meet the eyes of Salome. 'He was nine and I was seven. Grandmother thought he was wonderful.' Her laughter was dry and faintly bitter. 'She never had to live with him. But she was fair, my grandmother, fair at the end. She left her money to me. So sweet!'

If only she would tell him something significant, something to make him feel justified in setting in motion the machinery that would send this sprite-like creature, this breathless waif of a woman, to a long incarceration. And yet . . . Tamsin in Holloway, Tamsin coarsened, roughened in speech and in manners. It was unthinkable.

'That was nice for you,' he said stupidly.

'I loved her, you know, but she was a bit mad. Patrick's father committing suicide, it sent her over the edge. It gave her a sort of pathological fear of divorce.'

This is it, he thought. He needed to hear and at the same time he wanted to stop her. Almost unconsciously he fumbled along the window sill.

'Did you want a cigarette, Max?'

Taking one from the silver box, he said, 'I've given it up,' and lit it with shaking fingers.

'What was I saying? Oh, yes, about Grandmother. She knew I wasn't getting on all that well with Patrick. Funny, she made the match and she wanted us to make a go of it. Just because we were cousins she thought we'd be alike. How wrong she was! After she died we went along to hear the will read – like they do in books. Dramatic, I can't tell you! Patrick wasn't mentioned at all. I don't know if she thought he'd had enough from his father – that went on this house – or perhaps she resented it because he never went to see her. Anyway, she left all her money to me, the income, not the capital, on condition . . .'

She paused as the dog padded in and Greenleaf listened, cursing the diversion.

'On condition Patrick and I were never divorced!'

O God, he thought, how it all fits, a pattern, a puzzle like those things the boys used to have, when you have to make the ball bearings drop into the right slots.

'As if I wanted to be divorced,' she said. 'I can't support myself. They were too busy educating him to bother about me.'

But Patrick had been going to divorce her. She would have had nothing. Without money from her Oliver Gage would have been unable to marry her, for the costs of her divorce and Nancy's would have fallen on him. Like everyone else he must have been deceived about her income until she got cold feet and told him. He pictured her confessing to Gage; then, when he recoiled from her, running ashamed and wretched – for Tamsin, he was sure, was no nymphomaniac – to Marvell, her last resort. When Marvell refused her there was only one way out . . .

'Does anybody know?' he asked sharply, not bothering to conceal a curiosity she must take for impertinence.

'It was so humiliating,' she said, whispering now. 'Everybody thought I was quite well-off, independent. But if Patrick had divorced me I would have been – I would have been destitute.'

It was a sudden bare revelation of motive and it recalled him to the real business of his visit.

'Tamsin . . .' he began. The cigarette was making him feel a little dizzy, and to his eyes, focussing badly, the woman in the chair opposite was just a blur of brown and bright green. 'I came to tell you something very serious. About Patrick . . .'

'You mean Freda Carnaby? I know all about that. Please! They were the same kind of people, Max. They really suited each other. If Patrick could have made anyone happy it was Freda Carnaby. But you mustn't think I drove him to it. It was only because of that – Oliver and me . . . I was so lonely, Max.'

He was horrified that she should think him capable of repeating gossip to her and to stop her he blundered into the middle of it, forgetting his doctor's discretion.

'No, no. I meant Patrick's death. I don't think he died of heart failure.'

Was it possible that, immured here since her return, she had heard nothing of the gossip? She turned on him, quivering and he wondered if this was the beginning of the violence he expected.

'He must have,' she cried. 'Max, this isn't something that'll stop me going tomorrow, is it? He was so hateful to me when he was alive and now he's dead – I can feel him still in the house.'

So intense was her tone that Greenleaf half-turned towards the door.

'You see what I mean? Sometimes when I go upstairs I think to myself, suppose I see his writing in the dust on the dressing-table? That's what he used to do. I'm not much of a housewife, Max, and we couldn't keep a woman. They were all frightened of Queenie. When I hadn't cleaned properly he used to write in the dust "Dust this" or "I do my job, you do yours". He *did*.'

Were some marriages really like that? Yes, it fitted with what he had known of Patrick's character. He could imagine a freckled finger with a close-trimmed nail moving deliberately across the black glass, crossing the t, dotting the i.

Although he knew her moods, how suddenly hysteria was liable to wistfulness or vague reminiscing, he was startled when she burst out in a ragged voice:

'I'm afraid to go in his room! He's dead but suppose – suppose the writing was there just the same?'

'Tamsin.' He must put an end to this. 'How many wasp stings did Patrick have?'

She was still tense, hunched in her chair, frightened of the dead man and the house he had built.

'Four. Does it matter? You said he didn't die of the stings.' The air in the room was pleasantly warm but she got up and closed the door. It was stupid to feel uneasy, to remember the frightened charwoman, the Smith-King children. She sat down again and he reflected that they were shut in now with the strong watchful dog and that all the neighbours were away on holiday.

'How many did he have when he came in from the garden?'

'Well, four. I told you. I didn't look.'

'And after – when he was dead?'

He stubbed out the cigarette and held his hands tightly together in his lap. His eyes were on her as she coaxed the Weimaraner to her chair, softly snapping her fingers and finally closing them over the pearled fawn snout.

'There, my Queenie, my beauty . . .' Dry brown cheek pressed against wet brown nose, two pairs of eyes looking at him.

'I think he was stung by a bee, Tamsin.'

At a word from her the dog would spring. For armour he had only the long curtains that hung against the window blinds. Wrapped around him they would protect him for a moment, but the dog's teeth would rip that velvet and then . . . ?

'Stung by a *bee*?'

'Perhaps it was an accident. A bee could have got into the bedroom –'

'Oh, no.' She spoke firmly and decisively for her. 'It couldn't happen that way.' Her mouth was close to the dog's ear now. She whispered something, loosening her fingers from Queenie's dewlap. Greenleaf felt something knock within his chest like a hand beating suddenly against his ribs. But it was ridiculous, absurd, such things couldn't happen! The dog broke free. He braced himself, forgetting convention, pride, the courage a man is supposed to show, and covered his face as the chair skidded back across the polished floor.

15

For one of those seconds that take an age to live through he was caught up in fear and fettered to the chair. His eyes closed, he waited for the hot breath and the trickling saliva. Tamsin's voice came sweet and anticlimactic.

'Oh, Max, I'm awfully sorry. That floor! The furniture's always sliding about.'

I make a bad policeman, he thought, blinking and adjusting his chair back in its position by the window. But where was the dog and why wasn't he in the process of being mauled? Then he saw her, puffing and blowing under the sideboard in pursuit of – an earwig!

'You baby, Queenie. She'll hunt anything, even insects.' It was all right. The drama had been nothing but a domestic game with a pet. And Tamsin, he saw, had noticed only that he was startled by the sudden skidding of a chair. 'Talking of insects,' she said, 'it's funny about the bee. It's a coincidence, in a way. You see, that's what happened when Patrick first saw the picture. I'd never seen him before and I was watching from the garden. He ran into the conservatory and there was a bee on a geranium. He put out his hand and it stung him.'

The shock was subsiding now.

'What happened?' he asked rather shakily.

Tamsin shrugged and pulled Queenie out by the tail.

'Why, nothing happened. It made me laugh. Children are cruel, aren't they? Grandmother and my aunt, they made a dreadful fuss. They put him to bed and the doctor came. I remember I said, "He must be an awful coward to have the doctor for a bee sting. I bet you wouldn't have got the doctor for me," and they sent me to my room. I told him about it when we were older but he wouldn't talk about it. He only said he didn't like bees and he couldn't stand honey.'

'Didn't it ever occur to you that he might be allergic to bee stings?'

'I didn't know you could be,' she said, her eyes wide with surprise.

He almost believed her. He wanted to believe her, to say, 'Yes, you can go. Be happy, Tamsin. Drive and drive – far away!'

Now more than ever it seemed likely that the bee had got there by chance. Hadn't he opened the window in the balcony room himself? Wasps stung when they were provoked; perhaps the same was true of bees and Patrick's killer, alighting on his exposed arm, had been alerted into venom by a twitch or a galvanic start from the sleeping man. If Tamsin were guilty she would clutch at the possibility of an accident and no law could touch her.

'I asked you about an accident,' he said. 'Could a bee have stung him by accident?'

'I suppose so.' Marvell is wrong, he thought. She isn't clever. She's stupid, sweetly stupid and vague. She lives a life of her own, a life of dreams sustained by unearned, unquestioned money. But dreams can change into nightmares . . .

Then she said something that entirely altered the picture he had made of her. She was not stupid, nor was she a murderess.

'Oh, but it couldn't!' Dreamy, vague children often do best in examinations, drawing solutions from their inner lives. 'I know it couldn't. Crispin told me something about bees once. They're different from wasps and when they sting they die. It's like a sort of hara-kiri, Max. They leave the sting behind and a bit of their own inside with it. Don't you think it's horrid for them, poor bees? The sting would still have been in Patrick's arm if it had been an accident. We'd have seen it!'

Unwittingly he had given her a loophole. A guilty woman would have wriggled through it. Tamsin, in her innocence, was confirming that her husband had been murdered.

'Max, you don't mean you think I . . . ?'

'No, Tamsin, no.'

'I'm glad he's dead. I am. I tried everything I could to make him forgive me over Oliver and give that woman up. But he wouldn't. He said I'd given him the chance he'd been waiting for. Now he could divorce me and Freda's name wouldn't have to be brought into it at all. Oh, outwardly he was perfectly friendly to Oliver, but all the time he was having his flat in town watched. Oliver and Nancy must come to the party. Then, when he'd got everything lined up he was going to drop his bombshell.' She paused and drew a little sobbing breath, rubbing away the frown lines with her ringless fingers. 'He liked to make people suffer, Max. Even the Smith-Kings. Did you see how he was torturing Denholm at the party?' When Greenleaf said nothing she went on in a shaky voice that fell sometimes to a whisper, 'Oh, that awful party! The evening before, he went straight to Freda's house. I was desperate, I cried and cried for hours. Oliver came but I wouldn't let him in. All those weeks when we were at the flat he'd been hinting that he'd get Nancy to divorce him. My money would pay for that and keep us both. I had to tell him there wouldn't be any money. I did tell him at last, Max, I told him at the party.'

And Gage had sat beside her gloomily, Greenleaf remembered. There had been no close sensual dancing after that.

'He went on and on about it. He even tried to think of ways of upsetting the will. But d'you know something? I don't want to be married. I've had enough of marriage.' Her voice grew harsh and strident. 'But I'd have married anyone who would have supported me. Can you see me working in an office, Max, going home to a furnished room and cooking things on a gas ring? I'd even have married Crispin!'

'Marvell hasn't any money,' he said. 'His house is falling down and he won't get much for the land.'

She was thunderstruck. The mask slipped at last and her big golden eyes widened and blazed.

'But his books . . . ?'

'I don't believe he ever finishes them.'

To him it was the saddest of stories, that Marvell should have to leave the house he loved, that her nightmare of the room with the gas ring might become real to him. Because of this her ringing laughter was an affront. Peal upon peal of it rang through the room; hot laughter to burn and cleanse away all her old griefs. The Weimaraner squatted, alert, startled.

'What's so funny?'

She no longer cared what he might think or say.

'It's mad, it's ridiculous! He spent the night here, you know, the night Patrick died. He spent it with me. I was so scared when you made me sit on the bed in the back bedroom. I felt you must sense that – that I hadn't been alone. Oh, Max, Max, don't you see how crazy it is?' He stared, his hurt suspicion melting, for he saw that she was laughing at herself. 'I wanted to marry him for his money,' she said, 'and he wanted to marry me for mine, and the mad thing is we hadn't either of us got a bean!'

16

She walked with him to the gate. He shook hands with her and impulsively – because he was ashamed of the thoughts he had harboured – kissed her cheek.

'Can I go tomorrow? Will it be all right, Max?' She spoke to him as if he *were* a policeman or a Home Office official. In denying the possibility of accidental death she had declared, if not in words, that Patrick had been murdered. But Greenleaf knew she hadn't realised it yet. Sometime it would reach her, surfacing on to her mind through that rich, jumbled subconscious, and then perhaps it would register no more strongly than the memory of a sharp word or an unfriendly face. By then she might be driving away on the road that led – where? To another terse young company director who would be fascinated for a time by witchlike innocence? Greenleaf wondered as he drew his lips from her powderless cheek.

'Good-bye, Tamsin,' he said.

When he came to the Linchester Manor gates he looked back and waved. She stood in the twilight, one hand upraised, the other on the dog's neck. Then she turned, moving behind the willows, and he saw her no more.

He entered Marvell's garden by way of the orchard gate. The bees were still active and he gave the hives a wide berth. It occurred to him that Marvell might still be out but if this were so he would wait – if necessary all night.

By now it was growing dark. A bat brushed his face and wheeled away. For a second he saw it silhouetted against the jade-coloured sky like a tiny pterodactyl. He came to the closed lattice and looked in. No lamps were lit but the china still showed dim gleams from the last of the light. At first he thought the room must be empty. The stillness about the whole place was uncanny. Nothing moved. Then he saw between the wing and the arm of a chair that had its back to the window a sliver of white sleeve and he knew Marvell must be sitting there.

He knocked at the back door. No footsteps, no sound of creaking or the movement of castors across the floor. The door wasn't locked. He unlatched it, passed the honey-laden table and walked into the living room. Marvell wasn't asleep. He lay back in his chair, his hands folded loosely in his lap, staring at the opposite wall. In the grate – the absurd pretty grate that shone like black silver – was a pile of charred paper. Greenleaf knew without having to ask that Marvell had been burning his manuscript.

'I came earlier,' he said. 'I had something to ask you. It doesn't matter now.'

Marvell smiled, stretched and sat up.

'I went to tell Glide he could have the land,' he said. 'You can take your honey, if you like. It's ready.'

Greenleaf would never eat honey again as long as he lived. He began to feel sick, but not afraid, not at all afraid. His eyes met Marvell's and because he couldn't bear to look into the light blue ones, steady, mocking, unfathomably sad, he took off his glasses and began polishing them against his lapel.

'You know, don't you? Yes, I see that you know.'

Hazily, myopically, Greenleaf felt for the chair and sat down on the edge of it. The wooden arms felt cold.

'Why?' he asked. His voice sounded terribly loud until he realised that they had been speaking in whispers. 'Why, Crispin?' And the Christian name, so long withheld, came naturally.

'Money? Yes, of course, money. It's the only real temptation, Max. Love, beauty, power, they are the obverse side of the coin that is money.'

From his dark corner Greenleaf said: 'She wouldn't have had any if Patrick had divorced her. That was the condition in the will.' The man's surprise was real but, unlike Tamsin, he didn't laugh. 'You didn't know?'

'No, I didn't know.'

'Then . . . ?'

'I wanted more. Can't you see, Max? That place, that glass palace. . . . With the money from that and his money and her money, what couldn't I have done here?' He spread his arms wide as if he would take the whole room, the whole house into his embrace. 'Tell me – I'm curious to know – what did she want from me?'

'Money.'

He sighed.

'I thought I would know love,' he said. 'But, of course, I do see. That kind of sale is a woman's privilege. May I tell you about it?'

Greenleaf nodded.

'Shall we have some light?'

'I'd rather not,' the doctor said.

'Yes, I suppose you would feel that way. I think that like Alice I had better begin at the beginning, go on till I get to the end, and then stop.'

What sort of a man was this that could talk of children's books on the edge of the abyss?

'As you like.'

'When Glide told me about the house I thought I had come to the end of my world. The bright day is done and we are for the dark.' He paused for a moment and rubbed his eyes. 'Max, I told you the truth and nothing but the truth, but I didn't tell you the whole truth. You know that?'

'You told me one lie.'

'Just one. We'll leave that for the moment. I said I'd begin at the beginning but I don't know where the beginning was. Perhaps it was last year when Tamsin was helping me extract the honey. She said Patrick didn't like it. He was afraid of bees and everything associated with them, but he'd only been stung once. That was when he was a little boy at their grandmother's house. He'd been frightened by a picture of a girl holding a man's head on a plate and he'd run into the conservatory. A bee stung him on his hand.'

'Yes, she told me.'

'Max, she didn't know why the doctor had been sent for. She thought it was because Patrick was a spoiled brat. She didn't know why the doctor had given him an injection, had stayed for hours. But at the time I was reading a book about allergies. I was interested because of that damned hay fever. When she'd gone I looked up bee stings and I found why the doctor had stayed and what kind of an injection Patrick had had. He must have been allergic to bee stings. I didn't say anything to Tamsin. I don't know why not. Perhaps, even then . . . I don't know, Max.'

'Some people grow up out of allergies,' Greenleaf said.

'I know that too. But if it didn't come off, who would know?'

'It did come off.'

Marvell went on as if he hadn't spoken.

'It wasn't premeditated. Or, if it was, the meditation only took a few minutes. It began with the picture. I don't know this part – I'm only guessing – but I think that when Tamsin was offered the picture things were all right between her and Patrick, as right as they ever were. Of course she knew he'd hated it when he was a child but she thought he'd grown out of that.'

'When it arrived,' Greenleaf said slowly, 'she must have been trying to patch things up between them. He might think she'd sent for it to annoy him, so she had it put in her room, a room he never went into.'

'I saw it – and, Max, I told them about it in all innocence!'

'Tamsin was past caring then.'

He must be kind, not a policeman, not an inquisitor.

'Go on,' he said gently.

'It was only when Patrick reacted the way he did that I remembered the bee sting. The temptation, Max! I was sick with temptation. I don't know how I got down those stairs.'

'I remember,' Greenleaf said. 'I remember what you said. Something about the eye of childhood fearing a painted devil. I thought it was just another quotation.'

Marvell smiled a tight bitter smile.

'It is. Macbeth. It doesn't mean that in the text. It doesn't mean that Macbeth was looking with a child's memory, but only in a childish way. I suppose it was my subconscious that gave it that meaning. I knew that Patrick feared it because of what had happened when he *was* a child. Then the wasps got him. Even then I couldn't see my opportunity. I wasn't sure of Tamsin. I'd never made love to her. For all I knew I was just an old pedagogue to her, a domestic science teacher. At midnight she came into my orchard.'

'But she wasn't carrying that straw bag,' Greenleaf said quickly. 'It wasn't at all her style. Besides, when Oliver Gage came round with the bi-carb Tamsin was out but the bag was on the birthday table.'

Marvell got up and, crossing to the window, opened the casement. 'My one lie,' he said. Greenleaf watched him drawing in great breaths of the dark blue air. 'Will you be in a draught?'

'It doesn't matter.'

'I felt – I felt suddenly as if I was going to faint.' From shock? From fear? Greenleaf wondered with dismay if for months now Marvell hadn't been getting enough to eat. 'I'll close it now.' He shifted with precise fingers the long wisps of Tradescantia. 'I'd like the lamp. You don't mind?' When Greenleaf shook his head, he said urgently, 'Darkness – darkness is a kind of poverty.'

When the lamp was lit Marvell put his hands round it. They had the opacity age brings and the thought came to Greenleaf that had his son's hands covered that incandescence the light would have seeped through them as through red panes.

'It all happened as I've told you,' Marvell went on, 'except that I didn't say no to Tamsin. I told her I'd walk back with her but that I'd left my jacket in the orchard. I went down to the shed to get my gloves and my veil and a little box with a mesh lid. Someone had once sent it to me with a queen bee in it.

'When we got to Hallows I went in with her. She'd told me you'd given Patrick a sedative and we both knew I was going to stay with her. We didn't say it but we knew. She didn't want to look at Patrick and she went to take a shower. While she was in the bathroom and I could hear the water running I went into Patrick's room. I still wasn't sure the sting wouldn't wake him. There was a big pin-cushion on the dressing-table. I took a pin and stuck it very lightly into him. He didn't stir.'

Greenleaf felt a deathly cold creep upon him, a chill that culminated in a tremendous galvanic shudder.

'Then I put the bee on his arm and I – I teased it, Max, till it stung him.' He slid his hands down the lamp until they lay flat and fan-spread on the table. 'I can't tell you how I hated doing it. I know it's sentimental, but the bees were my friends. They'd worked for me faithfully and every year I took their honey away from them, all their treasure. They'd fed me – sometimes I didn't have anything but bread and honey to eat for days on end. Now I was forcing one of them to kill itself for my sake. It plunged its sting into those disgusting freckles. . . . My God, Max, it was horrible to see it trying to fly and then keeling over. Horrible!'

Greenleaf started to speak. He checked himself and crouched in his chair. They were not on the same wavelength, a country G.P. and this naturalist who could kill a man and mourn the death of an insect.

Marvell smiled grimly. 'I had to stay after that. I had to stay and see she didn't go into that room. She hated Patrick but I don't think she would have stood by and let him die.' He stood up straight and in the half-dark he was young again. 'I made love to Tamsin under the eyes of Herod's niece.' His shoulders bowed as if to receive age like a cloak. 'At the time I thought it a pretty conceit. I should have remembered, Max, that they might both understand the desires of old men. I thought it was love.'

He sat on the table edge and swung his legs.

'I left at four. She was asleep and Patrick was dead. I checked. The dog came upstairs and I shut her in with Tamsin.

'Perhaps I was vain, Max, perhaps I thought I had a kind of *droit de seigneur*, perhaps I'm just old-fashioned. You see, I thought that still meant something to a woman, that she would have to marry me. When she made it plain she didn't want me, I felt – My God! She'd wanted me before, but I'm fifty and she's twenty-seven. I thought . . .'

'Crispin, I *do* see.' It was more horrible than Greenleaf had thought it could be. He hadn't anticipated this grubbing into the roots of another man's manhood. 'Please don't. I never wanted to. . . .'

'But it was only money, always money.' He laughed harshly but quite sanely into Greenleaf's face. 'It's all better now, all better. I am Antony still!'

'But why?' Greenleaf asked again. 'Why tell me so much?' He felt angry, but his anger was a tiny spark in the fire of his other emotions: amazement, pity and a kind of grief. 'You led me into this. You made me suspect.' He spread his hands, then gripped the chair arms.

Marvell said calmly: 'Naturally, I intended to get away with it at first.' His face was a gentle blank. He might have been describing to the doctor his methods of pruning a fruit tree. 'But when I knew that I had killed Patrick in vain, for nothing, I wanted – I suppose I wanted to salvage something from the waste. They say criminals are vain.' With a kind of wonder he said: 'I *am* a criminal. My God, I hadn't thought of it like that before. I don't think it was that sort of vanity. All the moves in the game, they seemed like a puzzle. I thought a doctor and only a doctor could solve it. That's why I picked on you, Max.'

He made a little half-sketched movement towards Greenleaf as if he was going to touch him. Then he withdrew his hand.

'I meant to try to get you interested. Then Nancy started it all off for me. I've always thought hatred was such an uncivilised thing, but I really hated Tamsin. When you suspected her I thought, to hell with Tamsin!' He raised his eyebrows and he smiled. 'If it had come to it, perhaps. . . . I don't think I could have let her suffer for what I did.'

'Didn't you think what it would mean if I found out?'

Marvell moved to the fireplace and taking a match from the box on the mantelpiece struck it and dropped it among the charred sheets of the manuscript. A single spiring flame rose and illuminated his face.

'Max,' he said, 'I had nothing to hope for. I've had a fine life, a good life. You know, I've always thought that was the true end of man, tilling the soil, husbanding the fruits of the soil, making wonderful things from a jar of honey, a basket of rose petals. In the evenings I wrote about the things of the past, I talked to people who remembered like me the days before taxes and death duties took away almost everything that made life for people like me a kind of – a kind of golden dream. Oh, I know it was a dream. I wasn't a particularly useful member of society but I wasn't a drag on society either. Just a drone watching the workers and waiting for the summer to end. My summer ended when Glide told me about this house. That's what I meant when I said the bright day was done and I was for the dark.' As the flame died he turned from the fireplace and clasping his hands behind his back looked down at Greenleaf.

'I don't know what to do,' the doctor said. It was the phrase of despair, the sentence desperate people used to him from the other side of the consulting room table.

Marvell said practically: 'There's only one thing you can do, isn't there? You can't be a party to a felony. You're not a priest hearing confession.'

'I wish,' Greenleaf said, a world of bitterness making his voice uneven, 'I wish I'd kept to it when I said I didn't want to hear.'

'I should have made you.'

'For God's sake!' He jumped up and they faced each other in the circle of yellow light. 'Stop playing God with me!'

'Max, it's all over. I'll have a wash, I'll put some things in a bag. Then we'll go to the police together.' As the doctor's face clouded he said quickly. 'You can stay with me if you like.'

'I'll wait for you.' Not here though. In the garden. 'I'm not a policeman.' How many times had he said that in the past weeks? Or had he in fact said it only to himself in a repetitive refrain that irritated his days and curled itself around his sleep?

Marvell hesitated. Something leaped into his eyes but all he said was: 'Max . . . forgive me?' Then when the doctor said nothing he picked up the lamp and carried it before him into the passage.

The garden was a paradise of sweet scents. At first Greenleaf was too bemused, too stunned for thought. He moved across the grass watching his own shadow going before him, black on the silvered grass. The great trees shivered and an owl flying high crossed the dappled face of the moon.

In the house behind him he could see the lamplight through a single window, the bathroom window. The rest of Marvell's home was as dark and as still as if Glide had already bought it, as if it was waiting with a kind of squat resignation the coming of the men with the bulldozers. A year would elapse perhaps, only six months if the weather held. Then another house would arise, the mock-Tudor phoenix of some Nottingham business man, on the ashes of the cottages Andreas Quercus had made when George I held court in London.

The light was still on. No shadow moved across it. I must leave him in peace, Greenleaf thought, for a few more minutes. He has lived alone, loving loneliness, and he may never be alone again.

Avoiding the orchard where the bees were, he walked in a circle around the lawn until he came once more to the back door. He went in slowly, feeling his way in the dark. His fingers touched the uneven walls, crept across the plates, the framed lithographs. At the bathroom door he stopped and listened. No sound came. Suddenly as he stood, looking down at the strip of light between door and floor, he thought of another house, another bathroom where Tamsin had showered her slim brown body while her lover gave to Patrick the sting that was his own individual brand of death.

He paced the narrow passage, sickness churning his belly and rising into his throat. When he could stand it no more he called, 'Crispin!' The silence was driving him into a panic. 'Crispin, Crispin!' He banged on the heavy old door with hands so numb and nerveless that they seemed no part of his tense body.

In a film or a play he would have put his shoulder to that door and it would have yielded like cardboard, but he knew without trying how impossible it was for him to attempt to shift this two-inch-thick chunk of oak. Instead he groped his way back, wondering what that noise was that pumped and throbbed in the darkness. When he reached the open air he realised that it was the beating of his own heart.

He had to make himself look through that lighted window, pulling his hands from his eyes as a man pulls back curtains on to an unwelcome day. The glass was old and twisted, the light poor but good enough to show him what he was afraid to see.

The bath was full of blood.

No, it couldn't be – not all blood. There must be water, gallons of water, but it looked like blood, thin, scarlet and immobile. Marvell's face rested above the water line – the blood line – and the withdrawing of life had also withdrawn age and the lines of age. So had the head looked in Salome's silver platter.

Greenleaf heard someone sob. He almost looked round. Then he knew that it was he who had sobbed. He took off his jacket, struggling with it as a man struggles with clothes in a dream, and wrapped it around his fist and his arm. The window broke noisily. Greenleaf unlatched the casement and squeezed in over the sill.

Marvell was dead but warm and limp. He lifted the slack arms and saw first the slashes on the wrists, then the cut-throat razor lying beneath the translucent red water. Greenleaf knew no history but there came to him as he held the dead hands the memory of a lecture by the professor of Forensic Medicine. The Romans, he had said, took death in this way, letting out life into warm water. What had Marvell said? 'I am Antony still' and 'Max, forgive me.'

Greenleaf touched nothing more although he would have liked to drain the bath and cover the body. He unlocked the door, carrying the lamp with him, and left Marvell in the darkness he had chosen.

Half-way across the living room he stopped and on an impulse unhooked from the wall the olive-coloured plate with the twig and the apple. As it slid into his pocket he felt with fingers that had palpated human scars the bruise on the underside of the glazed fruit.

The wood with its insinuating branches was not for him tonight. He blew out the lamp and went home by Long Lane.

On Linchester the houses were still lit, the Gages' noisy with gramophone music, the Gavestons' glowing, its windows crossed and re-crossed by moving shadows. As he came to Shalom a taxi passed him, women waved, and Walter Miller's face, brown as a conker, grinned at him from under a pink straw hat. Home to Linchester, home to autumn, home to the biggest sensation they had ever known. . . .

Bernice opened the door before he could get his key out.

'Darling, you're ill! What's happened?' she cried and she put her arms round him, holding him close.

'Give me a kiss,' he said, and when she had done so he lifted her arms from his neck and placed them gently at her sides. 'I'll tell you about it,' he said, 'but not now. Now I have to telephone.'

VANITY DIES HARD

For the Savilles:
Patricia and Derek, Mark and Caroline

Vanity dies hard; in some obstinate cases it outlives
  the man,

Robert Louis Stevenson: *Prince Otto*

1

The rain stopped as they came into the town, but puddles lay everywhere, whipped and wrinkled by the wind. Wet leaves smacked against the windscreen and lay on the pavement like torn rags.

'This do you all right?' Hugo asked. He pulled the car on to a parking area marked with criss-crossed white lines as if for some intricate game. 'We're a bit tight for time, so if you think you can . . .'

'You might take her all the way,' said his wife. 'I call it mean, dumping people as if you were a bus. Besides, it's going to pour.'

'I said we were late,' Hugo snapped. He turned to his sister. 'O.K., Alice? Now the programme is, Jackie and I make a quick tour round Amalgamated Lacquers – there's some kind of a reception at four – but we should be through before five. Pick you up here again at five?'

'Lovely,' said Alice. She gathered up her umbrella and her handbag and opened the car door.

'Don't take any notice of him,' Jackie said quickly. 'Of course we'll call for you at Nesta's. Tell me the address again, will you?'

'Saulsby – S, a, u, l, s, b, y – Chelmsford Road, but I can easily —'

'Rubbish.' She glared at her husband and her black saucer-sized curls vibrated like antennae. 'If he had an ounce of – of chivalry . . . Oh, what's the use?' For Hugo had already started the car, was putting it in gear. In silent rage he held his left wrist extended, displaying the face of his watch. Alice stood on the pavement and gave a little wave.

'Love to Nesta and all that,' Jackie shouted. 'I hope she won't be in one of her moods. Mind you cheer her up before we come.'

In one of her moods. . . . It was not improbable; it would account for her long silence, her apparent refusal to answer most of Alice's letters. Perhaps she shouldn't have come. Certainly it would have been better to come in her own car, instead of impulsively begging a lift from her brother. Chelmsford Road might be anywhere, might be a mile away on the other side of the town.

So this was Orphingham, a narrow high street rather consciously unspoilt, houses that were called 'period' because they had mostly been built before the nineteenth century, a few new shops, plane trees from whose trunks the bark peeled like flakes of olive-coloured paint. Above her on a bright green mound Alice could see the castle; between gaps in the buildings the Orph could be seen winding between water-meadows. Alice thought it had changed little since the days when Constable painted it, a brown looped river walled with willows. A pretty place for a woman of taste, or a sanctuary for a weary spirit.

Outside the town hall there was a street plan, framed and glazed. Alice found Chelmsford Road at once. She smiled at her own trepidation when she realised that Nesta's street was one of the arms leading from the junction where she now was. As soon as she entered it she saw that it was literally what it called itself, the road to Chelmsford. Wider than the street by which she had entered, it was affluent rather than beautiful and suggestive at first of a wealthy suburb. Many of the houses lay back, half concealed by high walls with gates let into them under arched openings.

It was not quite what she had pictured for Nesta. She had imagined a cottage with espalier apple trees and a porch of cockle-shells. 'A little house,' in Herrick's words, 'whose humble roof is weatherproof.' There was nothing like that here, only huge gabled and turreted villas. Nesta probably had a flat in one of them.

A light drizzle had begun to fall. Alice put on her grey uncompromising 'Pakamac' and opened her umbrella. As she did so she couldn't help remembering how perfect Nesta always looked, how svelte. Her umbrella had been a pagoda-shaped affair, black with a slender handle that looked as if it was made of onyx. Alice sighed. Even without a mirror she knew exactly what she must look like, a pleasant, blue-eyed Englishwoman, no longer very young and never worth a second glance. She put up her left hand to smooth back a trailing strand of fair hair and as she did so a raindrop splashed her new wedding ring. The sigh changed to a smile. What did anything matter, age, indifferent looks, competition, when she had Andrew?

She began to walk briskly down Chelmsford Road. As she had supposed from Nesta's address, none of the houses had numbers. Orphingham Lodge – the abode surely of a successful dentist – El Kantara, The Elms. . . . On the opposite side she noted a succession of similarly obvious names. The last big house had a bungalow next to it, its barren garden planted with Japanese cherries whose stark branches stuck upwards like the spokes of umbrellas turned inside out.

Beyond it there remained only a single terrace. Alice's eyebrows went up in surprise. The block of coke-dark late-Victorian houses was so out of character in this prosperous street that she could hardly believe her eyes. They were small and cramped, incongruous against the background of swelling green hills, and they reminded Alice of miners' dwellings, blackened by smoke from pit chimneys.

Each bore a stucco plate under its eaves with its name and the date, 1872. Dirt and time had obscured the lettering. To read the plate on the first house she had to come right up to the iron gate, lean over it and peer.

Alice felt a bitter let-down, a cold stab of disappointment. The house was called Kirkby. Nesta's house was going to be one of these, of course it was. But Nesta *couldn't* live here. To come to this after Salstead? Helicon Lane and The Bridal Wreath had been so exquisite. Scotch pines sheltered the little shop with its steep steps and its iron railings; out of the pavement by its forecourt grew the historic Salstead Oak through whose split trunk it was said a man could ride on horseback and from whose branches mistletoe hung in a loose green ball.

She told herself not to jump to conclusions. That dark side of her character, that pessimistic side that had always been liable to fear the worst, had never manifested itself since her marriage. Andrew had taught her to be gay, frivolous almost. Stoically she looked up again. Kirkby,

Garrowby, Sewerby and – yes, Revesby. So it wasn't one of these, after all. She heaved a sigh of relief.

And yet . . . Wasn't it rather odd to come upon four houses whose names all ended in the same way as Saulsby and Saulsby not be one of them? Perhaps there were more – prettier than these or smartened up in some way – right at the end of the road. But the houses petered out after the next fifty yards and the pavements changed to grass verges blackened with mud and diesel. In this direction the only building was Orphingham Castle, standing out grey and gaunt against a background of fast-flowing cloud. She had come to the end of the town.

'Excuse me . . .'

A woman in a tweed suit and mackintosh was approaching the road from a field path. She clambered heavily over a stile and came diffidently up to Alice with the suspicious look people wear when accosted by strangers.

'Can you tell me where there's a house called Saulsby?'

'In Chelmsford Road?'

'Yes, Saulsby. I can't find it anywhere.'

The woman pointed in the direction of the terrace. Under the pall of cloud the squat houses seemed to frown back. Alice frowned too.

'That's Sewerby.'

'Canvassing, are you? They do make these mistakes over names. It'll be Sewerby you want, all right.'

'I'm not canvassing. I'm going to see a friend of mine.' Alice got out her address book. 'Look, Saulsby.' Interested, the woman peered over her shoulder. 'She wrote to me and told me her address.'

'Somebody's made a mistake somewhere, if you ask me. You take my advice and ask at Sewerby.'

You take my advice . . . Well, she had asked for advice and she might as well take it. There was no bell on the shabby front door of Sewerby, only a knocker in the shape of a Lincoln Imp. Alice tapped and waited. For a while – half a minute perhaps – she heard nothing. Then from within there came a shambling shuffling sound. The door was bolted and the bolt squeaked as it was drawn back. It opened and she saw a very old man, as pale and purblind as if he had been shut up for years in the dark. From the dim hole of a hall came a stench of boiled cabbage, unwashed clothes and camphor.

'Good afternoon. Is Mrs Drage at home?'

'Who?'

'Mrs Drage. Mrs Nesta Drage.'

'There's only me here, lady.' He wore an ancient over-large suit and his collarless shirt was fastened at the neck by a bone stud. His face was rough and wrinkled, the skin had the texture of rind on old cheese. 'Been all on my own since the wife went,' he said. 'All on my own since fifty-four.'

'But Mrs Drage used to live here,' Alice persisted. 'A young woman, a girl really. She's very pretty with fair hair. She came here about three months ago from Salstead. I thought she had a . . .' She paused, realising that the standards she had set for Nesta were falling all the time. '. . . a room or something,' she said.

'I never let no rooms. It'll be Mrs Currie at Kirkby you want, her what's got a girl nursing at the hospital, but she only takes young fellers.'

So it wasn't Sewerby. She *had* been right. From the page in the address book she read it again: Saulsby. Nesta had written to her – written to her twice – and although she had thrown away the letters, she had copied the address down at once. It was incomprehensible, absurd.

Slowly she walked back the way she had come. The Elms, El Kantara, Beechwood, St Andrew's, Orphingham Lodge and twenty more. But no Saulsby, no Saulsby in the whole street.

Suppose you knew the name of a house and the name of the street it was in, but you couldn't find the house, how did you go about finding it? 'Canvassing, are you?' That was it. The electoral register, the voters' list!

The police station was in the centre of the town between a public house called The Lion and Lamb and the cottage hospital. Alice went in. The station sergeant had naturally never heard of Saulsby but he provided a copy of the electoral register.

'She won't be on it,' he said, 'not if she's new here.'

But Saulsby would be. Here it was, Chelmsford Road.

'Kirkby, Garrowby, Sewerby, Revesby,' she read aloud and her voice faltered.

'She's written to you from that address, madam?'

'Of course she has, twice.'

'Well, now, I don't rightly know what to suggest.' He hesitated and then, suddenly inspired, added: 'What does she do for a living?'

'She's a florist. She used to have a flower shop in Salstead. You mean I could enquire at all the florists?'

'All two of them,' he said. 'Wouldn't do any harm, would it?'

At the first she drew a blank. The second was larger and busier. Inside the air was humid yet fresh with scent. That particular perfume, a mixture of roses, acrid chrysanthemums and the heavy languor of carnations, brought Nesta back to her as perhaps nothing else could. It seemed to go naturally with the plump pretty face, the golden hair and the commonplace prattle.

The woman ahead of her was ordering wedding flowers. Back in May, when Alice and Andrew had been married, Nesta had given them all the flowers for a wedding present, sewing with her own hands the white orchid to a length of satin ribbon Alice had carried in a prayer book; early in the morning she had come to Vair Place and banked the walls of Uncle Justin's drawing-room with Whitsun Lilies.

'Do you have a Mrs Drage working for you?'

She smiled and opened her eyes in wide delight when the manageressy girl replied: 'Yes, dear. She's just gone out the back to see to an order. She won't be a minute.'

The search was over. As she waited she felt a quick little twinge of shame and of – envy? Only a woman who had never had to work for her living would come looking for a friend who did work, come on a weekday and expect to find her at home. Of course Nesta would have to work and perhaps she wouldn't be able to leave the shop for long. But then, she comforted herself, something could surely be done to persuade the manageress to let her leave early, or at least get away for a few minutes. She, Alice, could buy something – she slipped her hand into her bag and felt the thick roll of notes she always carried – something extravagant to give to Nesta. Those orchids, possibly, or a dozen long-stemmed red roses.

'I'll give her a call, shall I? I'm sure I don't know what's keeping her.'

Alice wandered about the shop, making plans. It was going to be so good to see Nesta again. I do hope she's got over that depression, she thought. Surely the change of air and environment would have cured it by now. In a moment she would come through that door, ducking her head to avoid an ivy in a hanging basket. She would be wearing a black nylon overall and her hands would be damp, with leaf shreds adhering to them. A sleepy smile would cross her face, for she had always looked lately as if she had just been awakened from a disturbing dream, and she would come out with one of her characteristic, endearing catch-phrases.

'Well, this is a surprise. Long time no see!'

A surprise? No, she wouldn't say that, for Alice had written to her to tell her she was coming, and in five minutes the mystery of the house that wasn't there would be cleared up.

From the back of the shop came the sound of paper being crumpled, then footsteps. Alice smiled eagerly and took a step forward.

'Nesta . . .'

She blinked and put her hand up to her lips.

'This lady here is Mrs Drake. Sorry to have kept you.'

The disappointment was so sharp that she felt her face muscles fall into an almost comical dismay. Her eyeballs prickled. Mrs Drake was thin, red-armed and middle-aged.

'I said Mrs *Drage*.'

'I'm sorry, I'm sure, but I could have sworn . . .'

She shook her head and turned her back on them. So much frustration was past bearing. She stood on the pavement in the rain, the umbrella dangling from her wrist like a wet deflated pod, staring drearily at the shoppers. Nesta might be among them. Surely . . . ? She started, looked again, and began to run after the little figure in the black shiny raincoat whose bright hair was escaping under a scarf. But as she put out her hand to touch the sleeve the woman turned and showed a pig's face with rosy corrugated skin and scarlet lips.

A sob rose in her throat and with it the beginning of panic. It was an old familiar feeling, this sudden fear, this dread of something terrible about to happen. Familiar but old, half forgotten in the happiness of the past year. Calm, practical, matter-of-fact. That, she knew, was how everyone thought of her.

Suddenly she felt very young, almost childish. She wanted to cry and she wanted Andrew. Strange, because the two impulses were incompatible. In his eyes she was strong, calm and maternal. With a little catch of her breath she turned and caught sight of herself in the rain-dashed glass of a shop window, a tall substantial woman with broad shoulders made to cry on, not to shake with sobs.

Nesta had often cried on them. When you are young and pretty you can cry and nobody minds, nobody reprimands you. Why think of that now? Pull yourself together, she told herself in another of Nesta's clichés. She lifted her sleeve and glanced at the little platinum and diamond watch. Almost four. In an hour's time Hugo and Jackie would come looking for Nesta's house, driving up and down the street, growing angrier and more impatient. She could hardly sit on the wall outside Sewerby, waiting for them in the pouring rain. It was almost funny when you thought of it like that, not a crying matter at all.

In all her thirty-eight years Alice had hardly ever used a public telephone box. For communication with its outlying villages Orphingham had a complicated dialling system, a series of codes. What was the name of the firm whose factory Hugo was visiting? He had only mentioned it once. Amalgamated something – paints, varnishes, sprays. . . . She opened the directory and found it quickly. Amalgamated Lacquers, Orph Bridge. Away from Salstead and the people she had known all her life, Alice was always a little ill-at-ease, uncertain, shy. Never having had to make her own way in the world, she was daunted by the unfamiliar. Tentatively she studied the code and worked the dial slowly. Outside it was beginning to grow dark. Water drummed on the roof and washed down the glass walls.

'May I speak to Mrs Whittaker, please?'

She found she had to explain more fully than that. There followed clicks and trills as someone worked a switchboard, then Jackie's puzzled, slightly apprehensive voice.

'Hallo? Is that you, Mummy?'

'It's Alice.'

'Oh God! I thought there was something wrong with the kids. What's the matter?'

Alice told her. In the background she could hear voices, restrained laughter.

'You've obviously made a mistake,' Jackie said rather sharply. 'Got the address wrong. Have you got her letters with you?'

'I haven't got them at all. I threw them away.'

'Well, there you are, then. You got the address mixed up.'

'That's not possible, Jackie. Nesta left a ring at Cropper's to have it enlarged. I sent it to her at Saulsby and I sent letters too. She got the ring, she wrote to me and thanked me for it. She even sent two pounds to cover the cost of the enlargement.'

'You mean you sent letters and a parcel to a place that doesn't exist and you got answers?' Jackie's tone was gentler now, yet high-pitched with a sort of excitement. 'Listen, I'll come over and fetch you and then we'll come back for Hugo.'

2

'Now, let's see. She moved away from Salstead at the beginning of August and she was very vague about where she was going. She said she hadn't got anything fixed but she'd write and let you know when she was settled. Right?'

Alice nodded. 'I didn't like to bother her with a lot of questions, Jackie. She'd been so depressed lately. She'd been in Salstead three years at that shop and she said that was enough. It can't be much fun being a widow and having to earn your own living. She's so young.'

'Young!' Jackie stretched her trousered legs. 'She's older than I am. Twenty-eight if she's a day.' She added thoughtfully: 'A cross between a Jersey cow and a china doll, that's how she struck me.'

That was not at all how Nesta had struck Alice. Looking back to a couple of years before she was married, she remembered how she had gone into The Bridal Wreath when it had first come under Nesta's management. The wreaths of variegated laurel and the pots of solanum sprouting little orange balls had all been taken away and replaced by specie fuchsias and orchids in green metal trays. In her slow dreamy way Nesta had loved orchids. Their gleaming opaque flesh seemed to have an affinity with her own, their petals curved and pearly like her nails. Alice recaptured that first sight of her now, in one of the black dresses she always wore, the only brightness about her pale vivid hair, stacked and interwoven into a filagree cone.

'It was about a month after she moved that I went into Cropper's to get that watch for Andrew. Nesta had taken her engagement ring in to have it enlarged —'

'I'm not surprised,' Jackie interrupted. 'She was putting on weight like mad. I noticed the way her ankles absolutely bulged when she tottered about in those crazy high heels.'

'Anyway, she must have forgotten to collect the ring before she left. I told Mr Cropper I'd send it to her, but I didn't know her address.'

'Was that when you were going to put an advertisement in *The Times*?'

'I knew Nesta wouldn't read *The Times*, but I thought she might have a friend or a relative who would. I was still thinking about it when I had a letter from her. It was just a couple of lines, but I sent the ring and she wrote back and thanked me for it. But that's weeks and weeks ago now.'

From the scuffed handbag of tooled leather she always carried Jackie took a packet of Sobranie Cocktail cigarettes, selected a pale green one and lit it reflectively. The smoke curled up to the car roof like a feather or a branching flower. 'How could she have got the ring if you sent it to a place that isn't there?'

'I don't know,' said Alice.

Above them the rain pattered rhythmically. The sound it made was like the regular tap-tap of little scurrying heels or long-nailed fingers drumming nervously on metal.

'You'd better tidy yourself up a bit,' Jackie said as she started the car. 'You look as if you've got caught in a storm on a cross-country run.'

A year before Alice would have resented the remark. Now she only smiled. 'I'll never be a glamour queen.'

'A *glamour* queen? Where do you get these expressions, out of the ark?'

'I don't need to – to attract people. I've got a husband.'

'Your Andrew,' said Jackie slyly, 'is a very attractive man.'

'I know.'

'I always think dark men are much more sexy than fair men, don't you?'

'Oh, Jackie, I've never thought about it.'

'Well, you can take it from me, they are. Frankly, lovey – I known you won't mind my saying this, you're too sensible, aren't you? – frankly I've often wondered how you managed to catch Andrew in the first place. Picked him up at some tin-pot school sports, didn't you?'

'It wasn't a school sports, it was Founder's Day. And I didn't pick him up. I went with a friend whose little boy was at school there. We were talking to the English master. . . .'

'And the English master was Andrew.'

'Jackie, dear, I thought every Whittaker in the place knew the story by now. We wrote to each other and had dinner together. Isn't that how most women meet their husbands?'

'I met Hugo in a pub.'

'Yes, I remember, but for goodness' sake don't let Uncle Justin know.'

Jackie giggled. When they were about a mile out of Orphingham she took a left-hand turn down a recently concreted lane. The factory where Hugo was resembled a great fungoid growth, plaster-white and rubbery-looking among the fields. Presently he came out to the car. His manner was ebullient if slightly nervous and he launched at once into an account of the contract he assured them was 'in the bag'.

'Who cares, anyway?' said Jackie truculently.

'It's your bread and butter, isn't it? And Alice's, come to that. Shove over, you'd better let me drive. All you lot, you batten on Whittaker's like a bunch of parasites.' He gave an irascible grunt. Jackie lit a blue cigarette, elaborately calm. Hugo sniffed. 'Give me one, will you? Not one of those, a real cigarette. Couldn't care less about the works, could you?' All the Whittakers referred to their factory as 'the works'. 'Never think about it, do you? Grasshoppers living it up while the ants do all the work, the ants being Justin and me.' He grunted again. 'Oh, and Andrew of course,' he added as an afterthought and as a sop to Alice.

She was used to his quick gusts of temper, spurts of rage that evaporated quickly and usually meant nothing. 'I'm sorry Jackie had to come back,' she said peaceably, 'but I suppose you've gathered that I couldn't find Nesta. The house just wasn't there.'

'What d'you mean, wasn't there? Oh, damn and blast him!' He braked sharply, stuck his head out in the rain and shouted at the driver of a molasses tanker. The traffic was dense, a glittering sluggish caterpillar.

'It's useless trying to talk to you,' said Jackie. She gasped and exclaimed suddenly, 'Why didn't we think of it? We should have gone to the Post Office.' The car jerked almost into the tanker's tail lights and the big sign attached to its rear, *Caution, Air Brakes*, seemed to leap against the windscreen. 'Hugo!' she screamed. 'What the hell are you doing? Will you still love me when I've had plastic surgery?'

'Oh, Jackie,' said Alice miserably, 'I wish I'd thought of the Post Office. It was the obvious place. I went to the police, but I never thought. . . .'

'You went to the *police*?' Hugo sounded aghast.

'Only for the voters' list. Could we go back, Hugo? It's worrying me rather.'

'Go back? It'd worry me rather if I had to go back through this hell's delight in the middle of the rush. Besides, they'll be closed.'

'I suppose so. I didn't think.'

In fact it was difficult to see how anyone could turn and go back. The crawling queue remained unbroken and serpentine all the way to the Brentwood fork. Then one in three trickled away.

'Thank God this'll be a thing of the past when the by-pass opens next week.'

The whole stream came to a shivering stop as the first cars edged into the bottleneck of Salstead High Street. To her right Alice could see the white mouth of the twin-track road and across it a row of oil drums set about with red warning lights. The new lamps were in place but unlighted. It was a ghost road, a virgin stretch of concrete over which no tyre had yet passed. Still and silent, it dwindled away between dark embankments of piled-up clay. Alice could just make out the big flat direction sign in the distance and the acute-angled branch where the slip road forked away to meet the High Street in the centre of the town. On the other side of that slip road lay Helicon Lane. It was a stump now, its lower end lopped off to allow the passage of the by-pass, but The Bridal Wreath was still there, the oak and the swinging mistletoe. . . .

At the cross roads they left the High Street and turned down Station Road. The lights were on in the doctor's surgery and Mr Cropper was veiling his window display in the metal night guard that looked like a curtain of chain mail. At any rate, Nesta had got her ring. Somewhere in the elusive Saulsby she might even now be slipping it on above her wedding ring, twisting it and smiling as the light caught the facets of the diamond chips.

People were going into The Boadicea. It must be gone six. The car sped smoothly between new developments of semi-detached houses, under the railway bridge, past 'the works' – Whittaker-Hinton, est. 1856. The last of the workers were leaving, in cars, on bicycles, some on foot. Hugo slowed, raising his hand in a salute, and Alice recognised his secretary coming down the steps. Uncle Justin's Bentley and Andrew's Sprite were missing from the executives' car park. The car moved on quickly into the peace of the wet sequestered countryside.

Vair House was much smaller than Vair Place, but built at the same period and of the same tulip-red bricks, and it clung close to its side without being joined to it. It was

rather as if the parent building had actually given birth to
Vair House, had delivered a child unmistakably its own,
though not its replica.

The larger house topped the other by perhaps a dozen
feet and this extra space consisted of an overhanging roof
from which four dormers protruded. From these windows,
and indeed from all the upper windows of both houses, an
unscarred view was to be had of Salstead's outlying
meadows. Justin Whittaker, who lived at Vair Place, said
that just as there was nothing ugly or incongruous about
what he called the demesne, so nothing unsightly was
visible from it.

Even the new service station on the Pollington Road was
concealed by a fine wall of limes, whitebeams and larches.
Only St Jude's spire could be seen, a tenuous needle of
stone above a web of branches. By building their factory
just outside the station the Whittakers had for ever ruined
the visitor's first prospect of Salstead; their own dwelling
they had taken care to guard from depredations.

Alice and Hugo, orphaned as children, had been brought
up by their father's brother, the present head of the firm.
But when Hugo married he had chosen to build himself a
new bungalow a quarter of a mile away. Vair House fell
vacant when the last Hinton aunt died and had remained
so until Uncle Justin gave it to Alice on her marriage to
Andrew.

Andrew . . . It was just the place for him, she thought as
Hugo dropped her at the entrance to the drive and she
began to walk towards the house. She could hardly remember anything that had given her greater pleasure than that
first day she had shown him Vair House and had told him
it was to be their home instead of one of the stucco-fronted
bungalows reserved for married masters at Pudsey School.
Unless – unless it was giving him the little red Sprite for a
wedding present or the gold watch on his birthday or the
William and Mary bookcase for his Trollope first editions.

The Sprite was on the drive now, dwarfed by Uncle
Justin's Bentley on the other side of the hedge. Of course,
he would be home by now. Alice looked at her watch.
Almost half past six. She rounded the only bend in the path
and then she saw him waiting for her to come.

She knew he was waiting for her although he was not looking into the garden. The curtains had not yet been drawn and through the small square panes she could see the pink light from one of the lamps falling on his face and on the book he was reading. As she came up the steps, tiptoeing because she loved to come upon him unawares, she could see every detail of the cameo in the embrasure of the window: Andrew's long hands that always reminded her of the hands in Titian's *L'homme au Gant*, the signet ring on his finger, even the cover of one of his favourite Palliser novels, brown and duck-egg blue with the Huskinson drawing.

She let herself in quietly. In front of the hall glass she paused and looked at herself. When she had married and brought Andrew to Salstead she had made a firm resolution. Nothing about her appearance should be changed. Let them laugh and gossip because dowdy Alice Whittaker had found herself a husband at last – and what a husband! They would have laughed and talked more, she thought, if she had taken to wearing high heels and short skirts and had had her hair cut.

In the great hall at Pudsey she had looked the way she always did, a woman with a splendid figure – a fine woman, Andrew said – in a Macclesfield silk dress and sensible low-heeled sandals, her hair done in the way it had been since she had first put up the plaits when she was seventeen. Andrew had spoken to her, sat with her, fallen in love with her just the way she was. Why should she change?

Still . . . She remembered Jackie's reproaches and felt a tiny stab of doubt. The scarf might look better draped against the neck of her sweater with the brooch pinned to it, or knotted perhaps. She fumbled unsuccessfully; then, smiling at her small vanities, discarded the scarf and fastened the brooch again. Behind her the door swung and she knew he was standing there. His face appeared in the glass over her shoulder.

' "She well knew",' he quoted, laughing, ' "the great architectural secret of decorating a construction and never descended to construct a decoration." '

'Darling Andrew!'

'I was beginning to get worried about you.'

He put out his arms and she went into them, just as if they had been parted for a month.

'You weren't really worried?'

'I would have been if you hadn't come soon. Hungry?' She nodded. 'I sent Pernille off to the pictures. Apparently some early gem of Bergman has found its way to the Pollington Plaza. She'll be back in time to get dinner.'

He followed her into the drawing-room. The tea things were arranged on a low table with thin bread and butter and pastries from the cake shop in York Street.

'I waited tea for you.'

'Waited? Oh, Andrew, you got all this ready specially, didn't you?'

'*Madame est servie.*'

The fire was just beginning to come up. She imagined him letting it die down, not noticing. Then, when it was six o'clock and still she hadn't come, rushing to pile logs on the ashes. She warmed her hands at the thin yellow flames, remembering the first time he had ever handed her a cup of tea in the hall at Pudsey on Founder's Day.

He too had felt it or read her thoughts, for he said gravely, 'Do you take milk, Miss Whittaker?'

She laughed, lifting her face to his and meeting there a shared tenderness, an awareness of the miracle that had happened to them both. It was still impossible for her to believe that he loved her as much as she loved him, yet impossible to doubt when she saw in his eyes that glow of wonder and delight. Love had come to her late and unlooked for. 'It's so romantic,' Nesta had sighed, 'it makes me want to cry,' and her pale blue eyes had filled with tears. Nesta might be crying somewhere now because she had waited for Alice and Alice had failed to come. She drew away from Andrew, keeping hold of his hand. If Nesta had really been waiting for her, surely she would have telephoned.

'Tell me what you've been doing,' she said. 'Anything happened, anyone phoned?'

'Harry Blunden came in, ostensibly to lend me something and to return a book he'd borrowed. You see, he's torn the cover.' He shrugged, indicating a long rent in the jacket of the novel he had been reading. 'He's a ham-handed character for a doctor. I hope he never has to give me an injection.'

So Nesta, wherever she was, had kept silence and was content to do so. 'I haven't seen Harry for weeks and weeks,' she said. Harry might know, he had been Nesta's doctor. 'What did you mean, ostensibly?'

'Of course, he really came to see you, Bell.' He always called her Bell, for it was the Victorian diminutive of her second Christian name. 'I shall call you Bell,' he had said when she had told him she was called Alice Christabel. 'Alice is too hard for you. Alice is for old spinsters, not young wives. . . .'

'What did Harry want?'

He laughed. 'Just to see you, I imagine. He hung about flapping his great hands for half an hour, more or less tongue-tied, and then he had to take his evening surgery.'

'You don't like Harry, do you?'

'Naturally I don't like men who are in love with my wife,' he said lightly. 'I don't like men who treat her house as if it were a shrine and I don't like men who make a point of sitting in her favourite chair because they know she sat there last. He carries his torch aloft over the ground you tread on.' Smiling a little, he sat down on the floor at her feet. 'Which age-old platitudes,' he said, 'bring me to your friend Nesta. How was she? Tell me all about it.'

'There's nothing to tell. I didn't see her. It's awfully odd, darling, but I couldn't find her.'

'What d'you mean, Bell?' He listened in silence, relaxed and perfectly still, as she told him about it.

'What did you say the house was called?'

She took a pastry basket full of marzipan fruit and bit into it.

'Saulsby. I know Jackie thinks I've got it wrong, but I haven't. It's in my book. Wait a minute and I'll get it.'

'Don't get up now. I know you don't make mistakes like that.' He shifted comfortably, looking up at her. 'You really have the most delightful cushiony lap I ever rested my head in.'

'Have you rested it in many?'

'Hundreds.'

She smiled at that, pitying the other women that had been rejected when she was chosen. 'What ought I to do about Nesta?'

'Do? Why should you do anything?'

'It seems so strange.'

'There's probably some quite simple explanation.'

'I hope so. I can't help feeling she may be in some kind of trouble. Do you remember how depressed and strange she was when she left?'

'I remember she went around saying good-bye to everyone, metaphorically rattling her collecting box.'

'Oh, darling!'

'She foisted herself on us because she said everything was packed up for the move and she couldn't cook herself a meal.'

'Pernille was ill so I had to cook it, but the cheese soufflé went flat and it was ghastly.'

'It wasn't particularly ghastly,' he said, and added teasingly: 'You should have invited Harry as well. I'm sure he'd guzzle . . .' He paused, selecting the worst thing he could think of. '. . . chocolate-coated ants if he thought you'd cooked them.'

'Horrible!' Alice shuddered. 'And then she had one of her little weeps,' she went on, 'and you drove her back to The Bridal Wreath. Goodness knows why because she was going to spend the night with the Feasts. That was the first night they began moving the old graves to make room for the slip road. Nesta had a thing about it.'

'The uncontrolled imagination of the ill-educated,' Andrew said pompously. He grinned at her.

'Don't be so unkind. Even you wouldn't have been awfully keen on sleeping a hundred yards from where a lot of people were unearthing corpses. I know I wouldn't. They even had a policeman and the vicar there, and I think that made it worse. But she wasn't there, anyway. I do wish I knew where she is now, Andrew.'

'Bell?' He sat up suddenly. 'Could we give Nesta Drage a rest?'

She looked at him questioningly.

'I was glad when she went away,' he said. 'I never have been able to see what you saw in her, Bell. When you said she'd borrowed money off you – I didn't like that.' When she began to protest he went on soothingly: 'All right, she paid it back. Today when you went to Orphingham I confess I thought you'd come back several hundred pounds poorer and a partner in another hopeless bit of private enterprise like the last one. But you didn't see her. Darling, I'm not much of a one for signs and portents, but I can't help seeing this mix-up over addresses as the interposition of a kindly Providence.'

'I was going to go back to Orphingham tomorrow.'

'I wouldn't if I were you.' She had never been clever at concealing her thoughts. Now she felt disappointment must show in every feature, for he said impulsively, 'You're really worried about this, aren't you?'

She nodded.

He sat back on his heels and, taking both her hands, smiled at her tenderly. 'I'm so afraid you'll be hurt. Why not wait till Saturday and then I can come with you?'

'Oh, Andrew, I don't need a bodyguard!'

He was still looking at her with that strange mixture of solicitude and amusement. 'Not a bodyguard,' he said, and his voice held a kind of sad intensity. 'There are other kinds of vulnerability.'

'Sticks and stones,' she said lightly. 'You know how it goes on.'

'Perhaps the most insensitive proverb of them all, certainly the most obtuse.'

Alice went upstairs to dress. It was absurd of Andrew to be so protective. If any of her relatives had heard him they would hardly have been able to keep from laughing, knowing how strong and self-sufficient she was. Maternal was the word they used to describe her, a fit adjective for a woman who had married a man nine years younger than herself.

3

'And where,' asked Uncle Justin as he got out of the Bentley, 'do you think you're going? Why aren't you having your luncheon?'

He came towards the hedge and looked her up and down. What he saw must have displeased him, for he gave no hint of a smile.

Alice recalled that some wit had once said of the family that all the Whittakers looked like the descendants of a monstrous union between a golden cocker and an Arab mare, but that only the males favoured the distaff side. Certainly Justin Whittaker looked very like a horse. His forehead was low but saved from ignobility by its width. The distance between his eyes and his mouth was great and made illusorily greater by the deep parallel lines which his constantly compressed lips had cut from his nose to his chin. His large teeth were all his own but he seldom showed them, keeping his underlip in a position of what he called determination, others pugnacity.

'I'm going to the starvation lunch, Uncle Justin, the bread and cheese lunch for Oxfam,' said Alice bravely, remembering that she was a married woman now. 'They have one every Friday.'

'Roman Catholic rubbish.'

It was useless to argue with him. Better for him to think she was toying with the Church of Rome than for him to fling at her his most opprobrious taunt, 'Socialist!'

'You don't have to pay for it, do you?'

'Of course we pay for it. That's the point.' She drew a deep breath. 'The proceeds go to Oxfam. I told you. At the moment we're trying to raise enough to buy agricultural machinery for an Indian village.'

He frowned, shaking his head. His silver tie was always so tightly knotted that he had to hold his chin up.

'I wonder what you think we're going to do with all these people you're feeding on the fat of the land. You aren't going to like it, Alice, when they come over here and live in prefabs all over Vair.'

'I can't argue now, Uncle Justin, I'll be late.'

'A lot of old tabbies, I suppose.' His look indicated that he included her among them, not a real woman, a pretty woman. Women in his view should be seen, and should be worth seeing, but should seldom be heard. 'You don't get any men there, I'm sure.'

'Yes, we do.' Alice owned to herself that he was almost right, and then named the only four men who ever attended. 'Mr Feast from the dairy – he's the treasurer – and Harry Blunden often comes. The vicar's almost always there and Father Mulligan from Our Lady of Fatima.'

'There you are, what did I say? You'd much better come and eat your luncheon with me.'

She was almost tempted. Lunch at Vair Place was delightful. She pictured her uncle eating the meal that seldom varied. A small glass of Manzanilla always preceded it, then came a steak and an apple pie cooked by Mrs Johnson and served by Kathleen. His version of bread and cheese was Thin Wine biscuits and a triangle of Camembert.

'I must go,' she said. 'Don't forget you're having dinner with us tonight.'

It was now much too late to walk. By the time she had battled through the lunchtime traffic and found a place to park she saw that it was a quarter past one. But the pitch pine door of St Jude's Hall was still hopefully open.

The hall floor was covered with light brown lino that, because it was never polished, looked like milk chocolate that has been left too long exposed to the air. At a trestle table just inside the door, a table laden with collecting boxes and hung with posters, sat a very thin man. He was even more emaciated than the starved children who, with distended bellies and feverish eyes, stared hopelessly from the flapping photographs.

'I'm sorry I'm late, Mr Feast.' Alice had known him too long to be amused by or even to notice the incongruity of his name.

'Better late than never.' In his throat a huge bulge, like an Adam's Apple swollen to monstrous proportions, stuck out above his collar. It was the only prominent thing about him. If only, Andrew had once proposed, he could be induced to stand at the hall entrance in a loincloth even Uncle Justin's hostility to the cause would melt. The most reactionary would join the bread and cheese eaters, perhaps unaware of the true objects of their fast.

She passed on quickly.

'Good morning, Miss Whit – Mrs Fielding, I should say,' said the vicar. He had married her but it would take him more than six months to get over the habit of twenty years. 'We haven't seen as much of you lately as we should like.' It was the very phrase he used to church backsliders.

I have married a husband and therefore I cannot come, Alice nearly said. Instead she smiled. 'Well, I'm here now.'

'Yes, indeed, and most welcome.'

He led her to one of the long deal tables and hesitated between the many empty chairs. Her eyes travelled from the oil painting of James Whittaker, builder of this hall, splendid in frock coat, watch and chain, to the different pictures beneath. Under each piously Gothic window hung a poster of a hungry child with an empty bowl, so that from where she stood it seemed as if a queue of malnourished infants stretched the length of the hall, watching and waiting.

'Alice! Come and have a place in the sun.' Harry Blunden pushed back his bentwood chair and stood up. 'Here you are, the warmest place in the room.'

She smiled up into his lean ugly face, trying not to show the embarrassment she felt when she saw in his blue eyes so much naked love.

'Thank you, Harry.'

His extreme height had always been a nuisance to him – she imagined him ducking beneath hospital bed curtains, bending almost double over the sick – that he now had a permanent stoop. 'There, what's it going to be?' He eased her coat from her shoulders. 'Mousetrap or best-quality kitchen soap?' It was the no longer funny remark he always made when they met at the Friday lunch.

'Oh, mousetrap. But please not that bit with the evil-looking hole in it.'

The table was covered with a cloth of white plastic. There were bread rolls and rough-hewn chunks of French stick all tumbled together in Pyrex bowls, cheese in bricks as dry and unappetising as the wood of the table, and, in a jam-jar, a small bunch of attenuated watercress. Everyone had a plate, a knife and a Woolworth glass tumbler.

'Hallo, Mrs Fielding.'

Alice looked across the table and met the eyes of a thin girl with long shaggy hair that reached to her shoulder blades.

'Hallo, Daphne. You're the very person I wanted to see.'

Daphne Feast parted the strands of hair and peered at her.

'I know. I've been talking to your sister-in-law.'

'*Jackie*? Is Jackie *here*?'

Reaching a long arm rudely across the plate of a plump woman sitting two places from her, Daphne pointed to the far end of the table where Jackie sat between her two small children.

'She said you'd been looking for Nesta Drage. She'd given you a false address or something.'

'Well, it wasn't quite —' Alice stopped as Harry interrupted her. She wished he wouldn't always try to monopolise her.

'Gave you a false address?' he said. 'But you went to see her, didn't you?'

'Yes, I did, but . . .'

She lifted up her glass as the vicar approached their section of the table with a jug of water.

'How much do we have to pay for this?' asked the plump woman suspiciously.

The vicar beamed. 'Just whatever you would have paid for your normal lunch at home.'

'But I don't have any lunch at home! My mother-in-law won't let me. She says if I put on any more weight I'll get a coronary. I won't get a coronary, will I, Dr Blunden?'

Harry turned towards her reluctantly. 'Just as well to be on the safe side,' he said.

'I wish you'd come and sit by me, Doctor, and tell me what I ought to do so that I can tell my mother-in-law.'

Alice could see he didn't want to move. For a moment he hesitated. Then he got up and, smiling abstractedly, walked round the table carrying his plate.

'I thought you might know where Nesta really is,' she said to Daphne. 'You were such close friends.'

'Oh, I don't know. We used to have a bit of a giggle together. That's all.'

'Didn't she tell you where she was going either? She must have given you an address to write to.'

'She knew I'd never write, Mrs Fielding. We were – what-d'you-call-it? – ships that pass in the night. She never even said a proper good-bye, but I'm not breaking my heart over it.'

Alice was bewildered. 'But she stayed with you and your father on her last night. August the seventh, that Friday night. She had supper with us and then she went to stay with you.'

'She never turned up.'

'I though it was a definite arrangement.'

'Not what you'd call an arrangement. She did *say* she'd come and Pop and me waited for her, but there was a play on the telly and what with her having the phone cut off I couldn't get in touch with her. You know how it is.'

No, she didn't know. She wrote down all her engagements in a twin to the big address book and she had never failed to keep a coffee-morning date, let alone break a promise to spend the night in a friend's house.

'Didn't you go round to The Bridal Wreath to find out?'

The suggestion almost seemed to shock Daphne. She nibbled at her last fragment of cheese. 'I told you, there was this play on. Pop just went up to The Boadicea for a beer and I said, "Keep your eyes open for Nesta," but he never had sight nor sound of her. When it got to ten I gave her up.' She leaned confidingly across the table. 'Quite frankly, Mrs Fielding, I didn't go much on going down Helicon Lane in the dark, not with all those graves being turned up.'

Heavens! Alice gave herself a little shake. There was something ghoulish about Daphne's pallid face in which only the eyes were made up, the streaming hair that trailed across the bread bowl.

'Well,' she said, 'it's a mystery, isn't it? Before I sent the ring off to Nesta – when I didn't know anything of her whereabouts – I asked everyone in Salstead who knew her and no one had her address.'

'You asked me then,' said Daphne mournfully, 'and I asked Pop and all the shop people.'

On the other side of the table Harry looked as if his patience was being exhausted. The plump woman's voice rang out, 'I suppose there's nothing to stop me going into The Boadicea when I've finished this and having a proper lunch, is there?'

'On your own head be it,' said Harry. He came round behind Alice's chair, stopped and patted her shoulder. 'I wouldn't do too much of this, if I were you, Alice.' His voice had dropped and she swivelled round quickly because his words were plainly intended only for her ears. 'You need proper meals. You've been looking tired lately.'

'But I feel fine.'

The words were almost a whisper and she had to strain to catch them. 'If there's ever anything troubling you – *anything*, Alice, you'll come to me, won't you?'

'You know I'm never ill, Harry.'

He shook his head, increased the pressure of his hand and then withdrew it. Puzzled, she watched him cross to the table where Mr Feast sat taking the money. Harry was a doctor, *her* doctor. Why then had she received such a strong impression that the trouble he feared for her wasn't physical at all?

'You said it was a mystery,' said Daphne Feast. 'Well, I'll tell you something. There were a lot of mysteries about Nesta.'

At the hint of gossip Alice felt herself shrink. All she wanted was to find out where Nesta was and why she was hiding herself.

'For one thing she was involved with some man.'

'Oh, come!' Nesta had been devoted to the memory of her dead husband, even to the extent of still wearing mourning three years after his death. One day certainly she would get married again. Anyone as pretty as she was was bound to. But, involved with a man? Nesta had been lonely and forlorn. It was because of this and in an effort to save her from the company of people like the Feasts that Alice had made a point of cultivating her.

'She wouldn't tell me who he was,' Daphne said firmly, 'only that he was a big man in Salstead and that some people would have a bit of a shock when it came out.' She lit a cigarette and dropped the match among the crusts and cheese rinds on her plate. 'I reckon he was married. There was some reason he didn't want it known. Nesta said he'd have to marry her one of these fine days. We had a bit of a giggle about it.'

'That sounds like day-dreaming to me,' said Alice severely.

'There was another funny thing. Nothing to do with her love life, but a funny thing.' Daphne flicked her ash across the table.

I'm not surprised Nesta didn't want to stay with the Feasts, Alice thought.

'Did you ever notice her eyebrows?'

'Her *eyebrows*?'

'You think I'm daft, don't you? No, you wouldn't have noticed, not with her being so neurotic about the way she looked. Well, when she first came here she had thick sort of fair eyebrows and very long lashes. Right?'

Yes, Nesta had beautiful eyebrows and long soft lashes. Her blonde hair had been abundant too.

'Well, naturally she used to pluck her eyebrows, but one day she was a bit heavy-handed and she pulled too much out. She said she'd have to let them grow . . .'

'Well?'

'Well, they never did. That's all. They never did and she used to have to sort of pencil them in. I popped into her flat once – she didn't know I was coming and, God, she jumped out of her skin – she'd taken her make-up off and she hadn't got any eyebrows at all. I can tell you, Mrs Fielding, it gave me the creeps. Just eyes she had and then nothing till her hair started.'

Daphne, Alice thought, had missed her vocation. She would have made a startling impact on filmgoers as a kind of female Boris Karloff. First the graves and now this.

'Her eyelashes were – well, they were quite luxuriant.'

'False,' said Daphne Feast. 'I'm not kidding.'

So poor Nesta had had alopecia. Horrible, when you remembered how proud she had been of her appearance.

'Thanks, Daphne. I expect she'll turn up.'

She began to put on her gloves.

'When you do root her out you might tell her to come and collect her stuff.'

'Her stuff?'

'She got Snows to fetch round some stuff of hers the day before she left. I reckon it was a load of junk or some of those kids' jigsaw puzzles she was so crazy on doing. Anyway, you can tell her I'm fed-up with it cluttering the place up.'

'I'll tell her.'

The trouble with being a Whittaker was that everybody expected you to dispense largesse wherever you went. Glad that Uncle Justin would never know the extent of her generosity, Alice took two pound notes from her wallet and laid them on the table in front of Mr Feast.

'Quite a good —' She had nearly said 'audience', '– attendance here today, Mr Feast.'

He began mournfully on a long diatribe. 'Always the upper crust and the working class, though, you'll notice, Mrs Fielding. The bourgeoisie keep their feet under their own fat tables. That's why I've always said and always shall say, the Popular Front's an impossibility. The upper crust and the working class —'

'Do tell me, Mr Feast, which do I come in?' At Jackie's voice, Alice turned. 'I didn't know what to do with the brats so I brought them along to see how the other half lived.'

Alice bent down and swung the three-year-old up into her arms. 'He's getting heavy, Jackie! What did you think of your funny old dinner, darling?'

Her nephew flung his arms around her neck. 'I'm partial to cheese, aren't I, Mum?'

'Partial?'

'It's his latest word. Put him down, Alice. You'll strain yourself.'

'I've just made up my mind,' Alice said. 'I'm going back to Orphingham. Now. This afternoon.'

'And we're coming with you,' said Mark and Christopher together.

Smiling, Alice squatted in front of them.

'Would you like to? You can. I'd love some nice jolly company.'

'Well, you've had that for a start,' said Jackie. 'You're coming to the dentist with me.'

As the double wail went up she put her hands over her ears.

'It's a pity you haven't got any of your own, Alice. If you'd got married ten years ago you'd have had kids and all the jolly company you wanted.'

Ten years ago Andrew had been nineteen, in his second year at Cambridge. Alice wondered if Jackie knew what she had said, but although she felt the blood mounting in her own cheeks there was no sign of embarrassment on her sister-in-law's face. Jackie and Hugo, Uncle Justin, all of them, only thought of Andrew's luck, the sudden rapid step he had taken into affluence. They never considered what he had lost by marrying a woman on the verge of middle age.

She took a hand of each of the boys. 'If you're very grown-up about going to the dentist, I promise I'll have something lovely for you at Vair. You get Mummy to bring you at – let me see – half past five.'

'That's a vicious circle,' said Jackie. 'Fill their beastly little fangs and then rot them all over again.'

Alice walked out into the cold sunlight. If she made haste and started at once she would be in Orphingham by three.

4

The post office was crowded. Alice had to push her way in past prams and tethered dogs. Behind the rail on the counter top, three people were serving, a thin young man with a face so pale as to be almost green, a plump woman and another man, older and dignified, with a heavy grey moustache. Alice glanced ruefully at a legend on a poster: 'Someone, somewhere, wants a letter from you.' She joined the shortest of the queues. It was moving very slowly. Pension books were brought out and presented with dogged patience, secreted once more in bags and wallets.

'Next, please.'

'I've been sending letters to a house in Chelmsford Road,' Alice began. 'To a friend of mine. But when I went to Chelmsford Road yesterday I couldn't find the house.' Behind her an old woman pushed forward to listen. 'The name of the house is Saulsby, but there isn't a Saulsby in the whole street.'

'You mean your letters have gone astray?' The young man's voice was rough with impatience. He kept his head bent while he rummaged in a drawer. 'If they've been wrongly addressed they'll be returned to sender in due course. It's a wise precaution to put your own address. . . .'

'I don't think they can have gone astray. I've been getting replies.'

At last he looked at her. 'You don't want us at all, do you? What you want is the council offices. They'll let you have a street plan. Next, please?'

Standing her ground, Alice said desperately: 'I know the name of the street. I told you, it's Chelmsford Road. I'm sorry if you're busy . . .'

'Always busy on a Friday afternoon on account of everybody coming in then because it gets so crowded on Saturday.'

His lack of logic almost defeated her. She stepped back and immediately an arm in moth-eaten ocelot thrust across her and laid a pension book on the counter.

'Isn't there anyone I could talk to about this? Surely there must be someone who would know?'

'If you'd like to line up over there you could have a word with Mr Robson. He's the postmaster.'

To join Mr Robson's queue she had to go right back to the door. She counted fifteen people waiting while the postmaster served a woman in an orange sari. Five minutes passed and nobody moved. The Indian woman was buying half a dozen stamps of each denomination to send home to a philatelic relative in Calcutta. The queue began to mutter and shuffle.

Suppose I were to go back there just once more, Alice thought, and make another check on those house names now it isn't raining. Ignoring the queue, she walked straight up to the pale man's counter. 'Will it be less crowded if I come back later?'

'Pardon?'

'If I come back later?'

'You can come back later if you like.' Counting notes, he hardly bothered to look at her. 'It gets a bit slacker around half-five.'

'Do you mind not going out of your turn?' asked a tired young woman carrying a child.

Alice went back to her car and drove up the High Street to the Chelmsford Road turning. Even under the wintry sky the place had the higgledy-piggledy, typically English prettiness of a calender or a Christmas card. The townspeople evidently took pride in their rainbow variety of painted front doors, lime-washed walls and sanded steps. This place, she thought, but without malice or contempt, would have made a particular appeal to Nesta's snobbishness and her love of beauty kept within orderly bounds. Its residents could turn up their noses at certain utilitarian workaday aspects of Salstead.

Chelmsford Road was deserted. Dead chestnut leaves like ancient wrinkled hands, brown and crepitating, rustled in the gutters. None of the houses had numbers and none was called Saulsby. She walked up one side examining name plates and down the other.

The only sound to disturb the cathedral-like hush came from the front path of El Kantara where a woman was sweeping leaves. The round-topped gate in the wall was open and just inside was a sign which read:

Orphingham Hospital Management Committee, Nurses' Home.

'I'm looking for a house called Saulsby,' Alice said.

'Saulsby? I don't think . . .' It was almost sinister the way she whispered and looked furtively over her shoulder. She held the broom a foot from the ground and the leaves began to eddy back, covering the swept path once more. 'You don't mean one of the eyesores?' she said in a voice so low that Alice had to strain to catch it.

'The eyesores?'

'Four nasty little slums. If you've been up the road you must have passed them. They've been due for demolition goodness knows how long.'

Why whisper about it? Why keep glancing up at those blind closed windows? In the heavy shadowed silence of the tree-grown drive Alice suddenly felt a little thrill of fear. If only she had waited until tomorrow when Andrew could have come with her.

'No, it isn't one of those,' she said softly. She glanced behind her quickly into the thick bushes and jumped as the woman hissed suddenly:

'Sorry I had to keep my voice down.' She smiled, breaking the tension, and pointed the broom handle aloft. 'You see, the night-duty girls are all asleep.'

Alice almost laughed as she went once more into the street. She must be letting this business get her down. Of course that was the obvious explanation. Why read ridiculous nuances into it?

While she had been inside the gate someone had parked a bicycle beside her car, a red bicycle. A postman would have a red bicycle, she thought. But where was he? As she stood looking at the blank wall, the long row of gates all overhung with chestnut branches, holly and yellow-spotted laurel, a sudden gust of wind caught the bicycle and knocked it over into the gutter. Its wheels spun. She bent to pick it up. He must have heard the crash and the whirr of wheels, for he came running, slamming the gate of The Laurels.

'Thanks very much.' He was very young with yellow hair and a characterless face in which the colour was oddly distributed, for his chin, nose and forehead were chapped and reddish while his lips and cheeks had a sickly pallor. 'You shouldn't have got yourself dirty.' He hoisted his canvas bag on to the handlebars and stood waiting for her to go.

'Tell me,' she said, 'do you deliver letters down here in the mornings, all the letters? Are you the regular postman?'

'Been on here a couple of months. What were you wanting?'

'Have you ever delivered any letters to a Mrs Nesta Drage at a house called Saulsby?'

'Not what you'd call delivered. There's a redirection notice on Saulsby.'

She stared at him. Her heart had begun to beat very fast. At last the name made sense to somebody besides herself.

'What's a redirection notice?'

'It's like when you change your address, see? You fill in a form at the post office and all the post – well, it doesn't go to your old address. It goes to the new one. We do our own sorting and when we get mail for this said person, the one that's filled in the form, we write the new address on the envelope and it goes back in the post. Saves your letters getting lost like.'

'Would you be very kind and tell me where Mrs Drage's letters are going?'

He shook his head. 'Can't do that. That'd be an invasion of privacy.'

The wind had grown suddenly cold. Twilight was coming and with it a light, needle-sharp frost. She shivered. She was seldom angry but now she could feel herself growing edgy with frustration.

'I suppose it didn't occur to you that there isn't a Saulsby in Chelmsford Road, that it doesn't exist?'

'Now, look,' he said, truculent and defensive, 'it's on the notice. I've seen it on her letters, plain as a pikestaff.'

'Where is it, then? Show me.'

'Up there.' He pushed the bicycle up to the grey terrace and Alice followed.

'Sewerby, you see,' she said quietly, and she was glad she had made no more of this small triumph, for he stared aghast at the name plaque and the flush spread across his whole face, dark as a naevus.

'But I've never had no letters for Sewerby.'

'I'm not surprised. He's a very old man and he's all on his own. I don't suppose anyone ever writes to him, and if you've only been on here two months —'

He interrupted her raggedly. 'I don't know what come over me.' His voice was pleading and he turned towards her as if he would clutch at her clothes. She moved away, lifting her hand. 'I reckon I must have misread that name and what with them always coming and going at Kirkby and them houses not having numbers like . . . Mr Robson did say I was to check, but – I don't know – things kind of got on top of me.' His hands tightened on the handlebars. 'He'll have the hide off me,' he said.

'I don't want to make trouble for you. I only want to know where my letters are going.'

'That's easy,' he said eagerly. 'There was a letter come for her Wednesday.' Alice nodded. She had posted it herself on Tuesday night. 'One hundred and ninety-three, Dorcas Street, Paddington. I've got it by heart on account of my mother's name being Dorcas.'

Alice wrote it down. 'I won't say a word to Mr Robson,' she joked feebly. 'He's not an easy man to see.'

One hundred and ninety-three, Dorcas Street, Paddington. Of Paddington Alice knew only the station and that small pretty corner known as Little Venice. Those streets she had seen from Western Region trains taking her on holiday to Cornwall had been far from prepossessing. Could Dorcas Street be one of them? It sounded charming but its very euphony made her uneasy. In present-day civilisation the pretty names belonged to sordid venues while a street that was called The Boltons or Smith Square was all that was respectable and affluent.

This, then, was the most likely explanation: Nesta had gone to an ugly slummy part of London but she had been unable to bring herself to admit it. Snobbery, a desire to seem grand to her friends, had made her give Alice a fine-sounding address.

Her heart contracted with pity as she gave Chelmsford Road a last look. Nesta must have been to Orphingham and seen in its peace the sanctuary she longed for. Chelmsford Road was the very place she might have chosen for her home if circumstances had been different. Perhaps that too was the explanation of her languor and her depression. A day-dreamer continually baulked could have conceived such a plan. Only a woman with a deranged mind would have carried it out. Or – or a woman who lived puzzles, jigsaws, problems on television quiz programmes, the easier crosswords in the evening papers?

Suddenly Alice felt quite excited. Then doubt and disquiet returned. There could be nothing amusing in the
motives which had prompted Nesta. She must be rescued.
Friendship was pointless if it stopped short at material aid.
Alice felt in her handbag the shiny blue book whose
cheques never bounced. Why, oh why, instead of this constant effort to keep up appearances, hadn't Nesta told her?

'I'd rather you didn't go.'
'Why on earth shouldn't I, darling?' She was at the dressing-table, combing her hair, when Andrew had come in,
already dressed, slightly impatient. As soon as he had heard
she meant to go to Paddington he had said he would go
with her, but she had protested. Nesta was proud. She
might tolerate Alice enquiring into her affairs, never
Andrew.
'Do as you like, but it'll upset you, Bell, if you find she's
living with a man.'
'*Nesta*?'
He came towards her and in the mirror she watched him
approach and put his hands on her shoulders. 'You're such
a child in some ways. I don't mean you're immature and
God knows you're always exaggerating your age, but you're
innocent. I wonder what you'd do if you found her in some
horrible back room with a man – say, Nesta trailing about
in a black négligé and the lover not bothering to hide
himself, but bellowing things from the bedroom?'
'That's not funny, Andrew.'
'Darling, forgive me, but wouldn't you just whip out the
little cheque-book – money, the universal healer?'
She was hurt and she showed it.
'You mean I'm mercenary? I make a god of money?'
'Not a god – a key to open all doors. Bell, I have to tell
you this, but that's the way a child feels. Jackie brought
Mark and Christopher in tonight –' Diverted, she held the
comb poised. She was suddenly appalled because she had
forgotten all about them. 'It's all right. I gave them some
sweets I found in a drawer. Mark didn't want to go home.
D'you know what he said? Let's stay, Mummy. I'll give you
sixpence if you'll let me stay.'
'And I'm like that?'

'You're – you're an angel.' He dropped a kiss on to the top of her head. Still troubled, she looked up and in the glass he met her eyes.

Now, as she lifted the heavy mass of hair in both hands and, seeking some way of doing it more flatteringly, held it loosely above her head, he drew back, not touching her any more.

'What's the matter?'

'Don't do your hair like that. I don't like it.' He sounded ridiculously annoyed.

'I thought it made me look younger.'

'For heaven's sake, Bell, don't keep harping on your age as if you were a candidate for a geriatric ward!'

'Sorry.' Still twisting her hair into a soft loose coil, she averted her head from the glass and turned to face him. To her surprise he let out his breath in a sigh.

'It's not so bad, I suppose. I imagine I could get used to it.'

'You won't have to. The old way's easiest.' Rapidly she began weaving the two plaits. 'Look, darling, will you feel better if I promise you that when I find Nesta I'll try to help her without actually giving her money?'

'What other help could you give her?' He was still shaken and she wondered why.

'If she was in need I could bring her here.'

'Bring her *here*? I'd rather you gave her money to stay away than adopted her!'

'Andrew! Adopt – why did you use that word? What did you mean?'

He shook his head. 'Nothing. Forget it.'

Her hands travelled down over her useless, ageing body. Jackie had been there, Jackie with her two sons. It was not hard to unravel the workings of his subconscious.

'I'm ready now,' she said in a carefully neutral voice. 'Let's go down.'

'Good heavens,' said Uncle Justin, 'it makes you wonder what the Post Office is coming to! If you had any idea of your duty as a citizen, Alice, you'd report the whole thing to that fellow-what's-his-name? – Robson.' Suspiciously he ran his tongue round the rim of his glass. 'Where did you get this sherry, Andrew? I may be wrong but to me it has a distinct flavour of the Southern Hemisphere.'

'Well, it can't have,' said Alice firmly. She had recovered her poise, 'since it came from Jerez. What do *you* think I ought to do about Nesta?'

'Ah, yes, Mrs Drage.' Alice remembered with exasperation that he had to know someone for at least twenty years before venturing on the Christian name. 'A comely woman, very easy to look at. Not at all the sort of person one would expect to see keeping a shop. I daresay she found it difficult to make ends meet.'

'She borrowed some money off Alice once,' said Andrew. Why had she ever told him that? 'Before we were married. I'm afraid there might be a repetition and that's one reason why I think it's better for Alice not to see her.'

'She paid it back,' Alice said pleadingly, 'besides it wasn't much.'

'A couple of hundred pounds and you call it not much!'

'Not enough to make a song and dance about,' said Uncle Justin unexpectedly. 'I'm happy to say I was able to give her a little help myself occasionally in that direction.'

Dumbfounded, Alice looked at him. He was sitting stiffly, not resting his head against the soft back of the chair. His thinness and the straight set of his shoulders took ten years from his age. His hair was grey but abundant. The bone formation of his face and the sparse flesh had suffered few of the effects of time. There were lines and cavities, deep pouches under the eyes, but there were no wrinkles.

Of all the big men in Salstead he was the biggest. Just as she was wondering if she dare ask him the obvious question Andrew asked it for her. 'And may one ask if you ever got it back?'

His answer would make all the difference. As she waited, half terrified, half curious, for the outburst, the door opened and Pernille appeared on the threshold, beaming at them.

'Ah, dinner!' said Uncle Justin. 'I hope you're going to give us some of your Scandinavian delicacies. I'm particularly fond of those little cup things with asparagus.'

'*Krustader*, Mr Whittaker.'

'That's it. Crustarther. You'll have to give Mrs Johnson the receipt for those.'

Too far away from him to warn him off further indiscreet questioning with a touch, Alice gave Andrew a glance of loving anger.

But he said no more and now her uncle was beaming in happy anticipation of the meal. She felt a sudden impatience, a wish to get the evening over quickly, the night that must pass before she could go to a hundred and ninety-three, Dorcas Street, Paddington.

5

A kaleidoscope of green, grey and rose-pink whirled and rocked; then it began to spin round an intensely bright, burning vortex. But just as she thought it must engulf her and destroy the last remaining steadiness of balance the colours split and settled back into the bathroom décor. Just grey tiles, a rectangle of green soap and three pink towels hanging on a wickedly bright rail. The window was like a square of gingham, white bars crossing the black sky of early morning. It was still now, no longer bouncing or swimming in a mist. But the sickness remained. Alice sat down on the edge of the bath. She could not remember ever having felt so ill.

It must be very early. The cold she felt could have nothing to do with the true temperature, for she had turned on the heater when she had first staggered here from the bedroom. Shivers fluttered along her arms and legs and seemed only to increase when she put her hands on the hot rail. In Andrew's shaving glass her face looked white and aged by the bile that was moving again, rising horribly into her mouth. She twisted over to the basin and retched.

Presently, when the spasm had passed, leaving her drained and trembling, she made her way back to the bedroom. Andrew was asleep. The dark blue light that precedes a winter dawn showed her a boy's cheek and a hand curled like a child's round the pillow edge. She moved in beside him warily, afraid to let him see her in the ignominy of a repulsive illness.

But she was *never* ill. Something in Pernille's dinner must have disagreed with her, the pink *silde salat* perhaps, or the *krustader*. Andrew had opened a bottle of wine, *Entre Deux Mers*, a dry white Bordeaux, but she had taken less than a glassful. And afterwards they had eaten chocolates that Uncle Justin had brought. She shifted away from Andrew, keeping her head up. The very thought of food was bringing the sickness back and the shivers that made her teeth chatter.

She pressed her hands against her diaphragm, willing the nausea to go. Perhaps it had been the yoghurt she had grown so fond of lately and took every night for her supper. As she remembered the gelatinous curd, white, decomposing into whey as the spoon broke it, she threw back the bedclothes and rushed across the room. Let me make it to the bathroom, she prayed.

Of course it had awakened him. She clung to the basin rim, knowing that he was standing behind her.

'Go back to bed,' she said harshly, 'I don't want you to see —'

'Don't be silly.' She knew she would have been sick again if anyone had touched her and yet because he did not touch her she felt, in the midst of her misery, the deprivation.

'I'll be all right in a minute.'

'Why didn't you wake me, Bell? How long have you been like this?'

She ran cold water into the basin, splashing her hands and face. 'Hours,' she said. 'I don't know.'

'Come on.' He put his arm around her and she turned her face away. 'I'll get Pernille to bring you some tea.'

'Leave me alone, please, Andrew.' She fell on to the bed and buried her head in the warm hollow where his had been. 'You mustn't see me like this.'

'Darling, don't be absurd. Aren't you supposed to be the flesh of my flesh and the bone of my bone?' It was a phrase from one of his favourite Victorian novels, half joke, half sincere. 'I'll get Pernille.'

She couldn't drink the tea. It grew cold and bitterly yellow on the bedside table beside the dregs of hot milk Andrew had brought her the night before.

'Pernille,' she said feebly, 'that yoghurt, where did it come from?'

The Danish girl shook out the pillows and pummelled them. 'I took it home from Mr Feast's, Mrs Fielding.'

Alice felt too ill to do her duty and correct the usage. She would never appreciate the difference between 'to bring' and 'to take'.

'Did you have any of it?'

'I? No, thank you. Nobody takes yoghurt but you.'

Andrew came back softly, bringing the morning papers. She wished he would leave her to the dimness and not snap on the overhead light.

'Any better, darling?'

'I feel terribly ill, Andrew. Do you think we could get Harry?'

'Just because you feel a bit sick?' He sat on the edge of the bed and lifted the long fair hair from her cheeks. 'You'll be better in a little while.'

'And I was going to London today,' she wailed.

'In that case you'd better have Harry. I'm sure he won't let you go out, darling. It's bitterly cold.' To emphasise his words he drew back the curtain and showed the cruel windy morning, clouds white as piled snow, lurching across purplish-black cumulus. The wind was tossing scotch pine branches against the glass, fist-shaped bunches of needles tapping and jerking away again.

'He needn't come till he's finished his other calls.'

His quick jealousy was a better tonic than any medicine Harry could prescribe. 'Don't worry,' he said sharply. 'He'll come.' Catching her eye, he laughed at himself and added ruefully: 'You know very well, darling, if the whole of Salstead was down with bubonic he'd still be here first thing.'

'Andrew!' He must love her, looking not with the eyes but with the mind. 'Go and have your breakfast.' He kissed her, picked up the book he had been reading the night before, and went downstairs.

Harry came as soon as his morning surgery was over. She blushed a little when he came in. Andrew's prophecy had been fulfilled. Bubonic was an exaggeration, but surely Harry had countless patients awaiting him. Andrew must be sitting in the dining-room now, smiling a little, the man in possession. It gave her a little warm thrill to think that, though apart, they shared the same thoughts.

'How do you feel, Alice?'

'Not quite so bad now.' She gave him her hand and he put his fingers to the pulse. 'I was terribly sick earlier. Did Andrew tell you about it?'

His face was expressionless. 'He said something about it on the phone. I didn't disturb him when I came in.' Taking his hand away, he said in a repressed tone, 'He was reading.'

You make him sound like Nero, she thought resentfully, fiddling while Rome burns. Andrew's jealousy was reasonable, the natural corollary to a husband's love, Harry's pathetic.

'I just kept being sick, on and on. I suppose Pernille's dinner was too rich.'

He smiled in disbelief and put the thermometer in her mouth.

'It's more likely to be one of these viruses.'

When she was beginning to think she would vomit again if the glass tube remained any longer between her lips, he took it from her and went to the window.

'It isn't anything serious, is it, Harry? I wanted to go to London today, to Paddington.'

He shook the thermometer down with a swift jerky movement.

'Paddington? You're not going away, are you?'

Strange how to everyone Paddington meant only the station. She shook her head.

'You mustn't think of going out,' he said. 'You'd far better stay where you are. I'll look in again tomorrow.'

Illness was unfamiliar. It made her at once into a hypochondriac. 'You'd tell me if it was anything serious?' But she knew he wouldn't. Doctors never did.

'I told you, Alice. You've probably got a virus infection. I thought you were looking pale yesterday.'

'Is that why you said I was to come to you if anything was troubling me?'

He blushed as hotly as the young postman in the twilit street. 'Of course,' he said abruptly. At the best of times he had no poise, only a vulnerable boyish gaucheness. Now as, all thumbs, he bundled his instruments back into the case, she thought briefly back over the ten years since he had come to Salstead. She had lost count of how many times he had asked her to marry him. And yet for all that, their relationship had never advanced beyond friendship, he had never kissed her or even put his arm round her shoulders. They were doctor and patient. She almost smiled as she thought that in spite of the love and the proposals the question of ending *that* relationship had never arisen. Her physical health had been so splendid she had never had to call him in.

'I hope I'm not going to be ill long,' she said fretfully. It was going to be awkward and embarrassing if he had to come here daily to attend her.

'Here's someone to cheer you up,' he said.

It was Hugo. Muffled in a rugger scarf, he tiptoed up to the bed and dumped a squashy parcel on his sister's stomach. 'Grapes,' he said. 'Hallo, Harry.'

'How did you know I was ill?'

'News travels fast in this neck of the woods. Jackie bumped into Pernille Madsen at the shops.' He rubbed his hands and sat down heavily on the bed. 'You're in the best place. It's enough to freeze the —'

'All right, Hugo!' Alice laughed weakly. 'Good-bye, Harry. It was nice of you to come.' He hesitated, waiting – for what? What did he expect her to say to him, what could she say that was kind, generous and meaningless all at the same time? 'You mustn't think that because I'm a friend . . .' As the smile on his face gradually chilled, she blundered on, 'I mean, you mustn't neglect your other patients for me. . . .'

His hand was resting on the glass fingerplate of the door. Then she saw that it was no longer resting, but pressing, pressing, until the nails showed white.

'What makes you think you're different from anyone else, Alice?' he snapped. Hugo coughed and, making a great display of loosening his scarf, flung it on the bed. 'Are you criticising my professional conduct?'

She was horrified, almost at a loss for words. 'I didn't . . . I wouldn't . . . You know what I meant!'

'I'm sorry. Forget it.' He cleared his throat and managed a smile. 'I'll leave a prescription with Miss Madsen,' he said abruptly. 'Take care of yourself.' Then he was gone.

'What was all that about?' Hugo asked.

'I don't know.'

'He's very fond of you, you can see that. It's written all over him.'

'Never mind that,' said his sister impatiently. 'Oh, Hugo, I did so want to go up to London today. D'you think . . . ?'

'No, I don't. You'll get pneumonia.'

'You wouldn't go for me, would you?'

'Not on your life. We've got people coming to lunch. Why d'you want to go there, anyway?'

She told him about the postman and the redirection notice, and he laughed in grudging admiration of Nesta's cunning.

'Good psychology, that. Women always read such a hell of a lot into an address. I know Jackie always wants to pick our holiday hotels by their names, and when you get there the Miramar turns out to be a slum on top of the marshalling yards.'

'But Saulsby wasn't there at all.'

'I can't see why she bothered to write. Why not just vanish?'

Yes, why not? The second letter was explained by the receipt of the parcel. But why had Nesta written the first letter suddenly, out of the blue? She couldn't have known Alice had the ring, for she hadn't mentioned it then. It was uncanny that she should have been silent for a month and then have written just as Alice was going to advertise for her. It was, at any rate, a remarkable coincidence.

'I didn't keep either of the letters, but I remember what they said. The first one said something like this: *Dear Alice, just a line to let you know I'm settled in temporarily, but I shan't be staying for very long. I don't suppose we shall meet again, but thanks for the meal and everything. Best wishes to Andrew and your uncle.*'

'Just an ordinary sort of letter,' said Hugo. Alice sighed, knowing from experience that his own were very much like that. 'It told you the basic essentials.'

'It told me nothing,' said Alice unhappily. 'The second one was even worse. *Thanks for the ring. I enclose two pounds to cover cost.* . . . And, Hugo, that was another odd thing. I've only just thought of it. I'd paid Cropper's but I didn't say what it had cost and I didn't ask for the money. But the bill was for two pounds and Nesta sent me exactly two pounds.'

'Coincidence?'

'Well, it *must* have been. Then she wrote: *Don't put yourself out to answer this as I've never been much of a correspondent,* and then something about being too preoccupied to bother. Not as rude as I've made it sound of course. She ended up with the usual regards to Andrew and Uncle Justin.'

'Keen on him, wasn't she?'

Something seemed to grip her chest, something which released a cold bubble of nausea.

'What *do* you mean?'

'Justin.'

'Oh.' She was able to smile again. 'What makes you think so?'

'She used to make him up a buttonhole every morning.'

'You're romancing, Hugo. Those flowers came from the garden.'

'Did they hell! Not for the last two years they didn't. Your little Nesta had an eye for the men.' He smiled and in the smile was a kind of wry vanity. 'She made a pass at me once,' he said thoughtfully.

'She did what?'

'Come off it, Alice. You know what a pass is as well as I do.' He glanced at her doubtfully. 'Almost as well, anyway. She'd been baby-sitting for us and I drove her home. She said would I see her into the shop because she was nervous in the dark. You know how slow and languid she was. There wasn't much in it but she sort of swayed against me in the dark. I put out my arm to stop her falling and she – well, she took hold of me and said she was so miserable, I mustn't leave her alone. I yanked her upstairs, put all the lights on and got out double-quick.'

As Alice stared at him he went on hurriedly: 'The funny thing was after that, whenever we were alone together – you know, if we met in the street just for a moment – she'd talk to me – Oh, damn it! It's so hard to explain. She'd talk to me as if we'd had a full-blown affair and had to kind of – well, keep it secret. She kept saying Jackie mustn't ever know. But there wasn't anything *to* know. I don't mind telling you, just between ourselves, I used to wonder what she would say if she ever got to be alone with Jackie and she was manic as against depressive.'

Alice was rather shocked. 'Manic-depressive? You mean she was really ill in her mind? Oh, Hugo, I think it was just loneliness and perhaps envy.' He shrugged, disbelieving. 'I don't think we any of us realised how lonely she was.' She looked up at him, wondering how he would take sentimentality. 'She told me once losing her husband had been like losing a leg or an arm. Part of her was in the grave with him.'

'She was a mistress of the cliché.' The door had swung open and Andrew was on the threshold, holding the coffee tray. Alice sat up, startled by his silent, almost supernatural arrival.

'Oh, darling! I remember she said —'

'And I remember,' he interrupted her, 'how she used to call a sheaf a sheath and a corsage a cortège.' As Hugo chuckled he moved towards the bed and took her face gently in his hands. 'You're better, Bell. You've got some colour in your cheeks.'

With a word, a smile, he could make her feel like a beauty. Feeling warmth coming back to flush her face, she put up her hands to the things she was proud of, the white, still unlined neck and the long loose hair.

'I think I could drink some coffee,' she said.

'I've brought you another visitor.'

He brushed his lips against her forehead in a fluttering kiss. Embarrassed, Hugo shifted uneasily.

'What's supposed to be the matter with you?' asked Uncle Justin from the doorway. He was frowning. Alice noticed the chrysanthemum bud in his buttonhole and remembered the roses, wound and wired in silver foil, he had worn in the summer.

'I'm supposed to have a virus.'

'A virus! I don't know what we're all doing in here, then. That's a fine thing to spread about the works.' With extreme ostentation, he shook out a large white handkerchief and held it yashmak-wise across his nose and mouth. 'I suppose a virus is a new-fangled name for the flu?'

'I'll get up when I've had my coffee,' she said meekly, knowing he would discourage malingering.

His reply surprised her. 'I wouldn't.' He sat on the dressing-table stool as far away from the bed as possible. 'You've got Andrew here and what's-her-name to wait on you.' Pausing, he added characteristically: 'It isn't as if you've got anything to do.'

Perhaps it would be better to stay where she was. Certainly everyone was very anxious that she should stay in bed. The coffee tasted strong and bitter. Over the rim of the cup she watched them all in silence.

Harry hadn't actually said it was a virus, just that it probably was. He hadn't said that she had a raised temperature either. It was true what Uncle Justin said about a virus just being the flu, but she had never had flu before. Surely there would be more to it than these waves of sickness that came so chillingly and overmasteringly, but when they had gone, left her feeling well and even cheerful?

As she sipped the coffee a strange thought visited her. That was how Nesta had been, alternating between illness and health, only Nesta's had been not of the body but of the mind. Nesta had been manic-depressive, Hugo said. Why had she, Alice, she who was never ill, suddenly developed this strange illness, when she was on the point of finding Nesta?

The malaise returned sharply, washing over her, and drawing the blood from her face. She felt the pallor and the chill which came with it and her whole body jerked in a big convulsive shudder.

Hugo and her uncle were discussing some change at the works. Only Andrew noticed. He took her hand and held it until the spasm had passed. She leant back against the pillows, spent, and inexplicably afraid.

6

On Monday morning, as soon as Andrew had gone, she got up. After two days in bed she still felt tired, but in her weariness there was no desire for sleep, only a weakness that seemed to come from some inner core of her body. The sickness had passed, leaving her languid and strangely prone to tears. She had no appetite except for liquids, but even tea and the yoghurt she had lately grown so fond of tasted odd, bitter yet otherwise flavourless. The fluid seemed to burn her throat.

But there was nothing really wrong with her. Harry had come again on Sunday and shrugged off her fears. It was just a mild virus, he thought, not absolutely committing himself. His words were reassuring, but she hadn't liked the look in his eyes. There was bewilderment in them, doubt and concern.

The fresh air would do her good. It was a pity the wind was so strong, stirring the bare black branches of the Vair shrubs so that their tops looked like a dark and stormy sea, but it couldn't be helped. She would wrap up warm and wear a scarf on her head. Besides it was always warmer and more sheltered in London than in the country.

The thought that in less than two hours' time she would see Nesta again provided her with a little spurt of energy. The house in Dorcas Street might be a bit of a shock. Of course Nesta didn't own it, nor even have a flat in it, but a single poor little back room. She, Alice, would make a stoical effort not to show her dismay. If Nesta were out at work – as she probably would be, a very minor assistant in a huge West End shop – she would just ask the landlady where the shop was and make her way there. She would take Nesta out to lunch. Dizzily she thought of taxis, of the Savoy, of wine brought by a deferential waiter.

'When I've gone,' she said to Pernille, 'you can ring up Dr Blunden and tell him I'm so much better he needn't bother to call.'

'I am not good with the telephone, Mrs Fielding.' The Danish girl had brown skin, darker than her hair, and eyes as blue and pleading as a Siamese kitten's.

'Then you obviously need practice,' said Alice firmly. 'I'll tell you what, when I'm out I'll get you a five-shilling stamp and a half-crown one for your brother. Is he still collecting?'

Pernille's willing-to-please smile quirked up even further at the corners and she broke into a giggle. 'Oh, yes, Knud is a famous . . .' The word came out on a bubble of proud laughter, '. . . philatelist!'

'I won't forget.'

Nesta ought to have a present, too. Alice wondered why she hadn't thought of it before. It was unlike her to go and visit someone empty-handed. She felt ashamed of herself, almost thankful that she hadn't found Nesta in Orphingham. To arrive without a gift when Nesta was probably in need. . . . She was appalled and puzzled at her own thoughtlessness.

Alice sincerely believed that she knew London. You must know a city if all your life you had lived only twenty-five miles from it. In fact she knew it less well than certain holiday resorts. The City itself she had seen only from car windows, its buildings like a series of photographs in a guide book that has been quickly flipped through. She was well acquainted with a few square yards of pavement outside most of the theatres and could easily visualise the river between the Tower and Westminster Bridge. At the age of ten she had been able to name all the bridges in their correct sequence just as she could count up to twenty in French. In fact she knew her capital as well as most Englishwomen know it; all her knowledge was of the two or three streets in which she had bought clothes.

From Liverpool Street she took the Tube and she remembered how often she had made just this same journey with Nesta. They had always got out at Marble Arch and walked back, window-gazing. Nesta's tastes had been expensive – the black she always wore had to cost a lot if it was to look nice – and sometimes Alice had slipped her a couple of pounds when the salesgirl wasn't looking. It seemed cruel not to be able to have the sombre dresses you only wore out of respect for your dead husband's memory. Alice had bought nothing for herself, but only followed where Nesta led.

Today she had no guide. Still, it was easy to buy presents for someone as pretty and vain as Nesta, floral scent, a scarf of white silk scribbled all over with black. Alice came out of the shop and hailed a taxi. It was only the second time in her life she had ever done such a thing in London. The driver accepted her directions, questioned nothing. She felt brave and rather sophisticated. London was just a place like any other, Salstead or Orphingham magnified.

Once past Marble Arch again, she was lost. They might be anywhere, in any great city. She leaned back and closed her eyes. The tiredness was coming back and with it a physical unease that was too faint to amount to sickness or even the warning of sickness to come. It was just discomfort and nervous anticipation. She sat up and looked out of the window.

They were nearly there. As they turned out of a big busy thoroughfare she caught sight of a name on a house wall, Dorcas Street. This, at last, was where Nesta lived.

It was neither sordid nor romantic and it was not a slum. The houses were very tall and ranged in long plaster-covered terraces, each with a pillared portico and little iron-railed balconies. They had a shabby, neglected look. The roadway, treeless and uniformly grey, seemed like a reflection of the wind-stirred grey sky, itself an avenue between long architraves.

She couldn't see much of a hundred and ninety-three. Stopping directly outside it, the taxi's bulk hid everything but its two fat pillars and its flight of steps. At home Alice would hardly have thought twice about how much to tip Mr Snow. Now she was a little flustered. A ten-shilling note? It seemed all right, enough, at any rate, to evoke a large pleased smile. It was only after he had turned that it occurred to her she might have asked him to wait. Her new-found courage was unequal to calling after him.

She sighed and went to the steps. Where the number should have been on the column that supported the canopy was only a blank rectangle, a paler patch on the plaster. Slowly she lifted her head and let her gaze travel upwards. There on the pediment, scrawled in neon tubing with a frail attempt at smartness, were the words *Endymion Hotel.*

It was happening all over again. For a brief wild moment her brain registered a mad picture of another redirection notice, indeed a whole series of them, directing her from one house to another, back and forth the length and breadth of the country. No, that was impossible, just stupid panicky guesswork.

She stood under the canopy, looking up at the name, at the plaster patch where the number should have been, and suddenly as she waited, half afraid to take that first look through the glass, a violent spasm of nausea washed over her so that she swayed against the wall. It passed with slow cruelty, leaving her legs cramped and stiff.

She took a deep breath of not very fresh air and pushed the door open.

Because she had expected squalor her first sight of the foyer came as a pleasant surprise. It had been recently modernised. The Victorian panelled doors had been faced with hardboard, the moulded ceiling boxed in with polystyrene tiles and a new floor laid of black and white blocks. At ceiling level she could see a curly plaster leaf, part perhaps of a Corinthian capital, peeping between strips of plastic. Gladioli and roses, made out of wafer-thin wax, stuck out like a sunburst from a simulated marble urn. Behind the acid-yellow counter sat a young man on a high stool writing something in a book.

The doors had made no noise and for a moment he didn't see her. She stood by the flowers – seen close-to, they were grimed with dust which had settled into and become part of their petals and calyxes – and as she hesitated somebody opened a door at the back of the hall.

It swung back as if of its own accord and through it she caught a disillusioning glimpse of what the rest of the place must be like. She saw a passage, its walls faced with ochre-coloured lincrusta, its floor covered by threadbare haircord torn on the threshold into a frayed hole. Then someone pushed the door suddenly, a woman who heaved her back against it and whose hair was a bright gauzy blonde.

Sickness and shyness were dispelled by excitement. Alice went up to the counter.

'Can you tell me if Mrs Drage is in?'

'Not what you'd call *in*. She's not a resident.' His complexion had the thick bloodlessness of skin on wet white fish. He wetted his fleshy lips and stared at her with blank boredom, swinging his legs as if to the tempo of some silent but remembered pop tune.

'But you do know her? She has been here?'

He just glanced at her handbag and her expensive gloves, then at the delicate wrappings on Nesta's presents. 'I haven't seen Mrs Drage for, let's see – three months. Oh, it'd be all of that. It's funny you asking. I wouldn't remember her on account of all . . .' He grinned ironically and she felt the grin was aimed at her, '. . . all the thousands we get passing through our doors.' Alice shifted impatiently. 'I say I wouldn't remember her only Mr Drage come in himself about half an hour ago.'

'*Mr Drage* ?' Alice clasped the edge of the counter, longing for a chair. Before she could stop herself she burst out, 'But she's a widow, there isn't a Mr Drage!'

He didn't wink. He yawned very slightly and gave a faint shrug. His background was perhaps as different from hers as possible, his outlook as unlike hers as was consistent with their both being human beings and of British nationality. 'Is that so? Yeah, well, live and let live. Maybe she got married again. I'd say it was her business, wouldn't you?'

The telephone rang. He gabbled into it, using a good many yeahs. Alice stood looking at him helplessly. Nesta hadn't been at the Endymion for three months, but her letters had been sent on to her from Orphingham to the Endymion.

While he talked she got out her diary and turned back to August. Nesta had left Salstead on August the eighth. She put on her reading glasses and walked away from the counter to stand under the rather dim centre light. *August seventh, Friday, Pernille not well. Harry says mostly mental, probably homesickness. Must do what I can to cheer her up. Perhaps a really nice present? Nesta to supper. Still very hot.*

August eighth, Saturday. Nesta leaving today. Raining hard.

'Did Mrs Drage come here on August eighth?'

He put the receiver down. 'You the police?'

'Do I look like the police?'

Perhaps policewomen dressed like she did when they were in plain clothes. As soon as she had asked the question she wished instead that she had had the courage to sustain the bluff. On the other hand – how much did you tip or bribe people like him?

'If it's her address you want,' he said suddenly, 'I haven't a clue. Mr Drage only come in to collect her mail.'

'Her mail?' Alice's voice sounded hollow and echoing as if someone else had spoken the words.

'Yeah. Well, if that's all I've got things to do.'

The sickness was coming back. Fighting it off, she said rather wildly, 'Please tell me . . .' It wouldn't do to give him too little. She opened her handbag, and, firmly shutting away thoughts of Andrew's and Uncle Justin's horror, laid a five-pound note on the counter top.

For a moment his face hardly changed. Then the wet red lips melted into a knowing smile.

'What's she done, then?'

'Nothing. I can't find her. I only want to find her.'

'Yeah, well . . .' The plump little hand had long nails. It closed over the note and thrust it into the pocket of his jacket through which gold thread ran, appearing occasionally like a recurrent vein of ore. He opened the book he had been writing in when Alice arrived.

'August eighth, you said? Mrs Drage booked up for that night but she never come. Mr Drage called up and cancelled it. She never come at all but we got mail for her. Three or four letters it was and a little parcel.'

'And you gave them to this man who came in this morning?'

'I gave them to Mr Drage, yeah. Why not?'

A big man in Salstead. . . . If he could only give her some clue to the appearance of 'Mr Drage'. He wriggled a little on his stool and began to buff his nails on his jacket lapel.

'You knew him well?' she said tentatively.

'Sure I did. Him and his wife been coming here on weekends God knows how long. From the country it was – some dump in Essex.'

Her heart leapt. This man might well be someone she knew.

'Then you must often have had a close look at him,' she said, forcing a smile and trying to make her voice persuasive. A description, she prayed, make him give me a description. 'You were alone with him this morning. I'm sure you . . .' She stopped. Suddenly his face had become hideously aggressive and he got slowly and deliberately off his stool. What had she said? Was there some limit to how much the bribe would buy? He leant across the counter and thrust his face into hers.

'What are you getting at?' he said. He was no more than five feet four, small-boned and sinuous as a girl. 'You insinuating something, are you?'

Alice had no idea what he meant, but she sensed something foul and alien. With a little gasp she backed away from him, slipping on the waxed floor. Her hands found the door as if by instinct and she stumbled out into the windy street.

A taxi, she must find a taxi. Clutching Nesta's presents she ran along Dorcas Street until she came to the main road. It was full of office workers hurrying to lunch places. After her encounter with the Endymion receptionist it was a comfort just to be with ordinary people, but how strange, how frightening, to notice how many of them looked like Nesta! Little heels tapped, short skirts lifted by the wind showed plump knees; pretty dolls' faces, their pink mouths snapping as they chattered, were topped by twists and bunches and doughnuts of yellow hair. She realised, but not newly, rather as if subconsciously she had always known it, that this was supposed to be the ideal type of womanhood. The fairness, the silliness, the porcelain skin – these were what attracted the majority of men, what they made jokes about, yet coveted.

She came up to the wider pavement and mingled with the crowd of little blonde ghosts. Ghosts, why had she thought of that? It made her shiver.

The first taxi was taken, the second pulled in beside her as she gave a feeble wave. It had been a disastrous morning and suddenly she knew she couldn't face the Tube.

'Will you take me all the way to Liverpool Street?'

The notes she could feel in her wallet were as comforting as a drug.

'My poor Bell,' said Andrew, smiling, 'I wish I'd been there. I'd love to have seen you taken for a policewoman.'

'It was horrible.' She began to pull the curtains, shutting out the garden, the windy night and the dark orange moon that was rising above Vair Place. 'I suppose I shall have to give up looking for her now.'

Andrew pulled the sofa up to the fire and tucked a cushion behind her head. 'You suppose? I thought the mystery was solved.'

'It isn't really. Not all of it. How could she write and thank me for the ring when she hadn't even got it? And why did that man go to the Endymion only this morning to get the letters? It's – well, it's such a fantastic coincidence.'

'It would be, but for one thing.' She looked up at him enquiringly, hoping wistfully for reassurance. He dropped a quick kiss on her cheek. 'You don't know the letters and the parcel were yours at all, do you?'

'But I – Andrew, I didn't actually ask him where they came from. I just assumed . . .'

'You just assumed. If the place is used as an accommodation address they might have dozens of letters for her. The boy friend could have been coming in once a week to fetch them.'

'That wasn't the impression I got, darling. I'm sure he meant that that was his first visit and that he took *all* the letters.'

A flicker of impatience crossed his face and pulled at the mouth muscles. Then he controlled it and, smiling, looked at her searchingly.

'How can you talk about impressions when you say yourself you weren't feeling well?'

Firelight like candlelight is flattering. She could feel it playing on her face, then realised with a little pang that she had not powdered her nose or painted her lips since the morning. Was that why he was staring at her so closely?

'You were ill and nervous and uneasy,' he said. 'Don't underrate your imagination, Bell.'

'No, you're right. You're always right.' She curled her legs under her and rested her head on his shoulder. The book he had been reading lay face-downwards on the cushions, a book with a chocolate-brown jacket, its title and illustration enclosed in rectangles of greenish blue. She watched his hand creep across to it. There was something loving and hungry and at the same time surreptitious in the way he slid it on to his lap.

'Go on,' she laughed, 'you can read if you like. I won't disturb you.'

Compulsive reading was just escapism. Why should he want to escape, and what was he escaping from? He was tired, she thought, it was only natural.

The fireplace wall was lined with bookshelves. The Trollope clericals and politicals had pride of place at eye level on the third shelf from the top. All the politicals had that same blue and brown cover. She smiled to herself as she realised that she had never yet seen the complete set there on the shelves. At least one was always out, actually in Andrew's hands, on the table or by their bed.

She looked at him covertly but he was already too preoccupied to notice the movement of her eyes. Wasn't it rather odd for a man to keep reading the same novels over and over again? He must know them by heart. She wondered vaguely how important to him was the world they presented. By now it must be very real to him, part of his daily consciousness, a source of metaphor, a guide to speech. Amid these reflections came a sudden conviction that to be a true companion to him she ought also to be acquainted with that world. It was what people meant when they talked about 'having things in common'. You needed as much of that as you could get when you had disadvantages that couldn't be overcome – the difference in age, for instance, the threat of childlessness. . . .

She got up. He turned a page and smiled at some favourite expression that had caught his eye. Smiling like that, uninhibitedly, indifferent to observation as a child is, he looked terribly young, younger even than he was. She was suddenly very much aware of her thirty-eight years.

The dining-room door was ajar. As she crossed the hall she peered through the dark room towards the uncurtained french windows that showed the shrubbery and the side of Vair Place. It was unpleasant to think that she had sat on that lawn, under those trees, a big strong child nearly five feet tall and already reading quite grown-up books, when Andrew had not even been born.

She went upstairs into her bedroom and switched on the light over the dressing-table glass. Then she felt in the drawer for the only lipstick she possessed.

Slowly she lifted her head and her eyes met her own reflection. There was not much light in the room and the furniture behind her lay in shadow. Apart from her own face the mirror showed only vague shapes and the pale shimmer of flowers in a vase.

Her hair was very untidy, coming loose in front from its braids and irradiated into translucent gold by the overhead light. Puzzled, very slightly alarmed, she drew back and closed her eyes. After an interval she opened them again. The impression was still there. Her own face looked unfamiliar and at the same time familiar. It seemed fuller, blanker, drained of intelligence. In some ways it looked younger for the skin was clear and glowing and the eyes bright.

'Pull yourself together,' she said aloud, but the brisk, hackneyed phrase which she could see as well as hear herself speak only enhanced the – the what? Hallucination?

Quickly she combed back her hair. As she painted two lines of strawberry red on her mouth the illusion vanished. With a sigh of relief she straightened up. She was herself again.

7

A wicked wind from the north-east whistled down the twin-track road and howled away under the concrete bridge. At the entrance to the by-pass the oil-drums had been taken away and in their place someone had stretched a long white ribbon of the kind seen on wedding cars.

In spite of the cold a crowd had gathered to watch the official opening: children from the primary school, shepherded by a harassed teacher; shop assistants out for their lunchtime break; housewives with baskets. Behind the ribbon stood the Parliamentary Secretary to the Ministry of Transport, surprisingly feminine as if it were not surprise enough that she was female; Justin Whittaker who was chairman of the highways committee; the chairman of the council; and a host of hangers-on who had nothing to do but watch, applaud and ultimately eat smoked salmon and roast chicken with the great ones at The Boadicea.

'There can scarcely be an inhabitant of Salstead,' Justin Whittaker was saying, 'who will not regard the opening of this by-pass as an unmixed blessing. I think I speak for all of us when I say that it is with disquiet and apprehension that we have watched the daily shaking – nay, undermining – of our historic buildings by the constant passage . . .'

Andrew squeezed Alice's arm. 'Oh, adjourn, adjourn!' he yawned.

'Sssh!'

'Nor will it deprive us of the trade necessary to our continued prosperity, for the slip road which leaves it and meets the town centre will allow access to those vehicles whose entry is a commercial necessity. This slip road is a triumph of contemporary engineering. Not only is it a most modern highway of its kind, but its designers have seen to it that Helicon Lane, to which it runs parallel, remains untouched to continue as a beauty spot of which we may all be justly proud.'

An icy drizzle had begun to fall. He raised the collar of his barathea overcoat and stepping back, handed a pair of shears to the Parliamentary Secretary. She drew her furs more closely around her and, still clasping the violets presented to her by one of the schoolchildren, cut the ribbon.

'I declare the Salstead By-pass well and truly open.' She had a voice like the Queen's, high-pitched, poised, remote.

Andrew nudged Alice. 'And may God save her and all who drive on her,' he said. She laughed and held his arm more tightly, flinching from the bitter, rain-bearing wind.

The Parliamentary Secretary scuttled back to her car in thin court shoes. Her driver stood holding the door open. Presently the car moved off along the virgin track, followed by Justin Whittaker's Bentley, the chairman's Rolls and so on down to the Mini that belonged to the assistant sanitary inspector. The Parliamentary Secretary waved graciously, again like a royal lady in a state procession.

'Come along, children,' said the schoolmistress. 'I'd like the first dinner people in the vanguard, please.'

'Are you going to the luncheon?' Alice asked Harry Blunden.

'I'm not a local dignitary. G.P.s are hoi polloi these days.'

'We've got a double ticket,' Alice said. 'Nepotism, really, because I'm a Whittaker, but Andrew's got to get back to the works.' She realised suddenly what she had said and what he might expect. There was no reason why he shouldn't come with her in Andrew's place. Walking between the two men, she glanced quickly from the smooth handsome head to the tousled one. Then Andrew's hand holding hers pressed very gently, relaxing again at once. It was an indication that he wouldn't care for the substitution. 'Of course I shan't go,' she said too emphatically.

'And you're better now, Alice?' Again that odd, solicitous look. 'Miss Madsen rang me yesterday and said you were better.'

'Nearly back to normal.'

'I'll look in again in a day or two, shall I?'

Andrew was holding the Sprite door open for her.

'Really, I don't think that's necessary,' he said smoothly. Harry blushed, screwing up his face against the squally wind. 'We can always contact you if . . .' He paused and said emphatically, '. . . if my wife needs another prescription.' The speed with which he hustled her into the car was almost rough. 'We may as well take advantage of the triumph of contemporary engineering,' he said.

The slip road left the by-pass smoothly and gradually at a narrow acute angle. Inside this angle the end of Helicon

Lane could be seen, cut off by the great embankments of
still grassless earth. They were like the raw edges of a
wound made in the fields.

Reflecting that she had not been down Helicon Lane
since Nesta's departure, Alice leaned over and looked
down. The branches of the Salstead Oak seemed to sweep
the sky like the bristles of a huge brush. She could just see
The Bridal Wreath, its twin bow windows now filled with
skeins of wool and canvases printed for gros point. The
sign had been replaced by another, The Workbasket. She
sighed, losing sight of it in the mist her breath had made
on the glass.

The road passed between stretches of barren earth. A
fence had been put up almost against the nave of St Jude's
Church and nothing remained of the old churchyard. It
was rather awe-inspiring to think that the new concrete
over which they were driving covered what had once been
consecrated ground. Here had been green mounds, moss-
grown slabs and between them long yew-shaded avenues.
Mourners had walked there, country people in smocks and
print gowns, bringing stocks and nasturtiums from cottage
gardens. Alice shook herself and said prosaically:

'I can't very well go to the luncheon now.'

'For heaven's sake, darling!'

'How can I, after what I said to Harry?' And after what
you said, she thought.

'You can change your mind at the last moment,' he said
jesuitically. 'Pernille won't have anything for you at home.'
He glanced into the wing mirror. 'I'd better speed up if we
don't want to get involved with the motorcade, or whatever
it's called.'

Still doubtful, she let him drop her in the High Street. It
was full of people, mostly people she knew. What did it
matter if they saw him take her in his arms and kiss her full
on the mouth? They were still on their honeymoon and it
would go on being like this until they were both old, so old
that the nine years between them was nothing. She was still
radiant from the kiss as she crossed the road and went into
The Boadicea.

The lounge was already crowded. A waiter approached
her with a tray of glasses and she took one containing

something pale yellow with a crescent of lemon peel slotted on to its rim. Through the glass door that led by way of a beamed tunnelly passage to the dining-room she could see tables laid with white cloths, silver, late dahlias in long narrow vases. The door swung and stuck open as a waitress came through. With her drifted a pungent garlicky smell of soup.

Alice put down her glass abruptly, suddenly and sharply sickened. The dry martini trickled coldly down her throat meeting a fierce surge of something that made her gasp. It was exactly as if her chest and stomach were being scalded from within. She sagged against the table, avoiding the solicitous eyes of Mrs Graham whose husband kept the hotel.

How could she dream of eating in company, feeling as she did? Before she was half-way through that soup she would be jerking back her chair, flying for the door with a napkin pressed against her mouth. Far better to go now before people came with their questions and their steadying arms.

She staggered towards the door, burrowing between knots and guests. Their laughter and their bright brittle talk stabbed at her with little points of pain. The wind that met her was cruel too, assailing her with mischievous teasing gusts. Just as she gained the shelter of Mr Cropper's shop porch Uncle Justin and the Parliamentary Secretary left their cars. He hadn't seen her. She kept her back turned for a moment, gazing at the swimming mass of rings and brooches, until they had crossed the pavement.

Then she began to walk up the High Street. The cutting wind seemed to beat at her with little slaps. No wonder the ancients had personalised winds, she thought, seeing them as gods or puff-cheeked cherubs, blowing with capricious malice.

It was half a mile to Vair House and Andrew had taken the car with him to the works. The hourly bus service to Pollington which had formerly passed Vair had been diverted from this moment to the by-pass. The obvious person to help her was Harry, but she couldn't go to Harry now. I shall *have* to walk, she told herself fiercely.

She managed another twenty yards or so until her legs threatened to buckle and yield. Her whole body felt unutterably weak and beaten, empty of everything but urgent fear. She had never been ill in all her life and now when illness had come it was like some huge venomous snake that wrapped her in coils of pain and panic. Gasping, she tottered up to the seat on the war memorial green and sank on to the thick oak board.

There was only one thing to do. She would have to hire a car. When she had had five minutes' rest she could probably just make it to Snow's.

Presently the drumming in her ears stopped and the coils relaxed. It was, she imagined, just like having a bandaged limb unbound, only in this case it wasn't a limb but her entire body. She raised herself gingerly and set off again along the pavement.

'Salstead Cars. Self-drive or chauffeur-driven cars for every occasion.' They had hired her wedding cars from here. From the windows of one of these black limousines she had waved to Mrs Johnson as she and Uncle Justin drove off down the drive of Vair Place.

The office was a creosoted wooden hut around which the great glossy cars clustered like seals. Perched on a high stool, his hat pushed to the back of his head, the proprietor sat eating sandwiches off a copy of the *Daily Mirror*. He got off the stool when she came in.

'Oh, Mr Snow, I'm afraid I'm not very well. I suddenly felt so awfully faint and I wondered . . .' She tried to smile, averting her face from the slabs of bread and corned beef.

'Here, have a chair, Mrs Fielding.' She dropped heavily into a bentwood chair with a broken cane seat. 'You're as white as a ghost. Now, if you were to ask me, what I would advise is a little drop of brandy.'

'Brandy? Oh, no, I couldn't . . .'

'It's wonderful for settling the stomach.' Ignoring her objections, he fetched a quarter-bottle from the shelf and with it a surprisingly clean glass. 'Warm the cockles of your heart, that will.'

'Thank you. It's very kind of you.'

The effect of the brandy was immediate. Unexpectedly it didn't burn, but flooded her with soft civilising warmth like the newly inhaled scent of fresh flowers. Fountains and sprays, healing and gentle, grew and cascaded all over her body.

Mr Snow wrapped up his sandwiches and stood by the small grimy window, whistling softly through his teeth.

'Don't happen to have heard from Mrs Drage, do you?' he asked suddenly.

'Well . . .'

'I only wondered, you and her being so friendly like. Feeling better now, are you?'

'Much better. Mr Snow, why did you ask about Mrs Drage?'

'Well, it was in the way of business, Mrs Fielding. But I won't worry you now, you being under the weather.'

'Oh, no, really, I'd like to hear.'

'You understand there's no offence meant, Mrs Fielding?' He took the glass, rubbed it with a bit of newspaper and inverted it on the shelf. Firmly she suppressed a shudder. 'Only it's like this, we did a couple of jobs for Mrs D. and seeing as she didn't leave no address . . .'

'You mean she owes you money?'

He opened the booking ledger on top of the desk. 'August seventh it was. Seventh and eighth.' Alice bit her lip, once more uneasy. 'She booked one of my vehicles to take some stuff up to Feasts' for her. Three p.m.' Those were the words Daphne had used – 'some stuff', 'she left some stuff at our place!' We did the job and she says to come to The Bridal Wreath the next morning, August eighth, eight sharp, she said, and pick her up and take her to the station. She was staying the night at Feasts' but coming back the next morning to see to the removals. We was to take her to the station and stop at Feasts' for the stuff on route. Eight o'clock sharp, she said. I don't mind telling you I was a bit narked. I took the car round myself but she'd gone. Not a word from her. She'd flitted on her own.'

'Are you sure?'

'They were taking out the furniture, Mrs Fielding. Cox's from York Street it was. The doors were all open and I went up. Len Cox was there taking out her bits and pieces. Where is she then? I said, not wanting to hang about on account of Saturday always being busy. Gone, he said. We was here at seven and the key was in the door so we come up. The place was as neat as a pin, Len said, all packed up and ready to go. You can't just take it, I said, not without her here, but Len's very hasty. It was going into store, he said, and she'd paid up when he give her the estimate. I can't have some bloody woman messing me about, he said— Pardon me, Mrs Fielding, but that's what he said.

'Well, I wasn't laughing, I can tell you. I'd turned down two jobs for eight o'clock and one of them would have brought in five nicker. Not only that. There was what she owed me for going to Feasts' with the van in the afternoon.'

Alice said quickly, 'Of course I'll make that good, Mr Snow.' She found her cheque-book and began to write, surprised at the firmness of her hand. 'I suppose Mrs Drage changed her mind and forgot she booked your car.'

'That's what happened. It stands to reason. I'm not saying she did it deliberate.'

Alice folded the cheque.

'You wouldn't think folks could be that forgetful, would you? Being as she booked the vehicle and when she saw me in the afternoon she reminded me about the next morning. The funny thing was she rang up again about five and said I wouldn't forget, would I? I was a bit narked, Mrs Fielding, I can tell you.'

'I expect you were,' said Alice faintly.

The incident of the car was a wholly unexpected development. Of course, it was possible that Nesta had forgotten. Her nervous depression had made her forgetful. But still Alice didn't like it. Perhaps she was growing forgetful too, for it was not until she was back in the High Street that she remembered her original purpose in calling on Mr Snow.

She paused under a shop awning and took her diary from her handbag. *August eighth, Saturday, Nesta leaving today. Raining hard.* Raining hard. She thought back to that summer morning. Friday, August the seventh, had been the last day of a long heatwave. She had got up quite early. The rain had awakened her and, pulling back the curtains, she had said to Andrew over her shoulder, 'It's pouring with rain. The drive's almost flooded. It must have been coming down for hours.'

How could she be sure it was that Saturday morning? Because Andrew had answered, 'Nesta's furniture will get wet.'

If the drive was flooded at eight it must have been raining for hours. Helicon Lane was a long way from the station. Nesta wouldn't have walked. And yet she hadn't been there when Cox's came at seven.

Alice began to walk slowly back along the High Street. She was building in her mind a picture and a timetable of Nesta's last evening. In the middle of the afternoon Mr Snow had taken the stuff, whatever it was, round to Feasts', and at five Nesta had telephoned him to remind him of the morning call. She must have used the afternoon for tidying the flat and preparing the furniture for Cox's. Then, soon after that telephone call she had gone out to make her round of farewell visits. Mr and Mrs Graham at The Boadicea, Harry probably – he had been her doctor – Hugo and Jackie, then Uncle Justin, last of all to Vair House where she had had supper.

Very weary she had seemed, more depressed than ever. It had been a warm evening and she had worn no coat over her thin dress of black pleated lawn. Her ankles, Alice remembered, had been swollen, bulging over the vamps of flimsy black patent shoes. She had gone up to say good-bye to Pernille and then she had come down and shared the flat cheese soufflé with them. It was soon after eight when Andrew had driven her back to The Bridal Wreath.

'Why not stay the night here?' Alice had said, for Nesta, clasping her hand tightly, had looked so tired and there had been tears in her eyes.

'Too late to change my plans now. I've fixed up I'm stopping at the Feasts'.'

That night they had begun shifting the graves. The very discretion with which it had been done must have heightened the atmosphere of ghostliness. From Nesta's bedroom window you would have been able to see the tarpaulin screens and hear the sound of earth being moved. That in itself would have been bad enough, but worse, far worse, the aftermath, when just before the first of the light, the coffins had been shrouded, abandoned, to await the coming of the vans. Of course she hadn't gone to Feasts'. Was it possible that she had forgotten that arrangement too? She had forgotten about the car, even though she must have gone to all the trouble of telephoning Mr Snow from a call box. Her own phone, Daphne said, had been disconnected.

'I'm stopping at the Feasts',' she had said, and her face close to Alice's smelt of a summer garden. Then she had meandered down the drive in front of Andrew, moving languidly in the hot dusty air.

Mr Feast was stacking cream cartons against a wall tiled like Covent Garden Tube station in khaki and white. He looked thinner than ever in his grocer's coat. She noticed for the first time a certain resemblance in that bulbous brow and hollow cheeks to Abraham Lincoln; the same crusading fire burnt in his eyes.

'I wonder if I might have a word with Daphne, Mr Feast?'

'If it's about the Freedom from Hunger, Mrs Fielding . . .' He glanced almost apologetically about his land of plenty. 'That's more my province, if you know what I mean.'

'No, it's something personal.'

'I hope the yoghurt's been to your taste. We've had to switch to a different brand, but it's very good.'

'Oh, yes, delicious.' It was strange that in the past few days sometimes the only food she could face had been the thin sourish whey in the green and white cartons. 'If I could just . . .'

'Through there, then.' He opened the door behind him and shouted, unnecessarily loudly, she thought: 'Daph! Mrs Fielding to see you. Go right up, Mrs Fielding. You'll make allowances, I know, for a certain amount of disarray.' She smiled, murmuring something. 'Did you want to take any yoghurt today? That's right. I'll pop it in a bag for you when you come down. Eat wisely and you'll live long, that's what I always say.' His voice, harsh and bird-like with a mechanical chattering note, pursued her up the staircase. 'The tragedy is that so many who would eat wisely if they only had the chance are deprived by man's inhumanity of the bare. . . .'

Daphne came out on to the landing. 'You've got Pop started.'

'He makes me feel virtuous because I didn't go to the official luncheon.'

'Have a bit of something with me, will you?'

Alice shook her head. The half-eaten pork pie on the tray without a cloth might be what Mr Feast called 'the bare' but the sight of it brought back a wriggle of nausea.

'You said you were keeping some things for Nesta. I wondered . . . Daphne, would you show them to me? Could I see them?'

'Them? It's not them, it's it. It's a sort of box. As a matter of fact Pop's got it in his room. He's using it as a bedside table.'

Mr Feast's bedroom was a long narrow cell that overlooked the High Street. Alice crossed to the window and looked down. The street was quiet, almost empty of traffic. Of course! The by-pass was in use, the plan was working.

'This is it,' said Daphne.

Alice turned. She could see only a single divan with beside it what appeared to be a table covered by a cloth and laden with magazines – *Peace News, China Today*, the journal of the United Nations Association – medicine bottles, an alarm clock, a green Anglepoise lamp.

She took a step towards it, then jumped violently. From somewhere behind her a bell began to ring, insistent, shrill, growing louder and clearer. Daphne glanced up and shrugged.

'It's only an ambulance. Some mad-brain's come a cropper on the new road.'

Only an ambulance . . . Why had the bell seemed like a warning, Go away, don't look? She watched the big white van turn out of the slip road, its blue light revolving. Her hands had gone up to cover her ears. She drew them down and gave herself a little shake, turning her attention once more to the table.

'But that's a trunk!' she exclaimed. 'A huge trunk.'

'I told you she left a lot of stuff.'

It was a wooden trunk, old-fashioned and long ago painted vandyke brown. Where a corner of the cloth hung was a hasp secured by a padlock.

'Is it locked?'

'I don't know.' Daphne wrenched at the padlock. 'Yep. I can't shift it.'

'I wonder whether we should. I can't make up my mind if we're justified. . . .' She hesitated and all the things that had alarmed her came back to her mind: letters which had never been received yet had been answered; the Endymion Hotel; the man who called himself Mr Drage; a car expressly, doubly ordered, that had called in vain.

'I reckon she can't want it all that much,' Daphne said eagerly, 'otherwise she wouldn't have dumped it here.' Her eyes shone. 'Here, I wonder what's inside.' She pushed up the sleeves of her brown mohair sweater. It was less like a garment than an extension of her own shaggy hair. 'My God, it's heavy!' She had lifted the trunk by its leather handles and dropped it again, gasping. It made a dull thud on the square of matting by Mr Feast's bed.

'We could get a locksmith, I suppose, or perhaps your father.'

'Pop can't leave the shop unless I take over.' This Daphne was plainly unwilling to do. 'I don't mind having a go.'

'*You* ?'

At Vair when they wanted anything done they sent for the gardener or Uncle Justin's chauffeur. If it was too big a job for amateurs a man with the appropriate skill was summoned from Salstead. Nobody, least of all a woman, would attempt anything as violent as breaking a lock.

'All you want,' said Daphne, 'is a screwdriver.'

Alice sat down on the bed and watched her dubiously as she came back with a toolbox. Daphne's eyes troubled her. They moved like a ferret's, darting between beaded lashes.

'What's happened to her, anyway?' The first of the three screws was coming unloose now. Alice shrugged. 'She's sort of disappeared, hasn't she?' The screwdriver twisted smoothly. 'Here . . .' Daphne stopped and glared. 'You don't think she's in here, do you? In bits, I mean. You know, like you read about in horror books.'

'Of course I don't,' Alice said sternly. 'Don't be silly.'

A wave of colic washed over her. The Feasts' flat smelt of sour milk.

'Here she goes,' said Daphne. The hasp had come away and hung against the brown wood. 'If it's anything nasty I warn you I shall be sick.' Her suet-coloured face showed two red spots on the low cheekbones. 'You look a bit queer yourself.'

Alice was breathing quickly now, clenching her cold hands. Why did Daphne have such horrible ideas? There couldn't be anything "nasty" in the trunk. Nesta had been alive and well after it had been sent to Feasts'.

Daphne gave a snorting giggle and threw back the lid in a rush.

8

Alice sighed with relief and shuddered at the foul taste in her mouth. She gave a quick deprecating laugh. The trunk was full of clothes.

There was a black nightgown on top and underneath it a layer of underclothes. Daphne pulled them out and threw an armful on the bed. Beneath were dresses, skirts, trews, a black and white check suit and four topcoats.

'All her clothes,' said Alice in wonder. 'Oh, but it can't be!'

Daphne was burrowing in the trunk. 'There are ever so many pairs of shoes under the coats.' She emerged, her arms full of shoes, packed heel to toe and wrapped in tissue. 'Look, Mrs Fielding, every pair of shoes she had. No, I tell a lie. She had some old black patent things. They aren't here.'

'She was wearing black patent that night she came to us. I noticed them because the heels were so high and her ankles were swollen.'

Daphne dived again and came out clutching a flat case perhaps twelve inches by eight. It was covered in black leatherette and initialled N.D. Before Alice could stop her she had opened that lid as well and a sweet powdery scent tickled Alice's nostrils, dissipating for a moment the dairy smell. Together they looked at the array of bottles and jars, lotions, creams, green eye shadow and blue eye shadow, lacquer for the hair and lacquer for the nails, brushes for the lips and brushes for the lashes.

'It's what used to be called a vanity case,' said Alice.

'Fancy her leaving that! And all her best shoes and all her coats. Wouldn't you have thought she'd have gone away in her summer coat? Look, this white orlon thing.'

'Then which coat did she wear that Saturday morning?'

'She can't have worn a coat. She only had the four, Mrs Fielding. I know Nesta's wardrobe like I know my own. I'd been through it often enough. We used to swap clothes.'

'Then, what . . . Daphne, what did she take with her?'

'If you're asking me, I'd say nothing except what she stood up in. There's a black lawn dress missing. I reckon she was wearing that on the Friday night.' Alice nodded. 'What I don't understand is how she came to leave all her best things. She'd saved up for that check suit and it cost her twenty quid.'

'Why send them all here anyway? I can understand she might want a suit or a coat for the morning but she was only staying with you for one night.'

'That's easy. I told you we used to swap clothes. I reckon she meant us to have a good go through her things. You know how keen she was on black?'

'It was her mourning, Daphne.'

'Mourning my foot! She said she looked so smashing in the suit she had for her husband's funeral that she stuck to black ever after. If you don't mind me saying so, you are a bit naive, Mrs Fielding. Well, as I was saying, she meant us to go through her things. I've got a little black lurex number she'd had her eye on for ages, but when she didn't turn up I thought she'd changed her mind.'

'But what is she wearing now? She can't have lived for nearly three months in a cotton dress and a pair of court shoes.'

Lived? You needed clothes for living and if you were Nesta above all you needed the precious little case that smelt of musk and lilies and vanity itself. She closed the lid abruptly and as she did so the thought came to her that for dying you needed only a shroud, a thin, black shroud.

'Unless,' said Daphne doubtfully, 'she got herself a rich boy friend who bought her a whole new wardrobe.'

In that case, Alice reflected wretchedly, she would surely have given the lot to Daphne. Certainly she wouldn't have tried to drive a hard bargain to get possession of the dress esoterically described as a 'lurex number'.

'Mucky lot of stuff she wore next to herself, didn't she?' Daphne was shovelling through the underwear. Alice had already noticed how tattered it was, some of the garments hastily cobbled, most left in holes, shoulder straps coming away, elastic stretched and puckered. 'She was always one for top show was Nesta. I can't say I'm sorry I didn't get her for my step-mum, though it seemed a bit of a giggle at the time.'

'Your stepmother?' Alice was aghast. Mr Feast had seemed to belong to a different generation until she realised unpleasantly that he was perhaps no more than ten years older than herself. 'I had no idea . . .'

'Well, no. I reckon nobody had. We got to know Nesta at first at the Chamber of Commerce. Pop got into the way of seeing her home from the meetings. He was very keen on her but it sort of petered out. I don't know as I believe in marriages where there's a big age difference.'

Alice looked down, feeling the flimsy back stuff and hoping Daphne had not seen her blush.

'There were no hard feelings, you know. Not between me and Nesta, that is. If you ask me she'd got her sights set on someone a cut above Pop. Mind you, he felt it. Funny, you wouldn't think anybody'd be jealous at his age, would you? What d'you think I ought to do with the things, Mrs Fielding?' There was a flicker of desire in her eyes as they lingered over the suit and the knitted coat.

'Hold on to them. What else can you do?'

Daphne must have misunderstood her. She pulled the coat round her and thrust her arms into the sleeves.

Horrified, Alice said, 'I didn't mean . . .' She broke off and stood up suddenly. A lapful of brassières and petticoats fell on to the floor.

Mr Feast was standing in the doorway looking at them, his face twisted with anger.

'D'you fancy me in it?' said Daphne. She pirouetted clumsily and jumped when she saw her father.

'Where did you get all them things?' It must be a very strong emotion, Alice thought, to make him lapse into cockney. 'What you doing with my bed table?'

'It's not your bed table, Pop. It belongs to Nesta Drage. We got it open and it's full of clothes.'

He fell on his knees among the piles of garments and began scooping them back into the trunk. 'Haven't you any respect for other people's property?' he shouted. 'That box was in our care. We're responsible for it. That's why the world's in the state it is, big people riding roughshod over the feelings of little people.' Stiff with horror, Alice backed away from him. 'Hitler and – and all that lot,' he said wildly. His face had become a dark red, the blood pumping through raised veins. 'Smarming their dirty hands over the – the household gods of the people!'

With a little pettish gesture Daphne shrugged the coat from her shoulders. Her father grabbed it and clutched it against his hollow chest.

'Haven't you got no ethics? You're no better than a dirty little Fascist.' He crammed the clothes back, flung the cloth over the trunk and began replacing the copies of *Peace News*. 'Stealing her clothes, tarting yourself up . . . Now if you was in a Free People's Democracy —'

'Calm down, for God's sake,' said Daphne mildly. 'I'm sure I don't know what Mrs Fielding's going to think of you.'

'Mrs Fielding . . .' He seemed to see her for the first time.

'Come on. You're due at the Orphingham Branch at half-three.'

The name struck Alice like a burning point of fire in the midst of her swimming brain. Blindly she put out her hand, but it caught only at the empty air. She might have been standing on ice or in a quagmire for all the support the floor gave her. Her legs yielded at the knees and a great curtain of blackness, muffling and utterly silent, slid down over her eyes and her consciousness.

Daphne's voice, cheerful and excited, was the last thing she heard. 'Here, she's going to pass out!'

The children were sitting in the corner of the big untidy room helping themselves to Smarties out of a coloured canister. On the fireplace wall the huge green abstract painting seemed to be hanging crookedly. Perhaps it was only her eyes. The brightness of this familiar room hurt them, the red and citron chairs, the waxen snake-like house plants, the toys flung all over the carpet into which some-one's heel had ground a strip of plasticene.

'Jackie . . . ?'

'It's all right. Mr Feast phoned me and I brought you here because it was nearer.'

'Where's Andrew?'

'At work, of course. Where else? I phoned him, but you moaned something at me about not fetching him.'

'Yes, yes, I know. I remember now. I just thought he might . . .' Her voice trailed away. She tried to smile at Christopher and he stared back shyly. The crumpled dress felt hot and constricting. Suddenly she longed desperately for Andrew and the tears welled into her eyes. 'That awful man, Feast. He got into a rage, a violent rage, Jackie, because we opened a trunk full of Nesta's clothes. I can't get his face out of my mind, those burning eyes and that lump in his neck.'

'It's only thyroid,' said Jackie placidly. Mark rattled the Smartie box listlessly. 'An over-active thyroid. That's why he's so thin and always brimming over with vim and vigour. I know I was only a nurse for about a year but that's one thing I do remember. Too much thyroid and you get like Mr Feast, too little – that's called myxoedema – and you get fat and sluggish.'

'He was going to Orphingham,' Alice said. 'Did you know they'd got a branch there? I didn't. That means he knows Orphingham well. Oh, Jackie . . .' She stopped, looking at the children.

'Go and get Aunt Alice a glass of water, will you?' said Jackie promptly to her elder son.

'Jackie, I think Nesta's dead. No, I don't *think* so. I know she is. I'm certain of it. A woman doesn't leave her home late in the evening or very early in the morning in a thin cotton dress without a coat. It was an old dress, Jackie, and Nesta was vain. No matter how miserable she felt she wouldn't go off to make a new start somewhere dressed like that when she'd got a new suit to wear. Besides, it was pouring with rain. I don't think she ever left The Bridal Wreath.'

'But the letters, Alice.'

'She didn't write those letters. For one thing they were typed. I never thought of it before but I don't think Nesta could type. All right, she signed them, but anyone could forge a five-letter name like that, particularly someone who'd had letters from her before.'

'But that means . . .' Jackie hesitated and forced a bright absurd smile as Mark came back slopping water from a nursery rhyme mug. 'Thank you, darling. Now you can go over to the playroom and – and *play*.' Alice felt too weak and preoccupied to laugh.

'Here.' She felt in her bag. The disgruntled faces brightened at the sight of sixpences. 'Go and buy something nice.'

'And for God's sake, mind the road!'

The two women looked at each other after they had gone, at each other and away again in the embarrassment that comes from an awful incredible realisation. It was impossible. Such things couldn't happen in a world that also contained nursery rhyme mugs and green abstract pictures and empty boxes of Smarties.

'Suicide?' said Jackie.

'They would have found her, Jackie. Cox's or Mr Snow would have found her in the morning. Besides, if she killed herself, why the letters?'

'You mean *someone* killed her?'

Alice drank some of the water and looked at the design of Jack and Jill on the side of the mug. 'Daphne said her father had been in love with Nesta. He was jealous of her. If he was jealous there must have been other men. I've got a feeling now that she liked to get a hold on them.' With a kind of outrage she shivered violently. 'It's loathsome, I know. I hate women like that but that's what Nesta was. I've found out so many horrible things about her.'

'What sort of things?' Jackie asked in a small voice. She kept glancing about the room, looking fearfully over her shoulder towards the door.

'She had all those clothes, but dreadful scruffy underwear. She had alopecia too, but I couldn't quite understand it when you remember her lovely hair. You used to nag me to do my hair like Nesta's.'

'You mean you don't know? That topknot thing of Nesta's wasn't her own. It was nylon. Haven't you seen those switches hanging up in Boot's?'

Alice didn't answer her. She was wondering why she had always thought Nesta beautiful. Beauty couldn't consist of false hair, plucked and painted eyebrows, skin that showed dry and mealy when the light fell on it. Was it perhaps only Nesta's own desperate seeking after beauty, her confidence in her own good looks – a confidence that sometimes seemed shaky, feverish – that made Alice believe in it too? Nesta had been taken at her own valuation.

'Alice . . .' Jackie found one of her coloured cigarettes among a mêlée of plastic soldiers and tea cards on the bookcase. 'What do you think has happened to her?'

Alice said slowly: 'She wouldn't tell anyone where she was going. It didn't seem so odd to me at the time, but it does now. It must have been because she was going away with a man. I can't help feeling she was killed by someone who was jealous.' Her eyes, roving across the room as she sought for words, fell on the framed photograph of Hugo on the sideboard. *She made a pass at me once.* Hugo had said that, but suppose it had been the other way about? Oh, absurd, stupid . . . Her own brother? People always tell lies about sex. She had read that somewhere and it had appalled her. Perhaps it had shocked because it was so true. 'Jackie,' she said firmly, 'tell me exactly what happened when she came here to say good-bye to you.'

'I don't remember all that well.' Jackie wrinkled her brows. 'You see, I was putting the brats to bed and she was in here most of the time with Hugo.' Alice sipped some water. Had they been planning to elope, those two? Hugo often seemed bored with his marriage, his children. From business associations he knew Orphingham well. She remembered how he had refused to go back to the post office. 'She was very upset when she said good-bye to me,' Jackie continued. 'She kissed me – funny, really, we didn't know each other all that well. Then she simply ran away.' Thin and boyish, her face white and intense, she presented, Alice thought, a complete contrast to Nesta. 'I can't think why she was so emotional about it all.'

'Perhaps because she thought we'd think ill of her when we found out what she'd done.'

Jackie shrugged. 'She went on to Uncle Justin after she'd left us, then to you.'

'She was very quiet,' said Alice. 'While I was getting the dinner Andrew took her up to see Pernille. She came down ahead of him and I noticed she had to hang on to the banisters. I asked her if she was all right and she said she'd taken a couple of aspirins. I knew she'd been going to Harry about her depression but she'd told me he wouldn't give her anything for it. It was all in the mind or something. She slipped a little brown bottle into her handbag but I didn't take much notice – I thought it must be aspirins.'

'I wonder . . .' Jackie was suddenly thoughtful and excited, as if she was on the verge of a discovery. 'I wonder if it wasn't aspirin at all, but tranquillisers?'

'Harry had given her tranquillisers, or so she said, but they didn't do her any good and she wouldn't take them.'

'Someone else could have given them to her. People are such fools, Alice. I know that from my nursing days. They won't rely on their doctor but they'll take stuff that's been prescribed for other people. They think all sorts of drugs with awful side effects are all right for anyone to take. For instance, Mummy was taking some tablets when she was staying here in the summer – she's been feeling low since Daddy died – and she left the bottle behind when she went. Well, you'd hardly believe it, but Hugo wanted to take a couple just because some business thing had gone wrong. I soon put a stop to that. For one thing, they were the things you mustn't eat with cheese. . . .'

'With *cheese*, Jackie? You don't mean it.'

'I know it sounds funny, but it's a fact. It's quite a fashionable drug, lots of people have it. I can't remember what it's called but it raises the blood pressure and the cheese raises it some more.'

'We had a cheese soufflé for supper that night,' Alice said. 'Nesta always had a good appetite but she didn't eat much of it. It didn't taste very nice and I felt awkward about it. After we'd finished she lay back in her chair and put her hand on her heart. She said her heart felt all fluttery as if it was beating too fast.'

'Tachycardia.'

'What?'

'Fluttery heart-beat. Go on.'

'Well, there isn't any more. I asked her again where she was going, but all she said was something about a holiday and then "fresh fields and pastures new". I remember that because afterwards Andrew said it ought to have been "fresh woods". Then he took her home. She was very unsteady going down the path.'

She hardly knew how to put it but she was too worried for tact. 'What happened to your mother's tablets, Jackie?'

'Don't know,' said Jackie carelessly. 'I expect they got thrown away. They aren't there now, anyway. Hugo probably slung them out. You know what a mania your family have for tidying up. Look, Alice, I'm not saying she actually took that particular drug – I *wish* I could remember what it's called – it was just a suggestion.'

Smoothing things over quickly, Alice said, 'I suppose practically anyone in Salstead could have had them prescribed. So many people have neuroses these days.' She paused, pondering. 'Mr Feast's terribly nervous and jittery, don't you think?' If only I dared ask Harry, she thought, recalling how sensitive he was about his professional honour. 'But, no. It won't do, Jackie. Nobody would know Nesta was going to eat cheese at my house.'

Jackie took another cigarette from the packet. The table lighter she picked up was fashioned ridiculously like a Queen Anne teapot. In the light from the flame her face looked wary and ill at ease. Wasn't she smoking rather more than usual, almost chain-smoking?

'Most people eat cheese after an evening meal,' she said softly. 'You can more or less take it for granted. And, Alice – my God! – it was *Friday*. Nesta often went to the bread and cheese lunch. She told everyone she thought it would help her to lose weight. He might have given her the stuff in the morning, but she needn't have taken it until later.'

It was frighteningly true. And yet there was comfort in the thought that of all the three men Alice associated with Nesta only Mr Feast would have been likely to have encountered her that Friday morning. Mr Feast was jealous of Nesta – his own daughter had said so. He had a shop at Orphingham and would know the place as intimately as only a tradesman can. Besides, it was absurd to think of men as normal and matter-of-fact as Hugo and Uncle Justin stepping over the border of normalcy into homicide. But, if Jackie's hypothesis were true, Mr Feast was already disturbed, his violent nature intensified by disease.

'Then Nesta was poisoned,' she said. Poisoned? The word had come out quite naturally and impulsively. What she had meant to say, of course, was 'drugged'. It was she, not Nesta, who felt this dreadful burning in the stomach, this movement of bile as if her whole being was constantly longing to reject something alien.

Presently the children came back with bags of potato crisps.

'Cheese and onion flavour,' said Mark happily, thrusting the packet under her nose. 'You can have one if you like.'

The smell of grease and, above all, the smell of cheese, was so nauseating that she quivered with revulsion. The child stared at her. Then, at a repressive glance from his mother, he put down the crisps and stood on one leg. Alice could see he sensed the tension between the two adults. The room was quite silent, yet with a kind of vibration in the air.

Mark was so like Hugo and like his great-uncle as well. It was as if Jackie had contributed nothing to his looks but just been the vehicle through which another Whittaker had been bred. Because she was suddenly ashamed of her suspicions, and because she felt that soon if nobody moved she would scream aloud, she reached out and threw her arms round the child. It was a way of making amends, but Mark knew nothing of that. He struggled and pushed her away.

His rejection did more to hurt her and cow her than anything else. In it she sensed the scorn and dismissal of all her family.

'Why is Aunt Alice ill?' said Mark.

'I don't know,' said Jackie shortly. 'People do get ill sometimes. You know that.'

'Grandad got ill and he died.'

Alice wanted to cover Jackie's embarrassed giggle with reassuring, incredulous laughter. Her lips felt as rigid and as cold as pebbles.

'I'd better drive you home now,' said Jackie.

Andrew deposited the stack of novels carefully on the bed-side table.

'Are you sure you want to read all this stuff? You'll probably find it as dry as dust.'

'You don't.'

'No . . .' He smiled distantly. Couldn't he see that she was trying to create a new bond between them?

'Are all the Trollope politicals here, Andrew?'

'Not quite all. There are a couple I want for myself downstairs.'

Downstairs. That meant he wasn't going to sit with her any longer. Still, she must try not to feel even a shred of bitterness. A compulsive reader like Andrew had to read like others had to have drugs. Drugs . . . She shivered. It was unjust to admit the thought that he preferred reading a book he had read over and over again to sitting with his wife.

'Which ones are missing?' she asked brightly.

'Two volumes of *Phineas Finn*. It'll take you days before you get to them.'

'Days, Andrew? I won't be here for days. I'm going to get up tomorrow and go to the police. No, don't say anything. I've decided. I've got to do something about Nesta.'

Exasperation crossed his face and tightened his mouth.

'Oh, Bell! What are you going to tell them? Don't you understand you can't prove anything without the letters and you haven't kept the letters. Nesta simply tried to deceive you into thinking she was in Orphingham when she was really in London. . . .' She shook her head violently and touched his arm, but he pushed her hand away gently. 'Of course she's in London. Try to be realistic. What you're feeling is hurt pride. At best your going to the police can only lead to your appearing in court as a witness when they find Nesta Drage and summons her for some paltry offence against the Post Office. And they can't even do that without the letters and without the redirection notice.'

It was all true. What one logical reasonable man believed other men would believe. Only she and Jackie were convinced, largely by evidence that appealed to the feminine instinct, that Nesta was dead.

Somewhere she was dead – and buried. The florist who had wound so many garlands had been buried without a wreath of her own. Where was she lying now? They had begun to move the graves that night and you could get into the old graveyard quite easily from the garden of The Bridal Wreath. The ancient coffins would contain nothing now but dust. Who of the midnight men moving silently among the yew clumps would notice that one was a little heavier?

If the coffins were too risky there were always the cavities left in the crumbly brown clay. A little could have been spaded away and later restored. A week afterwards tons of concrete had been poured over the rifled ground to make the slip road.

She hesitated fearfully, certain, but afraid to put her thoughts into words. Fancies such as these, spoken aloud in the still-warm room, would only serve to make her sound a neurotic. As she looked at him, straight and young with his smooth black hair, she was suddenly more than ever conscious of her age and that she was on the threshold of a woman's foolish years. She put her hand to her lips, then to the forehead that no longer had the satiny feel of youth.

He went coldly, slowly, without another word. She closed her eyes. When she opened them again Pernille was standing at the end of the bed with the yoghurt and some thin bread and butter on a tray.

'Mrs Fielding, I do not like to ask before because you are ill, but the stamps?'

She had forgotten all about them. A little half-hysterical laugh crept up and struggled in her throat. Stamps! Of all the trivial, prosaic things to have to remember when so many tumultuous things had happened!

'I forgot. I'm sorry. I'll get them as soon as I'm allowed out.'

'Knud will be so pleased. They are of more value when they are not postmarked, you see.'

Postmarks. . . . In the absence of the letters themselves, in the absence of the redirection notice, it might help if she could only say where those letters had come from and could show a sample of the typing.

'Pernille,' she said thoughtfully, 'd'you remember – Oh, way back in September – I had two letters from Mrs Drage?'

Pernille nodded, her clear dark skin growing increasingly pink. She stopped half-way to the door and looked back at Alice warily.

'You didn't happen to notice the postmarks, did you? I thought you might have seen by accident when you were taking the letters in.'

If she had been wearing an apron she would certainly have twisted it. Her face was a comical mask of shame, guilt and self-justification.

'The second letter,' she said at last. 'I kept the envelope, Mrs Fielding. You had finished with it and when I empty the wastepaper basket, there is the envelope with the beautiful new stamp. I look at the date on the postmark and I know at once . . . Oh, I do not know how to say it in English!'

Alice's mind went back thirty years to a rainy afternoon at Vair Place. She and Hugo had been sitting on the attic floor and between them was Hugo's new stamp album. Hugo had pulled her plaits and made her cry because, anxious to take part in this masculine pastime, she had wanted to soak a certain stamp off a certain envelope.

'A first-day cover!' she cried. 'You kept it for your brother because it was a first-day cover.'

Pernille nodded. 'It is the same in Danish,' she said simply. 'You do not mind?'

'Of course I don't mind. I'm glad, very glad. . . .' Her face fell in sudden disappointment. 'But you've sent it to Copenhagen?'

'No, I wait for Knud to come. Next week he comes for his holidays and then I will give him all the stamps I have saved. I long for him to come, Mrs Fielding.' Not bothering to hide her emotion, she said softly, 'I have been so – so homesad.'

'Homesick,' Alice corrected her gently. Suddenly her heart went out to the girl. She had been too happy with Andrew to notice this unhappiness on her own doorstep. Without hesitation she got out of bed and pulled on her dressing-gown.

'We'll go and find the envelope,' she said, 'and we'll have a look at your room. See if we can do something to cheer it up.'

Perhaps she hadn't devoted as much care as she should have done to furnishing it. It had a maid's room look about it, the floor uncovered but for the two stupidly bright goat-hair rugs. The curtains didn't match the bedspread and there were no ornaments, no books. Pernille's tiny transistor stood forlornly on the bedside table between a tiny brown glass bottle and a jar of hand cream. The envelope they had come for was retrieved pathetically from a writing case stowed under the Danish girl's pillow.

Alice took it eagerly and stared. It was clearly postmarked Orphingham.

But Nesta had never lived in Orphingham. Whoever had posted it there had done so to sustain the deception. The threepenny stamp was one of the new issue of Forth Road Bridge commemoratives, violet, blue and black. Its design of the great suspension arcs beside the Queen's head was almost obliterated by the name Orphingham in the twin circles of the postmark.

Tomorrow morning she would take it to the police. Surely they could deduce something from it, trace the typewriter, even find fingerprints? Delicately, as with tongs, she held the paper between her nail-tips. That greenish-pale assistant at Orphingham Post Office might even remember to whom he had sold stamps on that first day of issue.

'Pernille,' she said, 'I'm ashamed I let you sleep in this ghastly room.' Gratitude and hope were making her generous. 'I think we could run to a proper carpet, and would you like your own television?'

The pale blue kitten eyes met hers and looked away. Then Pernille smiled and nodded her thanks. Was it illness that made her see a kind of pity in those curling lips?

'You're eating properly, aren't you? Plenty of milk and meat and cheese?'

'I eat meat, yes,' Pernille justified herself. She shivered slightly, affecting disgust. 'But milk and that yoghurt you have – no, thank you!'

Smiling, Alice said a brisk 'Good night' and stepped out on to the landing. It was almost funny a Dane disliking the dairy foods that were so closely associated with her native land. She was concentrating so hard on keeping back the hysterical laugh that had risen to her lips that she failed to catch Pernille's last words. Something about cheese and lucky she didn't like it.

Alice went back to bed and ate some of the yoghurt. Everything tasted strange these days. Wearily she pushed it away and opened the first of the Victorian novels, seeing only a blur of print and line drawings.

The house had been perfectly silent but as she turned the pages she heard from beneath her a faint tapping, chattering sound. She listened. No, it wasn't coming directly beneath but somewhere from the other side of the house where the morning room and the dining-room were with the kitchen behind them. It is always difficult, she knew, precisely to locate the invisible source of sound. Then a door closed and quiet returned. The noise must have come from some of Pernille's kitchen equipment, for whatever it sounded like, there was certainly no typewriter in the house.

9

The sun was as bright as on a spring day. The thick evergreen foliage on the bushes in the drive gave a look of spring too, but along the edges of the paths frost clung to the grass.

Alice turned away from the landing window and began to go downstairs. The sun made bright flame-coloured patches on the red turkey carpet in the hall. As she reached the half-landing where the stairs twisted before the final straight descent, she heard voices from the kitchen. The door was slightly ajar.

'Of course she's years and years older than him.' The voice was Mrs Johnson's, the subject of the conversation not difficult to guess at. Vexed, she bit her lip and stood still.

'I did not know.' That was Pernille. Dear Pernille! 'I do not think one would know that. She is so pretty, I think, and she has a lovely body.'

'We don't say that over here, dear. A lovely figure, or a nice bust if you want to go into details.' On the stairs Alice almost giggled. 'And she's got a beautiful head of hair, I grant you that. Always did have, even when she was a little tot.'

This was an instance of listeners hearing nothing but good of themselves. Alice took a step down, about to announce her presence with a cough when Mrs Johnson spoke again.

'Mind you I'm not saying anything against *him* . . .'

'Mr Fielding?'

'No names, dear, no pack drill. We know who we mean. Affection there may be, I don't doubt it. But as for taking him into the works that was a mistake. He's no more use to Mr Whittaker than the office boy.'

Alice froze again.

'Not that Mr Whittaker ever says anything, but you can tell from one or two things he's let slip. I'm a bit of a psychologist in my way, Miss Madsen, and I get to read between the lines. Every time there's anything in the paper about those schoolteachers wanting more money Mr Whittaker gets very hot under the collar. Scathing is the word. I said to Kathleen only yesterday, Blessed is he that sitteth not in the seat of the scornful.'

She could stand it no longer. Her grandmother would have burst in on them. Times had changed. Alice crept back to the landing and came down again, making an unnecessary amount of noise. Mrs Johnson's voice rang out loudly:

'I just popped over with an egg custard for Mrs Fielding, dear. Something light and sustaining. I'm not saying anything against continental cooking, but those made-up dishes are a bit highly seasoned when you've got gastric trouble.'

Alice opened the door. 'Good morning, Mrs Johnson.'

'Well, madam, this is a surprise.' Alice had known Mrs Johnson for thirty years. She had been a nanny to her, almost a mother. But when she came home from school at eighteen the Christian name had been replaced by 'miss' and from the moment she returned from St Jude's after her wedding, Mrs Johnson had begun to call her madam. 'We thought you were asleep and here you are dressed. Well, I always say it's better to keep going and not give way.'

'I feel much better this morning.'

'That's right, you keep going. When we had all that trouble over my cousin, I was that low, I can't tell you. Dr Blunden wanted to keep me under morphia day and night, but No, I said, I'll keep going with my usual. . . .'

'I'm going out, Pernille,' said Alice.

Now she was on the point of going to the police, something held her back; reluctance to put her fears into words, perhaps, or shyness. The overheard conversation had been upsetting and she felt a sudden bitter resentment against her uncle. What right had he to talk about Andrew like that, as if Andrew were mercenary? Even in the wind her cheeks felt hot with anger. They seemed to be muffled in warm, suffocating cloth.

Postponing her visit, she went first to the post office and bought the stamps, then into the carpet shop and took away a pattern book. Harry came out of his surgery on the other side of the street, waved at her, smiled his sweet smile and got into his car. Outside Mr Cropper's shop the jeweller was standing in the sunshine, talking to Mr Feast.

'Good morning, Mrs Fielding.' He looked at her as if he wanted to say more, apologise perhaps, but she passed on quickly. The sight of him, cadaverous, intense, febrile, a jealous, violent man, was the one spur she needed. She went up the steps into the police station.

The station was familiar but not this little room with C.I.D. on the door. The man on the opposite side of the table had a young handsome face creased with fatigue. She fancied strangely that so might Andrew have looked if his life had been different, without education and cloistered pedagogy. The face was like Andrew's and yet unlike. Fineness and grace were there but scarred, as it were, by the passing of a brutish hand in a rough glove. He had introduced himself and her heart sank a little when she heard he was only a detective constable.

She told him about the letters. His face was impassive. She told him about her illness and how it had inhibited her, preventing her from making all the enquiries she would have liked to make. Apparently listening, he asked her if she would smoke. Impatiently she shook her head.

'From what I've heard I think Mrs Drage may have been involved with several men. This is what I think happened: one of them wanted to kill her and he gave her some tablets he said were aspirins. But they weren't, you see. They were a drug that's potentiated by cheese. Everyone knew she went to the bread and cheese lunches because she wanted to slim. She didn't eat cheese that day until she came to my house.'

She stopped. Not until she was actually telling him had she realised that the meal which had contributed to Nesta's death had been eaten in her house, cooked by her. The realisation, appalling though it was, made her only the more anxious to find the truth.

His expression told her she had been talking in vain. Desperately she clenched her fists and brought them down hard on the desk. It was a mistake.

'So you've been unwell, Mrs Fielding?' he said.

'I'm not sick in my mind.'

'Nobody suggested such a thing. Don't you think being ill could have made you over-imaginative?'

'I haven't got a powerful imagination and I don't read sensational literature.' In her mind's eye she saw the Victorian novels she had left on her bedside table, but she couldn't smile.

'Well, if you could just show me the letters Mrs Drage sent you.'

'I've told you, I didn't keep them. I've shown you the envelope. The address is written down in my book. You see, it's like Sewerby and . . .'

'Yes,' he said. 'It's a very easy mistake to make. I know I've done it myself.'

'All right, suppose I made a mistake. Mrs Drage had never lived at Sewerby either. I spoke to the owner of the house and he'd never heard of her. Look, if you were to go – if you were to send someone to Dorcas Street, I'm sure that boy would tell you Mrs Drage hadn't collected the letters and the parcel.'

He corrected her gently, '*Some* letters and *a* parcel. Mrs Fielding, about the cheese and the drug. I'm interested in drugs and I keep a file. Would you like me to show you something?' It was a folder of newspaper cuttings. She glanced at them listlessly. 'The drug you're thinking of,' he said, placing his finger on the cutting he had been looking for, 'is a pep pill containing tranylcypromine.'

'Very possible, I . . .'

'It says here that if you take them with cheese they combine to produce a blood pressure rise which can be dangerous.'

She nodded eagerly. They were getting somewhere at last.

'Mrs Fielding, do you know how many deaths associated with this combination have been recorded in this country since 1960 out of an estimated million and a half patients?'

'Of course I don't.'

He closed the file. 'Fourteen,' he said.

'She could have been the fifteenth.'

He turned his graceful dark head from side to side in gentle incredulity. It might have been a younger, rougher Andrew sitting opposite her. He seemed to be growing more and more like Andrew every minute. There was the same black hair growing high on his forehead, the same narrow sceptical mouth. Suddenly she wondered if he thought she was mad. Mad women probably came in here and told him improbable stories. They would look like her with untidy hair and pale hectic faces.

'She wrote to me and told me her address.' No, that was wrong. Someone else had written. 'I had a letter from Orphingham but the address was false.'

'If she wrote to you, Mrs Fielding, I don't understand why you think she's missing.'

'Won't you do anything?' she pleaded. 'If you could just talk to that man Feast, if you could get some expert to go over the envelope . . .'

He got up and stood by the window. She could see she had made some sort of an impression on him and she leant across the desk, striving to make a last appeal. His eyes flickered. Suddenly she realised that he was silent not from dawning conviction but out of pity and a certain awe of her clothes, her manner and her name. It would not do to cry in front of him. She bent her head and began pulling on her gloves.

'Mrs Fielding . . .'

'It doesn't matter. You'd better forget I came in.' She put the envelope into the pocket of her fur coat.

'We keep a list of missing persons. I don't feel justified in putting Mrs Drage's name on it at present, but we'll keep our eyes open. In case of any unidentified . . .'

Bodies, he had been going to say. In the face of such disbelief how could she tell him that they should exhume the graves in the new cemetery?

'I should go back home, Mrs Fielding, if I were you. I think we could find a car to take you if . . .' He saw the ignition key in her fingers and stopped. 'The chances are,' he said, hearty and relieved because she was going, 'the chances are that you'll have a letter from your friend in a day or two.'

His solicitude was unbearable. When a spinster, Alice had never seen herself as an object of pity. Now she was a married woman, but she felt that to this young man she was exhibiting all the traditionally sad signs of ageing spinsterhood, frustration, loneliness, a longing to draw attention to herself, a desire to make and keep friends.

When she had gone he would talk about her to the station sergeant. 'Bit of a nut-case, that one.' He might even tap his head. And the station sergeant, from a longer experience, would add: 'They go that way when they're getting on and they haven't any kids.'

Who else was there for her to turn to? Not Andrew. His reaction was like the young detective constable's, a mixture of pity and scorn. Uncle Justin and Hugo were at the works. Who but Harry? He would listen to her and believe. The police would believe him.

She must find him, go to the surgery now and go over the whole thing with him in detail. As she came down the steps St Jude's clock struck one. Surely it wasn't as late as that? She looked up at the clock, half doubting, waiting for the other eleven strokes, and her gaze fell on the church hall, its doors wide open. Of course, it was Friday, the day of the weekly bread and cheese lunch. Harry would be there – Harry and Mr Feast. She must be brave and, if necessary, confront him with something like bravado.

But it was the vicar who sat at the deal table just inside the entrance, taking the money.

'Good morning, Miss Whit – Mrs Fielding. Such a pleasure to have you with us again.'

She could think of absolutely nothing to say to him. Instead she felt in her bag and dropped a pound note in front of him. I pay grossly, disproportionately, for everything, she thought as she passed down the hall. I pay my way into everything and out of everything.

Daphne Feast was sitting next to the wife of the council chairman. Alice nodded to them, unable to smile. Father Mulligan was bearing down on her, slopping water from an over-full jug. She paused, giving him a pointless, supplicating glance. Didn't the Catholic catechism cite murder as one of the four sins that cried aloud to heaven for vengeance? He smiled back at her, a pale holy smile from a face like a rack-stretched saint's.

Harry was sitting alone among the posters at the end table. He tried to take her coat from her, but she drew it more closely around her, suddenly realising how bitterly cold she was.

'Harry,' she said, bursting into the middle of things, 'you must tell me, have you ever prescribed tranylcypromine for anyone in Salstead?'

'Have I what? Alice, what is this?'

'Have you? That's all I want to know.'

'Yes, I have as a matter of fact . . .' He stopped, holding a wedge of bread six inches from his mouth. 'Alice, dear,

I can't possibly confide in you about things like that. You must understand that as a doctor . . .'

'Have you ever given it to Mr Feast?'

'Certainly not. That would be the last thing. . . . Please, Alice, will you tell me what you're getting at?'

'It's Nesta,' she said quietly. 'If you won't believe me I don't know what I shall do.'

He had seemed annoyed, prickly and pompous, because of the questions she had no right to ask. While she had been the suppliant, a child with an empty bowl, he had been distant, unwilling to grant favours. Now she felt suddenly that they had changed places. Suddenly his face wore that look of hungry anxiety she had formerly felt on her own.

'Nesta?' he said, and then in a forced casual voice, 'What has she been telling you?'

'Telling me? Nothing. How could she tell me anything? Listen, Harry, nobody will believe me except Jackie. I've been nearly out of my mind with worry and Andrew won't listen to me. He won't talk about her.'

She was going to go on, pour out the details of her search, when he interrupted her with a remark so strange that for a moment she forgot all about drugs and letters and Mr Feast. His voice was practical and frighteningly kind.

'That's natural under the circumstances.'

At once she felt that she was on the threshold of a dreadful discovery, and at the same time that she was the last of all of them to make it. For a long time it had been there, a snake sleeping in a box, sometimes showing life but never venom. Now it was beginning to uncurl and to pulsate.

'What do you mean?'

'Alice, I can't discuss it with you. You must see that. When you married a man so much younger than yourself you surely realised there might be problems of this sort.'

The chatter in the hall rose and fell. A glass clinked. She pressed her hands together, suddenly very conscious of tiny sounds. By the vicar's table someone dropped a purseful of small change on to the floor. She heard the coins rolling and the scrabbling noise of someone groping for them. Her eyes compulsively fixed on pictured poverty, she said:

'I don't understand.'

'We'll come to Nesta in a minute,' he said, 'but, Alice, for your own sake you must stop connecting her with Andrew. It's essential for your own peace of mind.'

'Andrew with Nesta? I'm not, am I?' She could feel her voice becoming shrill, slipping out of control. 'I didn't know I was, Harry.'

His understanding and his pity was more than she could bear. She pushed back her chair and its legs grated on the rough surface of the floor.

'I'm sorry,' he said. 'If I hadn't thought you knew already I wouldn't have said as much as I have. You must forget it, treat it like a bad dream.' He put his hand out to touch her arm but the fingers caught only at her fur sleeve. 'Oh God, Alice,' he whispered, 'I'd give anything to take back what I said.'

Nor all thy piety and wit . . . nor all thy tears wash out a word of it! 'Let me go,' she said. 'I want to go home.' She pulled away from him and walked blindly down the hall.

10

The car roared on to the Vair gravel. She was driving erratically, much too fast, and she saw that she had twice swerved on to the turf verges, breaking the edges and grinding down the grass. But she was home at last, home without giving way to the terrible temptation to burst in on him at the works, sobbing out violent reproaches.

'Are you all right, madam?' Mrs Johnson, aroused from silver cleaning by so much unaccustomed noise, reminiscent perhaps of rally driving and quite alien to the peace of Vair, was leaning out of a window. 'You're a bundle of nerves these days.'

'I'm just tired. And I'm cold.'

'You go straight in and get Miss Madsen to make you a nice cup of something hot. Nerves are very treacherous things, as I have cause to know.'

Alice leant against the bonnet of the car, almost spent with misery and the need to make stupid conventional conversation.

A cloud of plate powder flew out of the window as Mrs Johnson flapped her duster.

'It's a pity you can't bring yourself to have a nice confidential chat with Doctor about it. I know he brought me untold comfort.' The unconscious irony brought a hysterical sob into Alice's throat. 'Now, if you'll just hang on a minute, madam, I can let you have just the thing. . . .'

'No, no!' Alice cried wildly. If she looked any longer into that insensitive, nanny-ish face she felt she would scream. 'I'm going to lie down.' She fumbled with the lock, rushed upstairs and fell on to her bed.

Jealous. Whoever had killed Nesta had been jealous. A big man in Salstead, Daphne Feast had said. To someone with Nesta's background Andrew would have seemed like that with his academic past, his house, his Whittaker connections. But Andrew loved her, Alice. Of course he loved her.

Wretchedly she remembered the police station and the detective who, with his dark good looks and his patience that seemed occasionally to break into exasperation, had reminded her of her husband. He had shown her something she had refused to face before. Young men in their twenties *pitied* women like her, women who were approaching middle age and who had never been beautiful. If they were kind young men they pitied them, if they were not they laughed behind their hands. They didn't fall in love with them. Why had she never thought of it before?

But Andrew loves me, she thought fiercely, I know he loves me. 'For your own sake,' Harry had said, 'you must stop connecting Nesta with Andrew.' All those evenings when Andrew had driven her home, all those weekends before they were married when he had been too busy to come to Vair. . . . He had already met Nesta then.

Why had he married her, given up the job that was his life, changed his whole existence, unless he had loved her?

Because you are a rich woman, said a small cold voice, because Nesta lived in Salstead too.

When they had first gone out together he hadn't known she was rich and the signs of love had shown themselves at once. You fool, snarled the canker that was growing inside her. Everything about you proclaimed it – your clothes, your rings, the photographs you showed him of Vair Place. On the second occasion they met she had spoken to him of Whittaker-Hinton. She could remember it all so clearly and now she thought she could remember that then, at that very moment, he had lifted his eyes from the picture, smiled, touched her hand, begun to show her the marked attentions of a lover.

It was on his first visit to Vair that she had introduced him to Nesta. Beforehand she had arranged the theatre foursome, Andrew and herself, Nesta for Harry. But Andrew and not Harry had taken Nesta home. He had been away so long, while she and Harry talked desultorily about nothing, and he had come back talking lightly of flowers he had been shown and carrying a rose-pink cyclamen in a pot. That had been a present for her from Nesta, he said. A present – or a peace offering, a payment for services rendered?

She turned into the pillows with a dry sob that seemed to tear her throat.

He came home earlier than usual, pale, tired, his hair blown by the wind into Byronic disorder. She was lying flat on her back, staring at the ceiling.

'Why did it have to happen, Andrew?' she said stupidly. Her mind was so full of haunting pictures of him and Nesta, excluding everything else, that she thought he must know at once what she meant.

Apparently he didn't. If he felt any guilt, had any inkling of her meaning, concern for her drove it away. He came to the bed and bent over her. 'Why did what happen? What's wrong, Bell?'

'You and . . .' It gave her a physical pain in the mouth even to pronounce the name. 'You and – and Nesta!' She wetted her lips, shuddering. 'Harry told me.'

'Damn and blast him to everlasting hell!'

She had never heard him swear before. He had been pale when he came in but now he was white with rage.

'You were in love with her, weren't you?' she whispered.

He swung round, turning his back on her. He was a slight man, not broad or muscular, but now his shoulders seemed enormous, hostile, blocking out the light. She covered her eyes with her hands. With his soft careful tread he was walking away from her into the farthest corner of the room. She heard him close the door and the little metallic click, unnoticed a dozen times a day, was like a pistol shot. The mattress dipped as she felt him slump on to the other side of the bed with a heaviness that contained a world of despair.

'Andrew . . .' she moaned.

He would tell her now, confess, ask for her forgiveness, and at the same time admit what she could never forgive – a passion for the dead woman who had been her friend. Clasping her hands together tightly, she opened her eyes and waited.

'If I could only make you believe,' he said, 'how violently . . .' She let out her breath in a trembling sigh. 'How violently I loathed her! She was utterly repulsive to me. But you couldn't see it. I had to put up with that white slug of a woman with her false hair always around me because she was your friend. My God, Bell, I sometimes thought I'd strike her if I ever had to hear her call an anemone an *anenomee* again!' He shivered and she could see the tremor wasn't simulated. 'Those wrists of hers, so fat with a sort of dimple around them like a bracelet . . .!'

'Oh, my darling, why didn't you tell me? But, Andrew – there was something – something between you you wanted hidden, wasn't there?'

'If there hadn't been,' he said dryly, 'I suppose I should hardly have felt the subsequent revulsion.'

'Tell me, then. You can tell *me*.'

'You remember that night we all went to see that play. *Rain*, it was. I remember afterwards thinking how apt of you it was to provide me with a Sadie Thompson.'

'But Nesta was invited for *Harry*.'

'You didn't make that clear, my love. You and Harry seemed to get on so well. I thought you were breaking it gently to me that here was the marriage of true minds. So, you see, when you asked me to take Nesta home I said I would. And when Nesta asked me in, all among the oxlips and the nodding violets, I went in. Oh, Bell dear, she made it very obvious she expected me to kiss her. I thought, why not? That is why I was asked to this particular party.'

'And then?'

'Nothing. I swear to you, nothing. The next time I saw her I was engaged to you.'

All the time he had been speaking he had been waiting, she could see, for a sign from her. Now she gave it. First her hands went out to him, then the smile which had begun in her eyes spread until it irradiated her whole face. He got up swiftly, came to her and took her in his arms.

'Oh, Bell, I've been so afraid for us,' he said, holding her close. 'I wanted to forget it all – what little there was – but Nesta wouldn't let me. When we were alone together she used to speak to me as if we'd been lovers, as if we had some secret we had to keep from you. Then she'd say it might be better if you knew. I watched her disintegrate into the manic-depressive she'd become and I wondered when it would come out, the confidences, the lies, the excuses.'

She nodded and her cheek rubbed warmly against his.

'She was like that with Hugo,' she said. 'Andrew, how many more were there? Why was she like that and how did Harry know?'

'I don't know,' he said thoughtfully. 'Overweening vanity, perhaps. As to how many more . . . Bell, I'll tell you something now. I felt I couldn't before.' He sat back, keeping his arm tightly around her shoulders. 'Back in the summer I was in your uncle's office at the works. You know how he always treats me rather like a minion?' She nodded, a tiny cloud passing across her new happiness. 'Well, that's fair enough – I'm not much good. He had to write a cheque for somebody. He just flung the cheque-book at me, asked me to see if there was one left in it, and went out of the room. As it happens there was just one left, Bell. I noticed some of the stubs – I couldn't help it. You know he uses a new cheque book about once a fortnight, but just the same two stubs were filled in for payments of ten pounds a time to N.D.'

The initials on the vanity case. . . . 'That's horrible, Andrew!'

He said quietly, 'He may have been as innocent as I was.' Tilting her face up to his, he gave her a gentle, passionless kiss. 'Don't worry about it,' he said. 'We'll never see her again.' He jumped up, springy and light, more carefree than she had ever seen him. 'I'll get you some tea.'

We'll never see her again. For more than a week all her energies had been devoted to an attempt to see Nesta again, then to an effort to find who had killed her. Nothing had been allowed to stand in her way but her illness. Now she was almost glad of that illness. The last thing she wanted was to see or hear anything more that could evoke a plump tripping figure, eyes brimming with foolish tears, a black and white check suit seductively tight.

Andrew came back rather noisily and hastily for him.

'Oh, darling, it's a bore but your uncle's downstairs with Hugo. Apparently Mrs Johnson's spun them some tale that you're ill again.'

'I'm coming,' she said. She would have to begin putting suspicions out of her mind and now was as good a time as any.

The tea was already poured out when she entered the drawing-room. Justin Whittaker, his silver tie stiff as a sword pointing at and threatening to pierce his lifted chin, gave a pettish glance at her swollen eyes.

'What's all this I hear about nerves?'

Hugo handed her a cup of tea, slopping it slightly and cursing. 'I've just driven Uncle back from Orphingham,' he said. 'I was dropping him at the gates when Mrs Johnson came flying out in a tear saying you'd nearly driven the car through the garage doors.'

Because she could think of nothing to say, she sat down beside Andrew and sipped the lukewarm tea. Uncle Justin contemplated the ceiling.

'Ten thousand years of civilisation shed in an instant when you put a woman behind the wheel of a car.' He put down his cup as if he had seen it and realised he was holding it for the first time. 'What do I want with tea at this time of night?' he said to no-one in particular, then to

Alice, shaking his head, 'I don't know where you pick up these proletarian customs.'

She was about to make some angry rejoinder – why were they here, what right had they to question her behaviour? – when the thought came to her that her uncle's bluster covered concern.

'I was worried about something,' she said calmly, 'and I was tired. It doesn't matter, does it? I didn't hit the doors.'

'What you need is a tonic,' he said, 'something to knock all this nonsense about being tired out of you.' Reluctant to betray any emotion, he added brusquely: 'I may as well tell you, Alice, I'm worried about you. You've got something serious the matter with you and if Andrew here doesn't look to it he's going to find himself tied to an invalid – or worse.'

Appalled she jumped up and took a step towards him. Andrew was breathing steadily, evenly, not moving.

'Uncle Justin!' The burning pain which caught at her diaphragm was the worst she had ever experienced. It had come suddenly from nowhere and it diffused at once, pouring into her limbs and flecking brilliant, flower-like colours across her vision. Her legs had become numb and immovable and as she put out her hands into intangible voids, a spasm of sickness flooded her so that she could hear with her physical ears a roaring like the waves of the sea.

'What's the matter, Bell? What on earth's the matter?'

It was going to happen again, just as it had in the Feasts' flat. This time his arms were there to save her, but she fell so heavily that they both crashed against the loaded table. The last things she heard were Hugo's oaths, the shattering of china and the dripping of milk and tea on to the carpet.

She had been conscious for a long time, but there seemed to be no reason for opening her eyes. Blackness and withdrawal were all she wanted. She had been aware of comings and goings and now she realised that Harry only was in the room with her and Andrew. The two men were arguing in harassed angry whispers.

'I fully realise I'm not here because you want me,' Harry was saying, 'but since Mr Whittaker telephoned me, and

Alice is my patient, the least you might let me do is try and make a diagnosis.'

'Considering you've seen my wife almost every day since this trouble started, and so far all you've managed to come up with is some mythical virus, I should think "try" is the operative word.'

'Listen to me, Fielding, a virus is the last thing I'm considering at this moment, but something very different.'

'You make me tired!'

'Before I can be sure I shall have to make a very thorough examination and ask her some questions, so if you or Miss Madsen will help me get her upstairs . . .'

She felt his hand move under her arm. Then Andrew jerked it violently away. Still Harry didn't quite lose his temper.

'Come now. Alice won't mind talking to me. I think you forget she and I are old friends.'

'I've had about as much of this friend-patient stuff as I can stand. It's always been my impression that the less so-called friendship existing between a doctor and his woman patient the better.'

There was dead silence. When Harry spoke his voice was so quiet that she had to strain to catch it.

'If anyone – *anyone* – but Alice's husband had said that I'd have had him for slander.' She heard him take a deep breath. 'For heaven's sake let's leave personalities out of this. It's essential that Alice should see a doctor. She ought to have tests made, a special diet.' He stepped back clumsily and she heard his heel grind into broken china. 'What on earth has she been eating? Did she have any lunch?' His voice rose and suddenly she knew what he was trying to say and why his voice had that chilled, appalled edge to it. 'Fielding, can't you guess what's the matter with her, or are you too much of an escapist to face up to it?'

'I happen to be a layman,' said Andrew, 'not a provincial, back-street physician. Now, will you please go?'

She opened her eyes then and gave a faint moan. Harry was standing, looking down at her.

'Alice,' he said, hardly moving his lips.

'I understand,' she said. 'I should have realised before. Don't worry, I'll be careful now.'

'I have to go.' Harry's face was miserable and anxious; his blue eyes stared down at her, wide with shock. 'Promise me you'll call someone else in, get a second opinion.'

'Of course I will.'

'Get out!' said Andrew.

He went without looking back and she saw that for once instead of stooping he walked erect. As the door closed she leaned back, the tears streaming down her face.

Now that the worst of his rage had passed he stood beside her almost humbly, abject, with eyes cast down. Evidently he expected her to reproach him, but she could think of nothing but the awful momentousness of Harry's words. *What on earth has she been eating? We must have tests made. Fielding, can't you guess what's the matter with her?* Harry was a doctor and Harry had seen, had divined from her symptoms, what was the matter with her.

It should have been a surprise and yet it wasn't. Subconsciously she had suspected it all the time and that accounted for her fear, the dread which arose within her each time the nausea returned. Spasms of sickness had occurred at each fresh stage in her search for Nesta, or rather had occurred just before those stages were reached. Whoever had killed Nesta was frightened too, so frightened that he was prepared to make her ill, even to kill her, in his desperate effort to stop the truth coming out.

Harry would have helped her, but Harry had been sent away. Even if he had stayed there was nothing he could have done. Quite clearly there rose before her eyes a picture of them all as they had been before she had drunk that cup of tea, Hugo and her uncle watching her, waiting, talking to fill in time. The tea had been poured out before she had come into the room. One of them could have . . . Oh, it was horrible! But how could she allow Harry to make tests, discover whatever it was – arsenic, strychnine? – and then incriminate her uncle or her brother? It couldn't be possible. Yet Andrew had said Justin Whittaker was paying sums of money out to Nesta. An allowance perhaps, or blackmail? Hugo had confessed to his own small adventure with Nesta. Maybe it had been not a small but a big adventure, an escapade that he would do anything to prevent Jackie discovering.

'Bell, we'll get you another doctor,' Andrew said at last, 'someone who really knows, a specialist.'

'I don't know. I'm so afraid, Andrew.'

It might not be either of them. Other men had been involved with Nesta. Hadn't there been something almost sinister in the way Mr Feast had pressed her to take the yoghurt? He had known that no-one else in the house would eat it. She mustn't stop to think about consequences, about police in the house, endless questions, a trial at which she must give evidence, when her own life was in danger.

Perhaps it was too late. Perhaps the poison had already taken a grip on her from which there was no escaping except into death. As if providing an affirmative answer, pain suddenly gripped her chest, diffusing out in flowing branches of agony, and as she moaned and hugged herself with numb cold arms, she seemed to sense death's grinning presence.

'If I should die, Andrew . . .' She shook her head against his expostulations. 'No, darling, listen. If I die it's all for you, this house and, oh, ever so many shares in the works. And everything that's in the bank. I made a will when we were married and it's all for you.'

'*Die?*' he said. 'People don't die, my darling, because they have food poisoning. You're so tired and overwrought you don't know what you're saying.'

If only she could get up and call them all back, shout to them that they were wrong, abysmally wrong, if they thought she wanted to find Nesta now. All she wanted was peace, a return to the normalcy of last week, a body that no longer need wage a battle against something too strong for it.

'Don't leave me,' she said. 'Stay with me.'

'Of course I'll stay. Try and get some sleep.'

Then he did a curious thing. With the tips of his fingers he touched her eyelids lightly and obediently she closed her eyes. It was only afterwards, just as she was slipping into exhausted, stunning sleep, that her brain associated his gesture with the closing of the eyelids of the dead.

11

Tomorrow the specialist would come. She had lain in bed for three days now and it seemed to her that hardly an hour had passed in which she had not rehearsed the coming interview, but still she hadn't made up her mind what she would say to him. Her association with crime, even though she was just a victim, seemed to have degraded her, smearing her with underworld dirt, and she pictured the distaste on the face of the great man as the truth began to become obvious to him.

The air in the bedroom was quite fresh – indeed she kept the windows open day and night in spite of the gale – but it seemed to her that the place was filled with a kind of miasma. Poison was in the air, in the mind of someone and in her own body. She had frightened Andrew by her refusal to eat anything that had not been prepared by himself or by Pernille, and frightened him more by her refusal to say why.

'I don't want to see them, I don't want them to bring me things,' was all she would say.

'But you could see Jackie, darling. She's made you a jelly and brought you some wonderful flowers.'

She reared up in the bed then and he flinched at her outburst of incoherent terror. And Jackie had gone away, hurt and indignant, leaving behind her a bunch of chrysanthemums with blossoms like curly golden wigs. Alice had always loved flowers and she had told Pernille to put these in a corner of the bedroom, out of scent but disturbingly within sight. They reminded her of the huge plumed flowers Nesta had woven into wreaths for winter funerals. Nesta had sat in her workroom with the chrysanthemums spread about her, her own golden head like an enlargement of one of the giant blooms.

Alice sat in bed, reading continuously, absorbing perhaps only one word in every ten, but turning the pages, keeping herself sane. Even so she couldn't keep her eyes from roving compulsively towards the vase in the corner. Then her body seemed to crystallise into a block of fear, a pillar of salt, while she stared rigid and terrified at twelve golden heads which the wind whipped and ruffled.

'When will he come?' she kept asking Andrew, for she longed for and feared the arrival of the specialist.

'Sir Omicron Pie?' Andrew always called him that, affecting to have forgotten his real name, and calling him instead after an eminent physician in one of his favourite novels. 'Tomorrow at three. You can't summon him at a moment's notice like some village quack.' And his mouth curled with a kind of scorn. 'How do you feel this morning?'

'I don't know,' she said. 'I wish I knew.'

The sickness which had been physical had undergone a subtle change. Now more than anything it resembled the dyspepsia that accompanies an anxiety neurosis. So many things could bring it on, the sound of her uncle's voice booming out enquiries in the hall below, the gleam of the golden flowers at twilight, her own thoughts that kept returning to the dead woman. But sometimes it came without provocation, mostly at evening or when she first awoke, and then it was so savage and unremitting that she knew no mental turmoil could have caused it.

'Pernille,' she said when the Danish girl came in with her lunch, 'would you take those flowers away?'

With only a hazy idea of what it had all been about, she closed the last page of the second volume in the series. Pernille rested the tray on her knees and she noticed the smart blue coat that was undoubtedly 'best', the white gloves, the black shiny pumps. For a moment the sight of those jetty pointed toes brought Nesta back to her so forcibly that she sank against the pillows, feeling a scented languid presence and hearing a voice whispering sad yet urgent words too far away to catch. Then, recovering, she said in a tone that sounded falsely bright:

'Are you going out?'

'It is my afternoon off, Mrs Fielding.' Pernille lifted the vase and held it in front of her.

'Are you going somewhere nice?' A pang of envy struck her. The girl looked so free, so happy, so radiant with animal good health.

'I think it is nice, yes. Today my brother comes for his holiday and I go to the airport to meet him.' Above the nodding blossoms her eyes sparkled. 'I am so excited to see him again.'

'Yes, you must be. Don't bother about getting back early.'

'Just think, I have not seen him during a whole year.' She hesitated and then burst out, 'Knud stays with a friend he has known at the university and . . .'

'Yes?'

'Mr Fielding said perhaps I need not come back till tomorrow, but you are ill so I . . .'

'Of course you mustn't come back!' A beautiful new idea was taking shape in her mind. 'Look, why don't you take two or three days off? Mr Fielding will look after me.'

'He will be home by five and all is ready for your tea and for your dinner.'

'You're an angel!' What could she do for this girl in gratitude for leaving her in solitude with Andrew? 'Pass me my bag, will you?' The notes snapped from their rubber band as flat and crisp as the pages of a book. Pernille's face flamed and her fingers crushed the green paper. She must be too overcome to thank me, Alice thought, watching her vanish in a flash of blue and gold.

It was only when she had gone that Alice remembered what she had meant to ask her. 'Go downstairs and see if you can find a book of Mr Fielding's called *Phineas Finn*.' It couldn't be helped; she would have to go herself.

Pernille's bedroom door was wide open, tidy but for signs of last-minute packing. A crumpled scarf lay on the bedside table. Beside it she saw what she had seen before but which her brain had not recorded as significant: a small brown glass bottle. Nesta had been holding a bottle like that the night she died. It means nothing, nothing, she told herself, as the bottle seemed to grow to huge dimensions, filling the room until it glowed like a great amber coloured tower of glass. Pernille had been ill with homesickness. . . Abruptly she turned her back on the room and closed the door.

Although it was still early afternoon the hall was already dark. The old sash windows rattled in their frames and the doors shook. Alice wasn't really cold but the sound of the wind, sighing and keening, made her shiver. The kitchen looked starkly clean and bare. Of course she had often been alone in it before, but seldom, she realised with a reassuring laugh, when there was no-one else in the house. Her laughter echoed and she wondered why, all by herself as she was, she had made a noise at all.

Pernille had left the back door unlocked. Alice turned the key. She wanted to be alone, didn't she? The last thing she wanted was a visitor from the outside world, a malignant visitor bringing her some dainty prepared for an invalid.

Now to find the book. She walked softly into the drawing room and over to the shelves which lined the fireplace wall. Andrew had a complete set of Trollope and they were usually in the third shelf from the top. Yes, there were the clericals – from hearing him talk about them she knew their titles by heart – but where the politicals should have been was a long gap, just a stretch of blank polished wood with wallpaper behind it. Most of those volumes were in her bedroom – but where were the two parts of *Phineas Finn*?

Andrew was fanatically tidy about the arrangement of his books. It was unlikely that he could have stuffed these two precious volumes among the modern fiction and the poetry on the other shelves. Just the same, she looked, whispering the titles to herself as her fingers skimmed their spines. But the two books were missing. All the time really she had known they would be. The milk chocolate and blue design on their covers was too distinctive to miss even with only a cursory glance.

He wouldn't want her to take the first editions. She crossed to the antique bookcase she had given him to house them. Dull green and gilt, attractive only to a bibliophile, they looked forbidding behind the glass doors. The key was in the lock but it had been turned. The books seemed to say, touch us not.

Perhaps the missing copies were in the dining-room or the little dark morning room they seldom used because it gave on to the shrubbery. Andrew sometimes sat in there by himself, reading, always reading. As she approached the door a sound behind her made her stop dead. It was a kind of whirring crepitation, dull but quite clear.

But she was alone in the house. *She must be*. Her nerves, already on edge by the discovery of the bottle, the unlocked door and the blank space where the books should have been, now seemed to prickle and jump as if long feelers had been put out to snag her skin.

The whirring went on, piercing her ears as violently as a scream. She kicked open the kitchen door, holding her breath. Then she let it out in a sigh and shook her head impatiently.

'You fool!' she said aloud, for it was only the refrigerator, its pump working noisily as it did perhaps once an hour, reducing temperature. That must have been the sound she had heard the other night, she thought, contemptuous of herself. How could she have mistaken something heard so often and so familiarly for the tapping of a typewriter?

The morning room was empty, cupboardless, with neither desk nor chest that might conceal a book. She came to the dining room. Bleak winter light flooded it from the french windows. She felt a sudden settling, a new ease. After all, it was just an ordinary November day, and here she was alone in her own house, naturally anxious and on edge as any woman would be under the circumstances.

The books were nowhere to be seen. The only explanation must be that, incomprehensible as it was, Andrew had taken them to the works with him. She pulled open the sideboard drawers, but saw only silver slotted into velvet-covered mouldings, tablecloths, their two napkin rings both initialled A. A magazine or a newspaper would have to do instead. There was a pile of these on a stool. Impatiently she began to shift the topmost copies and as she did so two heavy volumes slid out on to the floor and with them a fluttering spray of white quarto sheets and carbon paper.

Brown and blue covers, a little line drawing of bearded men sitting round a club table . . . *Phineas Finn*, Volumes One and Two. Why on earth had careful meticulous Andrew hidden them like this? But, of course, it was absurd to suppose that he had. He must have left them on the table, meaning to bring them up to her, but he had forgotten and Pernille, hurrying to get away, had bundled them up with the papers.

She tucked them under her arm and went to the window. Vair Place seemed to frown at her, a tough old man of a house, gaunt and impregnable among the beating branches. As she stared at the red brickwork, the white facings against which shrub fronds tore vainly, she wondered afresh if it was possible that her uncle could have done this dreadful thing to her. Her uncle or her brother? Tomorrow when the specialist came it would be too late to stop the whole machinery of police procedure. They would have to be questioned, any man who had known Nesta would be questioned. . . .

Any man? Suddenly she felt a renewal of unease that had nothing to do with Hugo or Justin Whittaker. Then, as if with a healing balm flowing into and blocking all the dark frightened corners of her mind, the idea which had come to her when she was talking to Pernille returned. Why shouldn't they go away, she and Andrew? There was nothing to keep them in Salstead, every reason why they should leave a place that had become hateful to both of them. . . .

She went upstairs dreamily, pulled back the covers and got into bed. It was ridiculous to spend all that time hunting for a book and then to be too tired to read it. She would sleep for a little while and wake up refreshed for Andrew.

'Do you take milk, Miss Whittaker?'

She laughed, carefree, ecstatically happy to be alone with him. Looking back, it seemed to her that the whole hateful business had begun at tea-time and now at tea-time she was going to end it.

'Andrew, shall we leave here and go away? Permanently, I mean. Would you like that? We could go tomorrow. I've thought it all out.'

'Sir Omicron Pie is coming tomorrow.'

'We could put him off, couldn't we? I know I'll be all right if I can only get away from here.'

'But, Bell, what about Pernille?'

'I'll – Oh, I'll give her six months' money or something. She's longing to go home, anyway. She's terribly homesick.

Darling, we could just pack up and go – go to an hotel somewhere. . . .'

He wasn't looking at her, but down at the silk bedcover, the thick soft carpet, the shell-thin china on the tray. The expression in his eyes was so strange that for a moment she couldn't tell whether it was delight or dismay. His hands were clenched so tightly that great white patches showed on the skin where the pressure of his fingers had driven away the blood.

'Andrew . . . ?'

'When we were engaged,' he said slowly, 'I came down here for the weekend.' Clearing his throat, he added carefully: 'My second weekend at Vair. I meant to tell you then that I'd have to take you away, Bell, that my work couldn't be here. But almost as soon as I arrived you brought me to this house. You showed it to me and said it was to be ours. Your face was like a little girl's, showing off a dolls' house, and I hadn't the heart then to say all the things I'd meant to say. We had lunch with your uncle. His face wasn't in the least like a little boy's. I know little boys, Bell, they were rather an important part of my life. . . .' She started to speak, but he stopped her, shaking his head. 'He gave me a glass of sherry. God, it was as dry as a bone and I happen to like sweet sherry. But he couldn't know that since he hadn't bothered to ask. Then he said to me – barked is the better word – "We'll have to find a niche for you at the works, I suppose. I daresay you're not picking up more than twentyfive a week, are you, at Dotheboys Hall or whatever it calls itself?" The next thing I knew I was sitting at that enormous table with Kathleen spooning asparagus over my left shoulder.'

'Oh, Andrew, I never knew – I never guessed it was as bad as that!'

'I'd often wondered what it feels like to be a commoner married to a royal princess. Oh, it's very nice going on the Civil List, of course, but I confess I feel a certain blow to my manhood when the works foreman makes a slip of the tongue and calls me Mr Whittaker.'

'Why did you stand it? Why didn't you tell me?'

He took her hands and said almost harshly, 'Don't you know?'

She nodded, too ashamed to speak.

'Did you mean what you said just now, that we could go away and not come back?'

'Of course. It's what I want.'

Expecting him to kiss her, she waited, holding up her face. Instead he gave her hand an absent pat, and getting up, stood apart from her. He seemed dazed, like a man who, hearing the first tidings of unbelievable joy, cannot yet face or grasp them.

He would put the car away, he had said. Then he would see what Pernille had left them for dinner and bring something up to her on a tray. Or perhaps she felt well enough to come downstairs? He could put a match to the fire Pernille had laid.

After he had gone she remembered she hadn't touched the tea he had poured for her. It was almost cold and it had a stagnant look but she sipped it. She heard him lift the garage door and start the car. What was it Mrs Johnson used to say to her when she was a little girl? 'I always know I'm a bit off-colour, love, when the tea's got a funny taste.' She put the cup down and from the floor beside the bed where she had laid it, picked up the first volume of *Phineas Finn*.

All at once the house seemed very silent and stuffily still. A sound that had been part of her existence for a week now had ceased. Then she understood. While she had been asleep the wind had dropped.

For a moment or two, feeling a faint recurrence of malaise, she held the book unopened in her hands. The brown and blue cover was slightly torn. Andrew could bring her the Sellotape when he came up again and she would mend it for him.

If they were really to leave tomorrow she must make an effort, not just lie here listlessly. To see her reading would please him; he would understand that she was beginning to relax again, to take an interest in something apart from her own health.

Were Victorian women really attracted by husky men in Norfolk jackets, men with great bushy fair beards? She smiled at the delicate Huskinson drawings, lingering over them. Here was a winsome crinolined girl standing in front of a Gothic mansion and here a painfully real illustration of a hunting accident. The pictures were amusing but the text looked dreadfully political. How would she ever plough through all that stuff about the Ballot and the Irish Reform Bill? Besides the illustrations were few and the text vast, nearly three hundred and sixty pages in the first volume. She sighed. Like another Alice she wanted pictures and conversation.

Snuggling down in the warm bed, she turned back to the list of contents. The characters and the place names in the chapter headings were all new to her. 'Phineas Finn Takes His Seat', she read abstractedly, 'Lord Brentford's Dinner', 'The New Government', 'Autumnal Prospects'. Her eyes were beginning to close . . . Then, with a little gasp, suddenly wide awake, she struggled up, first rubbing her eyes, then bringing the print close to them.

No, it couldn't be! It must be a hallucination, a delusion. She shut her eyes tightly and frightened by the darkness and the drumming in her head, opened them again to stare and stare. Every number, every line on that page swam together into a greyish blur except two words in italics: *Saulsby Wood*.

12

With the drumming in her ears came a terrible swamping heat, a blaze comparable to that from an open furnace. Then the sweat broke from her rather as if an outer constricting skin was being shed.

Saulsby.

She looked at the page again and the print danced. There was no point in staring at it so compulsively. Did she think that by looking and willing she could work a miracle, change the name into something else?

Saulsby. She shut her eyes and slammed the pages together. Her body was wet, running with sweat, and her fingers left damp prints on the book jacket.

The names of the houses in the terrace in Chelmsford Road had been real places, but Saulsby wasn't a real place. An author had invented it for a country house. This wasn't a popular novel anyone might read; it was obscure, largely unknown. Only a connoisseur, an enthusiast would read it. She mustn't think along those lines, that way madness lay. . . . She pushed her fists into her eye sockets.

Others in Salstead could have read it besides – yes, she had to say it – besides Andrew. She began to feel dreadfully sick. Try to be detached, she urged herself, try to make a part of you stand aside and look at it as a stranger might. But who would know as well as he that she wanted to advertise for Nesta? He had known first, seen it all happen, because he was on the spot, here in the house.

You haven't any proof, she thought, this is your husband that you love. She had come up the path the first time she had been to Orphingham, and seen him sitting in the window reading this same book. Hadn't he shown her the cover then and told her it had been torn? It had all begun at tea-time and at tea-time it would end. . . . He had asked her the name of Nesta's house and she had told him.

'Saulsby. I've got it written down in my book. I'll get it.'

'Don't get up now. I know you don't make mistakes like that.'

Ten minutes before he had been reading it, perhaps reading the very name.

But how had he done it, what had he done? In all her theories about Nesta's disappearance she had never yet been able to put a convincing face on the lover who called himself Mr Drage. It had been stupid to think of Uncle Justin or Hugo or Mr Feast. How could any of them have gone to London on all those weekends? Andrew could. Before they were married, separated as they had been by a hundred miles, whole weeks passed by when they saw nothing of each other. *Andrew.* Shock had delayed the action of pain. It struck her now as with a blow to the heart.

One part of her mind was wounded, agonised, the rest suddenly clear and analytical. It had been easy for him, a gift to an intelligent man. Pernille had been given tranquillisers – that was what the little brown bottle had contained.

One white tablet looked very like another. When they had gone up to Pernille together, and Nesta had asked for aspirins, nothing could have been simpler than to have given her two tablets – or three? – from that bottle. And Andrew knew they were all going to eat cheese. Only fourteen deaths, the young detective had said, out of one and a half million people. But he had also said that this particular combination *raised* the blood pressure. Suppose Nesta's blood pressure had been high already? Bitterly she thought of the many opportunities Nesta would have had for imparting this fact to Andrew. Oh, Andrew, Andrew . . . She stuffed the sheet into her mouth to stop herself crying aloud.

He had done it for her. To prevent her discovering his infidelity – had she threatened that very night to tell Alice everything as a parting shot? – he had killed Nesta. Could she live with him, knowing what he had done?

He must have loved her more than Nesta. What he had felt for Nesta wasn't love at all. Suppose it had been love but the lure of money and position was stronger? He had talked about being a consort, about going on the 'Civil List', but perhaps he had only married her to attain that. Rather than lose it he would do – had done – anything. If he loves me for my money, she thought desperately, it's because I *am* my money. I am what my money has made me, inseparable from it, part and parcel of it. A girl could love a man because he was rich and authoritative and assured. Surely the principle remained if the roles were reversed.

She would never let him know that she knew. Every day she would think of it, every hour. But not for always. Time would take it away. After years had passed she would probably be able to forget it for whole days at a time. The great thing would be to support herself now, tonight, just while he sat with her and they ate their dinner.

Their dinner. . . . The words brought another rush of heat and a fresh flow of sweat. The shudder which took her jerked the bed and set the tea cup rattling. He had brought her that tea and bent over her, smiling. A man may smile and murder while he smiles. He had done it because he loved her. She tore the sheets from her body and rushed trembling from the bed. Why hadn't she seen the flaw in that argument? Whoever had killed Nesta had tried to kill her. Nesta's killer had tried to kill or, at least, seriously to incapacitate the woman who sought him.

Chocolates, yoghurt, a jelly, an egg custard . . . What a fool she had been! No-one outside the house would dare to poison food anyone inside it might eat. But Andrew had brought her food and drink with his own hands, knowing it would be touched by nobody but herself.

She fell against the door, pressing it with cold clammy hands. The foretaste of vomit was on her tongue and bent double with an excruciating shaft of pain, she remembered the foul taste of the tea. Suppose she died tonight? Harry had been sent away after an obviously staged quarrel. In her own innocence she had herself asked Andrew to cancel the specialist's visit.

Pernille was gone. Not she but Andrew had told her to stay away all night. Charitably he had sent her away so that he might be alone with his wife.

I must get away too, she said aloud. I must get out! With agonising slowness the sickness subsided. It seemed to draw away from her mouth and throat and travel into her limbs where it settled as a kind of paralysis. She stumbled to the window and wrenched back the curtains. Light from the drawing-room showed her the drive misted by a faint drizzle. The laurels and ilexes, still now after a week of turbulence, hung their immobile heads. Thank God Uncle Justin was next door!

She began to dress, clumsily and feebly because her hands were shaking. There was no time to plait her hair. She caught it up and twisted it into a coil on the back of her head, found the pins and stabbed them in haphazardly. A coat next. It would be cold out there tonight. She unhooked the fur from its hanger and seeking warmth, thrust her hands into the pockets. Something stiff and cool touched her right palm – Nesta's envelope, the first-day cover. The contact brought back humiliation. She had slipped that envelope into her pocket at the police station.

If he saw her on the stairs he would try to stop her.

'What are you doing, Bell?'

Nobody would ever call her that again. For ever now she would associate the diminutive with sweet insincerity, a subtle, smiling poisoner. Clutching at her body, she let out a little cry of pain.

But it was useless to think of that now. For that she had all the rest of her life. Now she must get out. Cautiously she opened the door. The house was full of light. Down the stairs next as swiftly as her weak legs would take her. The front door, could she make the front door without his hearing her?

There was a light in the dining-room and she thought at once of the french windows which faced the side of Vair Place. From the kitchen came the very faint clink as of plates being moved. She went into the room and reached for the curtains to draw them away from the lock.

The room was different, changed since she had visited it that afternoon. Something, some unfamiliar arrangement of objects, unnoticed at first, but registering by their very oddity on her subconscious, made her turn towards the table. She started and froze. On the table was a typewriter.

A pad of perhaps half a dozen quarto sheets were in the roller. She moved towards the machine fearfully as if it were alive, able to transmit her actions to its owner by some method of supernatural photography. Her breath made the sheets flutter. Where had she seen that perfect, print-like type-face before? Methodically, as if she really were an expert sent by detectives to furnish evidence, she slid the envelope from her pocket.

The lettering, the spacing, the little serifs were precisely identical.

Like a second degree burn the shock it gave her was mild in comparison with the searing her mind had suffered from the sight of the words in the book. This merely confirmed what had been almost a certainty. Had he still hoped, still thought to quiet her by other means than poison? Had he been going to forge another letter? She stood swaying, not shuddering at all, but hollow and sick with horror.

Even when she heard his steps behind her she didn't jump.

'Bell, darling!'

'I wanted to come down,' she said, and every word was an effort. It was as if she was speaking an unfamiliar language. 'To surprise you.' But why was she suddenly laughing, a merry trilling laugh that bubbled out gaily? 'Yes, I wanted to surprise you, Andrew.'

It must have been the high strained note in her voice that made him stare at her like that. Or perhaps it was the fact that she had seen the typewriter. The movement he made to pull out the sheets of paper was swift and furtive.

Her foolish laughter went on unchecked. She couldn't stop it, though the feeling it stemmed from and it in its turn caused, was more like grief than happiness.

'Stop it, Bell,' he said sharply. 'Come and sit down.' She stiffened her body to prevent the recoil. Then she began to laugh again, but the spasmodic giggling died suddenly as his outstretched hands rested on her shoulders, terribly near her neck, pulling her towards the armchair. 'Let me help you down.'

Her will was too weak to hinder the great shudder. She shook and the coat slid from her back.

He stooped down and gathered it up in his arms. 'You won't want it in here.' Some of her fear, although wordless, had communicated itself to him. First she saw in his eyes apprehension, then he made a quick recovery. His tone was velvety. 'You surely weren't thinking of going tonight?'

'No. Oh, no, no, no. . . .'

When his hand – a dry, calm hand – touched her forehead and rested there she gritted her teeth and tensed all her muscles. Another moment and she would have screamed aloud.

'We'll have dinner in here,' he said, 'and then I'm not going to let you out of my sight.' Her teeth had begun to chatter. 'What's the matter with you?' Stern, unsmiling now, he had moved away from her, but his eyes never left her face.

'I'm so cold.'

He wouldn't give her the fur. It looked feral, alive, hanging over his arm, a prey in the hunter's hands. She identified herself with this old valued possession and she held her cold hands pressed against her cheeks as he went towards the door.

'I'll get a rug for your knees,' he said.

It was only a dozen yards to the cloaks cupboard. As soon as he was out of the room she staggered from the chair to the french windows and, her knuckles knocking against the glass, undid the bolts. In the obliquely slanted light from the table lamps his long shadow came in before him, heralding him. She sat upright and stiff in the armchair, clutching the arms. He spread the rug across her knees.

'You're to stay there,' he said, no longer gentle. 'You're not to move, d'you hear?' She nodded, terrified. Her head moved up and down, fast at first, then more and more slowly and automatically, like the head of a doll that has been wound up and is gradually running down. 'The sooner we get all this cleared up,' he said, 'the better.'

Only once before had she seen that hatred in his eyes, the day he had sent Harry away. Thoughtfully and deliberately he said, 'I'll light the fire.' He struck a match and the paper and logs caught at once.

Everything he did, she thought, shivering, he did well. The cold yellow blaze filled the corners of the room with flickering light.

'I may be a little while,' he said.

She heard him lift the telephone receiver in the hall and begin to dial. He pushed the door and it clicked closed but not before she had caught his first words. 'Is that Welbeck . . . ?' He was phoning the specialist, telling him not to come.

It would be bitterly cold out there in the garden. She wrapped herself in the rug and edged towards the windows. The turning of the key in the lock made no sound. A dry sob rose in her throat but she was too frightened to cry. The door gave soundlessly and cold moist air seeped in to meet her.

13

The evergreens in the shrubbery were wet with black reptilian leaves. She pushed her way through them, holding her hands in front of her face to prevent it being cut by holly. As she passed the greenhouse she saw in the blaze of light that streamed from her own house, a pile of yellow lying on the compost heap. It was Jackie's chrysanthemums. Pernille must have tipped them there before she went out. Checked for a moment and breathless, she stared at them briefly in fascinated horror. Each with its golden curled head was evocative of Nesta, dead, discarded, because its usefulness had ended and it was in the way.

Only one light showed in the windows of Vair Place and that was in the hall. She couldn't remember that she had ever rung the bell before, always letting herself in at the back or by one of the casement doors. Through the panes of glass she could see a glimmer of red carpet, polished oak and pale porcelain. As she waited the desire to giggle uncontrollably returned, to giggle madly at colours and shapes and bushes that poked spotted leaf-fingers into her face.

The door was opened by Mrs Johnson. Alice was stunned now and she felt nothing, only that it was funny and foolish of Mrs Johnson to be wearing her winter coat and a felt hat in the house.

'Where's my uncle?'

'Whatever's the matter, madam?'

It was surprisingly easy to smile, only difficult to stop bursting into laughter right in Mrs Johnson's face.

'Where's my uncle?'

'Mr Whittaker's dining with Mr and Mrs Hugo, being as it's their wedding anniversary.' It was a sudden sharp shock, as salutary as the prescribed slap in the face. Other people were doing other things, things apart from her; the world was going on. A wedding anniversary – how funny, something she would never have! But she clung to the newel post, not wanting to laugh any more.

Mrs Johnson's eyes flickered over the plaid rug.

'Whatever possessed you to come out without a coat, madam?'

'I'll wait for my uncle. What time is it?'

'Just gone seven.' Grudgingly the door was opened a little wider. 'As to waiting for him, madam, me and Kathleen was just on our way to Pollington to see my cousin Norman. But if you wanted to wait here we could always cancel our arrangements. . . .'

The heavy feet in their thick suède-collared boots edged back a few inches.

'No, no, not if you were going out to enjoy yourself. . . .'

'It's not a matter of enjoyment, madam,' Mrs Johnson bridled. 'Only with Norman being laid up all these months, and Mr Whittaker being so good to him, I always feel it's the least I can do. Goodness knows, the Dawsons are an idle lot in all conscience and Norman not the least, but when it's a case of genuine illness . . .'

'It doesn't matter!' She stopped, putting the names together. N.D., Norman Dawson. Uncle Justin had been paying an allowance to his housekeeper's sick cousin. Another door was slammed, another question mark erased.

'Of course you must go. I can wait by myself.'

'There, and just this minute Kathleen's raked out the boiler all ready for the sweep in the morning. Half an hour and them pipes get as cold as charity.'

'It doesn't matter! It doesn't matter!' Alice cried. She could go to Hugo. It wasn't far, less than a quarter of a mile. She turned, shaking her head feebly, exhausted with the effort of talking. The door was held open just long enough to light her way down the path between the laurels. She began to run along the street, stumbling and catching at the fences.

He would never dare to come after her. Or would he? If only her legs were less weak, the pavement dry instead of greasy with mud and water.

Your husband is trying to kill you. He has killed one woman and because you know too much about it, and because he wants your money, he is trying to kill you too. It was no good. They were just words, words that might have come back to her out of a book she had been reading. The facts were all there, clear in her head, but the magnitude of the horror provided an anaesthetic that blanked out all emotion. Your husband is trying to kill you. Her mouth twisted into a silly smile.

Hugo's bungalow was the first of an estate of large modern houses built behind the elms in what had been a country lane. Lights glimmered behind a web of tangled black branches. She was going to spoil their celebration, burst in on a group of happy people just as they raised their glasses in the first toast. It couldn't be helped.

As she put her hand to the gate the lights of a car loomed out of the black hole between the arched boughs. It seemed to roar as it emerged like a train coming out of a tunnel and she flattened herself against the hedge, all the breath driven from her body. But it was only a shooting brake with a retriever gazing placidly from the rear window. Drizzle speckled on to her lifted face and a cascade of liquid mud splashed against her legs. This is how the hare must feel, she thought, afraid by instinct, but not knowing what it fears, running with hysterical leporine laughter.

The path to the bungalow was long, a causeway of crazy paving, slightly raised above wet grass. This was the last lap and it gave her a spurt of energy. She flung herself into the porch and hammered on the door.

Jackie was coming. Thank God Jackie would be the first to see her! With the sound of human movement, the certainty of immediate human contact, there returned in piercing violence the awfulness of reality. Andrew has killed Nesta, Andrew is trying to kill you . . . For a little while Jackie would hide her from the men, take her to her bedroom and warm her until the worst of the panic was gone. What would come after the panic she didn't dare to think.

The door was tugged open abruptly.

'Oh, Jackie, I thought I'd never . . .'

She gasped. There on the doorstep with Christopher in her arms stood Daphne Feast.

Wedding anniversary cards propped on vases covered the mantelpiece. A big one with a slightly more pithy greeting than the others had been pinned to the frame of the lop-sided green picture. A peasant, a displaced person with a blotchy white face under a cowl of tartan, looked back at Alice from the mirror. Christopher had begun to cry.

'They've gone to The Boadicea,' said Daphne. 'Didn't you know? It stands to reason she wouldn't want to mess about with cooking on her anniversary.'

The mirrored face mouthed out, 'What are you doing here?'

'Baby-sitting. And it's not funny round here. He's been yelling his perishing head off ever since they went.' She held the child out to Alice and stared at her. 'Here, you take him for a bit. If you're not in too much of a state, that is.'

It was as well the chair happened to be there. Alice fell into it without looking behind her. She clutched the child tightly, taking comfort from him. Diverted by a new face, he stopped crying. She pulled the comb from her hair and gave it to him. He fingered his own wet cheeks and then touched hers down which weary tears had begun to trickle, laughing as if he had made a happy discovery.

'Is there anything to drink?' Her voice sounded harsh, more like that of a hard-bitten woman propping up a bar than her own.

'I don't know. It's not my house.'

'There ought to be some brandy in the sideboard.'

Round-eyed, Daphne slid back the doors and handed the bottle and a glass to Alice. She dumped Christopher on the floor. He began combing the long mohair strands of the hearthrug. Alice poured some brandy and drank it. The comfort it brought and the new warmth staggered her.

'I reckon you ought to phone Mr Fielding and get him to come and fetch you.'

'I will,' Alice lied.

Fortunately the telephone was in the hall. She shut the door on Daphne. It was nearly a year since she had dialled this number, but she knew it by heart. Taking a deep breath, she waited for him to answer.

Perhaps there had been something in what Jackie said. If she had done her hair like this years ago, taken trouble with her face, it might never have happened. Jackie's dressing-table afforded an array of things Alice had never thought of buying.

Busily she brushed her hair, but baulked at the thought of plaiting it. Instead she twisted it into a cone on the top of her head and with a strange excitement, stepped back to study the effect. She gasped, then in mimicry gave a tight little smile. So that was the explanation!

It was with a sense of indulging in a secret vice that she began to make up her face. The lips were a pale glossy pink now, the eyelids blue. As the final step in assuming another identity, she drew in dark arched brows over her own fair ones. The transformation was almost complete.

She couldn't go out into the road again draped in a travelling rug. Jackie's wardrobe was full of coats. Tip-toeing now, she slid one in black bouclé off a hanger and without looking back at the glass put it on.

The stage was set, the curtain about to go up. She opened her eyes and turned. Yes, it was just as she expected. Nesta Drage was walking forward to meet her.

She sat down heavily on the bed, euphoria displaced by shock. Had they all seen it, all of them but herself? Was that why Jackie had said, You ought to do your hair like Nesta's, because with a little juggling, a tiny change of make-up, she looked like Nesta? Her forehead was higher, her eyes larger than the florist's, but there was the same plumpness of figure, the same bud of a mouth. In spite of her illness, her face had filled out, heightening the resemblance.

Justin Whittaker had seen it. His affection for Nesta had been an uncle's, seeing in her the pretty womanly woman his own niece could never be. Andrew had seen it. He had married her because she reminded him of Nesta. Cold pain stabbed her and the face in the mirror responded with Nesta's look of melancholy.

Daphne's voice called her out of the nightmare.

'You all right, Mrs Fielding?'

She answered in a tone that was exclusively hers, cultivated and authoritative.

'I've borrowed one of Mrs Whittaker's coats. She won't mind.' Turning out the light, she stepped into the hall.

'Aren't you going to wait for Mr Fielding?'

'I expect I'll meet him on my way.'

'You do look nice. Quite with-it, if you know what I mean.' If Daphne had noticed the uncanny resemblance she said nothing about it. Her face was wistful, for whatever was going on she had played her small part in it and in a moment was to be excluded. 'Scared stiff you looked when you came in. Someone hanging about in the lane, was it? I thought to myself. She's seen some man and he's scared her. Was it a man, Mrs Fielding?'

'Yes, it was a man,' Alice said.

On the telephone to Harry she had explained nothing. It had seemed to her then under the pleasurably numbing influence of the brandy that once she was with him everything would ease and fall into place. He had always loved her and, seeing her husband with the eyes of an outsider, anticipating the inevitable, waited his own chance. He would take her away somewhere, and one day, when it was all over . . .

She walked along Station Road, under the bridge, past the works, no longer afraid. In a moment his car would appear, swing in to the kerb beside her. 'If anything is troubling you – anything, Alice – you'll come to me, won't you?' But he was her doctor as well as her friend; she couldn't compromise him. For the time being all she could expect was a sympathetic listener, a friend when all other friends had failed.

Things seldom happen just as and just when you expect them to. But at the point when her thoughts said, Now he will come, the car twisted out from the High Street and swung alongside her. It was a little like falling in love for the first time the way her heart leapt. This perfect achievement of timing did more than anything to dispel her doubts. How had she ever thought him clumsy or gauche?

She was in the car beside him before she looked at his face. Then, as at last she looked up at him, his gaunt tiredness brought her a quick twinge of physical displeasure, and she thought visually of Andrew's beauty. Andrew. . . . Would she ever see him again? At some distant future time, sitting like this perhaps with Harry, she might catch sight of him far away, a stranger in a crowd.

'I'm glad you phoned me,' Harry said quietly. 'I thought you might. We began a conversation, didn't we, in the church hall? Perhaps we ought to finish it now.' He suddenly seemed to realise that it was night, that it had been raining and that she had walked. 'What's Andrew thinking of to let you . . . ?'

'I've left him,' she said flatly.

She knew he wouldn't be surprised. From the first he had expected it. He turned the car into the High Street without speaking. The orange lights on the slip road and the by-pass lit up the sky with a dull glare. It was as if some horizon town was on fire.

'Harry, I can't talk about it now. I thought I could right up until I met you, but it's too near, too recent. If you could just talk to me, be with me, till Hugo gets back . . . I don't want to be a nuisance, Harry. Perhaps it would be better if I went to an hotel. I just don't know any more.'

They passed The Boadicea. Hugo is in there, she thought, Hugo and my uncle. If she could not tell it to Harry, how could she ever tell it to them?

'I wish you could be with me,' Harry said under his breath. She began to cry. 'You'd feel better if you told me about it.' He gave her his arm and helped her out of the car across the pavement to the door with the brass plate beside it. In the waiting-room the chairs had been arranged against the wall and the magazines piled tidily. He didn't bother to switch on the light or lock the door behind him. 'You can lie down in here,' he said, 'and I'll give you something to calm you.'

Walking into the surgery in front of him, she saw her own reflection coming to meet her in the black rain-dashed window. At the sight of that gold and black blur she put her hand up to her eyes and sank into a chair. In silence he went to the medicine cupboard and handed her two tablets. The tumbler he gave her had about two inches of water in it. He had put on the light and the brightness hurt her eyes.

'Wouldn't you like to tell me about it now?' he asked gently.

She swallowed the tablets and took a deep breath. 'I wish I hadn't stopped you that day in the church hall,' she said. 'You were going to tell me, weren't you, Harry?' If only she had let him go on, not jumped up and run from him, she might have known it all before she had made those plans for herself and Andrew, plans that had been sweet and now seemed ludicrous. 'I could have borne it better, then.'

He was puzzled. 'I don't quite understand you, Alice.'

'Don't you remember? You said I mustn't connect Andrew with Nesta.'

'You haven't left him because of *that*?' He gave a little dry laugh. Surprised, she looked up at him.

'That – and other things.'

He sat beside her and a tremor of alarm crossed his features. 'Alice, I don't know what the other things were – I'm not asking you – but I wasn't going to gossip to you about your husband.'

'What, then?'

Frowning, he said, 'I merely thought the time had come to tell you a few things about Nesta Drage. Oh God, I'd held out so long, but when you started to talk about her I – I braced myself for a confession, Alice.'

'Talk about her? Everybody knew I was nearly out of my mind with worry about her.'

There was no mistaking the shocked incredulity in his face. 'Why didn't you tell me?'

Like a jet of icy water the realisation hit her. He was right, she had never told him about it. Of all the people she might have consulted she had never consulted him, because she was afraid – with his swift warnings he had made her afraid – of discussing a patient with her doctor!

'But, Harry . . .' she stammered, 'Nesta hadn't been ill. Why should I ask you?'

Again the dry bitter laugh. 'Hadn't been ill! Did you think it was normal for a woman to get fat and lose her hair and be as depressed as she was?'

'No, but – Harry, I don't care about all that. I beg you to tell me where – where Andrew came into it all!'

She was calmer now. The tablets he had given her were taking quick effect. She bent towards him, gripping the table.

Suddenly he had the air of a man who, coming to the end of his world, may say anything, admit anything, because nothing matters any more. 'There were only two men in Nesta's life,' he said. 'Feast – and I don't think he was ever alone with her for more than five minutes at a time – and one other.'

'Andrew?' she whispered.

'Alice, I told you not to connect them. I meant it. Andrew, Hugo, your uncle, they were just props for her ego. Believe me, you need props when you're a young pretty woman and suddenly, out of the blue, you get a loathsome disfiguring thing the matter with you. You need reassurance all the time – it's one of the signs. You want to be told all the time that you're still lovely and desirable.'

'What thing?' she cried. 'What thing? What was the matter with her?'

'You'll do anything to hide it,' he said slowly, 'but I think Feast sensed it. It might even explain the attraction, the drawing together of such physical opposites, one lacking what was such a burden to the other. I don't suppose you've ever heard the name. . . .'

A green picture, two children sent away out of earshot. . . . The difficult word Jackie had spoken came back to her and she faltered out the syllables.

'Myxoedema?'

'Clever of you.' He gave the ghost of a smile.

'But how do you know all this, about Feast, about Andrew and my uncle?'

'I made up my mind I'd tell you the lot once I'd started. You see, I was the other man.'

Mechanically her hand had gone to the telephone. She could only think, It's all right, I must phone Andrew. But he caught the fingers, stopping her. She was weak and his strength seemed suddenly great.

'Let me finish now. Don't desert me again, Alice. She reminded me a little of you, you see. There was an elusive something – like you in a distorting glass. I couldn't have you, but I had to live, didn't I?'

'I want Andrew, I must go to Andrew!'

Anger shook him. He grasped her wrists. 'Can't you forget him for a single moment? Don't you owe it to me to give me one last half-hour of your time?'

'All right, but . . .'

'We used to go to a place she knew – a sordid dump in Paddington. I think I'm shocking you, Alice.' She shook her head wearily. 'It had to be like that, secret, sordid, underhand, because I was her doctor. Not very pretty, is it? Oh, I stopped needing her long ago, but she needed me. She used to say that if I left her she couldn't be responsible for what she might say. I knew she'd got myxoedema – how could I help knowing, a doctor and so – so close to her? I knew that if she wouldn't be treated for it eventually she'd become like an idiot, helpless, bloated, quite unable to look after herself. But she was so vain, and it didn't make any difference when I told her her vanity was just another symptom. She kept saying: "Leave me alone. I'll get all right in time. You're persecuting me because you want to get rid of me." '

To get rid of her. The words were like worms wriggling across Alice's brain. Suddenly she wanted to stop him, to get out into the clean cold air of the night outside.

'Please don't get up,' he said. She hated that near-hysterical tone in his voice and beads of sweat broke on her upper lip. 'Let me tell you everything.' He paused and went on in a rush: 'She said she couldn't work any more. She couldn't stand the pace. With what she got for the shop she was going to stay at this place in Paddington for a bit and think things out. I could go and – and see her there, she said. In a way it was a relief, but it was worse too. My God, I was frightened to death! Sooner or later, I knew, she'd have to get herself another doctor – she'd *have* to – and then, what would she tell him about me?'

'I don't want to hear! I don't want to know!'

'Sit down, Alice. Please!'

'I know what you're going to tell me, that you gave her a drug and she ate cheese and . . .'

'It wasn't like that,' he said in wonder. 'That wouldn't have harmed Nesta. It would only have raised her blood pressure and people with myxoedema have *low* blood pressure. Oh, Alice – poor Alice – is that what you've been thinking?'

'What was it, then?'

'I had a key to The Bridal Wreath,' he said. 'I was going to meet Nesta there the night before she went away. When she got back from saying good-bye to everyone I was going to make a final effort to get her to have treatment.' He hesitated. 'Look, Alice, I did try to get her to take thyroid. It's extract of thyroid, you know, that people like Nesta lack. I gave her tablets of thyroid and told her they were pep pills, but she wouldn't take them. By that time she wouldn't take anything I'd prescribed.'

The structure he was building up was growing to the proportions of a house in a nightmare, a house with many rooms through which you mounted until at last you came to the secret in the attic at the top. She wanted to get out of the house and run screaming down the stairs he was forcing her to climb.

'Harry, please . . .'

'I didn't get there till half past nine. I called to her but she didn't answer. Then I went upstairs and found her lying on the bed. All the bedding was packed and she was lying there on the bare mattress.' Again he paused as if afraid to go on. Alice made a little inarticulate sound. 'She was . . . she was unconscious. I didn't know what had happened, what she'd taken. . . . God, I wish I could make you understand what I felt at that moment. To be safe, to be free . . . One tiny push over the edge – not that even – just to do nothing and let her die. No one would ever know. Why let anyone see her, come to that? Acres of earth were all turned up outside. I looked at her lying there with that false hair coming adrift, and then I looked out of the window at a ready-made burial ground.'

A cry of sheer terror broke from her.

'What are you trying to tell me?' And her eye fell on the empty glass on the edge of his desk. 'No, no, Harry, no!'

She had come up all those stairs in the nightmare house with him behind her, prodding her on. The rooms had been laid open, one by one, and she had seen their contents, objects that grew uglier and more terrifying as each stage of the journey was passed. Now they had come to the summit of the top flight and there was just one door left.

Doors – the past weeks there had been doors everywhere, opening on hope, showing glimpses of black clothes and bright hair, and closing on despair. This was the last door and in a moment it would open too.

She backed away from him on the brink of a scream. He started towards her, murmuring something, very tall and bulky against the square window. Behind the door she could hear footsteps tapping, muffled at first, then coming nearer. It *mustn't* open. She had to get out, back to Andrew!

Was it the real door, or the one in her vision? There was a faint click as the latch began to move. It was an old door with a black finger-plate and a curly iron handle that crept slowly downwards like a snake, writhing and crawling across the wood.

Alice's stiff hands went up to cover her eyes. But they wouldn't close, instead growing wider, fixed and staring. The door opened an inch, stopped and moved again.

A little wind blew through the crack and with it came a cone of honey-coloured hair, a black pointed toe stepping over the threshold.

Her whole body had frozen into a taut knot of screwed-up muscles and nerves. Somewhere inside her was a scream that the back of her closed dry throat held imprisoned. Shock kept her fingers pressed against her forehead, but through them she could still see the bobbing blonde chignon and the black and white check suit. Between gloved fingers the initials on the vanity case gleamed out at her.

'Well, this is a surprise! Hallo, Alice. Long time no see.'

14

Bent double in the chair with her head touching her knees, she knew that she had never quite lost consciousness. The rim of the glass Harry was holding to her lips chattered against her teeth and water slopped down Jackie's coat.

There was deep silence in the room. She was aware of her own heart beating heavily. Then the silence was broken by the sound of Harry's lumbering tread as he crossed to the sink, the gush of water as he rinsed the glass, the nervous cough he gave.

The staring eyes were not Harry's. She lifted her own and met them. A Jersey cow, a china doll, a white slug of a woman – all those descriptions she was now remembering, but none fitted the girl who sat on the edge of the desk, looking back at her, swinging long slim legs. Nesta was beautiful. Her golden hair, framing her face in a cloud, blazed against the old walls, the green baize. Surely her skin had never had quite that translucency? She remembered it as strangely thick, always heavily *maquillée*. Nesta was no longer fat, but slender. Instead of being like a second skin the check suit fitted as a suit should.

Speechlessly they gazed at each other. Nesta's silence, her lips parted as if she longed to speak but could not, only heightened the impression that this was just a vision. It was Harry who brought reality in to shatter the long dream. When he saw that Alice was recovering he went up to Nesta and said in a low angry whisper:

'It was inexcusable, creeping up on us like that. What are you doing, anyway? You're not due out till next week.'

Nesta blinked. Once she started to speak the words came tumbling out. 'I was as right as rain. They got fed-up with me so they gave me the push. I thought it was the least I could do to come and see my devoted physician.' Alice could hardly believe it. This was Nesta; every word, every phrase, was hers. But this was Nesta as she had been when she had first come to Salstead. She heard her foolish giggle, watched the fingers in their long black gloves tap the desk. 'I popped into Feasts' first, though, and dolled myself up. I wasn't going to be seen a minute longer than poss. in that ghastly red mac you bought me, Harry.' Turning again to Alice, she smiled conspiratorially, all girls together, and added: 'Red, I ask you!'

Without knowing why, unless it was from relief or as a prelude to forgiveness, Alice put out her hand and found

Nesta's. The little hand squeezed hers. Nesta bent her head and sniffed the red rose in her buttonhole.

'I reckon I owe you an apology, Alice.' She looked so contrite that Alice shook her head vehemently. 'Oh, yes, I do. I've been awful to you and I've got a sort of feeling I've upset you a bit.'

'That,' said Harry, 'must be the understatement of the year.'

'But where have you been?' Alice found herself blushing. 'I thought you were dead,' she said.

'I very nearly was. Those last weeks in Salstead I was so ill I nearly went off my rocker.' She hesitated, then gave her hair a nervous pat. Glancing at Harry, she went on quickly: 'Something went wrong with . . . Oh, my metabolism or something. Nothing anyone could *see*. Mostly in the mind really.'

'Rubbish!' said Harry.

She gave him an indignant look. 'I was in quite a state that Friday. The too bright smile made her thin-drawn eyebrows go up. 'It didn't make me feel any better, I can tell you, seeing the Grahams all jolly and bouncing at The Boadicea, and then Hugo and Jackie with their kids. By the time I'd got to your uncle's I was at a pretty low ebb. Well, I went into the kitchen to say good-bye to Mrs Johnson. . . .'

'And the silly old fool said she'd got just the thing for nerves and gave her a bottle with three Tofranil tablets in it,' Harry said. 'She *will* do it, hand out drugs I've prescribed for her to all and sundry.'

'She tried to give me some the other day,' said Alice, remembering.

'Nesta was a damned fool to take them.'

'When I'd been in to see Pernille,' said Nesta, 'I went into your bathroom and swallowed the lot with some water out of your tooth-mug.'

'Tofranil lower the blood pressure, the worst thing for someone with myxoedema.'

Nesta flinched at the word and Alice squeezed her hand.

'They have other side effects,' said Harry brutally, 'tremor, tachycardia, loss of appetite.'

'Well, I felt rotten when I got back and I thought I'd have a lay down. I must have passed out because I was nearly gone when Harry found me. I reckon I ought to be grateful to him and I am. They hadn't got a bed at Pollington so he whipped me off to hospital in Orphingham.'

'*Orphingham?* You mean you were there all the time?' It was unbelievable, yet truer than any of her conjectures. While she had gone to the police, to the post office, while she had pursued one shadow at the florist's and another down the pavement, the real Nesta had been lying a hundred yards away at the cottage hospital.

'Harry came down to see me two or three times a week. He didn't want anyone in Salstead to know about me and I went along with him in that. Then he told me I'd have to drop you a line. You were going to advertise for me in the paper, he said, and I'd have to let you know where I was. The nurse might see the advert or one of the patients. Well, I said, of course I'd write but – I don't know, Alice – I was a bit unbalanced and I thought it might upset you to see me so under the weather. . . .'

'That's nonsense and you know it,' said Harry testily. 'She was terrified to let you see her, Alice. They'd taken away that hair things she wears and they wouldn't let her use make-up. They couldn't have the symptoms masked, could they? She didn't want you or Andrew to see the bloated flabby wreck she'd become because of her own vanity.'

'Don't,' said Alice. She got up and put a protecting arm around Nesta. 'Don't be so cruel!'

'I got used to the nurses,' Nesta whispered, 'but it was bad enough having them poke and prod me. All except one. I used to have a bit of a giggle with her.' She sighed and lifted her head. 'She was a nice girl. Harry wasn't very sympathetic, nag, nag, nag all the time through visiting. As soon as I got a bit better he brought me a load of stodgy novels to read and he said I ought to do some therapy, learn a useful job for when I got out. My nurse used to buy me all the women's weeklies.'

'The upshot of all this, Alice,' said Harry impatiently, 'is that I simply lent her my typewriter.' Nesta gave him a resentful glance. 'Flower selling had been a dead loss, anyway.'

'I feel ever so ashamed, Alice. I don't know how to explain. You see, I didn't want you to worry about me, but at the same time I didn't want you to see me. Well, here goes. That nurse I told you about – Nurse Currie – she said, wasn't it funny I didn't get any letters? Perhaps no-one knew where I was. Why didn't I let her get me a redirection thing from the post office and have my stuff sent on to the hospital from Salstead? She said she didn't like to think of anyone not getting any letters. It reminded her of an old man who lived at a house called Sewerby in Chelmsford Road next door but one to her mum. He never got any letters, she said, and when he went into the post office for his pension he'd seen a notice that said *Someone, somewhere, wants a letter from you* and it had cut him to the heart. She laughed then and said it was a chance anyhow whether anyone in Chelmsford Road got their letters or not on account of the new postman being more or less half-witted.'

'Oh, Nesta!' Alice cried and she began to laugh weakly.

'You know me, Alice. I always was one for puzzles, crosswords, quizzes, something to occupy the mind.'

'Go on,' said Harry.

'All *right*. Only I want to tell it my way, d'you mind? I filled up the form, Alice, and put Sewerby as my last address.' Alice looked at her, but didn't interrupt. 'I thought I'd have the stuff sent on to the hospital – I did mean to, I swear I did – but then I thought, my God, Nurse Currie'll bring in my post and she'll see the Sewerby address, next door but one to her own mother, Alice, and then where'll I be? So I fixed on the Endymion. You see I knew they'd be safe there and I could pop up and fetch them when I got out. They were always saying, you'll be out in a week or two, Mrs Drage. How was I to know you'd keep writing and get all steamed up?'

'You did your best to stop me,' Alice said. 'Your letters weren't very encouraging.'

'That wasn't intentional, duckie. I never could get the hang of that machine. Just a few lines and that was about my limit. But, look, Alice, you're not to blame Harry. I never told him a thing.'

'I don't understand how you knew your plan was working, Nesta. I mean, the postman might have seen through it. I mightn't have sent off the ring . . .'

'That was where Harry came in. He hadn't seen you but he'd got wind of it by the old grapevine.'

Harry interrupted savagely, 'Let me tell her, will you? I met your sister-in-law, Alice. She said you'd been writing to Nesta. I didn't know the details and I didn't want to. I left it at that. You do see, don't you?'

Alice saw. He would have been too frightened, too apprehensive of the outcome to ask any questions.

'Nesta said she couldn't get on with the typing,' he went on, 'so I fetched the machine away. Andrew had told me he needed one and I took it in to him that day you came down to Orphingham. God knows I can't stand him – what's the use of pretending? – but I couldn't bear to think of him spending any more of your money. That car, that watch you gave him – I wasn't going to sit by and see him squander a hundred pounds on another expensive toy!'

She felt herself grow white with anger, but she set her teeth. When she spoke the rage vibrated through the mild words. 'You don't understand, Harry, you don't begin to understand . . .'

'I'm sorry. I shouldn't have said that. Never mind, skip it, forget it. Andrew told me you'd gone to Orphingham to look for Nesta. He said she was living there – living in a private house, I mean. God, I didn't know what was going on. I'd brought him back a book I'd borrowed – Nesta had been reading it – and I just dropped it on the table, muttered something about having to get down to the surgery and got out. Then, the next day I saw you at the bread and cheese lunch. You said you'd been looking for Nesta and you started asking Daphne Feast. I was going to tell you where Nesta was then, Alice, but there were all those people there – that damned woman wanted to talk to me about her diet . . . I said you were to come to me if anything was troubling you. It was a hint to come and see me by yourself, but you didn't come and . . .'

'And then I told him,' said Nesta, 'made a clean breast of the whole thing.' She giggled. 'They say open confession is good for the soul. My God, I thought he'd do me an injury, he was so mad. When I said all the stuff was going to the Endymion he nearly had a fit.'

'I went up and got the letters,' Harry muttered. 'I couldn't tell you about it after that, Alice. You'd have told Andrew and he'd have had me up before the Medical Council. I could just see it. Mr Drage, otherwise Dr Blunden, spending weekends with a patient in an hotel, and what an hotel!'

Nesta looked demurely down at her black gloves. 'Poor Harry would have been struck off,' she said. 'Can you picture him, Alice, all down at heel, peddling patent medicines from door to door? That's what happens to doctors who go off the rails. I've seen it on TV.'

'Oh, shut up!' said Harry. He turned to Alice. 'Once I'd got the letters, Alice, I thought it would all blow over. But when you started connecting Andrew with Nesta I knew I'd have to set things straight.'

'You don't have to go on,' said Alice. 'I can see it all, but for one thing. If you meant to give your address as Sewerby, Nesta, why didn't you?'

'I did. Of course I did.'

Her bewilderment was momentary. 'Did you enjoy *Phineas Finn*, Nesta?' she asked dryly.

'Did I what?'

'A Victorian novel with a blue and brown cover.'

'You mean Andrew's book? There are limits, Alice. I reckon Harry must have thought he was improving my mind. I flipped through it and had a look at the pictures and, believe me, that was enough.'

'Enough to make you have a mental aberration and write Saulsby when you meant Sewerby.' Recalling the young detective's words, she said softly, 'It's an easy mistake to make.'

Nesta put her hand up to her mouth. At last she said, 'No wonder I couldn't ever get those crosswords to come out.'

'I'll take you home, Alice,' said Harry wearily. He felt in his pocket and held out his hand to Nesta. Something in his palm winked and glittered as diamond chips caught the light. 'By the way, I've had this for a week. I forgot to give it to you.'

Slowly Nesta drew the black glove off her left hand. Then she waved her third finger showily.

'Somehow I don't think I'm going to need it.' The black diamond was large, square-cut and expensive-looking. 'My fiancé – oh, you don't know, do you? – he's quite a big man in his way. He broke his leg when his Jag ran into a lorry the first day the by-pass opened.' She laughed as they stared at her. Alice was remembering the ambulance she had heard that day at Feasts', and wondering strangely in the midst of that other greater wonder. That was the day she had first believed Nesta dead. Had the ambulance in fact been bringing her a new life? 'Of course he had a private room at Orphingham,' Nesta went on, 'but they've got a lovely lounge there – for first-and second-class passengers.' She giggled at her own joke. 'I've only known him a week. It's what they call a whirlwind romance. Don't look like that, Harry. I shan't tell him about you.' She drew on her glove and in a queer little gesture of hope, pressed both index fingers along the painted hairless lines of her brows. 'I've got something to lose now, too,' she said.

'I can't understand why I was so sure she was dead.'

'Perhaps you wished she was,' Harry said quietly.

'I wished Nesta was dead? But that's nonsense, that's horrible! I spent days and weeks looking for her. I was nearly out of my mind with worry. I spent pounds and pounds trying to find her.'

'Why did you try to make yourself look like her tonight?'

'I . . .' Why had she? She put her handkerchief up to her eyes and scrubbed at the blue on the lids.

He said impatiently: 'You're not really alike, you know. What you see in the mirror isn't the true image. It's lateral inversion. It's not what other people see, Alice. I believe you looked in the mirror and sometimes you saw her as if she were the other side of yourself.' She stared at him as he turned into Station Road and stopped the car. Then he turned to face her. 'You see, Nesta had succeeded where you had failed, Alice. You were a spinster at thirty-seven, rich but without a career. Nesta had married young, earned her own living, made herself attractive to men. It was only when she started to get ill that you really took her up.'

'I was *sorry* for her.'

'Perhaps you were. You weren't sorry for yourself any more because you were going to be married. Then Nesta moved away and disappeared. By then you'd changed places, but you didn't quite want to lose the other self that was lonely, just as you had been. Money would get her back just as money had got you everything.'

'No!' she cried, 'No, Harry, it isn't true.'

'Why not be detached about it? We all act this way. You began to find things out about her, the way she had attracted Andrew. Perhaps she'd been attractive to other people as well.' Alice put her hands up to her face. 'You were going to kill that other image with all the things it implied, particularly Andrew's infidelity.' With swift intuition, he added: 'Bury it deep in the coffins and make way for a new road. Maybe you had killed her. Where else did you get that mad idea about the cheese? Or if you hadn't Andrew had. Andrew had killed the young, the pretty, the desirable.'

'How you must hate me, Harry,' she said.

'Hatred, as Nesta might say, is akin to love.'

'Not your kind of hatred. Whatever Nesta was going to tell me about you it was enough to make you go to any lengths.' She sobbed and wrenched at the car door. 'Look, I can forgive you if you were only trying to make me ill, but . . . Why did you poison me? Why?'

She was breathing deeply, sobbing as she caught each breath. What he would do she hardly knew, but the orgy of fear she had experienced at Vair and afterwards at the surgery – a fear that had been none the less real because she now knew it was unnecessary – had left her indifferent to further terror.

As she was about to step out, he touched her arm. The question he asked her was totally unexpected, inconsequential, under the circumstances an insult.

'What d'you think? You talk to me about worry. How do you think it's been for me, ill, terrified to eat, suspecting everyone I loved of trying to kill me?'

'You aren't ill,' he said, 'and nobody's been trying to poison you. You're going to have a child.'

She said nothing, but she got out of the car. The air was cold and fresh. She leant against one of the wings and began to cry.

Presently he came out and stood beside her.

'I didn't know at first,' he said, 'but I guessed that day at the lunch when you got into such a state. When you fainted and I came up to Vair I wanted to examine you and make sure, but Andrew wouldn't let me.' He sighed heavily. 'I was glad in a way. You see, when you're in love with someone and she marries someone else the only way you can stop yourself going off your head is by self-deception. You can't face up to the facts and you tell yourself it's for companionship – what does the prayer book say? – the mutual society the one ought to have of the other. In your heart you know it isn't, it's a true marriage in every sense of the word, but you fool yourself, you get used to it and you achieve a kind of acquiescence.'

He looked at her as if he would have liked to take her hand. But she stood stunned, swaying a little, letting the wind play on her face.

'Then something else happens, what's happened to you. I couldn't fool myself any longer. I felt ten times worse than I did the day you told me you were engaged to him. It was as if the fact of the marriage had really been brought home to me at last. But I didn't want to have to tell you. The specialist could do that.' He gave a dry laugh. 'As if it needed a specialist! Any half-baked midwife could have seen it – the way you walked, the way your face had filled out and made you look ten years younger, that sickness. Why do you think you had all those fantastic ideas about Nesta? Didn't it ever occur to you – doesn't it now – that they were just the fancies of an imagination heightened by pregnancy?'

Still she was speechless. A thin rain had begun to fall, little more than a heavy mist. The cloying air was almost unbreathable. It dewed her face.

'Let someone else tell them, I thought. I knew I couldn't bear to see your happiness and his.' His voice broke and he cleared his throat. 'To see it,' he said, 'and to know it had nothing whatsoever to do with me.'

'I am happy,' she said.

She drew the black coat around her and pressed her hands to her waist. Happiness spiralled through her and seemed to burst into flower.

'Let's go,' he said.

'No.'

His eyelids fell and she looked into a face that was blank and blind.

'I'm going to telephone Andrew and get him to fetch me.'

'Andrew!' he said bitterly. 'Always Andrew. Funny, I always hoped, Alice. I thought it would only be a matter of time. He'd leave you and then – then you'd come to me.'

'Andrew will never leave me,' she said sternly.

She walked away from him quite fast, not looking back at all. The telephone box on the corner of the High Street and the slip road was empty. A gang of youths loitered outside The Boadicea and although her hair was coming down and she had bitten most of Jackie's lipstick from her mouth, one of them whistled. She slipped inside and closed the door, feeling her lips purse into that look of mock modesty and consciousness of beauty she had seen on the faces of other women but never felt on her own.

It was only when she lifted the receiver and touched the dial that she realised. She had no money. *She had no money.* For years now she had bought her way into everything and out of everything; always about her person had been the shiny blue book and the wad of notes. But at this moment when she wanted to do something that even the poorest could afford she had no money, not even a few coppers.

It didn't matter. She could walk. Independence was like a tonic, invigorating and joyous, and it was coupled with a new dependence – on Andrew.

The lights of the car caught her in their beam as she stepped from the box. For a moment she thought it was Harry returning for her and pity fought with indignation. Dazzled, she blinked and moved into the light. This car was small, red, gay.

'Andrew,' she said as calmly as if they were meeting by a long-arranged appointment.

'Bell, darling!' He jumped out of the car and took her in his arms. The loiterers again broke into whistles. Andrew didn't seem to notice them. 'I've been looking for you everywhere. I thought you'd run away from me. I've even been into The Boadicea to see if you were with Justin. Where have you been?'

'Seeing ghosts,' she said. I'll tell you all about it, she had been about to add. The words died and she smiled instead. Tell him about it, tell him that she had suspected her own husband of murder, of adultery, of outrageous deception? No marriage, especially so young a one as theirs, could survive it. Dependence and trust, she thought, time and patience. Time would clear up all the mysteries that remained.

Suddenly exhausted, the last spark of energy used up, she got into the car. She moved her body carefully, treasuring it and longing for the first stir of life. But when they got home he would ask her again where she had been and she would have to tell him. The answer came to her. To whom does a woman go when she suspects pregnancy but to her own doctor? Leaving Andrew without a word, running down to the High Street in the rain, all that was compatible with her hopes and fears.

For the moment she didn't speak. He was looking at her tenderly. 'I've just seen someone we used to know.' Hesitating, he chose his words with care. 'She was outside the Feasts', getting into an enormous Jaguar with a dented wing.'

'I know.'

'You've seen her too? I didn't speak to her,' he said. 'I was looking for you.'

Epilogue

Alice tucked the baby up in his pram. He was already asleep, a placid olive-skinned child with his father's black hair. She wheeled the pram into the shade of the diminutive porch. Andrew liked to see him there when he came home from afternoon school.

Now she had a whole two hours before her in which to read the book. It had arrived from the publisher's by the late post and for the hundredth time she read the title: *Trollope and The House of Commons* by Andrew Fielding. Some people said that artistic creation was like giving birth to a child and theirs had been a simultaneous gestation.

Her eye caught the name Saulsby in the second chapter. She smiled, shamefacedly recalling a different reaction. She had kept her resolution never to tell him what she had suspected, but some questions had to be asked.

'Why didn't you recognise the name when I asked you? You remember, I'd come back from Orphingham and you'd got my tea ready.'

He had laughed at her then, holding her tightly in his arms to take away the sting of mockery. 'What does Saulsby sound like when you say it with your mouth full of marzipan cake?'

'I see. Oh, Andrew, you thought I said *Salisbury*.'

'There must be one in every English country town.'

Still smiling, she turned the page, marvelling that a seven-letter word, once the cause of so much anguish, was now just a tiny jigsaw piece in the general pattern of contentment.

THE SECRET
HOUSE OF DEATH

**For
Dagmar Blass**

> Then is it sin
> To rush into the secret house of death
> Ere death dare come to us?
>
> *Antony and Cleopatra*

1

The man was heavily built and he drove a big car, a green Ford Zephyr. This was his third visit to the house called Braeside in Orchard Drive, Matchdown Park, and each time he parked his car on the grass patch in the pavement. He was in his early thirties, dark and not bad-looking. He carried a briefcase. He never stayed very long but Louise North who lived at Braeside with her husband Bob was always pleased to see him and admitted him with a smile.

These were facts and by now everyone who lived in the vicinity was aware of them. The Airedale who lived opposite and who belonged to some people called Winter obligingly kept them informed of the big man's visits. At day-long sentry-go behind his gate, the Airedale barked at strangers, kept silence for residents. He barked furiously now as the man strolled up Norths' path, knocked at the front door, and, thirty seconds later after a whispered word with Louise, disappeared inside. His duty done, the dog nosed out a brown earth-encrusted bone and began to gnaw it. One by one the women his outburst had alerted retreated from their windows and considered what they had seen.

The ground had been prepared, the seed sown. Now all that remained was for these enthusiastic gardeners to raise their crop of gossip and take it to market over the fences and over the tea-cups.

Of them all only Susan Townsend, who lived next door to Braeside, wanted to be left out of this exchange of merchandise. She sat typing each afternoon in her window and was no more proof than they were against raising her eyes when the dog barked. She wondered about the man's visits but, unlike her neighbours, she felt no lubricious curiosity. Her own husband had walked out on her just a year ago and the man's visits to Louise North touched chords of pain she hoped had begun to atrophy. Adultery, which excites and titillates the innocent, had brought her at twenty-six into a dismal abyss of loneliness. Let her neighbours speculate as to why the man came, what Louise wanted, what Bob thought, what would come of it all. From personal experience she knew the answers and all she wanted was to get on with her work, bring up her son and not get herself involved.

The man left forty minutes later and the Airedale barked again. He stopped abruptly as his owner approached and, standing on his hind legs – in which position he wriggled like a belly dancer – fawned on the two little boys she had fetched from school.

Susan Townsend went into her kitchen and put the kettle on. The side gate banged.

'Sorry we're so late, my dear,' said Doris Winter, stripping off her gloves and homing on the nearest radiator. 'But your Paul couldn't find his cap and we've been rooting through about fifty lockers.'

'Roger Gibbs had thrown it into the junior playground,' said Susan's son virtuously. 'Can I have a biscuit?'

'You may not. You'll spoil your tea.'

'Can Richard stay?'

It is impossible to refuse such a request when the putative guest's mother is at your elbow. 'Of course,' said Susan. 'Go and wash your hands.'

'I'm frozen,' Doris said. 'Winter by name and Winter by nature, that's me.' It was March and mild, but Doris was always cold, always huddled under layers of sweaters and cardigans and scarves. She divested herself gradually of her outer coverings, kicked off her shoes and pressed chilblained feet against the radiator. 'You don't know how I envy you your central heating. Which brings me to what I wanted to say. Did you see what I saw? Louise's boy-friend paying her yet another visit?'

'You don't know he's her boy-friend, Doris.'

'She says he's come to sell central heating. I asked her – got the cheek of the devil, haven't I? – and that's what she said. But when I mentioned it to Bob you could see he didn't have the least idea what I meant. "We're not having central heating," he said. "I can't afford it." There now. What d'you think of that?'

'It's their business and they'll have to sort it out.'

'Oh, quite. I couldn't agree more. I'm sure I'm not interested in other people's sordid private lives. I do wonder what she sees in this man, though. It's not as if he was all that to write home about and Bob's a real dream. I've always thought him by far the most attractive man around here, all that cool fresh charm.'

'You make him sound like a deodorant,' said Susan, smiling in spite of herself. 'Shall we go in the other room?'

Reluctantly, Doris unpeeled herself from the radiator and, carrying shoes, shedding garments in her wake, followed Susan into the living-room. 'Still, I suppose good looks don't really count,' she went on persistently. 'Human nature's a funny thing. I know that from my nursing days . . .'

Sighing inwardly, Susan sat down. Once on to her nursing days and the multifarious facets of human idiosyncrasy to be observed in a hospital ward, Doris was liable to go on for hours. She listened with half an ear to the inevitable spate of anecdote.

'. . . And that was just one example. It's amazing the people who are married to absolutely marvellous-looking other people and who fall in love with absolute horrors. I suppose they just want a change.'

'I suppose they do,' Susan said evenly.

'But fancy trusting someone and having complete faith in them and then finding they've been deceiving you all along. Carrying on and making a fool of you. Oh, my dear, forgive me! What have I said? I didn't mean you, I was speaking generally, I was —'

'It doesn't matter,' Susan cut in. She was used to tactlessness and it wasn't the tactlessness she minded but the sudden belated awareness on the part of speakers that they had dropped bricks. They insisted on covering up, making excuses and embarking on long disquisitions aimed to show that Susan's was an exceptional case. Doris did this now, giggling nervously and rubbing her still cold hands.

'I mean, of course, Julian *did* carry on behind your back, meeting what's-her-name, Elizabeth, when he was supposed to be working. And you've got a trusting nature like poor Bob. But Julian never did it on his own doorstep, did he? He never brought Elizabeth here.' Doris added transparently, 'I know that for sure. I should have seen.'

'I'm sure you would,' said Susan.

The two little boys came downstairs, their arms full of miniature cars. Susan settled them at the table, hoping Doris would take the hint and go. Perhaps she was overprotective but Paul was, after all, the child of a broken marriage and on her rested the responsibility of seeing he didn't grow up with too jaundiced a view of matrimony. She glanced at Doris now and slightly shook her head.

'Just listen to my dog,' Doris said too brightly. 'It's a wonder the neighbours don't complain.' She trotted to the window, gathering up shed garments as she went, and shook her fist at the Airedale, a gesture which inflamed him to a frenzy. He stuck his big woolly head over the gate and began to howl. 'Be quiet, Pollux!' Susan often wondered why the Airedale had been named after one of the Gemini. Orchard Drive must be thankful the Winters had no Castor to keep him company. 'It's the new baker's roundsman that's set him off this time,' Doris said sagely. 'He never barks at us or you or the Gibbses or the Norths. Which just goes to show it's fear with him and not aggressiveness, whatever people may say.' She glared at her son and said, as if instead of placidly eating bread and butter, he had been urging her to stay, 'Well, I can't hang about here all night, you know. I've got Daddy's dinner to get.'

Susan sat down with the children and ate a sandwich. If you had no 'Daddy's dinner' to get, you certainly prepared none for yourself and tea was a must. Paul crammed a last chocolate biscuit into his mouth and began pushing a diminutive red fire engine across the cloth and over the plates.

'Not at the table, darling.'

Paul scowled at her and Richard, whose hands had been itching to reach for a dumper truck, hid them under the table and gave him a virtuous glance. 'Please may I leave the table, Mrs Townsend?'

'I suppose so. Your hands aren't sticky, are they?'

But both little boys were on the floor by now, trundling their fleet of vehicles and making realistic if exaggerated engine sounds. They wriggled across the carpet on their stomachs, making for Susan's desk.

This was a Victorian mahogany affair full of niches and cubby-holes. Susan had sufficient empathy to understand its fascination for a five-year-old with a mania for Lilliputian vehicles and she tried to turn a blind eye when Paul used its shelves for garages, her writing paper boxes for ramps and her ribbon tins for turntables. She poured herself a second cup of tea and jumped, slopping it into her saucer, as the paper clip box fell to the floor and fasteners sprayed everywhere. While Richard, the ingratiating guest, scuttled to retrieve them, Paul stuck a jammy hand on Miss Willingale's manuscript and began to use it for a racing track.

'Now that's quite enough,' Susan said crisply. 'Outside both of you till bedtime.'

She washed the tea things and went upstairs. The children had crossed the road and were poking toys at Pollux through the curlicues of the wrought-iron gate. Susan opened the window.

'You're to stay on this side,' she called. 'All the cars will be along in a minute.'

The Airedale wagged his tail and made playful bites at a lorry bonnet Paul had thrust into his face. Susan, who hadn't been thinking about Julian nearly so much lately, suddenly remembered how he used to call Pollux an animated fun fur. This was the time Julian used to come home, the first of the commuting husbands to return. Pollux was still there and unchanged; as usual the children littered the front garden with their toys; the cherry trees were coming into bloom and the first lights of evening appearing in the houses. Only one thing had altered: Julian would never come again. He had always hated Matchdown Park, that detestable dormitory as he called it, and now he had a flat ten minutes from his office in New Bridge Street. He would be walking home now to vent upon Elizabeth his brilliance, his scorn, his eternal fussing over food, his didactic opinions. Elizabeth would have the joy and the excitement – and the fever-pitch exasperation – until the day came when Julian found someone else. Stop it, Susan told herself sternly, stop it.

She began to brush her fair shiny hair – thinner and less glossy since the divorce. Sometimes she wondered why she bothered. There was no one to see her but a little boy and the chance of a friend dropping in was almost nil. Married couples wanted to see other married couples, not a divorcee who hadn't even the advantage of being the guilty and therefore interesting party.

She had hardly seen any of those smart childless friends since the divorce. Minta Philpot had phoned once and cooled when she heard Susan hadn't a man in tow, much less was planning on remarriage. What had become of Lucius and Mary, of lovely remote Dian and her husband Greg? Perhaps Julian saw them, but he was Julian Townsend, the editor of *Certainty*, eternally sought after, eternally a personage.

The children were safely occupied on the lawn by now and the first homing husband had arrived, Martin Gibbs with a bunch of flowers for Betty. That, at any rate, awoke no painful memories. Julian had never been what he called a 'hothouse hubby' and Susan had been lucky to get flowers on her birthday.

And here, exactly on time, was Bob North.

He was tall, dark and exceptionally good-looking. His clothes were unremarkable but he wore them with a grace that seemed unconscious and his masculinity just saved him from looking like a male model. The face was too classically perfect to suit modern cinematic requirements and yet it was not the face of a gigolo, not in the least Italianate. It was an English face, Celtic, clear-skinned and frank.

Susan had lived next door to him and his wife since they had moved to Braeside two years before. But Julian had despised his neighbours, calling them bourgeois, and of them all only Doris had been sufficiently pushing and thick-skinned to thrust her friendship on the Townsends. Susan knew Bob just well enough to justify the casual wave she now gave him from her window.

He waved back with the same degree of amiable indifference, took the ignition key from his car and strolled out on to the pavement. Here he stood for a few seconds gazing at the ruts the green Zephyr had made in the turf. His face had grown faintly troubled but when he turned and glanced upwards, Susan retreated, unwilling to meet his eyes. Herself the victim of a deceiver, she knew how quickly a fellow-feeling for Bob North could grow, but she didn't want to be involved in the Norths' problems. She went downstairs and called Paul in.

When he was in bed, she sat beside him and read the nightly instalment of Beatrix Potter. Strong-featured, flaxen-haired, he was his mother's son, as unlike Julian as could be.

'Now read it all again,' he said as she closed the book.

'You must be joking. It's ten to seven. *Ten to seven.*'

'I like that book, but I don't think a dog would ever go to tea with a cat or take it a bunch of flowers. It's stupid to give people flowers. They only die.' He threw himself about on the bed, laughing scornfully. Perhaps, Susan thought, as she tucked him up again, he wasn't so unlike Julian, after all.

'I tidied up all your papers,' he said, opening one eye. 'I can have my cars on your desk, if I tidy up, can't I?'

'I suppose so. I bet you didn't tidy up the garden.'

Immediately he simulated exhaustion, pulling the bed-clothes over his head.

'One good turn deserves another,' Susan said and she went out into the garden to collect the scattered fleet of cars from lawn and flower-beds.

The street was deserted now and dusk was falling. The lamps, each a greenish translucent jewel, came on one by one and Winters' gate cast across the road a fantastic shadow like lace made by a giant's hand.

Susan was groping for toys in the damp grass when she heard a voice from behind the hedge. 'I think this is your son's property.' Feeling a little absurd – she had been on all-fours – she got up and took the two-inch long lorry from Bob North's hands.

'Thanks,' she said. 'It would never do to lose this.'

'What is it, anyway?'

'A kind of road sweeper. He had it in his stocking.'

'Good thing I spotted it.'

'Yes, indeed.' She moved away from the fence. This was

the longest conversation she had ever had with Bob North and she felt it had been deliberately engineered, that he had come out on purpose to speak to her. Once again he was staring at the ruined turf. She felt for a truck under the lilac bush.

'Mrs Townsend – er, Susan?'

She sighed to herself. It wasn't that she minded his use of her christian name but that it implied an intimacy he might intend to grow between them. I'm as bad as Julian, she thought.

'Sorry,' she said. 'How rude of me.'

'Not at all. I just wondered . . .' He had dark blue eyes, a smoky marbled blue like lapis, and now he turned them away to avoid hers. 'You do your typing at the window, don't you? Your writing or whatever it is?'

'I do typed copies of manuscripts, yes. But only for this one novelist.' Of course, he wasn't asking about this aspect of it at all. Anything to deflect him. 'I wouldn't consider . . .'

'I wanted to ask you,' he interrupted, 'if ever . . . Well, if today . . .' His voice tailed away. 'No, forget it.'

'I don't look out of the window much,' Susan lied. She was deeply embarrassed. For perhaps half a minute they confronted each other over the hedge, eyes downcast, not speaking. Susan fidgeted with the little car she was holding and then Bob North said suddenly:

'You're lucky to have your boy. If we, my wife and I . . .'

That doesn't work, Susan almost cried aloud. Children don't keep people together. Don't you read the newspapers? 'I must go in,' she stammered. 'Good night.' She gave him a quick awkward smile. 'Good night, Bob.'

'Good night, Susan.'

So Doris had been right, Susan thought distastefully. There was something and Bob was beginning to guess. He was on the threshold, just where she had been eighteen months ago when Julian, who had always kept strict office hours, started phoning with excuses at five about being late home.

'Elizabeth?' he had said when Susan took that indiscreet phone call. 'Oh, *that* Elizabeth. Just a girl who keeps nagging me to take her dreary cookery features.'

What did Louise say? 'Oh, *that* man. Just a fellow who keeps nagging me to buy central heating.'

Back to Miss Willingale. Paul hadn't exaggerated when he had said he had tidied her desk. It was as neat as a pin, all the paper stacked and the two ballpoint pens put on the left of the typewriter. He had even emptied her ashtray.

Carefully she put all the cars away in their boxes before sitting down. This was the twelfth manuscript she had prepared for Jane Willingale in eight years, each time transforming a huge unwieldy ugly duckling of blotted scribblings into a perfect swan, spotless, clear and neat. Swans they had been indeed. Of the twelve, four had been best sellers, the rest close runners-up. She had worked for Miss Willingale while still Julian's secretary, after her marriage and after Paul was born. There seemed no reason to leave her in the lurch just because she was now divorced. Besides, apart from the satisfaction of doing the job well, the novels afforded her a huge incredulous amusement. Or they had done until she had embarked on this current one and found herself in the same position as the protagonist. . . .

It was called *Foetid Flesh*, a ridiculous title for a start. If you spelt foetid with an O no one could pronounce it and if you left the O out no one would know what it meant. Adultery again, too. Infidelity had been the theme of *Blood Feud* and *Bright Hair about the Bone*, but in those days she hadn't felt the need to identify.

Tonight she was particularly sensitive and she found herself wincing as she re-read the typed page. Three literal mistakes in twenty-five lines. . . . She lit a cigarette and wandered into the hall where she gazed at her own reflection in the long glass. Tactless Doris had hit the nail on the head when she said it didn't matter how good-looking a person's husband or wife was. It must be variety and excitement the Julians and the Louises of this world wanted.

She was thinner now but she still had a good figure and she knew she was pretty. Brown eyes and fair hair were an unusual combination and her hair was naturally fair, still the same shade it had been when she was Paul's age. Julian used to say she reminded him of the girl in some picture by Millais.

All that had made no difference. She had done her best to be a good wife but that had made no difference either. Probably Bob was a good husband, a handsome man with a pleasing personality any woman might be proud of. She turned away from the mirror, aware that she was beginning to bracket herself and her next-door neighbour. It made her uneasy and she tried to dismiss him from her mind.

2

Susan had just left Paul and Richard at the school gates when Bob North's car passed her. That was usual, a commonplace daily happening. This morning, however, instead of joining the High Street stream that queued to enter the North Circular, the car pulled into the kerb a dozen yards ahead of her and Bob, sticking his head out of the window, went through the unmistakable dumbshow of the driver offering someone a lift.

She went up to the car, feeling a slight trepidation at this sudden show of friendship. 'I was going shopping in Harrow,' she said, certain it would be out of his way. But he smiled easily.

'Fine,' he said. 'As it happens, I have to go into Harrow. I'm leaving the car for a big service. I'll have to go in by train tomorrow, so let's hope the weather cheers up.'

For once Susan was glad to embark upon this dreary and perennial topic. She got into the car beside him, remembering an editorial of Julian's in which he had remarked that the English, although partakers in the most variable and quixotic climate in the world, never become used to its vagaries, but comment upon them with shock and resentment as if all their lives had been spent in the predictable monsoon. And despite Julian's scornful admonitions, Susan now took up Bob's cue. Yesterday had been mild, today was damp with an icy wind. Spring was certainly going to be late in coming. He listened to it all, replying in kind, until she felt his embarrassment must be as great as her own. Was he already regretting having said a little too much the night before? Perhaps he had offered her the lift in recompense; perhaps he was anxious not to return to their old footing of casual indifference but attempting to create an easier neighbourly friendship. She must try to keep the conversation on this level. She mustn't mention Louise.

They entered the North Circular where the traffic was heavy and Susan racked her brains for something to say.

'I'm going to buy a present for Paul, one of those electrically-operated motorways. It's his birthday on Thursday.'

'Thursday, is it?' he said, and she wondered why, taking his eyes briefly from the busy road, he gave her a quick indecipherable glance. Perhaps she had been as indiscreet in mentioning her son as in talking of Louise. Last night he had spoken of his sorrow at his childlessness. 'Thursday,' he said again, but not interrogatively this time. His hands tightened a little on the wheel and the bones showed white.

'He'll be six.'

She knew he was going to speak then, that the moment had come. His whole body seemed to grow tense beside her and she perceived in him that curious holding of the breath and almost superhuman effort to conquer inhibition that precedes the outpouring of confession or confidence.

The Harrow bus was moving towards its stop and she was on the point of telling him, of saying that she could easily get out here and bus the rest of the way, when he said with an abruptness that didn't fit his words, 'Have you been very lonely?'

That was unexpected, the last question she had been prepared for. 'I'm not sure what you mean,' she said hesitantly.

'I said, have you been lonely? I meant since your divorce.'

'Well, I . . .' Her cheeks burned and she looked down into her lap, at the black leather gloves that lay limply like empty useless hands. Her own hands clenched, but she relaxed them deliberately. 'I've got over it now,' she said shortly.

'But at the time, immediately afterwards,' he persisted.

The first night had been the worst. Not the first night she and Julian had slept apart but the night after the day when he had gone for good. She had stood at the window for hours, watching the people come and go. It had seemed to her then that no-one but herself in the whole of her little world was alone. Everyone had an ally, a partner, a lover. Those married couples she could see had never seemed so affectionate, so bound together, before. Now she could remember quite distinctly how Bob and Louise had come home late from some dance or party, had laughed together in their front garden and gone into the house hand in hand.

She wasn't going to tell him any of that. 'Of course, I had a lot of adjusting to do,' she said, 'but lots of women get deserted by their husbands. I wasn't unique.'

Plainly he had no intention of wasting sympathy on her case. 'And husbands by their wives,' he said. Here we go, Susan thought. Surely it couldn't take more than ten minutes before they got into Harrow? 'We're in the same boat, Susan.'

'Are we?' She didn't raise her eyebrows; she gave him no cue.

'Louise is in love with someone else.' The words sounded cold, deliberate, matter-of-fact. But when Susan made no reply, he suddenly burst out raggedly, 'You're a discreet, cagey one, aren't you? Louise ought to thank you. Or maybe you're on her side. Yes, I suppose that's what it is. You've got a big anti-men thing because of what happened to you. It would be different, wouldn't it, if some girl came calling on me while Louise was out of the house?'

Susan said quietly, although her hands were shaking, 'It was kind of you to give me a lift. I didn't know I was expected to show my gratitude by telling you what your wife does while you're out.'

He caught his breath. 'Perhaps that's what I did expect.'

'I don't want to have any part in your private life, yours and Louise's. Now I'd like to get out, please.'

He reacted peculiarly to this. Susan had thought refusal impossible, but instead of slowing the car down, he swung with hardly any warning into the fast lane. A car immediately behind them braked and hooted. Bob cut into the roundabout, making the tyres screech, and moved on a skid into the straight stretch. His foot went down hard on the accelerator and Susan saw his mouth ease into the smile of triumph. Indignant as she was, for a moment she was also genuinely afraid. There was something wild and ungoverned in his face that some women might have found attractive, but to Susan he simply looked very young, a reckless child.

The needle on the speedometer climbed. There were men who thought fast dangerous driving a sign of virility and this perhaps was what he wanted to demonstrate. His pride had been hurt and she mustn't hurt it further. So instead of protesting, she only said dryly, although her palms were wet, 'I should hardly have thought your car was in need of a service.'

He gave a low unhappy chuckle. 'You're a nice girl, Susan. Why didn't I have the sense to marry someone like you?' Then he put out the indicator, slowed and took the turn. 'Did I frighten you? I'm sorry.' He bit his lip. 'I'm so damned unhappy.' He sighed and put his left hand up to his forehead. The dark lock fell across it and once more Susan saw the bewildered boy. 'I suppose he's with her now, leaving his car outside for everyone to see. I can picture it all. That ghastly dog barks and they all go to their windows. Don't they? Don't they, Susan?'

'I suppose so.'

'For two pins I'd drop back to lunch one day and catch them.'

'That's the shop I want, Bob, so if you wouldn't mind ...'

'And that's my garage.'

He got out and opened the door for her courteously. Julian had never bothered with small attentions of this kind. Julian's face had never shown what he was feeling. Bob was far better looking than Julian, franker, easier to know – and yet? It wasn't a kind face, she thought. There was sensitivity there, but of the most egocentric kind, the sensitivity that feels for itself, closes itself to the pains of others, demands, grasps, suffers only when its possessor is thwarted.

She stepped out of the car and stood on the pavement beside him in the cold wind. It whipped colour into the skin over his cheekbones so that suddenly he looked healthy and carefree. Two girls went past them and one of them looked back at Bob, appraisingly, calculatingly, in the way men look at pretty women. He too had caught the glance and it was something of a shock to Susan to watch him preen himself faintly and lean against the car with conscious elegance. She picked up her basket and said briskly, 'Thanks. I'll see you around.'

'We must do this more often,' he said with a shade of sarcasm.

The car was still at the pavement edge and he still sitting at the wheel when she came out of the toyshop. How hard the past year had made her! Once she would have felt deeply for anyone in his situation, her own situation of twelve months before. She couldn't escape the feeling he was acting a part, putting all the energy he could muster into presenting himself as an object of pity. He said he was unhappy, but he didn't look unhappy. He looked as if he wanted people to think he was. Where were the lines of strain, the silent miserable reserve? Their eyes met for a second and she could have sworn he made his mouth droop for her benefit. He raised his hand in a brief salute, started the engine and moved off along the concrete lane between the petrol pumps.

In another *Certainty* editorial, Julian Townsend had averred that almost the only green spaces remaining in north-west London were cemeteries. One of these, the overspill graveyard of some central borough, separated the back gardens of Orchard Drive from the North Circular Road. From a distance it still had a prettiness, an almost rural air, for the elms still raised their black skeletal arms against the sky and rooks still nested in them. But, taking the short cut home across the cemetery, you could only forget you were in a suburb, on the perimeter of a city, by the exercise of great imagination and by half closing your senses. Instead of scented grass and pine needles, you smelt the sourness of the chemical factory, and between the trees the traffic could always be seen as if on an eternal senseless conveyor belt, numberless cars, transporters carrying more cars, scarlet buses.

Susan got off one of these buses and took the cemetery path home. A funeral had taken place the day before and a dozen wreaths lay on the fresh mound, but a night of frost and half a day of bitter wind had curled and blackened their petals. It was still cold. The clouds were amorphous, dishcloth-coloured, with ragged edges where the wind tore them. A day, Susan thought, calculated to depress even the most cheerful. Struggling across the bleakest part of the expanse, she thought that to an observer she must appear as she held her coat collar up against her cheeks like Oliver Twist's mother on her last journey to the foundling hospital. Then she smiled derisively. At least she wasn't pregnant or poor or homeless.

Now as she came into the dip on the Matchdown Park side, she could see the backs of the Orchard Drive houses. Her own and the Norths' were precisely identical and this brought her a feeling of sadness and waste. It seemed too that their occupants' lives were destined to follow a similar pattern, distrust succeeding love, bitterness and rupture, distrust.

Two men were coming down the path from Louise's back door. They had cups of tea in their hands, the steam making faint plumes in the chill air, and Susan supposed they were labourers from the excavations on the road immediately below her. They had been digging up that bit of tarmac for weeks now, laying drains or cables – who knew what they ever did? – but it had never occurred to Susan to offer them tea. To her they had merely meant the nuisance of having clay brought in on Paul's shoes and the staccato screaming chatter of their pneumatic drills.

She let herself out of the cemetery gate and crossed the road. Inside the workmen's hut a red fire burned in a brazier made from a perforated bucket. As she approached the gate in her own fence the heat from this fire reached her, cheerful, heartening, a warm acrid breeze.

The men who had the teacups moved up to the fire and squatted in front of it. Susan was about to say good morning to them when a third emerged from the trench that never seemed to grow deeper or shallower and gave a shrill wolf whistle. No woman ever really minds being whistled at. Does any woman ever respond? Susan fixed her face into the dead-pan expression she reserved for such occasions and entered her own garden.

Out of the corner of her eye, she saw the whistling man march up Louise's path in quest of his tea. The fence was six feet high between the two back doors. Susan could see nothing, but she heard Louise laugh and the exchange of badinage that followed that laughter.

Susan went through the house and out of the front door to bring in the milk. Contrary to Bob's prediction, there was no green Zephyr on the grass patch, but wedged into the earth at the far side of the garden she caught sight of its counterpart in miniature. Inadvertently she had left one of Paul's cars out all night.

As she stooped to pick it up, shaking the earth from its wheels, Doris appeared from Betty Gibbs's house with Betty following her to prolong their conversation and their last goodbyes as far as the gate.

'An endless stream of them,' Susan heard Betty say, 'always up and down the path. Why can't they make their own tea? They've got a fire. Oh, hallo.' Susan had been spotted. She moved towards them, wishing she felt less reluctant. 'Doris and I have been watching the way our neighbour runs her canteen.'

'No visit from lover-boy today,' said Doris. 'That's what it is.'

'Louise has been making tea for those men for weeks and weeks,' Susan protested, and as she did so she felt a violent self-disgust. Who decreed that she should always find herself in the role of Louise's defending counsel? The woman was nothing to her, less than nothing. How smug she must appear to these perfectly honest, ordinary neighbours! Smug and censorious and disapproving. There was earth on her hands and now she found herself brushing it off fastidiously as if it were a deeper defilement. 'Come,' she said and she managed an incredulous smile, 'you don't really think Louise is interested in any of those workmen?'

'I know *you* don't. You're too discreet to live.'

'I'm sorry, Doris. I don't mean to be a prig.' Susan took a deep breath. 'I just hope things will work out for the Norths, that's all, and that they won't be too unhappy.'

The other two women seemed for a moment taken aback. It was as if unhappiness as the outcome of the Norths' difficulties had never occurred to them. Excitement, perhaps, or huge scandal or further sensational food for speculation, but nothing as real as grief. Doris tossed her head and Susan waited for the sharp retort. Instead Doris said mildly and too loudly, 'I'll be in with Paul at the usual time.'

It was a sound characteristic of Louise North that had alerted her and caused the swift artificial change of subject. Behind them on the Braeside path came the sharp clatter of the metal-tipped high heels Louise always wore. Roped into this conspiracy of gossip, Susan didn't turn round. Her back was towards Louise but the other women faced her and it was both comic and distasteful to see the way they drew themselves up before Betty, the weaker of the two, managed a feeble smile and a twitch of the head.

Susan would have felt less weary of them and less sickened had they accorded the same treatment to Julian a year ago. But as soon as trouble between her husband and herself became evident these women had positively fawned on him. In Matchdown Park, surely the last bastion of Victorianism, the adulterer was still fascinating, the adulteress fallen. Deliberately she crossed back into her own garden and gave Louise a broad smile and a hearty untypical, 'Hallo, there!'

Her neighbour had come into the garden on the same mission as her own and in her hands she held two pint bottles of milk, their foil tops pecked to pieces by blue tits. 'Hallo,' said Louise in her little girl's voice that always had a whine in it.

'Bob gave me a lift into Harrow this morning.'

'Oh, yes?' Louise couldn't have sounded less interested, but just the same she approached the fence, picking her way across the soggy grass. Her heels sank in just as her lover's car tyres had sunk into the grass plot.

Louise always wore very high heels. Without them she would have been less than five feet tall, about the size of a girl of twelve, but like most tiny women she set herself perpetually on stilts and piled her hair into a stack on top of her head. Beneath it her little white face looked wizened and shrunken. Of course, it was particularly cold this morning and as usual Doris had begun to shout about the low temperature at the top of her voice, reiterating her urgent desire to get back to her fire as she made her slow way back across the road.

'Freezing! I've never known such weather. Goodness knows why we don't all pack up and go to Australia!'

'It isn't as cold as all that,' Louise whispered, and now she was leaning over the fence. It only reached to the average person's waist, but she rested her elbows on it and stared wistfully at Susan. 'There are worse things,' she said, 'than a bit of cold.'

'I must want my head tested, hanging about here,' Doris shouted, still on the pavement, still staring frankly at Louise. 'I'm a mass of chilblains as it is.'

'Well, I really am going in,' Susan said firmly and she closed the front door behind her. For a moment she had had the uneasy notion that Louise too wanted to confide in her, only it was impossible. She hardly knew the woman. The idea that an intimacy might be about to grow between her and the Norths really frightened her. Yesterday they had been the merest acquaintances, while now . . . It almost seemed that Julian had been right when he said you chose your friends but your neighbours were thrust upon you and the only protection was to hold yourself aloof. No doubt, she had been too forthcoming. It might even be that her reputation for discretion at which Doris had hinted had reached the North's ears, so that separately they had decided to make use of her as the repository of their secrets.

Susan shrugged, hardened her heart and settled herself at her desk. It was a bore, but there was nothing to be afraid of. And why did she suddenly feel this curious dichotomy, this desire both to be miles away and at the same time to go outside once more and look at Braeside, that strangely secret house where the windows were seldom opened and where no child ever played on the lawn? It was as if she wanted to reassure herself, to settle a doubt or allay a fear.

Presently she spread her hands across the keys and emptied her mind.

At half past three she went into the kitchen. A resolution had been forming subconsciously while she worked and now she brought it out into the open. In future she would have as little as possible to do with the Norths. No more accepting of lifts, no more garden talks. It might even be prudent to be on the alert for their comings and goings to avoid bumping into them.

The drills were screaming behind the back fence. Susan put the kettle on, watching the big elms sway in the wind with the pliability of grass blades. From here she could just see the workmen's fire glowing crimson in its punctured bucket and the workmen's faces, 'dark faces pale against that rosy flame' as they passed across the threshold of their hut. The sight of another's hearth which others share and enjoy always brings a sense of exclusion and of loneliness. The brazier, incandescent and vivid, its flames burning translucent blue against the red heart, brought to mind the improvised stoves of chestnut sellers and she remembered how she and Julian, on their way to a theatre, had sometimes stopped to buy and warm their hands.

The sky was blue now like arctic ice and the clouds which tumbled across it were pillowy glacial floes. Susan's kettle bumped, the drills shrilled and then, clearly and succinctly through the louder sounds, there came a gentle tap at the front door.

Pollux hadn't barked. It must be a neighbour or a familiar visitor to the street. Surely it was too early for Doris to be bringing Paul? Besides, Doris always came to the back door and Doris always shouted and banged.

The drills died away on a whine. Susan crossed the hall and the little tap was repeated. She opened the door and when she saw who her caller was she felt an actual dismal sinking of the heart.

What was the use of resolving to avoid people when those people intruded themselves upon you? Louise North wasn't wearing her little girl's size eight coat, but had wrapped it round her thin shoulders. She stepped inside, shivering, before Susan could hinder her and the little hammer heels rattled on the wood-block floor. Louise was trembling, she was scarcely steady on her feet.

'Spare me five minutes, Susan? Five minutes to talk?' She lifted her eyes, bending her head back to look up into Susan's face. Those eyes, the pale insipid blue of glass beads, were watering from the cold. But she's only come from next door, Susan thought, unless she's crying. She *is* crying. 'You don't mind if I call you Susan, do you? You must call me Louise.'

You're at the end of your tether. Susan almost said it aloud. Two tears coursed down Louise's thin face. She brushed at them and scuttled towards the living-room. 'I know the way, she muttered. 'It's just the same as my house.' Her heels left a twin trail of little pits, ineradicable permanent holes in the parquet.

Susan followed her helplessly. Louise's face was muddy with make-up applied over stale make-up and tear-stains. Now in the warm quiet living-room she dropped her head into her hands and tears trickled through her fingers on to the gooseflesh of her wrists.

3

Susan stood by the window and waited for Louise to stop crying. She was anxious not to prejudge her, but she felt impatient. Louise had no handkerchief. Now, in a feeble and embarrassed way, she was fumbling in the pockets of her coat and looking vaguely about her for the handbag she hadn't brought.

In the kitchen the kettle was bumping on the gas. Susan knew it was the sponge she had put inside it years and years ago to absorb the lime deposit the water made. The sponge had become petrified with time and the noise of this piece of rock lurching against the kettle lining made the only sound. Susan went into the kitchen, turned off the gas and fetched Louise a clean handkerchief.

'I'm ever so sorry,' Louise gulped. The tears had made her childish face pink and puffy. She put up a hand to her hair, retrieving wisps and poking them back into the piled lacquered structure that gave her an extra two inches. 'You must think me very uncontrolled, coming here and breaking down like this when we hardly know each other.' She bit her lip and went on miserably. 'But my friends are all Catholics, you see, and I don't like to talk to them about it. I mean, Father O'Hara and Eileen and people like that. I know what they'd say.'

Susan had forgotten Louise was a Catholic. Now she remembered seeing her go off to church sometimes with Eileen O'Donnell, black lace scarves in their hands to put over their heads at the mass. 'Of course, I can't get a divorce,' Louise said, 'but I thought – Oh, dear, I can't put it into words. I've taken up your time getting into a state and now I can't seem to say it.' She gave Susan a sidelong glance. 'I'm like you, you see, I'm rather reserved.'

Susan didn't altogether care for the comparison. Reserve doesn't take itself into a neighbour's house and weep and borrow handkerchiefs. 'Well, suppose you sit there and calm down a bit while I make the tea?'

'You're awfully kind, Susan.'

The drills began their deafening clamour while Susan was cutting bread and butter. She began to think what she should say to Louise when she returned to the living-room, but she feared any advice she could give would differ hardly at all from that proffered by Eileen or the priest. As to what Louise was about to say to her, she had no difficulty at all in guessing. It would be a defiant recital of how love gave you the right to do as you chose; how it was better to spoil one life now than ruin two for ever; how you must take what you can get while you were still young. Julian had said it all already and had expressed it more articulately than Louise ever would. Should there be any hesitations or gaps in her narrative, Susan thought bitterly, she could always provide excuses from Julian's own logical and entirely heartless apologia. She went back with the teacloth and the plates. Louise was standing up now, watching the quivering elms and the cold rushing sky, her face stricken with woe.

'Feeling a bit better?' Susan asked, and she added rather repressively, 'Paul will be in in a moment.' She hoped her face made it plain to her visitor that she didn't want her son, the child of a broken marriage and already the witness of grown-up grief, to hear yet again an adult's marital problems and see an adult's tears.

But Louise, like her husband, had little interest or concern to spare for other people's anxieties. 'Oh, dear,' she said pathetically, 'and Doris Winter with him, I suppose. Susan, I've been screwing up my courage all afternoon to come to you. It took me hours and hours before I dared. But you were so nice and friendly to me in the garden and I . . . Look, Bob's going to be late tonight and I'll be all alone. Would you come in to me? Just for an hour?'

The side gate clicked and slammed. For a second the two women's eyes met and Susan thought how innocent Louise looked. As if she wouldn't hurt a fly. Why bother with flies when you can torture people?

'Hi, there!' Doris called from the back door. 'Late again. I'm dying for a cup of tea.'

'Will you stay and have one?'

Louise shook her head and picked up her coat from the chair. Her face was still blotched and tear-stained. She looked up when Doris came in and a small pathetic smile trembled on her lips.

'Oh, I didn't know you'd got company,' said Doris, 'or I wouldn't have come bursting in.' Her eyes were wide with excitement at the idea she might by chance have come upon adventure at the least likely time and in the least likely place. She drew her stiff red fingers out of the woollen gloves and, turning towards Susan, raised an interrogatory eyebrow. Susan didn't respond and it amused her to see Doris's greedy anticipation gradually give way to chagrin until, like a battery in need of recharging from some source of power, she attached herself to the radiator and said sulkily, 'All right for some. I've been frozen all day.'

Then Louise said it. Afterwards Susan often thought that if her neighbour had kept silent or merely made some harmless rejoinder, the whole ensuing tragedy would have taken a different course or perhaps have been altogether averted. In spite of her determination not to be involved, she would have accepted Louise's invitation for that night out of weakness and pity. She would have learned and understood and been in a position to defend.

But Louise, fumbling with her coat and hesitating whether to pocket Susan's handkerchief or leave it on the chair arm, turned those watery glass bead eyes on Doris and said, 'I'll have my central heating next winter. They're soon going to put it in.' A tiny spark of enthusiasm brought colour into her cheeks. 'I expect you've seen the man here.'

Doris's always active eyebrows jerked as if she had a tic and almost disappeared into her fringe.

'I'll just see you to the door,' Susan said coldly. Rage bit off the christian name she had meant to use and which would have softened the dismissal. That Louise should come here and cry about her love affair, then persist in employing the blind she had used to deceive everyone, filled her with choking anger. The dishonesty and the duplicity were past bearing.

Louise tripped as she crossed the hall and Susan didn't put out a hand to steady her. The metal heel left a pit and a long gash in the parquet Susan and her cleaner, Mrs Dring, kept so carefully polished. Illogically, this wanton damage was more maddening than Louise's slyness and her lack of control. At the front door she stopped and whispered:

'You'll come tonight?'

'I'm afraid I can't leave Paul.'

'Come tomorrow then, for coffee,' Louise pleaded. 'Come as soon as you've taken Paul to school.'

Susan sighed. It was on the tip of her tongue to say she would never come, that the Norths and their problems were nothing to her. Bob would be away for once, so like a child, Louise wanted Susan's shoulder to cry on. Didn't it occur to her that Susan was always alone, that Julian had gone away for good? It was all Julian's fault. If he had been here, he wouldn't have allowed her to be the Norths' mediator and counsellor, but then if he had been here none of this confiding would have begun. It was only because she had been deserted and divorced that the Norths thought her a suitable adviser. Her experiences qualified her; she might be supposed to understand the motives of wife and husband; her knowledge gave her the edge over the priest and the devout unworldly friends.

'Louise . . .' she said helplessly, opening the door and letting the chill damp air wash over her hot face.

'Please, Susan. I know it's ugly and beastly, but I can't help it. Please say you'll come.'

'I'll come at eleven,' Susan said. She could no longer resist that look of agonised supplication. Still exasperated but almost resigned, she followed Louise outside to call the boys in for their tea.

Louise's heels tap-tapped away into the side entrance. Her shoes had pointed toes, curled and wrinkled at the tips where her own toes were too short to reach. In her long floppy coat and those absurd over-large shoes, she reminded Susan of a little girl dressing up in her mother's clothes.

For a moment Susan let her gaze travel over the Braeside façade. Of all the houses in the street it was the only one whose occupants had never troubled to improve its appearance. Susan was no admirer of rustic gnomes, of carriage lamps or birdbaths on Doric pediments, but she recognised a desire for individuality in the Gibbs's potted bay tree, a wistful need of beauty in the O'Donnells' window boxes.

Braeside was as stark now as it must have been when it was first built ten years before. Since that time it had never been painted and the perpetually closed windows looked as if they would never open. The house belonged to the Norths and yet it had an air of property rented on a short lease as if its owners regarded it as a place of temporary sojourn rather than a home.

No trees had been planted in the front garden. Almost every other house had a kanzan or cypresses or a prunus. The Braeside garden was just a big square of earth planted entirely with daffodils and with a few inches of turf bordering it. The daffodils looked as if they were grown by a market gardener to sell, they stood in such straight rows.

But Louise never even cut them. Susan could remember how in springs gone by she had sometimes seen her neighbour walk carefully between the rows to touch the waxen green leaves or stoop to smell the fresh and faintly acrid scent of their blossoms.

They were as yet only in bud, each tightly folded yellow head as sealed as the house itself and, like it, seeming to hold secrets.

Susan called the children and hustled them in through the side gate. The Braeside windows looked black and opaque, effective shutters for a woman to hide behind and cry her eyes out.

Coping repressively with Doris's curiosity and trying to give Paul an adequate but necessarily untruthful answer to his question as to why Mrs North had been crying, left Susan exhausted and cross. She badly needed someone with whom she could discuss this crisis in the Norths' lives and she thought rather wistfully of how Doris must be now regaling John with its latest phase. A man would see the whole matter more straightforwardly – and less subtly – than she could; a man would advise how to avoid involvement with kindness and tact.

When the phone rang at seven-thirty she knew it must be Julian and for a moment she thought seriously of casting her troubles on his shoulders. If only Julian were more human, less the counterpart of an actor playing a brittle role in an eternal drawing-room comedy! And since his new marriage he had grown even more suave and witty and in a way unreal. Contemptuous he had always been, misanthropic and exclusive, besides having this odd conviction of his that dwellers in a suburb were quite alien to himself, sub-human creatures leading a vegetable or troglodyte existence. He was indifferent to their activities, although the doings of his own circle often aroused in him an almost feminine curiosity, and as soon as Susan heard his voice her hopes went. Consulting Julian would be only to invite a scathing rebuff.

'You said this was the most convenient time,' said the drawling pedantic voice, 'so, since I aim to please, I've dragged myself away in the middle of my prawn cocktail.'

'Hallo, Julian.'

His habit of plunging into the middle of things without greeting, preamble or announcing who he was, always irritated her. Of course an ex-wife might be expected to recognise her ex-husband's voice; that was fair enough. But Susan knew he did it to everyone, to the remotest acquaintance. In his own estimation he was unique, and it was unthinkable to him that even the deaf or the phone-shy could mistake him for anyone else.

'How are you?'

'I am well.' This strictly correct but unidiomatic reply was another Julianism. He was never 'fine' or even 'very well'. 'How are things in Matchdown Park?'

'Much the same,' said Susan, bracing herself for the sneer.

'I was afraid of that. Now, listen, my dear, I'm afraid Sunday's out as far as having Paul is concerned. Elizabeth's mamma wants us for the weekend and naturally I can't chicken out of that even if I want to, which I don't.'

'I suppose you could take him with you.'

'Lady Maskell isn't exactly mad about having tots around the place.'

It had always seemed odd to Susan that Julian, the editor of a left-wing review, should in the first place have married a baronet's daughter and secondly should set so much store by the landed gentry to which his in-laws belonged.

'This is the second time since Christmas you've put him off,' she said. 'It seems rather pointless the judge making an order for you to have him every fourth Sunday if you're always going to be too busy. He was looking forward to it.'

'Oh, you can take him out somewhere. Take him to the zoo.'

'It's his birthday the day after tomorrow. I thought I'd better remind you.'

'Flap not, my dear. Elizabeth's got it down on her shopping list to make sure we keep it in mind.'

'That's fine then, isn't it?' Susan's voice shook with annoyance. It had been an impossible day, thronged with impossible people. 'You'd better get back to your steak,' she said in the nagging tone he both provoked and hated, 'or whatever's next on the menu.' Elizabeth had got it on her shopping list! Susan could imagine that list: canned prawns, peppers, cocktail sticks, birthday present for 'tot', fillet steak, chocs for Mummy. . . . How maddening Julian was! Strange that whereas remembered words and phrases of his could sadden her and awaken pain, these weekly telephon : conversations never did.

He was bound to send Paul something utterly ridiculous, an electric guitar or a skin-diving outfit, neither of which were outside the bounds of what Julian or Elizabeth would consider suitable for a middle-class suburban child on his sixth birthday. Susan went around the house bolting the doors for the night. Usually on this evening task she never bothered to glance up at the side of Braeside, but tonight she did and it disquieted her to see the place in darkness.

Could Louise already have gone to bed? It was scarcely eight o'clock. A simple curiosity, an inquisitiveness as indefensible as Doris's possessed her, drawing her into the front garden to stare frankly at the house next door. It was a blot of darkness amid its brightly lit neighbours. Perhaps Louise had gone out. Very likely she had gone out to meet her lover and was now sitting with him in some characterless North Circular Road pub or holding hands in a half-empty café. But Susan didn't think she had and it depressed her to imagine Louise lying sleepless in that house with her eyes open on the dark.

She listened, hardly knowing what she was listening for. She heard nothing and then, a little unnerved, she listened to the silence. Julian called Matchdown Park a dormitory and at night it was a dormitory indeed, its denizens enclosed like bees in their warm cells. And yet it was incredible that so many people should live and breathe around her, all in utter silence.

But if this was silence, it was nothing to the deep mute soundlessness of the back garden. Susan checked her back door lock, noticing that the wind had died. There was no movement in the black trees and, apart from the running river of traffic in the distance, no light but from the three red spots of the lamps the workmen had left on their pyramid of clay.

4

David Chadwick hadn't seen Bernard Heller for months and then, quite by chance, he bumped into him on a Tuesday evening in Berkeley Square. It was outside Stewart and Ardern's and Heller had his arms full of cardboard boxes. Some heating equipment, David thought, that he must going to dump at the offices in Hay Hill where *Equatair* had its headquarters.

Heller didn't look particularly pleased to see him, although he forced his features into an unsuccessful grin. David, on the other hand, was glad they had met. Last summer, on a generous impulse, he had lent Heller his slide projector and now he thought it was time he got it back.

'How are things?'

'Oh, so-so.' The boxes were stacked up under Heller's chin and perhaps it was this which gave to his face a set look.

'How about a drink if you're knocking off?'

'I've got some more stuff to unload.'

'I'll give you a hand,' David said firmly. He didn't want to lose him now.

'In the car, then.'

He still had the same green Zephyr Six, David noted as he lifted out the three remaining boxes from the boot which Heller had opened. The cardboard was torn on the top one and inside part of a gas burner could be seen.

'Thanks,' Heller said, and then, with an effort to be gracious, 'Thanks very much, David.'

Equatair's swing doors were still open. A couple of typists in white boots and fun furs passed them on the steps. Heller put his boxes on the floor of a small vestibule and David followed suit. Photographs of radiators and boilers and one of a lush living-room interior were pinned to the walls. It reminded David of his own designs for television film sets. That was how he had first met Heller, through work. *Equatair* made fireplaces too and David had borrowed one for the set of a series called, *Make Mine Crime.*

'How about that drink?'

'All right. I'm in no hurry to get home.' Heller didn't look at David when he said this and he mumbled something else with his head averted. It might have been, 'God knows, I'm not,' but David couldn't be sure of that.

He was a big heavy man, this heating engineer, with a round bullet head and hair that stuck up in short curly bristles. Usually he was almost irritatingly cheerful, inclined to slap people on the back while he told tedious jokes which, for all that, had about them an innocent slapstick quality. Tonight he had a hangdog look and David thought he had lost weight. His plump jowls sagged and they were greyish, perhaps not just because Heller, normally careful of his appearance, was in need of a shave.

'There's a nice little place in Berwick Street I sometimes go to,' David said. He hadn't got his car with him so they went in Heller's. For an engineer-cum-salesman, he was a lousy driver, David thought. Twice he was afraid they were going to go into the back of a taxi. It was his first experience of being driven by Heller as their encounters had usually been for a pre-lunch drink or a sandwich. Heller had been kindness itself over the fireplace and almost embarrassingly generous. It had been a job to stop him paying for all their drinks. Then, back in July, he had happened to say his twin brother had been staying with relatives in Switzerland – they were Swiss or half-Swiss or something – but couldn't show the slides he had taken because he hadn't a projector. For a long time David had wanted to show his gratitude, but it was difficult while Heller insisted on paying for everything. The loan of the projector had settled that question.

Paying off debts was one thing. He hadn't expected the man to hang on to it for eight months without a word.

'I wonder if I might have my projector back sometime?' he said as they crossed Regent Street. 'The summer's coming and holidays . . .'

'Oh, sure,' Heller said without enthusiasm. 'I'll drop it off at the studios, shall I?'

'Please.' It wouldn't have hurt him to say thank you. Still, he evidently had something on his mind. 'That's the place, The Man in the Iron Mask. If you're quick you can nip in between that van and the Mercedes.'

Heller wasn't very quick. Twice he bungled the reversing manœuvre. The pub was tucked between an Indonesian restaurant and a strip club. Heller gave the pictures of nudes on leopard skin a sick look.

Over the entrance to The Man in the Iron Mask was a sign depicting this apocryphal character, his head encased in a cage. David went in first. Inside the place was cosy and overheated and with its black and white tiled floor and walls panelled in dark wood, suggested a Dutch interior. But the hunting prints could only be English and nowhere but in England would you see the facetious slogans and the pinned-up cartoons.

The area behind the bar was suffused with red light, making it look like the entrance to a furnace, and this same light stained the faces of the man and the girl who sat there. Her fingernails showed mauve when she moved her hands out of the red glow to caress her boy-friend's shoulders. The discerning would have recognised his grey tunic as the upper half of a Confederate uniform.

'What are you going to have?' David asked, anticipating the usual. 'No, let me.'

'Lime and lager,' Heller said only.

'Big stuff. What are we celebrating?'

'It's just that I have to drive.'

David went up to the bar. He was trying to remember where Heller lived. South London somewhere. If he was going to have to make conversation with this semi-conscious man, he would need something strong.

'Double scotch and a lime and lager, please,' he said to the barman.

'You mean lager and lime.'

'I don't suppose it would matter at that.'

Heller rubbed his big forehead as if it ached. 'D'you often come in here?'

'Off and on. It's quiet. You see some interesting charac-ters.' And as he spoke, the Confederate kissed his girl on her oyster-coloured mouth. The door opened with an abrupt jerk and two bearded men came in.

They advanced to the bar and, because it was for an instant unattended, knocked sharply on the counter. The taller of the two, having given their order with a scowl, resumed an anecdote. The red glow turned his beard to ginger.

'So I said to this bank manager chappie, 'It's all very well you moaning about my overdraft,' I said. 'Where would your lot be without overdrafts?' I said, 'That's what I'd like to know. That's what keeps you banks going. You'd be out of a job, laddie,' I said.'

'Quite,' said the other man.

Heller didn't even smile. His florid skin was puckered about his eyes and the corners of his mouth turned down.

'How's work?' David asked desperately.

'Just the same.'

'Still operating in the Wembley-Matchdown Park area?'

Heller nodded and mumbled into his glass, 'Not for long.'

David raised an eyebrow.

'I'm going abroad. Switzerland.'

'Then we are celebrating. I seem to remember your once saying that's what you wanted. Haven't *Equatair* got a footing out there?'

'Zürich.'

'When do you go?'

'May.'

The man's manner was only just short of rude. If he went on like that it was a wonder he ever sold anyone a thermostat replacement, let alone a whole central heating system. It struck David suddenly that May was only two months off. If he ever wanted to see his projector again he had better look sharp about it.

'You're fluent in German, aren't you? Bi-lingual?'

'I went to school in Switzerland.'

'You must be excited.' It was a stupid thing to say, like asking a shivering man if he was hot.

'Oh, I don't know,' Heller said. 'Might have been once.' He finished his drink and a spark of something fierce flashed momentarily in his dark eyes. 'People change, you get older.' He got up. 'There doesn't seem much point in anything, does there?' Without offering to buy David a drink, he said. 'Can I drop you anywhere? Northern Line for you, isn't it?'

David lived alone in a bachelor flat. He wasn't going anywhere that night and he intended to eat out. 'Look, I don't want to be a bore about this,' he said awkwardly, 'but if you're going straight home, would you mind if I came along with you and collected my projector?'

'Now, d'you mean?'

'Well, yes. You're going in May and I dare say you've got a lot on your mind.'

'All right,' Heller said ungraciously. They got into the car and David's spirits improved slightly when the other man said, with a ghost of his old grin, 'Bear with me, old man. I'm not very good company these days. It was decent of you to lend us the projector. I didn't intend to hold on to it.'

'I know that,' David said, feeling much better.

They went over one of the bridges and down past the Elephant and Castle. Heller drove by a twisty route through back streets and although he seemed to know his way, he was careless about traffic lights and once he went over a pedestrian crossing with people on it.

Silence had fallen between them and Heller broke it only to say, 'Nearly there.' The street was full of buses going to places David knew only by name, Kennington, Brixton, Stockwell. On the left-hand side a great blank wall with small windows in it ran for about two hundred yards. It might have been a barracks or a prison. There wasn't a tree or a patch of grass in sight. At a big brightly lit Odeon Heller turned right and David saw that they were at a typical South London crossroads, dominated by a collonaded church in the Wren style, only Wren had been dead a hundred and fifty years when it was put up. Opposite it was a tube station. David didn't know which one. All he could see was London Transport's Saturn-shaped sign, glowing blue and red. People streamed out over the crossing, their faces a sickly green in the mercury vapour light.

Some of them took a short cut home through a treeless park with a cricket pavilion and public lavatories. Heller drove jumpily on the inside lane of the stream. The street was neither truly shopping centre nor residential. Most of the big old houses were in the process of being pulled down. Shops there were, but all of the same kind, thrust shabbily together in a seemingly endless rhythmic order: off-licence, café, pet foods, betting shop, off-licence, café . . . If he were Heller he wouldn't have been able to wait for May. The prospect of Zürich would be like heaven. What kind of a slum did the man live in, anyway?

Not a slum at all. A fairly decent, perhaps ten-year-old block of flats. They were arranged in four storeys around a grass and concrete court. Hengist House. David looked around for Horsa and saw it fifty yards ahead. Some builder with Anglo-Saxon attitudes, he thought; amused.

Heller put the car into a bay marked with white lines.

'We're on the ground floor,' he said. 'Number three.'

The entrance hall looked a bit knocked about. Someone had written, 'Get back to Kingston' on a wall between two green doors. David didn't think they had meant Kingston, Surrey. Heller put his key into the lock of number three. They had arrived.

A narrow passage ran through the flat to an open bathroom door. Heller didn't call out and when his wife appeared he didn't kiss her.

Seeing her gave David a jolt. Heller was only in his early thirties but he was already touched by the heavy hand of middle-age. This girl looked very young. He hadn't been thinking about her so he had no preconceived idea as to how she would look. Nevertheless, he was startled by what he saw and as he met her eyes he knew she expected him to be startled and was pleased.

She wore blue jeans and one of those skinny sweaters that there is no point in wearing if you really are skinny. Her figure was the kind that is photographed large and temptingly in the non-quality Sundays. Long black hair that a brush touch would set sparking fell to her shoulders.

'I don't think you've met,' Heller mumbled, and that was all the introduction David got. Mrs Heller peeled herself from the wall and now her glance was indifferent. 'Make yourself at home. I won't be a minute finding the projector.' He looked at his wife. 'That slide projector,' he said. 'Where did you put it when Carl brought it back?'

'In the bedroom cupboard, I suppose.'

Heller showed him into the living-room, if pushing open a door and muttering could be called showing anyone anywhere. Then he went away. The room had three white walls and one red one with a stringed instrument hanging above an *Equatair* radiator. A little bit of haircord clung to the centre of the floor space. Mrs Heller came in and rather ostentatiously placed cutlery for two persons on the table. It amused David to reflect on the domestic surroundings of real salesmen-executives. In the films and plays he did sets for they had open-plan apartments, forty feet long, split-level with wall-to-wall carpeting, room dividers festooned with ivy, leather furniture. He sat down in an armchair that was a woven plastic cone in a metal frame. Outside the buses moved in a white and yellow glare.

'Sorry to come bursting in on you like this,' he said. She put two glasses of water on the table. In his films they had bottles of Romani Conti served in straw baskets. 'I happened to run into Bernard and I remembered my projector.'

She swivelled, tilting her chin. 'Ran into him, did you?' Her voice had the remnants of a burr he couldn't place. 'D'you mind telling me where?'

'In Berkeley Square,' he said, surprised.

'Sure it wasn't Matchdown Park?'

'Quite sure.' What was all this? The man was legitimately employed in Matchdown Park, wasn't he? He watched her as she finished laying the table. An orchidaceous face, he thought. Horrible word, but it just described that lush velvety skin, the little nose and the full pink pearl lips. Her eyes were green with gold sparks. 'I hear you're going to Switzerland. Looking forward to it?'

She shrugged. 'Nothing's settled yet.'

'But surely Bernard said . . .'

'You don't want to listen to everything he says.'

David followed her into the kitchen because he couldn't hang about there any longer with the glasses of water and the mandoline or whatever it was. The blue jeans were provocative as she bent to light her cigarette from the gas.

He wondered how old she was. Not more than twenty-four or twenty-five. In the next room he could hear Heller banging about, apparently shifting things from a high shelf.

A pan of water was heating on the cooker. Already cooked and lying dispiritedly on a plate were two small overdone chops. When the water in the pan boiled the girl took it from the gas and emptied into it the contents of a packet labelled, 'Countryman's Supper. Heavenly mashed potatoes in thirty seconds.' David wasn't sorry they weren't going to ask him to share it.

'Magdalene!'

Heller's voice sounded weary and fed-up. So that was her name, Magdalene. She looked up truculently as her husband lumbered in.

'I can't think where it's got to,' Heller said worriedly, glancing with embarrassment at his dusty hands.

'Leave it,' David said. 'I'm keeping you from your meal.'

'Maybe it's up there.' It was the girl who had spoken, indicating a closed cupboard on top of the dresser. David was a little surprised, for up till now, she had shown no interest in the recovery of his property and seemed indifferent as to whether he went or stayed.

Heller dragged out a stool from under the table and stuck it against the dresser on which was a pile of unironed linen. His wife watched him open the cupboard and fumble about inside.

'There was a phone call for you,' she said abruptly, her full mouth pouting. 'That North woman.' Heller mumbled something. 'I thought it was a bloody nerve, phoning here.' This time her husband made no reply. 'Damned cheek!' she said, as if trying to provoke from him a spark of anger. 'I hope you didn't forget your manners on the phone.'

David was rather shocked. Uncouth, graceless, Magdalene might be, jealous even. She had hardly deserved to be reproved with such paternal gruffness in front of a stranger. She was evidently drawing breath for an appropriate rejoinder, but David never found out what it would have been. Heller, whose arms and shoulders had been inside the cupboard, retreated and, as he emerged, something heavy and metallic fell out on to the linen.

It was a gun.

David knew next to nothing about firearms. A Biretta or a Mauser, they were all the same to him. He knew only that it was some sort of automatic. It lay there glistening, half on Heller's underpants and half on a pink pillow slip.

Neither of the Hellers said anything. To break the rather ghastly silence, David said facetiously, 'Your secret arsenal?'

Heller started gabbling very fast then. 'I know I shouldn't have it, it's illegal. As a matter of fact, I smuggled it in from the States. Went on a business trip. The Customs don't always look, you know. Magdalene had got scared, being here alone. You get some very funny people about out there, fights, brawls, that kind of thing. Only last week there was a bloke down in the alley shouting at some woman to give him his money. A ponce, I dare say. Hitting her and shouting he was. In Greek,' he added, as if this made things worse.

'It's no business of mine,' David said.

'I just thought you might think it funny.'

Suddenly Magdalene stamped her foot. 'Hurry up, for God's sake. We're going to the pictures at seven-thirty and it's ten past now. And there's the washing-up to do first.'

'I'll do that.'

'Aren't you coming, then?'

'No, thanks.'

She turned off the oven, lifted the plates and carried them into the living-room. David thought she would return, but she didn't. The door closed and faintly from behind it he heard the sound of spy thriller music.

'Here it is at last,' Heller said. 'It was right at the back behind the hair dryer.'

'I've put you to a lot of trouble.'

Heller passed the projector down to him. 'That's one thing I won't have to worry about, anyway,' he said. He didn't close the cupboard doors and he left the gun where it lay.

Perhaps it was the presence of the gun, grim, ugly, vaguely threatening, in this grim and ugly household that made David say on an impulse, 'Look, Bernard, if there's anything I can do . . .'

Heller said stonily, 'Nobody can do anything. Not a magician, are you? Not God? You can't put the clock back.'

'You'll be better when you get to Zürich.'

'If I get there.'

The whole thing had shaken David considerably. Once out of the courtyard, he found himself a pub, bigger and brassier and colder than the Man in the Iron Mask. He had another whisky and then he walked up to the tube station, discovering when he was a few yards from it that it was called East Mulvihill. As he walked under the stone canopy of the station entrance he caught sight of Magdalene Heller on the other side of the street, walking briskly, almost running, towards the big cinema he and Heller had passed. She looked jerkily to right and left before she went in. He watched her unzip her heavy shoulder bag, buy a ticket and go alone up the stairs to the balcony.

The cause of Heller's misery was no longer in doubt. His marriage had gone wrong. One of these ill-assorted, very obviously incompatible people, had transgressed, and from what Magdalene had hinted of a telephone call, David gathered the transgressor was Heller. It looked as if he had found himself another woman. Had he dwindled to this taciturn shadow of the cheerful buffoon he once had been because it was not she but Magdalene he must take with him to Switzerland?

5

On the way to school they passed the postman and Paul said, 'I don't have to go to school tomorrow until after he's been, do I?'

'We'll see,' Susan said.

'Well, I shan't,' he said mutinously for Richard's benefit. Richard ran ahead, jumping into the air at intervals to grab at the cherry branches. 'He'll be early anyway,' Paul said in a more conciliatory tone, taking his mother's hand. 'Daddy's going to send me a watch. He promised.'

'A watch! Oh, Paul . . .' Of all the vulnerable and ultimately – when Paul fell over in the playground as he did two or three times a week – tear-provoking presents for a six-year-old! 'You'll have to keep it for best.'

They reached the school gates and the two little boys were absorbed by the throng. Susan looked at the children with different eyes this morning, seeing them as potential adults, makers of misery. A cold melancholy stole over her. Determinedly she braced herself, waved to Paul and turned back towards Orchard Drive.

It was ten to nine, the time she usually saw Bob North. His car regularly passed the school gates about now. Susan didn't want to see him. She remembered their last encounter with distaste. He wouldn't offer her a lift today as he would be able to see she intended to go straight home, but she was certain he would stop. Probably he had found out about Louise's visit to her and their appointment for this morning and he would be anxious to put his own story across before Louise could blacken his character. People in Louise's situation always blamed their marriage partners. Julian had spent a long time pointing out her deficiencies as a wife, her nagging, her dislike of his more *avant-garde* friends, her old-fashioned morality, before embarking on the tale of his own infidelity.

She felt very exposed as she walked back under the cherry trees, nervously aware that any time now Bob's car would nose or back out of the Braeside drive. She thought wildly of bending down to retie her shoelace or, if this ploy failed, diving into the house of someone she slightly knew. The trouble was she hardly knew anyone well enough for that.

It was a still day, not quite foggy, but uniformly grey. Rain threatened in the clammy air. Susan quickened her pace as she approached Braeside and then she remembered. Bob's car was in for a service. He would go to work by train today, so therefore he had probably left much earlier, had certainly left by now. Her spirits lifted absurdly. Really, it was stupid to work herself up to such a nervous pitch because in a couple of hours time one of her neighbours was going to confide something rather unorthodox to her. That was all it amounted to.

Braeside had a dull dead look. The upstairs curtains were all drawn as if the Norths were away. Perhaps Louise was lying late in bed. Unhappiness made you want to do that. Jane Willingale would have attributed it to a desire to get back to the womb but Susan thought it was only because you felt there was nothing to get up for.

As usual there was not a single open window, not even a fanlight lifted an inch or two. It must be cold and stuffy in there, the air stale with angrily exhaled breath and tears and quarrels.

Mrs Dring would arrive at any moment. Susan let herself into her own warm house and began to grease tins and beat mixture for Paul's party cakes. Her hall clock chimed nine and as the last stroke died away, the pneumatic drills began.

Breaking across this shrill sound, the Airedale's bark sounded hollow. He was used to Mrs Dring by now and wouldn't bark at her arrival. Not for the first time Susan wondered why this canine summons was impossible to resist. Hardly anyone really interesting ever came to Orchard Drive and yet Pollux never barked in vain. She was as vulnerable to the alert as any of the women, although, unlike them, a change of delivery man or a new meter reader left her indifferent. She didn't want to speculate as to why Fortnum's van had called at Gibbs's or a couple of nuns at O'Donnells'. Sometimes she thought she rushed to the window when Pollux barked because, against all experience to the contrary, she always hoped the roar announced a newcomer into her own life, someone who would change it, who would bring hope and joy.

How pathetic and childish, she thought as, in spite of herself, she ran into the living-room and drew aside the curtain. Winters' gate clanged between its concrete posts and Pollux, who had half-mounted it in his rage, dropped back on to the path with a thump.

Susan stared. On the grass patch in the pavement, its tyres buried in the ruts they had made on Monday, stood the green Ford Zephyr.

Once again Louise North was entertaining her lover.

'Good morning, dear. Did you think I wasn't coming?'

Mrs Dring always bellowed this question on a triumphant note if she was more than a minute late. A large raw-boned redhead of forty-five, she put immense value on herself and the work she did, confident that her employers, in the event of her non-appearance, must be reduced to a helpless and desperate panic like abandoned infants.

'I'll do downstairs, shall I?' she said, putting her head round the door. 'Make it nice for the boy's party.' Cleaning a room before a children's party seemed pointless to Susan, but it was useless arguing with Mrs Dring. 'Want me to come and give you a hand tomorrow? There's nothing anyone can tell me about running kids' parties. Famous for them I am.'

Mrs Dring didn't explain how she came to know so much about the organisation of children's parties. She had no children of her own. But she was always making statements of this kind in a dark tone, as if implying that all her acquaintances were aware of her omnipotent versatility and took repeated advantage of it. She had a good word for no one except her husband, a man whose competence in the most unlikely fields rivalled her own and who possessed in equal measure to his manual and administrative skills a superhuman intelligence quotient.

'There's nothing that man doesn't know,' she would say. Now she advanced into the room and went straight up to the window where she stood tying up her hair, almost scarlet this morning, in a scarf.

'I've been meaning to ask you,' she said, her eye on the green car, 'what's going on next door?'

'Going on?'

'You know what I mean. I got it from my friend who helps Mrs Gibbs. Mind you, my friend's a proper little liar and I reckon anyone who'd believe a word Mrs Gibbs says must want her head tested.' Drawing breath, Mrs Dring proceeded at once to place herself in this lunatic category. 'She says Mrs North is carrying on with the central heating fellow.'

'Do you know him?' Susan couldn't stop herself asking.

'I've seen him about. My husband could tell you his name. You know what a wonderful memory he's got. We was thinking about central heating ourselves and I said,

You want to talk to that fellow – Heffer or Heller or something – who's always about in a green car. But my husband put the pipes in himself in the end. There's nothing he can't do it he puts his mind to it.'

'Why shouldn't he be calling on Mrs North just for business?'

'Yes, funny business. Well, it stands to reason he's in the right job for that kind of thing if he fancies it. It's her I'm disgusted with.' Seeing Susan wasn't to be drawn, Mrs Dring dropped the curtain and pulled two kiss-curls, as fluorescent red as Day-glo paint, out on to her forehead. 'What d'you think of my hair? It's called flamingo, this shade. My husband did it last night. I always tell him he ought to have gone into the trade. He'd have been in the West End by now.'

Susan began typing desultorily. Mrs Dring was never silent for long and these mornings she was on edge, constantly distracted from work by futile remarks. Her cleaner, engaged in the first place 'to do the rough' had soon made it clear that she preferred polishing and cleaning silver to heavy work and her favourite tasks were those which kept her at a vantage point near one of the windows.

Now, having observed all there was to see in Orchard Drive, she had stationed herself at the french windows with the plate powder and a trayful of Susan's silver ornaments. It was half past nine. Although it had begun to rain, the drills had scarcely ceased in the past half-hour. Susan could hardly believe there was anything of interest to see from that window, but Mrs Dring kept craning her neck and pressing her face against the streaming glass until at last she said, 'They won't get no tea this morning.'

'Mmm?' Susan looked up from her typewriter.

'Them men. Look, he's going down the path now.' The summons couldn't be refused without rudeness. Susan joined her at the window. A tall workman in a duffel coat, its hood pulled up over his head, was making his way down Norths' garden from the back door towards the gate at the far end. 'I heard him banging on the back door. Wants his tea, I said to myself. Canteen's closed this morning, mate. Madam's got other things on her mind. Funny that dog of

Winters didn't bark, though. Have they got it shut up for once?'

'No, it's out.'

It was raining steadily. The workman opened the gate. His companions were deep in their trench where one of them was still plying his drill. The solitary man warmed his hands at the bucket fire for a moment. Then he turned, his shoulders hunched, and strolled off along the road that skirted the cemetery.

Nodding her head grimly, Mrs Dring watched him disappear. 'Gone to fetch himself a cup from the café,' she said and added because Susan had retreated, 'Is the car still there?'

'Yes, it's still there.' The rain streamed down its closed windows and over the pale green bodywork. Someone else was looking at it, too, Eileen O'Donnell, who was putting up her umbrella after scuttling out of Louise's garden.

'Mrs O'Donnell's coming round to the back door, Mrs Dring,' Susan said. 'Just see what she wants, will you?'

She was sure she would be called to the conference that was about to ensue, but after a short conversation at the back door, Mrs Dring came back alone.

'Mrs North asked her to bring some fish fingers in for lunch in case her husband comes home. She says she's banged and banged at the front door but she can't make no one hear. She says the upstairs curtains are all drawn but that's on account of Mrs North not wanting the sun to fade the carpets. I reckon some folks go about with their eyes shut, don't know they're born. Sun, I said, what sun? A kid of five could tell you why she's drawn them curtains.'

Susan took the package, noting with amusement that it was wrapped in last week's edition of *Certainty*. How pained Julian would be! Its use as insulating material for frozen food was only one step up the scale from wrapping it round fish and chips.

'What am I supposed to do with them?'

'Mrs O'Donnell said you was going in there for coffee. And could you take them in with you just in case that poor wretch she's doing dirt to comes home for his lunch?'

But Susan had begun to doubt whether she was expected to keep that appointment. By the time Mrs Dring had finished the living-room and moved into what used to be Julian's study it was half past ten and the car was still outside. It looked as if Louise had forgotten. Love was generally supposed to conquer all and, although this was perhaps not what the adage meant, it certainly in Susan's experience, banished from the lover's mind firm promises and prior engagements. Curious, though. Louise had been so insistent.

But between ten-thirty and eleven the time went slowly. There was no need to watch the window. The Airedale, now sheltering in Winters' porch, would warn her of the man's departure. Eleven struck and on the last stroke Susan's oppression lifted. The rain was filling Monday's ruts with yellow clayey water, making pools round the wheels of the green car. Its driver was still inside Braeside and Susan sighed with relief. She wouldn't have to go now. There was no need for tact or kindness or firm advice because, by her own actions, Louise had cancelled the consultation.

Mrs Dring wrapped herself in a cocoon of blue polythene and trotted off into the rain, pausing to glower at the car and the curtained windows. Susan tried to remember how many times and for how long each time the car had been there before. Surely not more than three times and the man had never stayed as long as this. Didn't he have a job to go to? How could he afford to spend so much time – an entire morning – with Louise?

She opened the refrigerator door to make sandwiches for her lunch. The fish finger packet lay slightly askew on the metal slats. Did Bob ever come home to lunch? Eileen O'Donnell had seemed to think he might and now, as Susan considered, she remembered how Bob himself had told her he might come home one lunchtime.

Well, let him come home. Let him find them together. A show-down might be the best way out of this mess for all of them. But Susan took the packet from the refrigerator and went round to the front of the house from where she could see Braeside.

There was no one sitting in the through-room or in the little room at the other side of the front door. They must be still in the bedroom behind those closed curtains. Susan glanced at her watch and saw that it was gone half past twelve. How would she have felt if she had walked into that hotel, or wherever they had met, and found Julian in bed with Elizabeth? It would almost have killed her. Julian had been far more discreet than Louise – he was far cleverer – but still the process of discovery had been dreadfully painful to his wife. If Bob North came now it would be a far worse pain than that which would meet him.

That decided her. It was all very well deciding to have as little as possible to do with the Norths. Circumstances altered cases and this was a hard case with circumstances as different from those of everyday life as Susan's present existence was from that of a year ago. She went back into the house and slipped her arms into the sleeves of her raincoat. Then she banged hard on Norths' front door, banged and rang the bell, but no one came. They must be asleep.

Reluctantly she went round to the side. What she was about to do would save Louise, at least for a time, from ignominy and possibly from violence, but Louise wouldn't be grateful. What woman would ever again be able to bear the sight of a neighbour who had found her in what the lawyers called *flagrante delicto*?

Better not to think about it. Get in, wake them up and go. Susan cared very little what Louise thought of her. She was going to give the Norths a very wide berth in future.

The back door was unlocked. If Louise was going to carry on with this sort of thing, Susan thought, she had a lot to learn. Julian would have made her a good adviser. The kitchen was untidy and freezing cold. Louise had stacked the breakfast things in the washing-up bowl but not washed them. There was a faint smell of cold fat from a water-filled frying-pan.

On the kitchen table stood the briefcase Susan had once or twice seen Louise's lover carrying up the path, and over the back of a chair was his raincoat. Susan put her package down and moved into the hall, calling Louise's name softly.

There was no answer, no sound from upstairs at all. In the little cloakroom a tap dripped. She came to the foot of the stairs and stood by the wall niche in which a plaster Madonna smiled down at her Child. It was grotesque.

No fires had been lighted in the house this morning and the ashes of yesterday's lay grey in the living-room hearth. All the windows streamed with water so that it was impossible to see out of them. Such heavy rain as this enclosed people like hibernating creatures, curled up dry, yet surrounded by walls of water. So it must have been for Louise and her lover, kissing, whispering, planning, while outside the rain fell and blotted out time.

Susan went upstairs. The bathroom door was open and the bathmat, a purple affair with a yellow scroll design in its centre, lay crookedly on the tiles. It looked as if none of the routine morning cleaning had been done. All the bedroom doors but one were open. She stood outside the closed door and listened.

Her reluctance to burst in on them had grown with every step and now she felt a strong revulsion. They might be naked. She put her hand to her forehead and felt a faint dew of sweat. It must be at least ten to one and Bob could be turning the corner of Orchard Drive at this moment.

She grasped the handle and opened the door gradually.

They were both on the bed, but the man appeared to be fully clothed. Only Louise's stockinged feet could be seen, for her lover lay spreadeagled across her, his arms and legs flung wide in the attitude of someone crucified on a St Andrew's Cross. His face was slightly turned as if he had fallen asleep with his lips pressed to Louise's cheek. They were both utterly still.

No one slept like that.

Susan came round the side of the bed between it and the dressing table and as she did so she stumbled over something hard and metallic that lay on the carpet. She looked down on it, breathing fast, and at first she thought it was a child's toy. But the Norths had no little boys to run up and down the stairs, shouting, Bang, bang, you're dead!

Momentarily she covered her face with her hands. Then she approached the bed and bent over the couple. One of Louise's shoulders was exposed. Susan touched it and the man's head lolled. Where his ear should have been was a neat round hole from which something sticky had run and dried. The movement revealed a mat of blood, liquid and caked, grumming their faces together and smothering the front of Louise's nightdress and housecoat.

Susan heard herself cry out. She put her hand up to her mouth and backed away, stumbling, while the floor eddied and rocked beneath her and the furniture swayed.

6

The police asked her to wait there until they came. Susan's voice had shaken so much on the telephone that she was astonished she had made herself understood. She was almost numb with shock and long after the kind voice had stopped talking and told her to do nothing and to touch nothing, she sat staring at the Madonna while the receiver hung from her hand.

A rushing splash of water at the front of the house announced the arrival of the car. Susan was surprised she could stand. She made her way to the front door, clinging to the furniture and groping like a blind person.

The Airedale hadn't barked, but in her present state this didn't warn her. Then, in a kind of horror, she watched the latch turn from the inserted key.

Bob had come home to lunch.

He had dived through the rain from the newly serviced car to the door and he had stepped inside, shaking the drops from his hair, before he realised who waited for him in the cold shadowy hall.

'Susan?' She couldn't speak. Her lips parted, she drew a long breath. He looked at her, then past her at the dead ashes in the grate, the briefcase on the kitchen table. 'Where's Louise?'

Her voice came in a cracked whisper. 'Bob, I . . . She's upstairs. I . . . I phoned the police.'

'Tell me what's happened?'

'She's dead. They're both dead.'

'You came to coffee,' he said stupidly and then he plunged for the stairs.

'You mustn't go up there!' Susan cried. She caught his shoulders and they were stiff, without a tremor, under her hands. He gripped her wrists as if to free himself and then the dog Pollux began to bark, dully at first, then furiously as the police car splashed through the puddles in the street. Bob dropped limply on to the stairs and sat with his head in his hands.

There were three policemen, a little brown-faced inspector called Ulph, a sergeant and a constable. They spent a long time upstairs and questioning Bob in the kitchen before they came to her. The sergeant passed the open living-room door with a sheaf of papers that looked like letters in his hand. Susan heard Bob say:

'I don't know who he is. I don't even know his name. Ask the neighbours. They'll tell you he was my wife's lover.' Susan shivered. She couldn't remember ever having felt so cold before. They were searching through the brief-case now. She could see them through the serving hatch and see Bob, sitting pale and stiff, by the table. 'No, I didn't know he was married,' Bob said. 'Why would I? Bernard Heller, did you say his name was? Of course I never ordered central heating.' His voice rose and cracked. 'Don't you understand? That was just a blind.'

'What about your own movements this morning, Mr North?'

'My car was in for a service. I left for work on foot. About half past eight. My wife was all right then. She was in her dressing-gown, making the bed, when I left. I'm a quantity surveyor and I went to Barnet to look at a building site. Then I collected my car from Harrow where it was being serviced and drove back here. I thought . . . I thought my wife was expecting me home for lunch.'

Susan turned her head away. The sergeant closed the door and the hatch. The coat Louise had worn the day before lay slung over the back of one of the chairs. There was something very casual about that coat as if it had been put down only for a moment and any minute now Louise would come in and envelop her childish body in its com-forting warmth. The tears came into Susan's eyes and she gave a little sob.

Upstairs the police were tramping heavily about. Then she heard someone descending the stairs and the small brown-faced inspector came in. He closed the door behind him and said gently to Susan, 'Try not to upset yourself, Mrs Townsend. I know this has been a great shock to you.'

'I'm quite all right, really. Only it's so cold in here.' He might think her eyes were watering from the cold, but she didn't think he would. He had compassionate eyes. Not the sort of policeman, she thought, who would be briskly hearty in the face of death or make jokes about it with his companions.

'Did you know Mrs North was on intimate terms with this man, Heller?' Inspector Ulph asked presently.

'I . . . Well, it was common knowledge,' Susan began. 'I know she was very unhappy about it. She was a Catholic and couldn't be divorced.' Her voice shook. 'She was terribly distressed when she came to see me yesterday.'

'Distressed to the point of taking her own life, or to agreeing to a suicide pact?'

'I don't know.' This sudden taking of responsibility frightened Susan. Her hands were icy cold and trembling. 'A Catholic wouldn't commit suicide, would she? But she was in a bad state. I remember thinking she was at the end of her tether.'

He asked her quietly about the events of the morning and Susan, trying to keep her voice steady, told him how she had seen Heller's car outside soon after nine; how she had waited and waited for Heller to leave; how Mrs O'Donnell had called and how, at last, she had come here to Braeside to alert Louise and Heller, believing them to be asleep.

'No one else came to this house during the morning?' Susan shook her head. 'Did you see anyone leave?'

'Only Mrs O'Donnell.'

'Well, that's all for now, Mrs Townsend. I'm afraid you'll have to be present at the inquest. Now, if I were you, I should telephone your husband and see if he can come home early. You shouldn't be alone.'

'I'm not married,' Susan said awkwardly. 'Well, that is, I'm divorced.'

Inspector Ulph made no reply to this, but he came with Susan to the door, lightly supporting her with one hand under her elbow.

As she came out into the garden, she blinked and started back. The crowd on the pavement affected her as bright sunlight shocks someone coming out of a dark room. Wrapped in coats, Doris and Betty and Eileen stood outside Doris's gate with the old woman who lived alone next to Betty, the bride from Shangri-La, the elderly couple from the corner house. Everyone who didn't go out to work was gathered there and everyone, their tongues stilled, was silent.

Even Pollux had been stunned into silence by those unprecedented comings and goings. He lay exhausted at his mistress's feet, his head between his paws.

The rain had ceased, leaving the roadway a glistening mirror of pools and wet tarmac. Raindrops dripped steadily from the cherry buds on to umbrellas and coat collars. Doris looked colder and more miserable than Susan had ever seen her, but for once she said nothing about the cold. She stepped forward, putting her arms around Susan's shoulders, and Inspector Ulph said:

'Will one of you ladies kindly look after Mrs Townsend?'

Susan let Doris lead her past the green Zephyr, the police car and the black mortuary van and into her own house. All the time she expected to hear her neighbours' chatter break out behind her, but there was only silence, a silence broken only by the steady drip-drip of water from the trees.

'I'll stay with you, Susan,' Doris said. 'I'll stay all night. I won't leave you.' She didn't cite her nursing experience as qualification for this duty and she didn't clutch at the radiators. Her face was grey and huge-eyed. 'Oh, Susan, Susan . . . ! That man, did he kill her and himself?'

'I don't know. I think he must have.'

And the two women, friends only from propinquity and mutual practical need, clung together for a moment, their heads bowed on each other's shoulders.

It was curious, Susan thought, how tragedy seemed to bring out in everyone the best qualities, tact, kindness, sympathy. Afterwards the only really tactless action she could remember was the arrival of Roger Gibbs at Paul's party with the present of a toy revolver.

'I reckon some women are downright daft,' said Mrs Dring. 'Fancy, a gun! You'd think Mrs Gibbs'd have had more thought. And she's sent that boy of hers with a streaming cold. What'll I get them on playing? Musical Parcel? Squeak, Piggy, Squeak?'

Murder was the favourite party game among the under-tens in Orchard Drive. When no one suggested playing it, Susan knew they must have been forewarned by their mothers. Had those mothers told their sons what she had told Paul, that Mrs North had had an accident and been taken away? What do you tell someone who is old enough to wonder and be frightened but too young, far too young by years and years, to understand?

'I hope to God,' said Mrs Dring, 'young Paul won't have an accident with that watch his dad sent him.' She was unusually subdued this afternoon, softer-voiced and gentler, for all the dazzling aggressiveness of her red hair and the lilac suit she declared her husband had knitted. 'Has Mr Townsend been in touch yet?'

The watch had arrived by the first post and with it a card bearing a reproduction of Van Gogh's *Mills at Dordrecht*, a gloomy landscape that Julian had evidently preferred to the more suitable teddy-bear mouthing, 'Hallo, six-year-old'. He approved of culture being rammed home during the formative years. But there was no note inside for Susan and he hadn't phoned.

'He must have read about it,' said Doris indignantly, passing with a tray of sausage rolls.

Mrs Dring frowned at her. 'Perhaps he'll put something about it in his own paper.'

'It isn't that sort of paper,' said Susan.

It was only because she had wanted to keep Paul's interest from the tragedy next door that she had decided to go ahead with the party as planned. But now, as the little boys shouted and romped to the loud music from the record player, she wondered how much of this noise was reaching Bob. Since Louise and Heller had been found, he had only left Braeside for two visits to the police station. All the curtains, not just those upstairs, remained drawn. Gossip had reached the workmen on the cemetery road and today none of them had come up to the back door for their tea. Susan didn't care to think of Bob alone in there, living, moving, sleeping in the house where his wife had been shot. If he heard the children, would he take their merriment as the outward sign of her own indifference to his sorrow?

She hoped he wouldn't. She hoped he would understand and understand, too, that she hadn't yet called on him because she felt as yet he was better alone. That was why she hadn't been among the stream of tip-toeing housewives who knocked almost hourly at the Braeside door, some of them with flowers, some with covered baskets, as if he was ill instead of sick at heart.

Doris met Susan after the inquest was over and took her back for lunch in the over-heated room the Winters called their 'through-lounge'. An immense fire was burning. Susan saw that Doris's gentle, sympathetic mood had passed now. Her curiosity, her avidity for gossip, had returned, and, wondering if she was being just, Susan recognised in the huge fire, the carefully laid tray and the gloss of the room, a bait to keep her there for the afternoon, a festive preparation in return for which she must supply the hostess with every juicy tit-bit the inquest had afforded.

'Tell me about the gun,' Doris said, helping Susan plentifully to fruit salad.

'Apparently this man Heller smuggled it in from America. His twin brother was in court and he identified the gun and said Heller had tried to commit suicide in September. Not with the gun. The brother found him trying to gas himself.' Doris made eager encouraging noises. 'He shot poor Louise twice, both times through the heart, and then he shot himself. The pathologist thought it rather strange that he'd dropped the gun, but he'd known that happen before in cases like this. They asked me if I'd heard the shots, but I hadn't.'

'You can't hear a thing when those drills are going.'

'I suppose that's why I didn't. The verdict was murder and suicide by Heller, by the way. Apparently he was always threatening suicide. His brother and his wife both said so.'

Doris helped herself to more salad, picking out pieces of pineapple. 'What was the wife like?'

'Rather beautiful, I thought. Only twenty-five.' Susan recalled how Carl Heller and Magdalene Heller had both tried to speak to Bob while they all waited for the inquest to begin and how Bob had turned from them, brushing off their overtures as if stung. She thought she would never forget how that big, heavy man had approached Bob and attempted to talk to him in his strongly accented English, and Bob's near-snarl, his bitter contempt for the woman whose dead husband had killed Louise. She wasn't going to tell Doris any of that, nothing of Bob's frenzied outburst in court when Magdalene Heller had accused him of driving his wife, through his own neglect, into another man's arms; nothing of the girl's stony, stunned horror that had broken at last into vituperative ravings at Bob.

'She knew about Louise,' Susan said. 'Heller had promised to give her up and try to patch up his marriage but he didn't keep his promise. He was miserable and suicidal about it. He'd been like that for months.'

'Had they ever met before, she and Bob?'

'Bob didn't even know Heller was married. No one knows how Louise and Heller met. Heller worked for a firm called *Equatair* and the managing director was in court. He said Heller was going as their representative to Zürich in May – apparently he'd always wanted to go back to Switzerland. He was born and brought up there – but he didn't show any interest when he was offered the post. I suppose he thought it would take him away from Louise. The managing director said *Equatair* got their custom by sending out business reply cards to people, but they hadn't sent one to Louise and everyone seemed to think Heller must have given her one just so that she could fill it in and arrange for him to call. That would make his visits look innocent, you see.'

Doris digested all this with satisfaction. She poked the fire until it crackled and blazed. Then she said, 'I wonder why they didn't just go away together?'

'I gathered from the letters that Heller wanted to but Louise wouldn't. It seemed as if Louise had never even told Bob about it, not in so many words.'

'Letters?' Doris said excitedly, discarding the rest of this fresh information. 'What letters?'

The police had found them in a drawer of Louise's dressing table, two love-letters from Heller to Louise which had been written in November and December of the previous year. Carl Heller had identified his brother's handwriting which, in any case, had been confirmed by an examination of Heller's work notes. When they were read in court Bob's face had grown grey and Heller's widow, covering her face with her hands, had buried her head in her brother-in-law's massive shoulder.

'They were just love-letters,' Susan said, sickened by this inquisition. 'They only read out bits.' Strange and horrible that they had picked out those bits which most cruelly maligned Bob. 'I can't remember what he'd written,' she lied.

Her expression must have shown her unwillingness to talk about it any more, for Doris, realising that she had gone as far as she dared, dropped the subject with a, 'It'll all be in the paper, I expect,' and suddenly became solicitous for Susan's welfare. 'I'm a beast, aren't I?' she said. 'Pestering you after all you've been through. You don't look at all well, as if you're sickening for something.'

'I'm all right.' In fact, Susan had begun to feel dizzy and rather sick. Probably it was only nerves and the hothouse temperature in this room. She would be better at home.

'Now I hope your place is really warm,' Doris twittered in the icy hall. 'I know it usually is. The great thing with shock and all this upheaval is to keep in an even temperature.' She hunched her shoulders and wrapped her arms around her chest. 'An even temperature, that's one thing my sister tutor always impressed on me.'

For Susan's neighbours the inquest had been a kind of demarcation. It was over and with it most of the excitement, the terror and the scandal. Those involved and those looking on had reached a point at which they must again take up the strings of their lives. Susan had found two dead bodies, but Susan couldn't expect to be the centre of attraction, of sympathy and of comfort for ever.

But for all that, it gave her a slight shock to realise that Doris wasn't going to accompany her home. Mrs Dring had stayed with her last night, but she had said nothing about coming back. Quietly and as cheerfully as she could, Susan said good-bye to Doris and thanked her for lunch. Then she crossed the road, keeping her eyes averted from Braeside.

Work is generally recommended as the remedy for most ills and Susan went straight to her typewriter and Miss Willingale's manuscript. Her hands trembled and, although she flexed them and held them against the radiator, she found herself unable to type at all. Would she ever again be able to work in this house? It was so dreadfully like Braeside. With all her heart she wished she had minded her own business on Wednesday, even though that meant the discovery would have been Bob's and not hers.

Her first impression of it, her first sight of its interior, had left on her mind an image of a house of death and now her own, its facsimile, seemed contaminated. For the first time she wondered why she had ever stayed on here after her divorce. Like Braeside, it was a house where happy people had lived together and where that happiness had died away into misery. Now nothing remained of that happiness and there was nothing to replace it while these walls reflected back the sorrow they had seen.

Susan heard Bob's car come in but she couldn't look up. Now that it was all over, she might have been able to comfort him. He had needed a counsellor for loneliness and here she was, alone. She knew she had neither the physical strength nor the will-power to go out and knock on his door. It was a cold ugly place, this corner of suburbia, where a young man and a young woman could live next door to each other in identical houses, two walls only between them, yet be so bound by reticence and by convention that they could not reach out to each other in common humanity.

Many times she had cursed the daily arrival of Doris at teatime, but when Paul came in alone she missed her bitterly. A craving for company, stronger than she had felt for months, made her want to lie down and weep. A child of six, no matter how much beloved, is no company for a woman who feels as troubled and insecure as a child and Susan wondered if in her eyes he saw the same bewilderment, masked by a determined effort to make a brave show, as she saw in his.

'Roger Gibbs says Mrs North got shot by a man.' Paul said it quite casually, stretching his white face into a broad manly smile. 'And she was all over blood,' he said, 'and they had a trial like on the TV.'

Susan smiled back at him and her smile was as matter-of-fact, as bravely reassuring as his. In a light even voice she embarked on a bowdlerised explanation.

'He says this man wanted to marry her and he couldn't, so he shot her. Why did he? He couldn't marry her when she was dead. Daddy didn't shoot Elizabeth and he wanted to marry her.'

'It wasn't quite the same. You'll understand when you're older.'

'That's what you always say.' The smile had gone, and with a quick glance at her, Paul went over to his toy box. The gun Roger Gibbs had given him lay on top of the little cars in their coloured boxes. He picked it up, looked at it for a moment and then dropped it listlessly. 'Can I wear my watch?' he said.

'Yes, darling, I suppose so.'

'Can I wear it right up until I go to bed?'

Susan heard Bob's car reverse out into the road. This time she went to the window and watched him. For a long time she stood there, staring at the empty street and remembering how she had told him of her loneliness on the night Julian had gone.

7

The inquest report was given a four-column spread on an inside page of the *Evening Standard*. David Chadwick bought a copy from a West End newsvendor and, reading it as he went, strolled along through the evening rush to where he had parked his car some ten minutes' walk away. Wednesday's evening paper had carried photographs of Magdalene Heller, of Robert North and of the young woman, a neighbour, who had found the bodies, but tonight there was only a shot of Mrs Heller leaving the court arm-in-arm with a man. The caption said he was Bernard's twin brother and from what David could see of him – his face and the girl's were shielded by a magazine he was holding up – the resemblance between the brothers was striking.

It must be he for whom the slide projector had been borrowed. David had unwrapped it on Tuesday night, a little amused by the care Heller had taken of it, swaddling it in newspapers under its outer covering of brown paper. And then he hadn't been quite so amused, but moved and saddened. For one of the newspapers, some South London weekly, yellowed now and crumpled, contained a tiny paragraph reporting Heller's wedding to a Miss Magdalene Chant. David only noticed it because the paragraph was ringed in ink and because Heller had written, just outside the ring, the date 7.6.62.

He had kept that paper as a souvenir, David thought, as simple people will. He had kept it until his marriage went wrong, until he had met Mrs North and wedding souvenirs were only a reminder of an encumbrance. So he had taken it, perhaps from a pile of other significant newspapers, and used it for wrapping someone else's property.

In the light of this notion and when he read of Heller's death, David had looked again at the sheets covering his projector and found, as he had suspected, newsprint commemorating Heller's success in some suburban swimming event and his inclusion among the guests at a darts club annual dinner. To Heller, evidently, these tiny claims to distinction, these printed chronicles, had once afforded the same pride as the record of his Order of Merit in *The Times* might give to a greater man. They had meant much and then suddenly, because his life had somersaulted and lost its meaning, they had meant nothing at all.

David thought of all this as he walked along Oxford Street and he thought also how strange it was that he, an acquaintance merely, should have been with Heller on the eve of his death, should indeed have spent more time with him on that occasion than at any time during the two or three years since their first meeting. He wondered if he should have attended the inquest, but he could have told them nothing that was not already known. Now he asked himself, as men do under such circumstances, whether he had failed Heller in his last hours, if he could have shown more sympathy and, worst of all, if there was any word he could have spoken of hope or encouragement that might have deflected the man from his purpose.

Who could tell? Who could have suspected what Heller had in mind? Nevertheless, David felt guilty and a sense of failure and inadequacy overcame him. He often thought of himself as a hesitant and indecisive person. Some men, hearty and brash perhaps but still the salt of the earth, would have sensed the depths of Heller's misery and, undeterred by his initial refusal to unburden his soul, have stayed and pumped his grief out of him. Others, the more sensitive of the do-gooders would have taken warning from that gun and linked its presence with Heller's confessed *weltschmerz*. He had done nothing, worse than nothing, for he had made his escape from that flat with obvious relief.

And on the next day Heller had shot himself. David felt bleakly depressed. He was driving, but he needed a drink, and all the breathalysers in the world could go to hell for all he cared. Folding the newspaper and cramming it into his pocket, he made for Soho and The Man in the Iron Mask.

It was early and the pub was nearly empty. David had never been there on a Friday before. He usually went home early on a Friday. Often he had a date and, anyway, to him the weekend started at five on Friday afternoon.

He didn't want to be alone yet and he looked around him to see if there was anyone here he knew well enough to sit with and talk to. But although all the faces were familiar, none was that of a friend. A man and a woman in their fifties were walking about, looking in silence at some new cartoons the licensee had pinned to the panelling; an elderly man who looked like an out-of-work character actor sipped Pernod at the bar; the men with beards sat at a table near the pub door. As he passed, David heard one of them say, ' "But that's share-pushing," I said in my naive way. "Call it what you like," he said, but he had a very uneasy look on his face.'

'Quite,' said the other.

' "Some people will do anything for money," I said. "Money's not everything." '

'That's a matter of opinion, Charles . . .'

The couple who had been looking at the cartoons sat down and David saw that behind them, in the most dimly lit corner, was a girl alone. Her back was turned to him and she had only a blank wall to stare at. He ordered a light ale.

'Buying on a margin like that,' said the man called Charles. 'Apart from the ethics of the thing, I personally like to sleep quiet in my bed. Shall we go?'

'I'm ready when you are.'

They went and while David was waiting for his change, he looked curiously at the solitary girl. He could only see her back, made shapeless by the vinyl jacket she wore, a head of glossy black hair, long legs in velvet trousers twined round the legs of her chair. She sat quite still, gazing at the brown panelling with the raptness of someone watching an exciting television programme.

He was surprised to see a girl in there alone. It used to be the practice, a kind of unwritten law among West End licensees, not to serve women on their own. Probably still was. However, this girl didn't seem to have a drink.

There was something familiar about the set of her shoulders and he was wondering whether he ought to know her when the door opened to admit four or five young men. The sudden cool draught caused her to turn her head swiftly and nervously. Instantly, but almost incredulously, David recognised her.

'Good evening, Mrs Heller.'

The expression on her face was hard to analyse. Fear? Caution? Dismay? Her curious green eyes, speckled with gold and iridescent like a fly's wing-cases, flickered, then steadied. David wondered what on earth she could be up to, by herself in a West End pub on the very day of her dead husband's inquest.

'Is this your local or something?' she asked in a discouraging voice.

'I come here sometimes. Can I get you a drink?'

'No.' The negative exploded from her so loudly that several people turned to look. 'I mean, no, thanks. Don't bother. I'm just going.'

David had considered whether he ought to write her the conventional letter of condolence, but because offering sympathy to a woman released by death from an obviously unhappy marriage seemed misplaced, he had thought better of it. Now, however, he felt it incumbent on him to say something, if only to show he was aware of Heller's death, and he embarked on a little stilted speech of regret. But after murmuring, 'Yes, yes,' impatiently and nodding her head, she interrupted him inconsequentially.

'I was meeting someone, but she hasn't come.'

She? David thought of all the possible meeting places for two women in London in the evening. An office where the other girl worked? One of the shops that stayed open late? A café? A tube station? Never, surely, a pub in Soho. Magdalene Heller got up and began buttoning her coat.

'Can I take you to your station? My car's not far away.'

'Don't bother. It's not necessary.'

David drank up his beer. 'It's no bother,' he said. 'I'm sorry your friend didn't come.'

Politeness wasn't her strong suit, but in everyone except the savage, convention forbids actually running from an acquaintance and slamming the door in his face. That, he thought, was what she would have liked to have done.

They approached the door and she fumbled in her bag with fingers he thought none too steady. The cigarette was eventually found. David got out his lighter and held the flame up to her face.

Behind her the door opened. It opened perhaps a foot and then stuck. Magdalene Heller inhaled, turning her head. David didn't know why he kept his finger pressed on the light, the flame still flaring. The man who had opened the door stood on the step, staring in.

Again Magdalene Heller faced him. Her lips parted and she said with an unexpected effusiveness, 'Thank you so much, David. I'm glad we ran into each other.'

David was so taken aback by this sudden *volte-face* that he too stared into her beautiful, suddenly flushed face. Her cigarette had gone out. He lit it again. The man backed abruptly the way he had come, leaving the door swinging.

They were ready to go, on the point of leaving, but she opened her bag again, rummaging aimlessly in its contents.

'D'you know that fellow?' David asked and then, feeling that he had been rude, added truthfully, 'I'm sure I do. Might be someone I've come into contact with on television, of course. His face seemed awfully familiar.'

'I didn't notice.'

'Or I could have seen his picture in a newspaper. That's it, I think, in connection with some case or other.'

'More likely on TV,' she said casually.

'He seemed to know you.'

Or had it been that this girl was so outstandingly good-looking that even in the West End where beauty is common, men stared at her? She put her hand on his arm. 'David?' She was lovely, the face close to his as they came into the street, flawless with its orchid skin and gold-specked eyes. Why then did her touch affect him strangely, almost as if a snake had flickered against his sleeve? 'David, if you haven't anything better to do, would you – would you drive me home?'

All the way to the car she chattered feverishly and she clung to David's arm. She had an accent, he noticed, that wasn't from London or from the North. He couldn't quite place it, although he tried while he pretended to listen to what she was saying, whether she would be able to keep her flat, her future, her lack of training for any sort of job.

She didn't look like a new widow. The clothes she was wearing were not those he had seen in the inquest report picture, although those had been indecorous enough. Now she was dressed shabbily, casually and – he observed this for the first time as she got into the car – provocatively. He disliked fly-fronted trousers on women and these were far too tight. She took off her shiny jacket and draped it over the seat. Her breasts, though undoubtedly real, had an inflated rubbery look and they were hoisted so high as to suggest discomfort, but as if the discomfort were worth suffering for the sake of the erotic appeal. All this was fair enough in a beautiful girl of twenty-five, all this sticky seductive make-up, long cheek-enveloping hair, and emphasis given to a bold figure. But she wasn't just a girl of twenty-five. She was a widow who that morning had attended the inquest on her husband and who was supposed to be, if not grief-stricken, stunned by shock and subdued by care.

They had been driving along for perhaps a quarter of an hour when she put her hand on his knee. He hadn't the courage to remove it and he began to sweat when the fingers caressed and kneaded his flesh. She smoked continuously, opening the window every couple of minutes to flick ash out into the street.

'Is it straight on,' he said, 'or left here?'

'You can take the back doubles. It's shorter.' She wound down the window and threw her cigarette-end on to the pavement, narrowly missing a little Chinese. 'Take the next exit. I'll navigate for you.'

David obeyed her, going left, right, left again, and plunging into a web of mean streets. It was still quite light. They came to a bridge with huge concrete pillars at either end, carved columns vaguely Egyptian, that might have come from the Valley of the Kings. Underneath was a kind of marshalling yard, overlooked by factories and tower blocks.

'Down here,' Magdalene Heller said. It was a narrow street of tiny slum houses. Ahead he could see a tall chimney, a gasometer. 'What's the hurry?'

'It's not exactly a beauty spot, is it? Not the sort of place one wants to hang about in.'

She sighed, then touched his hand lightly with one fingertip. 'Would you stop a moment, David? I have to get cigarettes.'

Why couldn't she have bought them in London? Anyway, the three or four she had smoked had come from a nearly full pack. He could see a shop on the corner and he could see that it was closed.

Reluctantly he pulled into the kerb. They were quite alone and unobserved. 'I'm so lonely, David,' she said. 'Be nice to me.' Her face was close to his and he could see every pore in that smooth fungoid skin, mushroom skin, rubbery as he could guess that too-perfect, pneumatic body to be. There was a highlight on her lips where she had licked them. 'Oh, David,' she whispered.

It was like a dream, a nightmare. It couldn't be happening. As if in a nightmare, for a moment he was stiff and powerless. She touched his cheek, stroking it, then curled her warm hands around his neck. He told himself that he had been wrong about her, that she was desperately lonely, devastated, longing for comfort, so he put his arms around her. The full wet lips he by-passed, pressing his cheek against hers.

He stayed like that for perhaps thirty seconds, but when her mouth closed on his neck with sea-anemone suction, he took his arms from her shoulders.

'Come on,' he said. 'People can see us.' There was no one to see. 'Let's get you home, shall we?' He had to prise her off him, a new and quelling experience. She was breathing heavily and her eyes were sullen. Her mouth drooped pathetically.

'Come and have a meal with me,' she said. Her voice had a dismayed whine in it. 'Please do. I can cook for you. I'm a good cook, really I am. You mustn't judge by what I was giving Bernard that night. He didn't care what he ate.'

'I can't, Magdalene.' He was too embarrassed to look at her.

'But you've come all this way. I want to talk to you.' Incredibly, the hand came back to his knee. 'Don't leave me all alone.'

He didn't know what to do. On the one hand, she was a widow, young, poor, her husband dead only days before. No decent man could abandon her. He had already abandoned the husband, and the husband had killed himself. But on the other hand, there was her outrageous behaviour, the clumsy seduction attempt. There was nothing cynical in concluding her offer of a meal was just eyewash. But was he justified in leaving her? He was a grown man, reasonably experienced; he could protect himself, and under the peculiar circumstances, do so with tact. Above all, he wondered why he need protect himself. Was she a nymphomaniac, or so unhinged by shock as to be on the edge of a mental breakdown? He wasn't so vain as to suppose against all previous evidence to the contrary, that women were spontaneously and violently attracted to him. The wild notion that he might suddenly have developed an irresistible sex appeal crossed his mind to be immediately dismissed as fantastic.

'I don't know, Magdalene,' he said doubtfully. They passed the prison or barrack wall and they passed the lighted cinema. There was a long bus queue at the stop by the park. David heard himself let out a small sound, a gasp, a stifled exclamation. His hands went damp and slithered on the wheel. Bernard Heller stood at the tail of the queue, reading his evening paper.

Of course, it wasn't Bernard. This man was even bigger and heavier, his face more ox-like, less intelligent than Bernard's. If David hadn't already been jumpy and bewildered he would have known at once it was the twin brother, Carl who had borrowed the slide pojector. But they were uncannily alike. The resemblance made David feel a bit sick.

He pulled the car in alongside the queue and Carl Heller lumbered into the back. Magdalene had gone rather pale. She introduced them snappily, her accent more pronounced.

'David's going to have dinner with me, Carl.' She added as if she had a part-share in the car and more than a part-share in David, 'We'll drop you off first.'

'I can't stay for dinner, Magdalene,' David said firmly. The presence of Bernard's twin both discomfited him and gave him strength. Here were capable hands in which he could safely leave the girl. 'I'm afraid I don't know where you live.'

Magdalene said something that sounded like Copenhagen Street and she had begun on a spate of directions when David felt a heavy hand, grotesquely like the comedy scene hand of the law, lower itself on to his shoulder and rest there.

'She's in no fit state for company tonight, Mr Chadwick.'
The voice was more guttural than Bernard's. There was
more in that sentence than a polite way of telling someone
he wasn't wanted. David heard in it self-appointed owner-
ship, pride, sorrow and – yes, perhaps jealousy. 'I'll look
after her,' Carl said. 'That's what my poor brother would
have wanted. She's had a bad day, but she's got me.'

David thought he had never heard anyone speak so pon-
derously, so slowly. The English was correct and idiomatic,
yet it sounded like a still-difficult foreign tongue. You
would grow so bored, exasperated even, if you had to listen
to this man talking for long.

Magdalene had given up. She said no more until they
reached Hengist House. Whatever she had been trying on,
she had given it up.

'Thanks for the lift.'

'I'm glad I saw you,' David said untruthfully. Carl's face
was Bernard's, unbearably pathetic, dull with grief, and
David heard himself say in a useless echo of his words to
the dead man, 'Look, if there's anything I can do . . .'

'No one can do anything.' The same answer, the same
tone. Then Carl said, 'Time will do it.'

Magdalene lagged back. 'Good night, then,' David said.
He watched Carl take her arm, propelling her, while she
tugged a little and looked back, like a child whose father
has come to fetch it home from a dangerous game with the
boy next door.

8

Julian and Susan had tried to be very civilised and enlight-
ened. They had to meet for Julian to see his son. It had
seemed wiser to try to maintain an unemotional friendship
and Susan had known this would be difficult. How difficult, how nearly impossible, she hadn't envisaged. When
life went smoothly, she preferred not to be reminded of
Julian's existence and his telephone calls – incongruously

more frequent at such times – were an uncomfortable disruption of peace. But when she was unhappy or nervous she expected him to know it and to a certain degree be a husband to her again, as if he were in fact a husband separated from his wife for perhaps business reasons, who had to live far away.

She knew this was an impossible hope, totally unreasonable. Nothing on earth would have made her disclose this feeling to anyone else. Julian had his own life to lead.

But was it so unreasonable to expect at this time some sign of concern from him? Louise's death had been in all the newspapers; tonight both evening papers featured the inquest. Julian was an avid reader of newspapers and the fact that the two Evenings had been delivered to her house, were now spread on the table before her, was a hangover from her marriage to Julian who expected his wife to be well-informed.

That he still hadn't phoned showed a careless disregard for her that changed her loneliness from a gathering depression to a panicky terror that no-one in the world cared whether she lived or died. To spend the evening and night alone here suddenly seemed a worse ordeal to pass through than any she had encountered since her divorce. For the first time she resented Paul. But for him, she could have gone out tonight, gone to the pictures, rooted out a friend from the past. Here in this house there was nothing else to think about but Louise and the only conversation possible an interchange between herself and her *alter ego*. The sentences almost spoke themselves aloud, the answerless questions. Could she have helped? Could she have changed the course of things? How was she going to stand days, weeks, months of this house? Above all, how to cope with Paul?

He had gone on and on that evening about Louise and the man. Because someone had told him Louise had loved this man, he found curious childish parallels between her case and that of his parents. Susan too had found parallels and she couldn't answer him. She reproached herself for her inadequacy but she was glad when at last he fell silent and slid the beloved cars out of their boxes, playing with absorption until bedtime.

So it was unforgivable to feel this mounting anger when she went to her desk and saw how he had left it, a multi-storied car park with miniscule bonnet and fender protruding from every slot and cranny. Black tyre marks were scored across each of the top three sheets of her typescript. Unforgivable to be angry, cruel perhaps not to control that anger.

But the words were out when she was halfway up the stairs, before she could stop herself and count to ten through set teeth.

'How many times have I told you to leave my things alone? You're never to do it again, never! If you do, I won't let you wear your watch for a whole week.'

Paul gave a heart-breaking wail. He made a grab for the watch, pulling it from its velvet-lined case, and cradling it against his face. Desperately near tears herself, Susan fell on her knees beside him and took him in her arms.

'Stop crying. You mustn't cry.'

'I'll never do it again, only you're not to take my watch.' How quickly a child's tears evaporated! They left no trace, no ugly swollen redness. Louise's weeping had left her face furrowed, old, distraught.

Paul watched her with a child's sharp intuition. 'I can't go to sleep, Mummy,' he said. 'I don't like this house any more.' His voice was small and muffled against her shoulder. 'Will they catch the man and put him in prison?'

'He's dead too, darling.'

'Are you sure? Roger's mother said he'd gone away, but she said Mrs North had gone away too. Suppose he isn't dead and he comes back here?'

Susan left the light on in his bedroom and the light on on the landing. When she got downstairs again she lit the twentieth cigarette of the day, but the smoke seemed to choke her, starting a long spasm of coughing. It left her shivering with cold. She ground out the cigarette, turned up the central heating and, going to the phone, dialled Julian's number.

Tonight, when nothing went right and all things seemed antagonistic, it would have to be Elizabeth who answered.

'Hallo, Elizabeth. Susan.'

'Susan . . .' The echoed name hung in the air. As always, Elizabeth's gruff schoolgirlish voice held a note of doubt. The impression was that she knew quite ten Susans, all of whom were likely to telephone her and announce themselves without surname or other qualification.

'Susan Townsend.' It was grotesque, almost past bearing. 'May I have a word with Julian?'

'Sure, if you want. He's just finishing his mousse.' How those two harped on food! They had plenty in common; one day, no doubt, they would share obesity. 'Good thing you rang now. We're just off for our weekend with Mummy.'

'Have a good time.'

'We always have a great time with Mummy. I do think all this killing in Matchdown Park is the end, and you up to your neck in it. But I expect you kept cool. You always do, don't you? I'll just fetch Julian.'

He sounded as if his mouth was full.

'How are you, Julian?'

'I am well.'

Susan wondered if her sigh of exasperation was audible at the other end. 'Julian, I expect you've read about all this business out here. What I want to ask you is, d'you mind if we sell this house? I want to move as soon as possible. I can't remember the way our joint property is tied up but I know it's complicated and we both have to agree.'

'You must do exactly as you like, my dear.' Had he brought the mousse with him? It sounded as if he was eating while he talked. 'You're absolutely free. I shan't interfere at all. Only don't think of taking less than ten thousand and wherever you choose to make your new home, see it's within distance of a decent school for my son and a good prep school when the time comes.' He swallowed and said breezily, 'Just put it in some agent's hands and let him do the lot. And if I meet anyone pining to vegetate in salubrious Matchdown Park I'll send him along. Tell me, were we ever on more than nodding terms with these Norths?'

'You weren't on more than nodding terms with anyone. Sneering terms might be more accurate.'

For a moment she thought he was offended. Then he said, 'You know, Susan, you've got a lot more waspish since we parted. It's rather becoming, almost makes me . . . well, no I won't say that. Rather a sexy-looking fellow, this North, as I recall, and a quasi-professional job, surely?'

'He's a quantity surveyor.'

'Whatever that may be. I suppose you and he are living in each other's pockets now, popping in and out of each other's houses. No wonder you want to move.'

'I don't imagine I shall ever speak to him again,' said Susan. Julian muttered something about finishing dinner, packing, setting off for Lady Maskell's. She said good-bye quickly because she knew she was going to cry. The tears rolled down her cheeks and she didn't bother to wipe them away. Every time Julian talked to her she hoped for kindness and consideration, forgetting for the moment that this was how he had always spoken to other people, waspishly, lightly, frivolously. She was the other people now and the tender kindness was Elizabeth's.

And yet she didn't love him any more. It was the habit of being a wife, of coming first in a man's scheme of things, that she missed. When you were married you couldn't ever be quite alone. You might cling on your own which was different. And whoever she begged to come to her now would look on her necessarily as a nuisance, a bore that separated them from the person they would prefer to be with.

For all that, she considered phoning Doris or even Mrs Dring. Her pride prevented her as her fingers inched towards the receiver.

Paul had fallen asleep. She covered him up, washed and redid her face. There was no point in it, but she sensed that if she were to go to bed now, at seven-thirty, it might become a precedent. You went to bed early because there was nothing to stay up for. You lay in bed late because getting up meant facing life.

She was going to move. Cling on to that, she thought, cling on to that. Never again to see the cherry trees come into crêpe paper bloom, the elms swaying above the cemetery, the three dull red pinpoints burning by the roadworks trench. Never again to run to a window because a dog barked or watch Bob North's headlights swing across the ceiling and die in a wobble of shadow against the wall.

They were glazing through the room now. Susan pulled the curtains across. She opened a new packet of cigarettes and this time the smoke didn't make her cough. Her throat felt dry and rough. That must be the intense heat. Why did she keep feeling alternately cold and hot? She went outside to adjust the heating once more, but stopped, jumping absurdly with shock, when the front door bell rang.

Who would call on her at this hour? Not surely those friends of her marriage, Dian, Greg, Minta, their consciences alerted by the evening papers? The dog hadn't barked. It must be Betty or Doris.

The man on the doorstep cleared his throat as she put her hand to the latch. The sound, nervous, gruff, diffident, told her who it was before she opened the door. She felt an unpleasant thrill of trepidation that melted quickly into pure relief that anyone at all had come to call on her. Then, coughing again, as nervous as he, she let Bob North in.

At once he made it clear that this wasn't a mere doorstep call and Susan, who had told Julian she would probably never be on more than remote terms with her neighbour, was curiously glad when he walked straight into the living-room as if he were a friend and a regular visitor. Then she told herself with self-reproach, that Bob had far more cause to be lonely and unhappy than she.

His face now bore no sign of the misery and bitterness to which he had given vent in court and although he again apologised for Susan's involvement in his affairs, he said nothing of why he had come. Susan had already put her sympathy and her sorrow for him into awkward words and now she could find nothing to say. That he had come with definite purpose was made clear by his nervous manner and the narrow calculating look he gave her as they faced each other in the warm untidy room.

'Were you busy? Am I interrupting something?'

'Of course not.' His loss made him different from other men, a pariah, someone you had to treat warily, yet appear to be no different. She wanted to behave both as if the tragedy had never happened and at the same time as if he were deserving of the most solicitous consideration. An odd reflection came to her, that it was impossible to feel much pity for anyone as good-looking as Bob. His appearance called for envy from men and a peculiarly humiliating admiration from women. If the tragedy hadn't happened and he had called like this, she would have felt ill-at-ease alone with him.

'Won't you sit down?' she said stiffly. 'Can I get you a drink?'

'That's very sweet of you.' He took the bottle and the glasses from her. 'Let me.' She watched him pour gin into a glass and fill it high with bitter lemon. 'What can I get you? No, don't shake your head . . .' He gave a very faint crooked grin, the first smile she had seen on his face since Louise's death. 'This is going to be a long session, Susan, if you'll bear with me.'

'Of course,' she murmured. This, then, was the purpose of his visit, to talk to one near enough to listen, far enough to discard when the unburdening was complete. Louise had tried to do the same, Louise had died first. Somewhere in all this there was a curious irony. Bob's dark blue eyes were on her, fixed, cool, yet doubtful as if he had still a choice to make and wondered whether he was choosing wisely.

She moved away from him to sit down and the sofa suddenly seemed peculiarly soft and yielding. A moment ago she had been glad to see Bob; now she felt only deeply tired. Bob walked the length of the room, turned sharply and, taking a roll of paper from his pocket, dropped it on the coffee table between them. He had an actor's grace, an actor's way of moving because he had studied and learnt those movements. Susan thought this with slight surprise and then she wondered if his gestures looked calculated because he was keeping them under a painful control.

She reached for the papers, raising her eyebrows at him. He nodded sharply at her. Could these quarto sheets be connected with some legal business? Could they even possibly be Louise's will?

Susan unfolded the first page without much curiosity. Then she dropped it with a sharp exclamation as if it had been rolled round something red-hot or something slimily disgusting.

'No, I can't possibly! I can't read these letters!'

'You recognise them, then?'

'Parts of them were read in court.' Susan's face burned. 'Why . . .' She cleared her throat which had begun to feel sore and swollen. 'Why do you want me to read them?' she asked fiercely.

'Don't be harsh with me, Susan.' His brow puckered like a little boy's. She thought suddenly of Paul. 'The police gave me these letters. They *belonged* to Louise, you see, and I've – well, I've inherited them. Heller sent them to her last year. *Last year*, Susan. Since I read them, I haven't been able to think of anything else. They haunt me.'

'Burn them.'

'I can't. I keep on reading them. They've poisoned every happy memory I have of her.' He put his face in his hands. 'She wanted to be rid of me. I was just an encumbrance. Am I so loathsome?'

She avoided the direct answer, for the question was absurd. It was as if a millionaire had asked for her opinion on the low state of his finances. 'You're overwrought, Bob. That's only natural. When people are having a love affair, they say things they don't mean, things that aren't true, anyway. I expect Julian's wife said a lot of exaggerated unpleasant things about me.' She had never considered this before. It cost her an effort to put it into words.

He nodded eagerly. 'That's why I came to you. I knew you'd understand.' Swiftly he got up. The letters were written on stiff quarto-size paper and they had once again sprung back into a roll. He flattened them with the heel of his hand and thrust them at Susan, holding them a few inches from her face.

She had spoken of the possibility of Elizabeth's having written defamotory things about her. If this had happened and such a letter come into her possession, nothing would have induced her to show it to a stranger. And yet the majority of strangers would jump at the chance. She must be exceptionally squeamish or perhaps just a coward, an ostrich. How avidly Doris, for instance, would scramble to devour Heller's words if, instead of coming here, Bob were baring his soul in the house across the street!

Susan reached for a cigarette. The thought came to her that she had never read a love-letter. During their courtship she and Julian had seldom been separated and when they were they phoned each other. Certainly she had never read anyone else's. Bob, who valued her for her experience, would be astonished at such innocence.

Perhaps it was this innocence that still held her back. Louise's love affair, a housewife and a salesman, a hole-in-the-corner ugliness, seemed to her merely sordid, unredeemed by real passion. The letters might be obscene. She glanced up at Bob and suddenly she was sure he would expose her to nothing disgusting. With a little sigh, she brought Heller's looped sloping writing into focus, the address: Three, Hengist House, East Mulvihill, S.E.29, the date, November 6th, '67, and then she began to read.

My darling,
You are in my thoughts night and day. Indeed, I do not know where dreaming ends and waking begins, for you fill my mind and I go about in a daze. I am a bit of a slow stupid fellow at the best of times, sweetheart – I can picture you smiling at this and maybe (I hope) denying it – but it is true and now I am half-blind and deaf as well. My love for you has made me blind, but I am not so blind that I cannot see into the future. It frightens me when I think we may have to go on like this for years, only seeing each other occasionally and then for a few snatched hours.

Why won't you make up your mind to tell him? It's no good saying something may happen to make everything come right for us. What can happen? He is not an old man and may live for years and years. I know you say you don't wish him dead but I can't believe it. Everything you say and the very look on your face shows me you feel he's just a burden to you. The rest is superstition and in your heart you know it. He has no rights, no hold over you that anyone would recognise these days.

What it boils down to, what you're really saying is that we just have to hang on and wait till he dies. No, I'm not trying to persuade you to put something in his tea. I'm telling you for the hundredth time to make him understand you have a right to your own life, to take it from him and give it to your loving but very miserable,

Bernard

No, it wasn't a disgusting letter – unless you happened to know the man Heller referred to as a tiresome encumbrance. And if you didn't know the man, you might even find the second letter poignant. If you didn't know the man and hadn't lived next door to the wife from whose betrayal Heller had drawn his insinuations.

The address was the same, the date nearly a month later. December 2nd, '67, Susan read, and then:

My sweet darling,

I can't go on living without you. I can't go on existing and working miles and miles away from you, thinking of you with him and wasting your life being a slave to him. You must tell him about me, that you have found someone who really loves you and will give you a proper home at last. You half promised you would when we met last week, but I know how weak you can be when actually with him.

Does he really need all this care and attention and wouldn't a housekeeper be able to do everything you do now? He has always been harsh and ungrateful, God knows, and you say sometimes violent. Tell him tonight, darling, while you are with him in what I can only call your prison.

Time goes on so quickly (it seems slow to me now but I know it really flies) and what will you be like in a few years time, growing older and still tied to him? He will never come to appreciate and love you now. All he wants is a servant. You will be bitter and soured, and do you really think our love can still last under those conditions? As for me, I sometimes think that without you I can only make an end to myself. I just can't envisage life dragging on like this much longer.

Write to me or, better still, come to me. You have never seen me happy yet, not happy as I will be when I know you have left him at last.

Bernard

Susan folded the letters and they stared at each other in a deep, sickened silence. To break it, she shied away from touching on the emotional content of the letters and, seizing on something mundane, said, 'Were there only these? Didn't he write any more?'

'Aren't they sufficient?'

'I didn't mean that. Only that I should have expected more, a whole series.'

'If there were more, she didn't keep them.'

'She may have been ashamed of them,' Susan said bitterly. 'They aren't exactly couched in deathless prose, not literary gems.'

'I hadn't noticed. I'm no judge of that sort of thing. Their meaning is clear enough. Louise hated me so much she was prepared to tell any lies about me.' He took the letters from her hand and kept hold of the hand, clutching it sexlessly, desperately, like a lifeline. 'Susan,' he said, 'you don't believe it, do you, that I was a violent, harsh, slave-driver?'

'Of course I don't. That's why I don't think there's any point in keeping the wretched things. You'll only read and re-read them and torture yourself.'

For a dreadful moment she thought he was going to cry. His face twisted and it was almost ugly. 'I can't bring myself to destroy them,' he said. 'Susan, would you do it, would you – if I left them here?'

Slowly she took them from his lap, expecting her wrist to be seized again. She felt rather as she did when each night she surreptitiously slipped the watch from Paul's hands while he slept. Here was the same held-breath caution, the same fear of a cry of protest. But Paul loved his watch. Was a kind of love curiously combined with Bob's hatred of these letters?

He let her take them. 'I promise, Bob,' she said, and a trembling weariness washed over her. 'I promise, as soon as you've gone.'

She thought he would go then. It was still early, but she had forgotten about precedents, about giving in to depression and tiredness. Now she only wanted to sleep.

But, 'I ought not to bore you with all this,' he said in the tone of someone who has every intention of doing so.

Evidently her tiredness didn't show. 'I've got to talk to someone. I can't bear to keep it all to myself.'

'Go ahead, Bob. I understand.'

So she listened while he talked of his marriage, his once great love for Louise, their disappointment at their childlessness. He speculated as to where Louise and Heller had met, what they could have had in common and how strange it was that Louise's faith had deserted her. He spoke with violence, with passion, with incredulity and once he got up to pace the room. But instead of exhausting him as they exhausted Susan, his outbursts seemed to invigorate him. Cleansed and renewed, he talked for half an hour, while Susan lay back, nodding sometimes and assuring him of her sympathy. The stubs in her ashtray piled up until they looked like the poster picture in the doctor's surgery. Her throat had become rasping, rubbing sandpaper.

'My God, I'm sorry, Susan,' he said at last. 'I've worn you out. I'll go.' She was beyond polite dissuasion. He took her hands impulsively and as he bent over her his dark vivid face went out of focus and swam above her. 'Promise I'll never see those foul things again,' he said. She nodded. 'I'll let myself out. I'll never forget what you've done for me.'

The front door closed and the sound of its closing reverberated in her head to settle into a steady throbbing. Long shivers were coursing through her now and her back had begun to ache. She closed her eyes and saw Bob's face suspended before them. Heller's spidery writing danced and the beating in a corner of her brain became the sharp clicking of Louise's heels.

When she awoke it was midnight. The air was foul with smoke. The heating had shut itself off and it was the cold which had awakened her, eating into her bones. Sometime before she slept she must have taken the glasses to the kitchen and emptied that spilling ashtray. She remembered nothing about it, but as she staggered to her feet she knew very well that her inertia and the sharp pain in her throat had little to do with the emotional vicissitudes of the day.

Symptoms like these had real physical cause. She had the flu.

9

Since Julian's departure Susan had slept in one of the two spare bedrooms at the back of the house. It was a small room with a north light but now she was glad she had chosen it. To be ill in a bedroom that was the twin of Louise's bedroom, to lie in a bed placed just where hers was, was the worst medicine Susan could think of.

She had passed a miserable night, getting sleep only in short snatches. By morning the bed was piled with every surplus blanket in the house, although Susan only dimly remembered fetching the extra ones. She took her temperature and found it was a hundred and three.

'Go over to Mrs Winter, darling,' she said when Paul pottered in at eight. 'Ask her to give you breakfast.'

'What's the matter with you?'

'I've just got a bad cold.'

'I expect you caught it off Roger Gibbs at the party,' said Paul, adding as if praising a friend for remarkable altruism, 'He gives his colds to everyone.'

The doctor came, arriving simultaneously with Doris who stood at the end of the bed, confirming his diagnosis and chipping in every few seconds with suggestions of her own.

'I don't want you to catch it, Doris,' Susan said feebly after he had gone.

'Oh, I shan't catch it. I never catch things.'

It was true. For all her vulnerability to low temperatures and her huddling into cardigans, Doris never even had a cold. 'I got immune to all that in my nursing days,' she said, punching pillows like a boxer. 'Just listen to my dog. He's kicking up a racket because all the funeral cars have come next door.' Cocking her head, she listened to the distant barking and what might have been an undertaker's subdued footfall. 'One thing, I've got an excuse for not going and it'd be suicide for you to get up.' She clapped her hand over her mouth. 'Oh dear, that's a dirty word round here, isn't it? I've heard the Catholics won't have Louise in their cemetery. Shame, really, when it was Heller who did it.' The dog barked hollowly, a door slammed. 'I've seen Bob and he sent his best wishes for a speedy recovery. Fancy, with all his troubles, he wanted to know if there was anything he could do. I said to John, Bob North's got a terrific admiration for Susan in his way, and John agreed with me. I've turned your heating full on, my dear. I hope you don't mind, but you know what a chilly mortal I am. I wonder if he'll get married again.'

'Who?'

'Bob, of course. Well, marriage is a habit, isn't it, and I should think it would be funny adapting yourself to the single life. Oh God, there I go again, both feet in it!' Doris blushed and hugged herself in her big double-knit jacket. 'Could you eat a cut off the joint? No, better not. By the way, I tidied up for you and dusted through. Not that it needed it, was was all as neat as a pin.'

'You're being awfully kind.'

'Just bossy and managing, lovey.' Doris's sudden unexpected self-analysis endeared her to Susan more than all her expert attention. She wished her painful throat and her huge weariness would allow her to speak her gratitude. She croaked out something about Paul and Doris said, 'He's gone with Richard. You can leave him with us for the weekend. What are you going to do with yourself? Maybe we could have the telly fetched up here.'

'No, really, Doris. I might read a bit later on.'

'Well, if you get bored, you can always watch the workmen slogging themselves to death.' And, twitching the curtain, Doris laughed loudly. 'They're as bad as I am, must have their fire and their tea.'

Watching three workmen fill in a trench and dig another one six feet up the road would hardly have been Susan's idea of compelling entertainment when she was well. She had often thought, as most people do, that if she was ever confined to bed, mildly sick, she would use the time to read one of those classics that demand uninterrupted concentration. So when Doris returned at lunchtime she asked her to fetch *Remembrance of Things Past* from the collection of books Julian had left behind him.

But Proust defeated her. She was uninterrupted, but her powers of concentration were so diminished as to leave her mind a vague blur of half-remembered worries, disjointed fears and thoughts of her removal from Matchdown Park. She put the book down after ten minutes of peering at the dancing print and, impatient to find herself yielding to Doris's silly suggestion, turned her eyes to the window.

The sky was a pale cloudy blue across which the elm branches spread their black lace tracery. She could just see the sun, a yellow puddle in the clouds. It all looked dreadfully cold and she could understand the workmen's need of a fire. The three of them were standing round it now, stirring tea in mugs Susan could see were coarse and cracked. Louise had given them china cups with saucers.

She propped the pillows behind her so that she could see better. Oddly enough, there was something peculiarly diverting in watching three unknown people moving about and talking to each other. That she couldn't hear what they said only increased the piquancy. There was an oldish man, a younger man and a boy. The two older men seemed to be chaffing the boy, but he took their shoving and their laughter good-humouredly. It was his task to collect the three mugs and take them back into the shelter of the hut. Susan saw him shake the dregs on to the clay-plastered pavement and wipe the insides of the mugs out with newspaper.

Presently they clambered back into their trench and the old man bowed his body over the broad handle of the drill. The boy had got hold of a muddy tangle of cables and capered about with them at which his companion started a mock fight. Only their heads and their flailing hands were visible over the ridge of the trench, but the boy's laughter was so shrill that, far away as she was, Susan could hear it above the reverberations of the drill.

Then a girl in a short red coat appeared around the corner of O'Donnells' fence and immediately, ceasing their sparring, the two younger men whistled her. She had to pass the roadworks and she did so with her nose in the air. The boy ogled her and shouted something.

Susan relaxed against her pillows. She had forgotten Louise and Bob, Paul's terrors, Julian's flippant unconcern. A much older woman crossed the road this time, but she too earned a heartening whistle. Susan smiled to herself, a little ashamed of getting amusement from something so puerile. How old did a woman have to be, she wondered, to escape this salute, thirty-five, forty, *fifty*? Certainly there was an open-hearted generosity in this lack of discrimination. Perhaps you were never too old or perhaps the old man, silent and grim while the other two acknowledged passing femininity, reserved his personal whistles for his female contemporaries.

At three the boy fetched a black kettle from the hut and began to boil it on the fire. Did they know Louise was dead? Had the news reached them somehow on the winged winds of gossip? Or had one of them come innocently to the back door on Thursday to be met by Bob's bitter staring eyes and Bob's abrupt dismissal?

The tea was made, the mugs refilled. The amount of tea they drank, they obviously preferred brewing their own to fetching it from the café two hundred yards away. No doubt it had been a blow to them when their emissary had gone to bang on Louise's door on Wednesday and got no reply. They hadn't sent the boy that time, Susan thought, but the man in his twenties who was pulling a blue jersey over his head as he crouched by the brazier.

The trench cut halfway across the road now and, having collected the mugs, the boy stationed himself on a pile of earth, a flag in his hand, to direct what little traffic passed. He swaggered, fancying himself a policeman on crossing patrol, but presently, after only two cars had passed, the blue-jersey man beckoned him back into the hole with fierce gestures. Susan felt that she was watching a silent film that would launch soon into knockabout farce, or perhaps some modern epic from Italy or Sweden, fraught with symbolism, where movement and facial expression are of deep significance and the human voice a vulgar intrusion.

And it was thus that Doris found her when she brought Paul home to put him to bed at six. The workmen had gone home and Susan lay back, looking dreamily at the dull crimson lights they had left behind them. She was absurdly disappointed that it was Sunday tomorrow, resentful like an avid viewer who knows he must wait two days for the next instalment of the serial.

'I've brought you a visitor,' Doris said on Sunday afternoon. 'Guess who.'

It couldn't be Julian, for he was staying in the country with Lady Maskell, part, no doubt, of a jolly gathering that would include Minta Philpott, Greg and Dian, and heaven knew who else. Besides, Julian avoided sickrooms.

'It's Bob.' Doris glanced nervously over her shoulder as his tread sounded on the stairs. 'He *would* come. I told him that in his low state he was vulnerable to every germ that's going, but he *would* come.'

His arms were full of daffodils. Susan was sure they were the ones that grew in the Braeside front garden and now she pictured that big square bed covered with the stubble of broken stalks. Louise had loved her bulbs and Bob's action in picking these flowers reminded Susan of a story she had once heard of the gardeners at Lady Jane Grey's home lopping the heads off all the oaks on the estate when she was killed. She said nothing of this to Bob. At first the sight of him embarrassed her and she wondered if he regretted his lack of reserve on Friday evening. But he showed no awkwardness, although his manner, until Doris had left them, was somewhat guarded.

'I rather expected you'd have gone away,' Susan said. 'Not exactly for a holiday, but just for a change.'

'There's nowhere I fancy going. All the places I've ever wanted to go to, I went with her.' He fetched a vase and arranged the daffodils, but clumsily for so graceful a man, crowding the stalks together and snapping them off roughly when they were too long. 'I'm better here,' he said, and when Doris thrust her head round the door with a bright smile. 'I've a lot of things to see to.'

'You're unlucky with your holidays, anyway,' Doris said. 'I remember last year Louise was ill and you were in that boat disaster.' Bob didn't say anything but his face darkened dangerously. 'Poor Louise had just what you've got now, Susan, and Bob had to amuse himself as best he could. Poor Louise said the holiday was just a dead loss as far as she was concerned. Oh dear, would you rather I didn't talk about her, Bob?'

'Please,' Bob said tightly. He sat down by Susan's bed, scarcely concealing his impatience as Doris twittered on about Paul's refusal to clean his teeth, his insistence on keeping the new watch under his pillow. 'Thank God she's gone,' he said when at last the door closed. 'Doesn't she drive you mad?'

'She's a good friend, Bob. Awfully kind.'

'She doesn't miss anything that goes on in this street. That dog of hers nearly sent me out of my mind when the funeral cars came.' He gave an unhappy sigh and suddenly Susan had for him what he had seemed to want all along, a fellow-feeling. Pity welled up in her so that, had she been well, she would have wanted to take him in her arms and hold him close to her as she might have held Paul. The thought startled her. Had it come to her because he looked so young, so pitiably vulnerable? He was older than she, four or five years older. For a moment she was embarrassed, almost dismayed.

He went to the door, opened it a fraction, then closed it softly. She thought he moved like a cat. No, like something less domestic. Like a panther. 'Got rid of those letters all right, did you?' His voice had the elaborate casual lightness of someone asking a question intensely but secretly important to him. 'That scum Heller's letters,' he said. 'You said you'd burn them.'

'Of course I did,' Susan said firmly. But the question jolted her, bringing the singing back to her head as if her temperature had swiftly taken a sharp rise. Until now she had forgotten all about the letters. They had been distasteful to her, she thought, and perhaps what had taken place in her mind was what Julian called a psychological block. Now, in spite of what she had said so reassuringly to Bob, she simply couldn't remember whether she had burnt the letters or not. Had she before, after or even during that dream-filled two-hour sleep that had almost been a coma, dropped the letters into the disused fireplace and set fire to them with her lighter? Or could they possibly be still on the table, exposed for Doris or Mrs Dring to read?

'I knew I could rely on you, Susan,' Bob said. 'Sorry if I was a bore the other night.' He picked up the book she had left face-downwards. 'Highbrow stuff you read! When I'm ill I only want to lie still and look out of the window.'

'That's what I did yesterday. I just watched the workmen most of the day.'

'Fascinating pastime,' he said rather coldly, and then, 'A rotten lonely life you lead, Susan. All these months you must have been lonely and I never gave it a thought.'

'Why should you?'

'I lived next door to you. I should have realised. Louise might have realised . . .' He paused and said, his voice charged with a dull anger, 'Only she was too busy with her own affairs. Or should I say affair? How old are you, Susan?'

'Twenty-six.'

'Twenty-six! And when you're under the weather you're stuck in a suburban bedroom with no-one to look after you and nothing better to do than watch four or five labourers dig up the road.'

It would be useless to tell him that for a few hours that suburban bedroom had been like a theatre box and the men actors on a distant comedy stage. Bob was such a physical, down-to-earth person, a prey to strong emotions but hardly the sort of man to get pleasure from the quiet observation of human behaviour. With his looks and his extrovert attitude to life, he had probably seldom experienced the taking of a back seat. He was looking at her now with such concern that she wondered why she had ever thought him selfish. She tried to laugh but her throat was too sore.

'But I'm not alone all the time,' she said, her voice rapidly disintegrating into a croak. 'And Doris is looking after me beautifully.'

'Yes, you said she'd been a good friend. I wish you'd said it of me. I wish things had been different so you *could* have said it of me.'

There was no reply to that one. He got up abruptly and when he came back, Paul was with him, the watch still strapped round his wrist at the edge of his pyjama sleeve.

'I can't kiss you, darling. I'm all germs.'

'You haven't got a clock in here,' Paul said. 'Would you like my watch, just for tonight?'

'That's a kind thought, but I wouldn't dream of depriving you.'

His look of relief was unmistakable. 'Well, good night, then.'

'Here, let's see if I can lift you.' Bob put out his hands to clasp the boy's waist. 'You've got so tall. I bet you weigh a ton.' It gave Susan a faintly sad shock to see that hard bitter face so suddenly tender. He had no children of his own, but now . . . Of course he would marry again. Perhaps because it was too soon to have such hopes for him, the thought was vaguely displeasing.

Paul let Bob pick him up, but when the man's arms tried to swing him high as if he were a tiny child, he struggled and said babyishly, 'Put me down! Put me down!'

'Come on now, don't be silly.' Susan was tired now. She wished they would all go and leave her. Paul would take a long time getting off to sleep tonight. Let Bob think her son had protested because he didn't care to be babied; she knew that there was another darker reason.

'Good night, Susan.' The rejection hadn't upset him at all and now he gave her the charming boyish smile that made her forget how sullenly that dark face could cloud. It was such a frank, untroubled smile, ingratiating almost. She felt strangely that he had made these overtures to her son to please her rather than from a fondness for children.

'Good night, Bob. Thank you for the flowers.'

'I'll come again soon,' he said. 'Don't think you've seen the last of me.' They were alone now. He went to the door and hesitated. 'You've been my lifeline, Susan. You've been a light in the darkness.'

Less than a week ago she had been prepared to go to any lengths to avoid him. Now it seemed a cowardly, impossibly exclusive way to have behaved. Far from being selfish, he was kind, thoughtful, impulsive, all those things that Julian had never been. But she didn't know why she should compare him with Julian at all – they were so utterly different, in looks, in temperament, in manner to her – unless it was because her former husband was the only other man she could truthfully say she knew.

When the repetitive sing-song, the 'Tick-tock, tick-tock', softly chanted from Paul's bedroom ceased, Susan put on her dressing-gown, checked that her son was asleep, and made her way downstairs. Her legs were weak and each step sent a throbbing through her body up into her head.

The living-room was neater than Mrs Dring ever left it. Susan's eyes went immediately to the coffee table where she last remembered having seen Heller's letters, but there was only a clean ashtray on the polished circular expanse. She moved slowly about the room, leafing absurdly through a pile of magazines, opening drawers. This, she thought, putting her hand to her forehead, was how an underwater swimmer must feel, struggling to make a free passage through a cumbersome, unfamiliar heaviness. The air in this room seemed thick, dragging her limbs.

Doris would have loved to read those letters.

It was an unforgivable thought to have about so kind a friend. Besides, Doris would never have taken them out of the house. Susan moved aside the firescreen and peered into the grate. There was no paper ash on the clean bars.

For all that, she must have burnt them herself. And now as she cast her mind back to those dazed fever-filled hours, she could almost convince herself that she remembered holding the letters in the fireplace and watching her lighter flame eat across the pages to devour Heller's words. She could see it clearly just as she could picture Doris tidying the grate, dustpan and brush in her hand.

Her relief nearly equalled total peace of mind and if she was again shivering uncontrollably it was only because she was still ill and had disobeyed the doctor's instructions to stay in bed.

10

The soft insinuating voice at the other end of the line was peculiarly persistent. 'Bernard thought such a lot of you, David. He often talked about you. It seems a pity to lose touch and I know Carl wants to meet you again. We were both disappointed when you couldn't stay and have a meal on Friday, so I wondered if you'd make it another time. Say tomorrow?'

'I'm afraid I couldn't make it tomorrow.'

'Tuesday, then?'

'I can't make it this week at all. I'll ring you, shall I?' David said good-bye firmly and hung up. Then he went back into the untidy, cluttered but interesting room he called a studio and thought about it.

She had a face like Goya's *Naked Maja*, full-lipped, sensuous. It didn't attract him. He was always finding resemblances between living people and people painted long ago. Portraits were pinned all over his walls, Ganymede reproductions, picture gallery postcards, pages cut out of Sunday paper colour supplements. Vigee Le Brun's *Marie Antoinette* was there, stuck up with Sellotape next to an El Greco *Pope*; Titian's *L'homme aux Gants* had a frame which was more than he had accorded to his Van Gogh peasants or the Naked Maja herself.

A peculiar inconsistent woman, he thought, and he wasn't thinking about the Goya. She had been surly to him on the night before her husband's death and actually dismayed to see him in The Man in the Iron Mask. And then, after five minutes stilted courtesy on his part and absent-minded rejoinders on hers, she had changed her entire personality, becoming sweet, seductive and effusive. Why?

They said that no man can resist a pretty woman who throws herself at him. His nature is such that he succumbs, unable to believe such good fortune. And if he has not himself made the slightest overture, he congratulates himself, while despising the woman, on his irresistible attractions. But it hardly ever happens that way, David thought. It had never happened to him before. There had been no difficulty at all in resisting. From the first he had been bewildered.

And yet he would have done nothing about it. The incident would have been dismissed to the back of his mind, along with various others of life's apparently insoluble mysteries. People were peculiar, human nature a perennial puzzle. You had to accept it.

But she had telephoned him, talking like an old friend who had every hope and every justification for that hope of becoming much more. From a vague uneasiness, his bewilderment grew until it crowded everything else from his mind. No matter how carefully he thought about it, going over and over the events of Friday night, he could only justify Magdalene Heller's conduct by assuming her to be not quite sane. But he knew that this conclusion is always the lazy and cowardly resort of a poor imagination. Mad she might be, but there would be method in her madness. Young widows do not go into West End pubs on the day of their husband's inquests; they do not dress in tight trousers and tight sweaters; above all they do not make inexplicable unprovoked passes at casual acquaintances.

She said she had been there to meet someone and he had never for a moment believed that someone was a woman. Then he remembered the man who had come in, who had stared at her, hesitating, before retreating in haste. From that precise moment her manner towards David had changed.

Suddenly David knew quite certainly that her appointment had been with this man. She had arranged to meet a man at the pub, but the meeting must be a secret one. Why else had she failed to make the necessary introductions, denied recognising that face which now, as David remembered it, had worn in that first instant a look of satisfaction, of pleasurable anticipation? She knew him. She guessed that David's curiosity had been aroused, so she had staged the scene in the car to blind him, to seduce him and, ultimately, to make him forget what he had seen.

It must be terribly important to her, he thought, and he recalled her nervous gabbling and the urgency of her caressing hand. She had detained him in the pub after the man had gone. Because, having speculated as to the man's identity, he might have looked for him in the street, and seeing his face in daylight, have made absolute recognition certain?

But he and the Hellers had, as far as he knew, no acquaintances in common. How could he have recognised a friend of Magdalene's? And, supposing he had, why did it matter so much to her?

Suddenly it had grown too warm for a fire, even outside. The roadmen had brought a spirit stove with them and the boy boiled their kettle on it inside the hut. For the first time, as if lured out by the fine weather, the man in the blue jersey was working above ground, and for the first time too, Susan saw him standing erect.

She was surprised to see that he was rather short, or, rather, short in the leg. Perhaps it was the length of his torso which had deceived her. She had a strong impression that she associated this man with height, but she didn't know why.

Then it came to her that on one previous occasion she had seen him walking along on level ground. She had seen him in Louise's garden on the day of Louise's death, and now, as she thought about it, the impression of a much taller man strengthened and grew vivid. Surely that man had been quite six feet tall and more slightly built than Blue Jersey who, swinging a pick, showed a thick waistline and a heavily muscled back.

The answer must be that at that time there had been more than three men working on the road. When he brought the daffodils, Bob had spoken of four or five men and no doubt he was better-informed on this matter than she who had scarcely spared the labourers a second glance until illness brought them into compelling perspective.

That illness was now receding and by the middle of the week Susan had lost interest in the workmen. Their doings had lost their freshness or her own standard of entertainment, lowered by fever, had risen. She read her Proust, hardly distracted even by the spasmodic scream of the drill.

'Mr North popped in with some books.' Mrs Dring piled a stack of new magazines on the bed. 'I reckon it's been the best thing that could have happened for him, you being ill. It's taken him out of himself, stopped him brooding. He coming in here again tonight, is he? You want to mind your neighbours don't get talking. That Mrs Gibbs has got a tongue as long as your arm.'

'Oh, rubbish,' Susan said crossly. 'You said yourself he only comes for something to occupy his mind.'

'And he's the type that occupies his mind with women.

You needn't look like that. I dare say there's no harm in it. Men are men when all's said and done. My husband's different, but then he's one in a million as I've always said. And talking of men, if you're going to start sitting up you want to watch that lot in the road don't see you all in your nothings.'

Mrs Dring's manner was more that of a nanny than a charwoman. Susan let her draw the curtains half across the window and accepted, with a meek shrug, the bedjacket that was tossed on to the pillow.

'How many men are there working on the road, Mrs Dring?'

'Just the three.'

'I thought there were four or five last week.'

'There was never more than three,' said Mrs Dring. 'That was your temperature making you see double. There's always been just the three.'

Magdalene Heller phoned David again on Wednesday evening. She was very lonely, she said, she hardly knew a soul but Carl.

'What about your friend you were meeting in the pub?'

'I don't know him that well.'

'Better than me, surely?' Did she know what she had said? He muttered a quick good-bye. Her voice after that fatal sentence had sounded stunned. This was no fear of being caught out in a clandestine adventure, no fear of scandal. David sensed that she was deathly afraid. He had guessed right and located the source of her fear, her sudden change of heart, her advances to himself, and briefly he was elated. She wouldn't bother with him again.

Of course she had set herself up as very pure, the essence of wronged womanhood in the coroner's court. It would look funny if it turned out she had a man friend of her own, and he remembered how he had thought she was going to meet a man when he had watched her visiting the cinema. It might be a thought to read that inquest report again and see just what she had said.

Presently he unearthed the old newspaper – he always kept newspapers for weeks and weeks, finally bundling them up and putting them on top of his tiny dustbin – but the report was brief and very little of what Magdalene had said was quoted. With a shrug, he folded the newspaper again and then his eye was caught by a front-page photograph on the previous Wednesday's copy of the *Evening News*. The caption beneath it said, 'Mr Robert North and his wife Louise, who was today found shot with Bernard Heller, a 33-year-old salesman. This picture was taken while the Norths were on holiday in Devon last year. Story on page 5.'

David's eyes narrowed and he looked searchingly into the photographed face. Then he turned quickly to page five. 'I had never even heard Heller's name,' North had told the coroner, 'until someone in the street where I live told me that *Equatair*'s rep. had repeatedly called at my house. I never saw him till he was dead and I certainly didn't know he was a married man.'

But six hours later he had walked into a Soho pub where he had arranged to meet that married man's widow.

A regular weekly feature of *Certainty* was a kind of diary written entirely by Julian Townsend and called 'Happenings'. In fact, as few things ever happened to Julian and he was incurably lazy, the diary consisted less of accounts of events attended by him than a *mélange* of his opinions. There was usually some local war going on for Julian to condemn and advise negotiation or arbitration; some bill being placed before Parliament which enraged him; some politician whose way of life annoyed him and offered him an occasion of mischief-making. When, as occasionally happened, a freak silly season occurred, Julian vented his vituperation on old-established customs and institutions, spitting venom at the Royal Family, the Church of England, horse racing, musical comedies and the licensing laws.

This week 'Happenings' was as usual headed by Julian's name writ large on a streamer beneath which the writer's face scowled from a single column block. The high bumpy forehead, glossy with the sweat of intellect, round metal-framed glasses and supercilious mouth were familiar to David as a constant reader of *Certainty* and now he scarcely noticed them. A girl-friend of his, a television actress called Pamela Pearce, claimed acquaintance with *Certainty*'s editor and occasionally threatened to introduce him to David. But up till now he had steered clear of the encounter, preferring to keep his illusions. Townsend could hardly be as pompous, as self-opinionated and as pedantic as his articles led the reader to believe. David felt he might lose his zest for 'Happenings' if its writer turned out to be unassuming.

There was always a discourse on food and today Julian had gone to town, devoting the whole of his first column to recipes for aphrodisiac meat dishes and puddings, with erudite references to Norman Douglas, and half his second to a violent condemnation of the lunch he had eaten in a country hotel while week-ending with his aristocratic in-laws.

Smiling, David passed on. Apparently the fellow was going to fill up the rest of his space with an attack on the suburbs of London. 'Happenings' was a misnomer for this spate of vitriol. 'Rural England castrated by the entrenching tool, the pneumatic drill,' David read, amused. From the ravaged countryside, Julian sped towards the metropolis. 'Matchdown Park, where never a month passes without the demolition of yet another Georgian jewel . . .'

Rather odd. Years went by without a mention of Matchdown Park and now it was constantly in the news. David was surprised to find Townsend actually lived there. But he evidently did. 'The present writer's knowledge,' the paragraph ended, 'is based on five years' sojourn in the place.'

David fetched the blue S to Z telephone directory and there it was: Julian M. Townsend, 16 Orchard Drive, Matchdown Park. He hesitated, pondering. But when he began to dial, it wasn't the number on the page in front of him.

'Julian Townsend?' said Pamela Pearce. 'You're in luck, as it happens, darling. I'm going to a party tomorrow night and he's bound to be there. Why not come along?'

'Will his wife be there?'

'His wife? I expect so. He never goes anywhere without her.'

A Mrs Susan Townsend had found Heller's body, and she lived next door to the Norths in Orchard Drive. It was all in the paper and it must be the same woman. What he would say when he met her David hardly knew, but it should be easy to bring the conversation round to the North tragedy. It would still be a hot topic with her. She had been a friend of Mrs North. Didn't the paper say she had been paying an ordinary morning call? She would know if North and Magdalene Heller had known each other before the inquest and, since she had been in court, could tell him if North's statements – 'I didn't even know he was a married man' and so on – had been misreported or if, when heard in their full and proper context, were capable of a different, innocent interpretation. If she were co-operative, she could set his mind at rest.

For it was active and troubled enough now. North had come to meet Magdalene in The Man in the Iron Mask six hours after the inquest. That was just explicable. He could have done so and still not have lied to the coroner. But if something else which David suspected were true, he had lied blackly and irredeemably.

They had arranged to meet there. That he knew for certain. Had they ever met there before?

11

'It's a crying shame the mess them floors get in,' said Mrs Dring on all-fours. 'There's holes in this parquet you could put your finger in.' Louise's heels, Susan thought with a pang. Probably they would never be eradicated, but at least the new occupant need never know how they had been caused. Of this prospective buyer she now had high hopes, for, once well again, her first task had been to call at the estate agent's. She watched Mrs Dring obliterating small clayey footmarks, her interest caught when she said, 'Let's hope we've seen the last of all this mud. Did you know they've finished the road at last? The three of them filled up that hole of theirs last night and good riddance.'

She had seen the last act of their play, then. Settling at her typewriter, Susan wondered why they had ever dug that series of trenches and whether life in Matchdown Park would have been brought to a standstill without the monotonous rhythm of those drills and the renewing of those glimpsed cables. Her ability to concentrate and reason normally, rediscovered in the past two days, brought her intense pleasure. It seemed to her that her illness had marked the end of a black period in her life and during that illness she had found fresh resources, decided to break away from Matchdown Park and made a friend in Bob North.

But as she worked, congratulating herself on her recovery, a tiny thread of doubt crept across her mind. For some unexplored reason she was troubled by her recollections of the roadmen and although she should have shared Mrs Dring's relief at their departure, she began instead to feel a curious dismay.

There had never been more than three men, Mrs Dring insisted, and yet while Louise was lying dead with Heller she had seen a fourth man in Louise's garden. That man had knocked at Louise's back door – Mrs Dring had heard him do so – and then walked away, not to join the others, but off by himself down the road. Recapturing the scene, lifting her eyes from the type which had blurred, Susan remembered quite clearly that the three others, the old man, Blue Jersey and the boy, had been in their trench while he stood for a moment, hooded, anonymous, to warm his hands at their fire.

'Mrs Dring.' She got up, feeling a faint sickness, the aftermath of her flu. 'I've just remembered something, something rather worrying. I suppose I was getting this flu while I was at the inquest. Only – only they asked me if I'd seen anyone call next door during the morning and I said I hadn't. I said . . .' She stopped, appalled at the curiosity which almost amounted to hunger on Mrs Dring's uplifted face.

'Well, you didn't see no one, did you?'

'I'd forgotten. It can't matter now. We all knew what the verdict was going to be, but still . . .' And Susan bit her lip, not because of what she had said, but because she had said it to this woman, this bearer of malice, this arch trouble-maker who had no kind word for anyone but her husband. Then she managed a strained smile and, convincing herself she was changing the subject, said, 'You'll have a chance to get the floors nice now Paul won't be bringing in any more clay on his shoes.'

Gin and the 'something fizzy' he always liked to drink with it, coffee cups on a tray, the last of the daffodils displayed in a vase. Susan had only made these preparations once before but already they were becoming a ritual. Bob would be late tonight – he couldn't be with her until ten, for he had a business call to make – but she had already given up going to bed early. There was something to stay up for.

'It's always so wonderfully warm in here, Susan,' he said as he entered the living-room. 'There's a lot to be said for central heating. I don't know why I didn't have it put in years ago.'

She turned her head away to hide the blush, but, although she was aware of his solecism, she felt a rush of elation. In saying such a thing, he had showed her that while Louise's death was fresh in his mind, the circumstances which had led up to it were fading. Would it be right to trouble him now with the question she had been intending to put to him all day? In all their talks they had scarcely yet discussed any subject but that of Heller and Louise, and just the same she hesitated, waiting for him to begin as he always did, obsessively, minutely on the details of their love and death.

A lightness and a sense of relief came to her when instead he asked her casually if she knew of anyone who would do the Braeside housework for him.

'My Mrs Dring might. I'll ask her.'

'You've done so much for me, Susan, and here I am still asking favours.'

'A very small favour. She may not be able to.'

'Somehow I feel she will if you ask her. You're one of those people who make things come right. D'you know, in the past week I've often thought that if we'd really bothered to get to know you, if you and Louise had been friends, none of this would ever have happened.'

They were back to it again. Subject normal.

'If I'm really so powerful,' Susan said, an urgency entering her voice, 'if I can really make things come right, I'd like to begin by telling you to stop all that, Bob. Try to forget it, put it behind you.'

He reached out and took her hands, both her hands in a strong warm grasp. For a comforter, a safe refuge, she suddenly felt strangely weak and enervated.

Pamela Pearce was a pretty little blonde with a taste for glitter. Metallic threads ran through the materials of most of her clothes; she liked sequins and beads and studs, anything that sparkled. Tonight she wore lamé, and against the cobbles and the grey brick walls of the South Kensington mews she glittered like a goldfish in murky waters.

'Hadn't you better tell me who my host and hostess are?' David said as he locked his car. 'I don't want to feel like a complete gatecrasher.'

'Greg's one of those society photographers. You must have seen those lovely things he did of Princess Alexandra. His wife's called Dian and she's absolutely lovely. You'll fall madly in love with her. Believe me, just to see her is to adore her.'

The trouble was David was never quite sure whether he had seen her. He was hardly in a position to fall madly in love with her as nobody bothered to introduce him to anyone and, Pamela having been borne off up the narrow staircase, he found himself alone on an island of carpet, surrounded by indifferent backs. Presently he forced his way between barathea-jacketed backs and half-naked backs, moving his arms like a swimmer doing the breast stroke, and finally squeezing into a little lyre-backed chair. A screen behind him was perilously loaded with lighted candles which dripped wax on to an improvised bar.

For some minutes no one took any notice of him and Pamela didn't reappear. Then a voice behind him said incomprehensibly, 'Do you think you could get outside some cup?'

David looked over his shoulder, first at the young man with butter-coloured hair who had addressed him, then at the bar where, in a bowlful of pale golden liquid, cherries and pieces of cucumber were floating. Before he could say he would avoid this at any price, a ladleful had been scooped up and dribbled into a glass.

It tasted like fruit juice which someone had poured into a cough mixture bottle. David put his glass down behind a plate of smoked eel canapes, observing that everyone else seemed also to have shunned the cup.

The room was too small to accommodate so large a party, but even so the guests had succeeded in huddling themselves into distinctly isolated groups. The largest of these had for its nucleus a tall man with an enormous forehead and he stood beneath the central lamp which effectively spotlighted him. David had no difficulty in recognising Julian Townsend.

The editor's prim mouth was opening and shutting nineteen to the dozen while he gesticulated sweepingly with a large hand in which he held a sausage roll. Five women stood around him in a circle, hanging on his words.

One of them must be his wife, David thought, the innocent neighbour of Heller's mistress, she who had found the dead couple. There was a statuesque brunette with a cigar, two nearly identical blondes, a teen-ager in brown and an elderly lady who evidently intended to spend the rest of the weekend in the country, for she wore a tweed suit, mesh stockings and tall boots. Pamela was nowhere to be seen, although he could hear her shrill giggle occasionally from upstairs, and he felt a stab of annoyance. Short of introducing himself as a reader and a fan, he couldn't see how he was going to talk to Townsend without her.

Then the teen-ager detached herself from the sycophantic circle and made for the bar. Her movements had the rapid and entirely selfish directness of the very young and, to avoid her, David backed into the bamboo screen.

'Good gracious, you nearly set your hair on fire!' The butter-haired barman had seized his arm and David backed away from naked candle-flame.

'Thanks,' he said, his face inches from the girl's.

'You need someone to look after you, don't you?' said the barman. 'It quite upsets me to see you standing there all lost. Take him under your wing, Elizabeth, do.'

Having refused the cup and helped herself to brandy, the girl said baldly, 'I'm Elizabeth Townsend. What's your name?'

'David Chadwick.' He was very surprised and perhaps he showed it. In her very short shapeless dress of the colour and texture of brown bread and with her long untidy brown hair she looked about seventeen. No doubt accustomed to being in the company of a man never at a loss for words, she fixed him with an incredulous glare. 'I believe you live in Matchdown Park,' he heard himself say in exactly the tone of wistful awe someone might use when enquiring if an acquaintance had a grace and favour apartment at Hampton Court.

'My God, no. Whatever gave you that idea?'

'I read it in *Certainty*,' David said indignantly. 'You *are* Mrs Julian Townsend?'

'Of course I am.' She looked deeply affronted. Then her brow, furrowed with impatience and some imagined slight, cleared. 'Oh, I see it all now. You've dropped a clang.' His discomfiture stirred a gurgle from the depths of the brown bread dress. 'That's his ex you're thinking of, my – well, what would you call her? – wife-in-law might fit, don't you think?' She giggled happily at her own joke. 'Wild horses wouldn't make me live in Matchdown Park.' She said this with violent defiance, but almost before the words were out something quick and sharp came into her expression to change it and make it assume a slight concupiscence. 'Why d'you ask, anyway? Have you got some sort of yen to live in the place?'

'I might,' David muttered, not knowing where all this was leading. Never in all his life had he met anyone so brutally direct and unselfconscious as this girl. He wondered on what her confidence was built, plain, dumpy and charmless as she was.

'Only my wife-in-law . . .' She grinned with delight at her invented expression. '. . . my wife-in-law wants to move, so Julian's got this house in Matchdown Park on his hands. It's a very good sort of house.' She seemed sublimely unconscious that two minutes before she had denounced its environs with a shudder. 'Julian would be absolutely ecstatic if I'd found a buyer for him.'

Next door to Norths, inhabited by the woman who knew the Norths, who had found Heller's body. The candles flared behind David's head and their reflections, tall, smoky, yellow-white, danced in Elizabeth Townsend's glass. 'How big is it?' he said cautiously.

'Come and meet Julian. He'll tell you all about it.' She grabbed his arm, her fingers, urgent and almost affectionate, digging into his elbow. 'Julian, do shut up a minute! Listen, I've found a bloke who actually wants to live in Matchdown Park!'

Susan hadn't warned Paul that Bob was coming in for the evening. She didn't want him to awaken and, troubled by fears and fantasies as he was, hear a man's voice downstairs. In his present world men who called on solitary women brought guns with them . . .

Murmuring an excuse to Bob, she went up to Paul's bedroom, tucked him in again, restored his watch to a more secure position on the bedside table and went out again, leaving the light burning. She was half-way down the stairs when the phone rang.

'I don't suppose you've sold the house yet?' Julian's voice sounded unnaturally enthusiastic against a background of music and hilarity.

'Hardly,' Susan said dryly.

'That's what I thought. However, not to worry. Now tell me, are you doing anything on Monday night?'

She no longer loved him but it was horrible to be asked such a question by the man who had once been her husband.

'Why?'

'I've told some fellow he can come and look over the house. Chadwell, Challis – something like that. He's here with me now as a matter of fact – well, not exactly with me but we're all at Dian's and Elizabeth picked him up.'

'I thought you must be. I can hardly hear you for the racket. How is Dian?'

'Absolutely lovely as usual.'

Susan cleared her throat. 'What time does this man want to come?'

'Eightish. By the by . . .' He lowered his voice to a barely audible mumble. 'I shouldn't mention that peculiar affair next door. It might put him off.'

'Julian, you must be more naive than I think you if you imagine anyone could go through all the fuss of buying this house without finding out about Louise's suicide.' She stopped, aghast. All the doors were open and Bob must have heard. Too late now. 'Oh, Julian!' she said, exasperated.

'He might not find out,' Julian said craftily, 'until he'd signed the contract. Don't tell me you're indifferent to the prospect of five thousand pounds. Now I must return to this do. I suppose you're all alone?'

'In point of fact,' Susan said, 'I'm not. A friend is with me, so if you'll excuse me, Julian, I'd better get back to him.'

Bob sat where she had left him, on his face the blank look of someone who has been unable to help overhearing a private conversation but who must pretend, from politeness, to a temporary total deafness.

'Sorry about that,' Susan said crisply. 'You must have heard.'

'I couldn't help it. I gather you're thinking of moving, Susan?'

'The atmosphere here isn't right for Paul, and besides that . . . I suppose I wasn't well, I was almost hysterical at the end of last week. I wanted to get away as soon as possible, but that was before . . .'

Before what? What had she been about to say? Confused, she turned her head away. She had waited for him to finish the sentence for her and instead his glance was cool, analytical, assessing.

'When d'you think you'll go?'

'As soon as I can,' she said evenly, and then she made herself smile, crushing down the absurd disappointment. Had she really supposed this widower, this lost soul almost, came to see her because he was growing fond of her? He wanted a shoulder to cry on merely, and hers was waiting.

'I can understand you want to shake the dust of this place off your feet,' he said, 'put all the misery behind you. You'll soon forget about Louise and me, won't you?' Then, obsessively, forgetting perhaps that he had said it all before a dozen times, he began step by step to go over every word, action and suspicion that had led him to suspect Louise's love affair, to search again into the circumstances of her death.

'Bob,' Susan said sharply, 'you'll have to stop this. You'll turn yourself into a neurotic. What do you hope to gain by it? They're both dead, it's all over.' He looked at her, shocked and silenced. For the first time she was asking herself why, when another man would put up an outward show of courage, he should be so obsessed by his wife's death. A little thrill of nervousness, not quite fear, at the enormity of what she was about to say, ran through her. 'It isn't because . . .' she began slowly, 'it isn't because you doubt that it *was* suicide, is it?'

He made no answer. His smoky blue eyes had a glazed look and his face went dead so that the lamplight seemed to fall on a copper mask.

Susan's own words had startled her and now that they were out she was sure they would have been better unsaid. She had no grounds at all for saying them, only a vague unease that during the day and the previous day had held her standing sometimes in a dream or sent her upstairs to stare meaninglessly out of the window.

'It's just that, while I was ill . . .' She blushed hotly. Was this how Doris felt when she made one of her gaffes? 'There were one or two things,' she said, 'one or two odd things that made me wonder.'

'You were delirious.'

'Come now, I wasn't that ill.'

'I shouldn't want,' he said, 'I couldn't bear . . . Susan, it was his gun, they found the powder marks on his hand. How could there be . . . ?'

'If you don't think so,' she said, 'of course there can't be any doubt.' And she felt cold and sick because he was on his feet now. She had been his comforter and now he must think her just like all the others, stirring up trouble for him, making use of him as a topic for speculation. Wordlessly, he had moved out into the hall to stand on the spot where Louise's heel had pierced the parquet.

'Bob,' she said, going to him.

'Susan?'

'I was delirious.'

He touched her shoulder, bent down and brushed her cheek with his lips. It seemed like ages since anyone but Paul had kissed her and as she felt the light touch of his mouth she fancied she could still hear quite clearly the laughter and the music from that party far away, as if the telephone was still open, still transmitting it. A loneliness that was abysmal and a desire to end that loneliness at all costs, made her put out her hand and take his, holding it tightly.

'Forgive me?'

He nodded, still too shaken to smile. She heard him walk swiftly into Braeside but although, after a sick empty interval, she too went out into the garden, she saw that no lights had come on in the house next door where the windows were always closed.

12

The trees which grew from rectangles in the pavement were the kind David most disliked, sterile ornamental cherries and prunuses which bear no fruit. They were in full blossom now and he guessed that he had picked for his visit the one day in the year on which Orchard Drive justified its name. The buds had all opened, not a petal had yet fallen, and the flowers reminded him of crêpe paper. Behind the pink cloudy masses street lamps glowed with the acid drop quality of milky quartz.

He drove along slowly, following the route Heller had taken to see his love. The houses would only appear large to those with small horizons. They were not all the same – he counted four different types – but each was detached, each had an integral garage and a biggish lawned or landscaped front garden. He passed doors painted lilac and doors painted lime; he noted here the pretentious bay tree and there the pair of mass-produced carriage lamps. No raised voice, no subdued strain of music, no footfall disturbed the silence. He was beginning to see why wild horses wouldn't have dragged Elizabeth Townsend to live here.

Rather like a wild horse herself or perhaps a shaggy Shetland pony, she had tugged him towards the group where the editor of *Certainty* was holding forth. With a shout of 'Do me a favour, Mintay', and 'Mind your backs!' she had shoved him unceremoniously under her husband's nose.

Julian Townsend raised his eyebrows and one deprecating hand in his wife's direction. '. . . And just that essential dash of cointreau,' he finished. 'It makes all the difference between common *potage* and *haute cuisine*. Now, what was it you wanted to say, my darling?'

The female sycophants edged away. David looked awkwardly into the face that each week launched a thousand outraged letters. A faint dew glistened on Townsend's bulbous forehead and it creased and smoothed again as his little brown wife introduced David inaccurately.

'A private transaction would be nice, of course,' the great man said at last. 'Not that I'd consider less than ten thousand.'

'Not exorbitant these days.'

This casual rejoinder threw Townsend slightly off balance. It was apparent that he was thinking quickly, perhaps dismayed that he had named so paltry a sum. But, the mobile supercilious face having worked for some seconds, he seemed to abandon that line to say almost meekly, 'It's a delightful area, *rus in urbe*, you know. The house itself is in excellent condition. Do you know the district well?'

David, who had occasionally passed through it on the tube and heard it twice mentioned by Bernard Heller, said that he did. Townsend beamed at him.

'I really do think this calls for a drink.' He made no move to fetch drinks himself, but a kind of telepathy seemed to pass between him and the woman called Minta. She trotted off and returned with a trayful of whiskies. Townsend raised his glass and shouted something which sounded like '*Tervey-deksenne!*'

'A Finnish toast,' said Minta reverently.

So Townsend had gone off to find Dian and get her permission to use her phone. 'I do hope you buy it,' said his wife, tucking her arm into David's. 'We could do with our half-share in the ten thou. Give my love to poor old Susan.'

Well, he would see poor old Susan in a minute. This was the place next door to Braeside, innocent, respectable-looking Braeside where Heller had found something the green-eyed Magdalene could not give him and into which he had taken death.

Or had death come to him?

That, David thought, was presumably why he was here. To try to find out. To disturb this all-enveloping, blanket-like silence. The pale, dry papery flowers brushed his face as he got out of the car. He slammed the door and from behind him out of the dark stillness came an appalling frenzied roar. He jumped, wheeled round. But it was only a dog, a great ginger and black curly-coated thing with a monstrous horror-film shadow that cavorted wildly in an opposite garden. David noted that a sturdy iron gate separated it from him. That was that. The noise put paid to all thoughts, very tempting natural thoughts, of giving up and returning the way he had come. Poor old Susan would have been alerted by now, was probably eyeing him from between those drawn curtains.

He marched up the drive, suddenly dreading the encounter. Would she be a facsimile of Elizabeth, strident and indiscreet, or a taboo-ridden housewife from whose genteelisms Townsend had thankfully escaped? The dog's fury pursued him embarrassingly. He rang the bell. The fact that it rang instead of evoking a carillon of Westminster chimes slightly cheered him. The hall light came on, the door opened and he stood face to face with the woman who had found Heller dead.

She was not what he had expected. Taking in the fair hair, the broad brow and the slender tilted nose, he knew at once where he had seen that face before. In the Tate Gallery, but not on a living woman. Effie Ruskin, he thought, Millais, *The Order of Release*. She smiled at him in a businesslike way.

'I'm sorry about the dog,' she said. 'Deafening, isn't it? He always barks like that at strangers.'

'Only at strangers?'

'Oh, yes. You needn't worry that he'll bark at you if you come to live here. Won't you come in? I'm afraid it's rather late for you to see the garden.'

A sudden dismay seized him. Pulling a fast one over Julian Townsend and his current wife was all very well. Shallow, unscrupulous, insincere, they had seemed to ask for it. This woman, who received him in good faith, impressed him at first sight as utterly honest. He sensed an old-fashioned integrity about her and it made him feel like a spy. For the past few days he had been living in a spy story world where the unconventional and the 'not done' thing was suspended. She brought him up against the hard brick wall of reality with a jolt.

Following her inside and watching her meet her own reflection, tall, shapely stylish, in the long wall glass, he thought of her supplanter and his opinion of Julian Townsend sank still further. Very probably he would give up taking *Certainty*.

'This is the living-room,' she said, 'with a dining area, you see, and that door leads to the room my – Julian, that is – used to have for his study. I'll show you in a moment.'

There was something that looked like a manuscript – perhaps she wrote – on a desk, a full ashtray beside it – she smoked too much – and on the sofa arm a copy of *Within a Budding Grove*. She had a mind too. For a prospective buyer, he was looking at all the wrong things. It was not she that was for sale.

'I'm sure you won't mind if I ask you to keep fairly quiet when we go upstairs. My little boy is asleep.'

'I didn't know you had a child.'

'Why should you?' Her cool voice chilled. She began to instruct him in the controls of the central heating plant and he thought of Heller. On the sideboard he could see a tray with a gin bottle on it, a can of some fizzy mineral water, two glasses. She was expecting someone, a man probably. Two women alone together would drink coffee or tea or perhaps sherry.

Presently she led the way upstairs. The child slept in a lighted room and he liked the way she approached the bed, tenderly and gently, to rearrange the tumbled bedclothes, but he was less happy about her troubled frown and for the first time he noticed a gauntness in her face.

Nobody slept in the main bedroom now. Bachelor though he was, he could tell an unused bed and detect that nothing lay between mattress and counterpane. She must have moved out when Townsend left her. Damn Townsend! It gave him a very real pleasure to envisage the man's disappointment when the expected 'five thou' wasn't forthcoming. For two pins he'd keep him hanging on while he, David, ostensibly made up his mind. He could take weeks about it, months. Only there was this girl. As she talked and pointed out the amenities of the place, he began to feel sick. He was practising on her a monstrous deceit, all the more reprehensible because she probably needed the sale.

She closed the bedroom door and said quietly, 'There's something I think you ought to know before we go any further. I don't know if you like the house, but I couldn't let you make an offer without telling you there was a double suicide next door. Only three weeks ago. It was in all the papers but perhaps you haven't connected it.'

Her honesty, in contrast to his deceit, brought the colour into his face. 'I did . . .'

'It wouldn't be fair not to tell you. Some people might feel superstitious about it. Mrs North and the man – a man called Heller – shot themselves in her bedroom. *This* bedroom. The houses are just the same inside.' She shrugged. 'Well, now you know,' she said.

He walked away from her and rested his hands on the banister rail. 'I did know,' he said, and in a rush, 'I knew Bernard Heller. I knew him quite well.'

The silence behind him was thick and almost frightening. Then he heard her say, 'I don't quite understand. You knew and yet you wanted . . .'

He began to go downstairs, all his natural diffidence depriving him of words. She came slowly after him. Without looking back, he felt a quite disproportionate sorrow that the tentative friendly harmony established between them had been destroyed.

At the foot of the stairs she stood a little distance from him. 'You want to buy a house next door to the one your friend died in? I really don't understand.'

'I know Mrs Heller too and I'll try to explain . . .'

She looked towards the front door, back at him. 'It's hardly my business, but it is my business to know if you want to buy this house or not. If you're a journalist or a private detective, you ought to be next door, not here.'

'Mrs Townsend . . .'

Her eyes opened wide – grey eyes, unbearably clear – and the Effie Ruskin mouth curled as it curled in the painting. 'What exactly *did* you think? That I'd gossip, give you revelations? I don't know anything about Mrs Heller, I only saw her once, but hasn't Mr North had enough?'

She glanced up upstairs, then trying to move casually, edged past him. She was frightened. It had never occurred to him that she might be frightened, for he had never before put himself into the shoes of a lonely woman who finds herself closeted with a strange man, an impostor. He felt his face go white with shame as he watched her eye the telephone, that lifeline, that communication with protection, and he moved away, his heart pounding.

In her eyes he was the salesman who wedges his foot in the door, the soft-spoken mechanic turned rapist, the insurance collector with warped desires, latent sadism. Her hand creeping towards the receiver, she said bravely, 'Mr North is a friend of *mine*. I don't understand what you're doing, only that he isn't going to be hurt any more. Tell Mrs Heller that.'

He opened the front door. The pink crêpe paper blossom covered the street light like a lampshade. He stepped out into the porch and once again the dog began to roar. She must know now that she was safe. 'Perhaps Mrs Heller has already told him,' he said loudly above the din.

'She has never spoken to him.' Abandoning the telephone, she lifted her head high. 'Now will you please go?'

'O God,' he said, stammering a little, cursing the dog, 'I won't hurt you. I'm going and you can phone the police if you like. I expect I've done something against the law, false pretences probably.' He couldn't meet her eyes, but he had to say it. 'Mrs Townsend, they do know each other. On the very day of the inquest they planned a meeting in a London pub. I saw them.'

The door slammed in his face, so near to his face that he had to jerk backwards quickly. The dog was so incensed by now that its antics made the gate rattle and clang. He got into his car, his hands actually shaking.

As he moved off another car passed him and swung smoothly into the Braeside drive. Only someone who did that manœuvre every day could perform it with such practised ease. David slowed. The man got out and David saw his head in his driving mirror, a dark head, neat, perfect, a gleaming, almost metallic coin relief in the pinkish-white lamp glow. Robert North. He had only seen that face in the flesh once before.

David braked and sat still. Without turning his head, he continued to observe North in the mirror. The other man was raising his garage door now, approaching his car, changing his mind. David wondered why the silence seemed wrong somehow and then he realised that the dog had ceased to bark. No one had taken it into the house. Its long monstrous shadow, magnified into a Hound of the Baskervilles, wriggled fawningly between the shadowed bars of the gate as North approached it and patted its head. The big black silhouettes quivered. North turned away and still the dog was silent. Susan Townsend had said it only barked at strangers. . . .

North's shadow moved across the road. It was much larger and more sinister than the man who cast it. David watched him go up to Mrs Townsend's front door and ring the bell.

They were on close terms those two, he thought as he drove away. The gin and the can of fizzy stuff were for him. No wonder the girl had reacted as she had! She was not merely a good discreet neighbour; she was emotionally involved with him. Why not use old-fashioned, more realistic terms? She was in love with him. On his looks alone, he was a man any woman might love. And he, David, had thought he could sound her about North's behaviour, North's attitude.

He must have been mad to suppose he could enter into a conspiracy with a strange woman, even if that woman had not been in love, enter with her into a plot to bring about North's downfall. This was not one of those serials for which he designed sets, but the real unromantic world. Had he really supposed that at a word from him she would break the barriers of convention and loyalty and confer with him as to her friend's actions and motives?

It seemed that he had. He had genuinely believed in the possibility of setting up with Mrs Townsend a kind of amateur detective bureau and, without prior contact, they were to have banded together in a scheme to overthrow two lives.

Bob put his arm gently around her shoulders and led her to a chair. 'What's happened, Susan? You look as if you've had a shock.'

'Someone was here,' she said, breathing quickly. 'A man . . . He said – insinuated, if you like – that you'd met Mrs Heller secretly on the day of the inquest.'

'So I did,' he said coolly. 'I met her in a London pub, but there was nothing secret about it.'

'You don't have to tell me.' Susan moved slightly to free herself from his encircling arm. 'It isn't my business, only I thought you didn't know her. I had the impression you'd never met till the inquest.'

'We hadn't. But afterwards I talked to her – she apologised to me, as a matter of fact, for the way she'd behaved in court. I was sorry for her. She's almost destitute, you know. That swine Heller hadn't left her a penny to live on. I felt I was bound to help and that's why we met. However, when we got there I found her with a man.'

'This Chadwick who came here?'

'Yes. Susan, the last thing I felt like was talking to strangers. I'm afraid I just bolted and then I came to see you. Of course, I've seen Mrs Heller since at her home. I've just come from there now.'

'How cruel people are,' she said wonderingly.

'Some are. And then you find someone who's sweet and good and lovely like you, Susan.'

She looked up at him incredulously.

'I meant that,' he said softly. 'Come here, Susan. You lived next door to me for years and years and I never saw

you. And now, I suppose it's too late . . . I wonder . . .
Would you kiss me, Susan?'

He would touch her forehead, brush her cheek, as he had
done the other day at the door. She lifted her face passively
and then, suddenly, it was not like the other day at all. She
was in his arms, clinging to him, mouth to mouth and eyes
closing at last on their loneliness and their shared rejection.

13

Detective Inspector Ulph knew that Robert North had
killed his wife and his wife's lover. He knew it, not as he
knew he was James Ulph, forty-eight years old, divorced,
childless, but he knew it as a juror must, beyond a reasonable doubt.

There was nothing he could do about it. His superintendent laughed at him when he talked of North's motive
and North's opportunity. Motive and opportunity cut no
ice, unless it can be proved the man was there, the gun to
which he had access, in his hand.

'Ever heard of a small point,' said the superintendent
scathingly, 'of tracing the weapon from its source to the
killer?'

Ulph had. It had perplexed him all along. Half-way
through his interrogation of North he had met the man's
eyes and read in them, under the simulated grief, a defiance
which seemed to say, You know and I know it. It can never
be proved. And as in a match there comes a point where
one of the contestants knows the other will win – will win,
at any rate, this hand or this game – Ulph knew that North
held the good cards, that he had stacked them subtly long
before-hand.

The gun was Heller's. Both Heller's widow and Heller's
brother swore that it was in his possession the night before
the killing. Except by unimaginable feats of burglary, by
breaking into a flat of whose very existence North was
certainly ignorant, he could not have gained possession of

that gun. After the deaths Ulph had tested Heller's hand for powder burns and then, as if it were an embarrassing formality, North's hand also. Heller had fired shots, North none. Heller had been seen to enter Braeside at ten minutes past nine by a Mrs Gibbs and a Mrs Winter and during the rest of the morning no one had left the house. North, carless as he was once every four weeks, had been in Barnet.

And yet Ulph knew that he had killed his wife. The picture, as in a peculiarly vivid and impressive film sequence, of how he had done it first came to him during the actual process of the inquest and since then it had returned often with the insistence of a recurring dream.

No one had seen North leave his house that morning, but this, this negative thing, this not seeing, not noticing, was pathetic, laughable, when it came to a question of proof and circumstantial evidence. 'I didn't see him leave,' Mrs Gibbs had said, 'but I often don't see him leave. Not seeing someone's no help really, is it? I saw Heller come.'

Because the dog had barked . . . North knew that, of course, that no-one in Orchard Drive ever saw anything unless the dog barked. Ulph's dream picture unfolded at this point, or just before this point. North had shot his wife while she was making the bed and then, when the dog barked, he had gone downstairs to admit the lover.

Ulph had only seen the man dead, but again and again he saw how that heavy earnest face must have looked when the door was opened, not by his mistress but by her husband. North would have stood well behind the door so that his neighbours, watching, saw only the door itself sliding inwards. And who would have questioned this secretive and surreptitious method of admitting Heller, this action so typical of a woman conducting a clandestine adventure?

Then, after the first shock, the adrenalin rushing into Heller's bloodstream, came the quick gathering of his forces. The cover story, the subterfuge . . . But North would have forestalled him, saying mildly that he was becoming genuinely interested in this idea of a heating installation. He had stayed at home to discuss it. And Heller, concealing his dismay, had followed him upstairs, entering as best he could, into this unlooked-for, fantastic conversation about radiators.

Ulph saw the dead woman lying on the bed and heard North's cry of alarm. His wife must have fainted. What more natural than for Heller to join him at the bedside, bend over – with a very real concern – the body of Louise North.

North had shot him then, shot him through the head. Had he been wearing rubber gloves? Had he perhaps come to the door with those gloves on and a tea-cloth in his hands? Ulph pictured those gloved hands closing the dead man's bare hand around the gun, aiming it at the dead woman's heart, pressing the trigger for the third time.

The picture stopped there, as if the projector had suddenly broken down.

North must have left the house. It was inconceivable that he could have done so and no one see him. All eyes had been on Braeside, regardless of the dog, waiting for Heller to come out. But North hadn't come out. He had come *in* at one-fifteen in his newly serviced car.

And the gun? Sometimes Ulph played fantastically with the idea that North might have taken it from him, out of his briefcase, while it stood on the kitchen table. But Heller never took that gun out of his flat. He would only have brought it with him to commit suicide. . . .

That part of Ulph which was a policeman wanted North brought to justice; that part which was an ordinary man had for him a sneaking fellow-feeling. His own wife had left him for another man and he had divorced her, but there had been times when another fantasy had occupied his mind, a fantasy not unlike that in which he saw North playing the vital role. He knew what it was like to want to kill.

That North's actions showed a long and careful premeditation did not, in Ulph's estimation, make the killing any less of a crime of passion. North had been cool, he thought, with the coolness that is a thin veneer lying on humiliated burning rage, unbearable jealousy. And the grief he had at first believed simulated might in fact be real, the horror of an Othello, who unlike Othello, had real and undeniable grounds for his crime.

So Ulph felt no desire to act as the instrument of society's revenge on North. His interest was academic, detached. He simply wanted to know how the man had done it, to a lesser extent why, when in this case divorce was the easy and obvious solution, the man had done it.

But the whole matter was closed. The coroner and the superintendent between them had closed it.

Afterwards David wished he hadn't telephoned her to apologise. Her voice still stung in his ears.

'Mr North has arranged to lend her some money. It's a pity some of her friends of longer standing didn't think of that.'

She had crushed him with cool pointed sentences, calculated to wound. But as he listened to her meekly, he could only think of the first impression she had made on him, an impression of utter sincerity. He bore her no ill-will. Unable to forget her face, he went into the Tate Gallery after work, found *The Order of Release* and then bought a postcard copy. He had made no mistake in likening her to Effie Ruskin, but now as he made his way out on to the Embankment and hailed a taxi, he found that the card which he still held in his hand brought him no pleasure, nor any satisfaction at the accuracy of his visual memory. He had the feeling that to pin it on his wall with the others might curiously depress him.

When he got to The Man in the Iron Mask the two bearded men were the only customers and they sat at their usual table, drinking shorts.

'Covenanting's all very well, Sid,' David heard Charles say, 'for the other fellow, the one who benefits, but it's a mug's game for number one.'

'Quite,' said Sid.

'What's in it for you, I mean? Sweet Fanny Adams, unless you get a kick out of doing the Inland Revenue in the eye.'

The barman eyed David curiously as, with an anxious frown, he pretended to scan the empty room.

'You look as if you've lost something.'

'Someone,' David corrected him. 'A young lady.' The genteelism grated rather. 'I hoped to find her here.'

'Stood you up, has she?'

'Not exactly.' Sid and Charles weren't going to bite. Why should they? It wasn't going to be as easy as all that. He edged diffidently towards their table. 'Excuse me.' Charles gave him an indignant glare. David thought it a bad-tempered face. 'Excuse me, but have you been in here since they opened?'

'We have.' Charles seemed about to add So what? or did David want to make something of it?

'I wondered if you'd happen to see a girl come in, striking-looking dark girl. You saw me in here with her a couple of weeks back.'

'Rings a bell.' Charles's surly expression softened and he began to look less like Rasputin. 'Wait a minute. Dishy-looking piece in tight pants, would it be?'

'Come now, Charles,' said Sid.

'No offence meant, old man. Intended as a compliment actually.'

'That's all right.' David managed a quite easy, natural laugh. 'She used to be my secretary and now my present girl's leaving me, I thought . . . The fact is I believe she's often in here and as I don't know where she's living, I came in on the off-chance of catching her.' He marvelled at his own ability to lie glibly. 'You know how it is,' he said.

'She's not been in tonight,' said Charles. 'Sorry we can't help you. I wish I'd had the nous,' he said to Sid, 'to buy a hundred Amalgamated Asphalts last week. They touched thirty-eight-and-six this morning.'

'Quite.'

'Can I get you a drink?' David asked desperately.

'You could have knocked me down with a feather. Six months they've been stuck at twenty-five bob and . . . Did I hear someone say the magic word drink? That's very nice of you, old man.'

'Brandy,' said Sid, apparently for both of them.

David bought two brandies and a beer for himself. The barman tightened his lips. His expression was meaningful but David couldn't interpret that meaning.

'Her boy-friend would do,' he said as he put the glasses down. 'All I want is her address.'

'*Salud y pesetas*,' said Charles. 'Not that I'd say much for the peseta at this moment. You still worrying about that girl, old man?'

Casting aside caution, David said, 'Have you ever seen her in here with a man?'

Charles gave Sid a lugubrious wink. 'Time and time again. Tall, good-looking dark bloke. Always drank gin with something fizzy in it, didn't he, Sid?'

'Quite,' said Sid.

Excitement caught at David's throat, making him stammer. That Sid and Charles obviously thought him Magdalene Heller's cast-off lover, didn't bother him at all. 'Always?' he said. 'You mean they've been in here often?'

'About once a week for the past six months. No, I'm wrong there. More like eight months. You can put me right on that, Sid. When did we give up The Rose and start coming here?'

'August.'

'August it was. I remember it was August because the first day I got back from Majorca Sid and I went as usual to The Rose and, damn it, if they didn't short-change me. I've had about as much of this as I can stand, I said to Sid, and so we came here instead. Your girl and the dark bloke were here then.'

'I see. And they've been meeting regularly here ever since?'

'Not for the past fortnight.' Charles glanced in the barman's direction and then leant towards David confidingly. 'It's my belief they got fed up with this place. There's a lot of skulduggery goes on. Just before you came in that fellow tried to pull a fast one on me. Said I'd given him a pound when it was a fiver. Disgusting!' His brows drew together angrily and he rubbed his beard.

'It looks as if I'll have to advertise for a secretary after all.'

Sid glared at him derisively and, getting up suddenly, spoke the longest sentence David had ever heard him utter. 'Don't give me that, that secretary stuff, d'you mind? We're all men of the world, I hope, and personally I don't care to be talked down to like a school kid. You don't want another drink, do you, Charles?' He swung the door open. 'Secretary!' he said.

'Quite,' said Charles, reversing roles. They went.

David turned towards the bar and shrugged.

'Couple of comedians they are,' said the barman energetically. 'If you like your humour sick.'

Keyed up and tremendously elated by his discovery, David had felt he couldn't stand the pub a moment longer. He was filled with an urgent energy, and wasting it on chit-chat with the barman made him impatient. Nor did he want to drink any more, for drink might cloud his thought processes. He went out into the street and began to walk about aimlessly.

His excitement lasted about ten minutes. While it lasted he felt as he had done at other high spots in his life, when he had got his diploma, for instance, when he had landed his present job. There was no room for anything else in his mind but self-congratulation. Heller was temporarily forgotten in a pride and an elation that had nothing to do with morality or justice or indignation. He had found it out, done what he had set out to do and now he could only reflect with wonder on his achievement.

But he was not naturally vain and by the time he came, by a circuitous route, to Soho Square his swagger was less confident. It might have been someone he had passed that recalled her to his mind, a girl with straight fair hair like hers or one whose grey eyes met his for a moment. Her image entered his mind with startling clarity and suddenly he came down to earth with a bump. He sat down on one of the seats under the trees and as his hand touched the cold metal arm a shiver ran through him.

She ought to be told. She ought not to be left there alone with no one to protect her, a prey to North. It seemed absurd to equate her with the classic detective story victim who, knowing too much, must be silenced, but wasn't that in fact what she had become? Already she had alerted North, informing him of David's early suspicions. There was no knowing how much else she had seen, living next door to North as she did, what tiny discrepancies she had observed in his behaviour. David didn't for a moment believe North sought her company from honest motives of affection. She was in danger.

He knew he couldn't warn her off. He was the last man in the world she would listen to. For all that, he got up and made slowly for a phone box. There was someone inside and he waited impatiently, pacing up and down. At last he got in. He had found her number, begun to dial when his nerve failed him. There was something better he could do than this, something more responsible and adult. As soon as he thought of it, he wondered why he hadn't done it days ago. The green directory then this time. . . . He took a deep breath and, tapping his fingers nervously on the coin box, waited for Matchdown Park C.I.D. to answer.

Inspector Ulph was a small spare man with a prominent hooky nose and olive skin. David always tried to find counterparts in art for living human beings. He had likened Susan Townsend to Millais' portrait of Effie Ruskin, Magdalene Heller had about her something of a Lely or even a Goya, and this policeman reminded him of portraits he had seen of Mozart. Here was the same sensitive mouth, the look of suffering assuaged by an inner strength, the eyes that could invite and laugh at esoteric jokes. His hair was not as long as Mozart's but it was longer than is usual in a policeman, and when he was a boy it had no doubt been the silky pale brown of the lock David had seen preserved at Salzburg.

For his part, Ulph saw a tall lean young man, intelligent-looking, not particularly handsome, whose eager eyes for a moment took ten years off his age. He poured out an impulsive story and Ulph listened to it, not showing the excitement which the name of North had at first evoked. What had he expected to hear? Not this. Disappointment succeeded his small elation and he stalled, summing his visitor up. Only one sharp pinpoint of his original excitement remained, and he left it glimmering to say briskly:

'You're telling me that Mr North and Mrs Heller have been meeting, to your certain knowledge, at a London public house called The Man in the Iron Mask? Meeting there at regular intervals before her husband and his wife died?'

David nodded emphatically. He had hoped for a sharper reaction than this. 'Yes, I am. It may be far-fetched, but I think they met there to plot, conspire, if you like, to kill the others and make their deaths look like suicide.'

'Indeed?' Ulph's eyebrows had gone up. No one looking at him now would have supposed him to be a man obsessed by thoughts of a gun and a subtly-contrived exit. He looked as if David's suspicions, the bare idea that North might be anything but totally innocent, were a revelation to him.

'I'm sure he did it,' David said impulsively, 'and if he did it she must have been in it too. Only she could have told him when Heller would arrive at Braeside and only she could have given him the gun. I visited Heller's flat the night before he died and I saw the gun. Later I saw her go into a cinema. I think North was inside that cinema, waiting for her to hand him the gun in the dark.'

The gun. This was the only way, Ulph thought, that North could have got it. Not by burglary, not by the unimaginable sleight of hand necessary to filching it from Heller himself, but through a conspiracy with Heller's wife. Immediately he saw pitfalls and he said, 'You say North and Mrs Heller first met at this pub in August?'

'Yes, I think it was this way. Bernard Heller had met Mrs North, fallen in love with her, started this affair of theirs, and North found out about it. So he got in touch with Magdalene Heller.' David paused and drew a deep breath. He was beginning to feel proud of himself again. His theory was forming as he spoke and it sounded good to him. 'They arranged to meet and discuss – well, the wrong that is being done them. For a while they don't do anything more. Bernard tried to commit suicide in September – I read that in the paper – and it must have shaken them. But when he took up with Louise again, they went on with their meetings and decided to kill the others.'

It was so full of holes, so remote from life as Ulph knew it, that he almost laughed. But then he remembered that, absurd as this theory was, a farrago of nonsense, he owed to it the one clue he had as to how North had come into possession of the gun, and he only sighed. The proper study of man is mankind, he thought, and he wondered how anyone as intelligent, as articulate and as alert as this man who confronted him, could have lived nearly thirty years on this earth yet be so blind to man's cautiousness and the pull convention exerts over his conduct.

He said gently, 'Listen to me, Mr Chadwick.' For this, he thought, is going to be quite a long speech. 'An ordinary middle-class quantity surveyor discovers that his wife is unfaithful to him. There are several things he can do. He can discuss it with her; he can discuss it with the man; he can divorce her.' Under the desk he felt his hands begin to clench and he relaxed them. Hadn't he done all these things himself? 'He can do violence to one or both of them, kill her, kill them both. Also he might just contact the wife of his wife's lover and reveal his discovery.

'This last is a possibility. You or I,' Ulph said, 'you or I might not do it, but it has been done. The innocent pair confront the guilty pair. More violence or more discussion follows. What the innocent pair do not do is meet in a pub and plot a murder. Strangers to each other? Knowing nothing of each other's emotions, propensities, characters? Can you hear it? Can you see it?'

Ulph began to speak in a tone quite unlike his natural voice, boyishly, impulsively. Was this North's manner of speech? David had no idea. He had never heard it. ' "We both hate them, Mrs Heller, and want to be rid of them. Suppose we make a foolproof plan to kill them? Suppose we plan it together?" ' But Magdalene's voice he did know and he flinched a little, so uncanny was Ulph's imitation of her long vowels and her sibilants. ' "What a lovely idea, Mr North! Shall I help you work it all out?" '

David smiled in spite of himself. 'Not in those words, of course, but something like that.'

'Wouldn't she have run from him? Called the police? Are you saying that two people, brought together only because their marriage partners were lovers, found in each other a complementary homicidal urge? It says much for your virtue. You've evidently never tried to involve a stranger in a conspiracy.'

But he had. Only two days ago he had attempted just that with Susan Townsend. He had gone to a stranger in the absurd hope she would help him to hunt North down.

Why hadn't he learned? Recent experience should have taught him that people don't behave like that.

'Suppose I go back to the pub,' he said diffidently. Was that amusement in Ulph's eyes? 'Suppose I get the names of those two men?'

'As long as you don't get yourself into trouble, Mr Chadwick.'

David walked slowly out of the police station. He felt humiliated, cut down to size by Ulph's expertise. And yet Ulph had only shown him that his reasoning had been at fault. He had done nothing to alter David's conviction of North's guilt or diminish the growing certainty that North was pursuing Susan Townsend to find out how much she knew.

14

It was just his luck that Sid and Charles weren't in The Man in the Iron Mask tonight. Perhaps they never came in on Thursdays. He couldn't remember whether he had ever been there on a Thursday himself before. Certainly he couldn't remember any occasion when he had been there and they hadn't. He hung about until eight and then he went home.

On the following night all the regulars were there, the middle-aged couple, the old actor, the girl with the mauve fingernails and her boy-friend, this time wearing a Battle of Waterloo tricorne hat, everyone but Sid and Charles. David waited, watching the clock, the door, and at last he asked the barman.

'Those two bearded characters, d'you mean?'

'That's right,' David said. 'You called them comedians. There's something I wanted to see them about.'

'I doubt if you'll see them in here.' The barman looked at him meaningfully, setting down the glass he had been polishing. 'Keep it under your hat, but I had a bit of a ding-dong with them yesterday lunchtime. Always money, money, money with them it was. Like a disease. The very first time they came in here they started on me about giving wrong change, over-charging, that sort of guff.' He lowered his voice. 'You wouldn't believe the insinuations. Well, yesterday I'd had about enough. Get the police if you're not satisfied, I said. We've nothing to hide. I'm within my rights to refuse to serve you, I said, and if you come back tomorrow I will.'

'The same sort of thing happened to them last August at The Rose,' David said hopelessly.

'I shouldn't be at all surprised. I'm right in thinking they're not friends of yours, aren't I?'

'I don't even know their names.'

'A pub crawl,' said Pamela Pearce. 'Well, I don't know, darling. It could be dreary.'

'There are two chaps I want to find. I've got to find them.'

'I suppose they owe you money.'

'No, they don't,' David said crossly. 'It's much more serious than that, but I'd rather not explain. Come on now, it might be fun having a drink in every pub in Soho.'

'Intoxicating. Still, I don't mind if it's Soho. But, darling, it's pouring with rain!'

'So what? You can wear your new raincoat.'

'That's a thought,' said Pamela, and when he came to pick her up she was glittering in silver crocodile skin.

At Tottenham Court Road tube station he said, 'They've both got beards and their conversation is almost exclusively concerned with money.'

'Is that all you've got to go on?'

He nodded and avoided meeting her eyes. It had occurred to him that Sid and Charles, when at last run to earth, would certainly make cracks about his concern to find a striking-looking dark girl, his ex-secretary. Pamela knew very well he had never had a secretary. Strange that this didn't worry him at all.

They would go first to The Man in the Iron Mask. There was just a chance some of the other regulars might remember North and Magdalene. But David doubted this. He had been a regular too, but he had no recollection of ever having seen the couple – the conspirators? The lovers? – until the inquest day. Did Sid and Charles only remember because like the majority of men they had been susceptible to Magdalene's beauty?

He must find them.

Pamela walked along beside him in silence while the rain fell softly and steadily through grey vapour.

It was Sunday and Julian Townsend was taking his son out for the day. Hand in hand they walked down the path towards the parked car. Susan watched them go, amused because the Airedale who only barked at unknown inter- lopers, had suddenly begun to roar at Julian. He had become a stranger.

She shrugged and went indoors. In the hall glass her reflection walked to meet her and she stopped to admire herself, the fair hair that had a new gloss on it, the grey eyes alight with happy anticipation, the new suit she had plundered her bank balance to buy. The fee from Miss Willingale could be used to make that good, for she had only four more chapters to complete.

Bob's footsteps sounded in the sideway. No more formal front door calling for him. Susan looked at the mirrored girl and saw in her face pleasure at the new intimacy, the beginning of taking things for granted.

She went to meet him a little shyly. He came in and took her in his arms without a word. His kiss was long, slow, expert, almost shocking in its effect on her. But they were only friends, she told herself, friends in need, each other's comforters. She broke away from him, shaken, unwilling to meet his eyes.

'Bob, I . . . Wait for me a moment. I have to get my gloves, my bag.'

Upstairs the gloves and the bag were ready where she had left them on the dressing table. She sat down heavily on the bed and stared at the sky, hard blue this morning, at the elms that swayed lazily, seeing nothing. Her hands were shaking and she flexed them, trying to control the muscles. Until now she had thought that the year passed without a man, a lover, had been nearly insupportable on account of the lack of companionship and the pain of rejection. Now she knew that as much as this she had missed sexual passion.

The Secret House of Death   411

He was waiting for her at the foot of the stairs. She remembered how the girl in Harrow had turned to look at him, how Doris had spoken of his looks and his charm, and these opinions, the spoken and unspoken views of other women, seemed suddenly to enhance him even more in her eyes. All but his own wife were overpowered by that physical presence, that quintessence of all that a man should be and should look like. She thought of his wife fleetingly now as she came down towards him. Why had this one woman been impervious, indifferent?

He smiled at her, holding out his hands. There was something shameful in wanting a man because of his looks and because – ugly, shameful thought – you wanted a man. She came closer and this time it was she who put out her arms to him and held her face up to be kissed.

'We'll have lunch,' he said, 'in a little country pub I know. I've always liked little pubs.'

She held his hand, smiling up at him. 'Have you, Bob?'

He said nervously, 'Why did you say it like that? Why do you look like that?'

'I don't know. I didn't mean to.' She didn't know, nor did she know why Heller and Heller's widow had suddenly come into her mind. 'Let's make a pact,' she said quickly, 'not to talk about Heller or Louise while we're out today.'

'God,' he said, and she felt him sigh as briefly he held her against him, 'I don't want to talk about them.' He touched her hair and she trembled a little when she felt his fingers move lightly against her skin. Her relief should have matched his own, but she felt only a vague dismay. Had they anything else to talk about, anything at all in common? There was something painfully humiliating in the thought which had crept into her mind. That instead of going out with him she would have preferred to stay here like this, holding him, touching her cheek to his, in an eternal moment of warmth and of desire. Outside this room they would have, it seemed to her, no existence as a pair, as friends.

The sharp bright air shocked her as if out of a dream. She walked ahead of him to his car and she was appalled at herself, like someone who had committed an

indiscretion at a party and now, in the light of day, is afraid
to face both his neighbours and his partner in that fall from
grace.

Doris looked out of her window and waved. Betty looked
up from her gardening to smile at them. It was as if she
and Bob were going off on their honeymoon, Susan
thought, and the pink cherry petals fell on to her hair and
her shoulders like confetti on a bride. She got into the car
beside him and then she remembered how harsh he had
been with her the day he had driven her to Harrow, violent
almost as he drove deliberately fast to frighten her. It was
the same man. He smiled at her, lifted her hand and kissed
the fingers. But she didn't know him at all, she knew
nothing about him.

Whatever she said it would come back to Heller. It
always did. But she had promised not to mention him or
Louise and now she realised that although Bob himself
would do so and derive a strange comfort from the tragedy,
he became uneasy if she took the initiative herself. It was
as if the double suicide was his private possession that no
one, not even she, might uncover and look at without his
permission.

The idea was very disagreeable to her. He was thinking
about it now. She could see it in his face. For the first time
she put into silent words what she had known since that
other drive in this car with him. He thought about it all the
time, day and night without rest.

She must talk to him about something. 'How are you
getting on with Mrs Dring?' she asked desperately.

'All right. It was good of you to persuade her, Susan,
sweet of you.'

'She can only come on Saturdays?'

'Yes, when I'm there.' He took one hand from the wheel,
touched her arm. Not from desire, she thought, not out of
affection. Perhaps simply to assure himself that she was
really there. Then he said, his voice very low, as if they
were not alone in a car but walking in a crowded street
were anyone could hear unless he whispered, 'She talks to
me about it. I try to keep away from her, but every chance
she can, she talks to me about it.'

'She's rather thoughtless,' Susan said gently.

He set his mouth, but not defiantly. He was controlling the trembling of his lips. 'She opens the windows,' he said.

And thereby let fresh air and sound into the secret thing he kept there? Susan suddenly felt cold in the stuffy car whose heater blew out a hot breeze. In a monotone, low yet rapid, he began to tell her about the questions Mrs Dring had asked him, of her maudlin tactless sympathy.

'I'll have a word with her.'

But he hardly seemed to hear her. Once more he had returned to that morning, to his arrival at Braeside, to the couple on the bed. And, pitying him, not wanting him to know she was also a little afraid, Susan put her hand on his arm and rested it there.

'I couldn't find them,' David said. Ulph's expression was that of an indulgent father listening to a child's tall stories. Perhaps he had never really believed in the existence of Sid and Charles. He made David feel like a crank, one of those people who go to the police with wild accusations because they want to make mischief or attract attention to themselves. And it was on account of this that he said no more of his quest with Pamela Pearce, of their visits to eighteen different pubs, of the perpetually repeated enquiries, all in vain. Nor, naturally, did he say anything of their subsequent quarrel when their tempers were frayed by frustration and the incessant rain.

'I should think they work in the City,' he said, feeling foolish. 'We could try the Stock Exchange or Lloyds, or something.'

'Certainly *you* could try, Mr Chadwick.'

'You mean you won't? You wouldn't put a man on it?'

'To what end? Do any of the other regulars at this pub remember seeing Mr North and Mrs Heller there?' David shook his head. 'From what you have told me of their conduct, your two bearded acquaintances aren't remarkable for their probity. Mr Chadwick, can you be sure they weren't – well, having you on?'

This time David nodded stubbornly. Ulph shrugged, tapping his fingers lightly on the desk. He too had much in his mind his professional discretion prevented him from revealing. There was no reason to tell this obstinate man how, since his last visit, North and Mrs Heller had again been separately questioned and had emphatically denied any knowledge of the other prior to the suicides. Ulph believed them. Mrs Heller's brother-in-law and Mrs Heller's neighbours all knew Robert North by now. They knew him as the kind benefactor who had first shown his face in East Mulvihill five days after the tragedy.

And, because of this, Ulph had lost his faith in David's theory as to the gun. He still believed in North's guilt, still had before his eyes that moving picture of North's actions on that Wednesday morning. But he had acquired the gun some other way. Ulph didn't know how, nor did he know how North had got out of the house. Answers to these questions would help him to get the case reopened, not unfounded theories as to a conspiracy.

'You see, Mr Chadwick,' he said patiently, 'not only do you have no real evidence of conspiracy existing, you have no theory to convince me such a conspiracy would be necessary. Mrs Heller offered her husband a divorce when she first discovered his infidelity and only failed to petition because for a time he wanted them to try to keep their marriage going. He couldn't have prevented her divorcing him as the guilty party. It wasn't even as if he tried to conceal the truth from her. He loved Mrs North, was committing adultery with her, and he told his wife so. As to North, he might have committed a crime of passion from jealousy or hurt pride. That's a very different matter from conspiring for months with a comparative stranger. His anger would cool in that time. Why take the enormous risk premeditated murder entails when with all the evidence he had, he too had only to seek a divorce?'

He said no more. Show me, he thought, how this man in the jealousy and the rage I can understand came into possession of a gun he could not have possessed and left a house unseen.

She had invited him often enough and yet, he thought, she would be dismayed to see him. By now North would have told her of his visit to Matchdown Park. He stood on the doorstep for a second or two, hesitating, before he pressed the bell. The red and yellow glare from the neon signs, the passing buses, rippled and flickered on the peeling wall and the chalk graffiti.

It was the brother-in-law who let him into the flat. In the half-dark it might have been Bernard Heller and not Carl on whose face the slow smile dawned, Bernard who stood aside to let him enter.

The flat smelt of greens and gravy. They had shared a meal and the dirty plates were still on the table. Magdalene Heller was standing against the wall underneath the mandoline, an unlighted cigarette in her fingers.

'I thought it was time I looked you up,' David said, and with a sense of rightness, of retribution, of destiny almost, he stepped forward with his lighter. The flame threw violet shadows on her face and her eyes widened. She said nothing for a moment but David felt that she too recalled the parallel forerunner of this scene and had, as he had, a sense of having been there before. He half-expected her to glance quickly over her shoulder, searching for North's face. She sat down, crossing her long beautiful legs.

'How are you getting on?'

'All right.' Her gruffness, her gracelessness almost, reminded him a little of Elizabeth Townsend. But whereas Mrs Townsend's sprang from the confidence born of background, upbringing, connections, Magdalene's was the attitude of a woman sure of her own beauty, of the lily that needs no gilding.

It was Carl who said, 'People have been very kind, Mr North most of all.' David fancied that the girl stiffened a little at the name. 'He's lent Magdalene money to tide her over.' Carl smiled bovinely as if to say, There, what do you think of that? 'More like an old friend,' he said, and when David slightly raised his eyebrows, 'The police even came here and asked Magdalene if she'd known him before.'

David's heart seemed to run a little, to trip. So Ulph *was* interested. . . . 'But of course she hadn't,' he said innocently.

Magdalene crushed out her cigarette. 'Why don't you put the coffee on, Carl?'

While Bernard's twin lumbered off to do her bidding, she fixed David with those green eyes in which the gold specks, particles of metal dust, moved sluggishly. 'Tell me something.' Her accent was strong tonight. 'Did Bernard ever tell you how he met that woman?'

'He told me nothing,' David said. 'How did they meet?'

'It was last August in Matchdown Park. She was in a friend's house and he came to fit a spare part to the heating. She'd been ill and she had a bad turn so he said he'd drive her home. That was how it started.'

Why are you telling me this? he wondered. The words had been bare, almost all monosyllabic.

'He told me it all,' she said. 'Bob North didn't know a thing. I had to tell him. It's not surprising, is it, we got together after the inquest? We had plenty to tell each other.'

'But the police somehow believe you and North had met before?'

Pure hatred flashed briefly in her eyes. She knew why the police had questioned her and who had alerted them, but she dared not say. 'I never set eyes on Bob till three weeks ago,' she said brusquely, tossing her head so that the black hair swept her shoulders. 'I'm not worried. Why should I be?'

'No coffee for me,' David said when Carl came in with the tray. He had a strong revulsion against eating or drinking anything in this flat and he rose. 'I suppose *Equatair* have given you something?' he said baldly, for there was no longer any question of impertinence or of tact between him and her. The memory of her full pink mouth pressed against his skin sickened him.

'Precious little,' she said.

'I don't suppose it was easy for them getting someone to go to Switzerland in Bernard's place.' David turned to look at Carl. 'Not in your line, I suppose?'

'I speak the language, Mr Chadwick, but, no, I am not clever like Bernard was. I shall go to Switzerland for my usual holiday. I was born there and my relatives are there.'

Magdalene poured her coffee very slowly as if she were afraid her hands would shake and betray her. Suddenly David felt sure he must keep in touch with her brother-in-law. Once before he had failed to secure an address. He nodded to the widow, keeping his hands behind his back, and he met her sullen eyes before following Carl into the hall.

'I may go to Switzerland myself,' he said when they were out of earshot, side by side, almost touching in the narrow passage. 'If I wanted a bit of advice . . . well, would you let me have your address?'

Carl's sad face lit with pleasure. He looked a man whose counsel is seldom sought. David gave him a pen and an old envelope on which he wrote in a long sloping hand his address and a landlady's phone number.

'Any time, Mr Chadwick.' He opened the door, peered out. 'I thought we might have the pleasure of seeing Mr North tonight,' he said. 'Once or twice I've been here when he has called to see Magdalene. But he is a busy man and his neighbours take up so much of his time . . .'

His neighbours. One neighbour, David thought. He crossed the street and as he slipped the envelope into his pocket his hand touched the card he had bought in the National Gallery. Under a street lamp he stopped to look at it. Was North with her now? Was North making love to her, just as Magdalene Heller had tried to make love to him, David, and for the same reason?

She was very lovely, this girl that Millais had painted, had wrested from Ruskin and had finally married. Susan Townsend was exactly like her, as like as Carl was to Bernard. It might have been her photograph which, bent and a little soiled now, David carried with him in his pocket. He wondered how he would feel if, instead of buying it, he had received it from her as a gift.

At East Mulvihill station he bought his ticket and then, swiftly, before he had time to dwell too much on what he was about to do, he went into a phone box.

15

'Mrs Townsend, this is David Chadwick. Please don't ring off.' Did his voice sound as intense to her as it seemed to him? 'I wanted to talk to you. I couldn't just leave things.'

'Well?' It could be a warm word, a word denoting health or things excellently done, but she made it the coldest in the world. On her lips it was onomatopoeic, a well indeed, a place of deep, dark and icy waters.

'I haven't phoned to talk of – what I mentioned to you last week. I don't intend to discuss Mr North.'

'That's good, because I wouldn't discuss him.' She was neither scathing nor hectoring. It was hard to say what she was. Iron-firm, implacable, remote.

'It was appalling what I did last week and I apologise profoundly. Can you understand when I say I want to see you and explain that I'm not a lout or a practical joker? Mrs Townsend, would you have dinner with me?'

Unable to see her, he couldn't define the atmosphere of her silence. Then she said, but not scornfully, '*Of course not*,' and she laughed. In her laughter he detected neither mockery nor outrage. She wasn't even amused. She was incredulous.

'Lunch, then,' he persisted. 'In some big crowded restaurant where I couldn't – couldn't frighten you.'

'I was frightened.'

In that moment he fell in love with her. ¯ntil then it had been a silly dream. Why had he been s. h a fool as to telephone and create for himself in five minutes a load of sorrow?

'I was frightened,' she said again, 'because I was alone and it was dark.' Again the silence fell and the pips sounded, remote, careless of what they terminated. He had his coin ready, his breathless question.

'Are you still there?'

Her voice was brisk now. 'This is rather a ridiculous conversation, don't you think? I expect you acted in good faith and it doesn't matter now, anyway. But we don't really know each other at all and the only thing we could talk about – well, I wouldn't talk about it.'

'It isn't the only thing,' he said fiercely. 'I can think of a hundred things just offhand like that.'

'Good-bye, Mr Chadwick.'

He went down the escalator and when he was alone in the passage that led to the platform he dropped the picture card to be trampled underfoot in the morning rush.

She was almost sure Bob hadn't overheard that conversation, but when she returned to the living-room he lifted his eyes and they had a haunted look. Should she lie to him, tell him it was someone the agent had put on to her, a prospective buyer of the house?

'I heard,' he said. 'It was that fellow Chadwick.'

'Only to ask me out to dinner,' she said soothingly. 'I shan't go. Of course, I shan't.'

'What does he want, Susan? What's he getting at?'

'Nothing. Don't, Bob, you're hurting me.' His hands which were so soft when they stroked her cheek, seemed to crush the bones in her wrists. 'Sit down. You were saying, before he phoned . . .?'

The hard fingers relaxed. 'About Louise,' he said. 'I was telling you how she and Heller met and how he drove her home. Magdalene Heller's told me the whole story. After that they used to meet when I had to work late.' His voice was feverish, desperate. 'In cafés, in pubs. He got in such a state he tried to kill himself. I wish to God he'd succeeded then. He started writing those horrible letters to her . . . Susan, you *did* burn those letters, didn't you?'

She was past caring now whether she told the truth to him or lied. What, anyway, was the truth? 'I burnt them, Bob.'

'Why can't I forget it all, put it behind me? You think I'm going mad. Yes, you do, Susan, I can see it in your face.'

She put her head in her hands, running her fingers through her hair. 'Keep away from Mrs Heller, if she upsets you,' she said presently. 'You've done enough for her.'

'What d'you mean?'

'You've given her money, haven't you?'

He sighed and he sounded infinitely weary. 'I'd like to get away, go far away. Oh, Susan, if only I didn't have to go back to that house tonight! Or ever again to see Magdalene Heller.' He paused and said as if he were stating something profound, yet at the same time novel and appalling, 'I don't ever want to see Magdalene Heller again.'

'Nor me, Bob?' Susan asked gently.

'You? It would have been better if I'd never met you, never seen you . . .' He got up and his face was as white and strained as if he were ill or really demented. 'I love you, Susan.' His arms went round her and, his lips almost touching hers, he said, 'One day, when I'm – when I'm better and all this is past, will you marry me?'

'I don't know,' she said blankly, but she kissed him on a long sigh and it seemed to her that no kiss had ever been so pleasurable and so sweet. 'It isn't the time yet, is it?' she said as their mouths parted and she looked up into that strained haunted face.

'There's the boy, I know,' he said urgently, reading her thoughts. 'He's frightened of me. That'll pass. We could all go away, couldn't we? Away from Mrs Dring and this Chadwick and – and Mrs Heller.'

The play for which David had designed the sets ended and the credit titles came up. He thought he might as well watch the news. The first item was the result of some West Country by-election which interested him not at all and he had got up to turn it off when he stopped, intrigued by the voice of a speaker who had suddenly replaced the announcer. That lilting intonation, those stressed r's were familiar. He had heard them before that evening on the lips of Magdalene Heller. Her accent, far less strong than that of the commentator, had always puzzled him and now he located it at last. She came from Devon.

Immediately he remembered the newspaper picture of Robert and Louise North. That had been taken in Devon while they were holidaying there last year. Did it mean anything or nothing?

Very carefully he repeated in his mind the conversation he had had with Magdalene two hours before and it seemed strange to him that she had taken such pains to tell him how her husband and Louise North had met. Because the circumstances of that meeting caused her real distress, or because in fact they had not met that way at all? Of course it was possible that Bernard had driven her home because she was unwell, had promised perhaps to enquire after her subsequently, and that from this beginning their love affair had grown. But wasn't it far more likely that they had all met on holiday?

Once more David felt excitement stir. Suppose they had met, the two couples, in an hotel or on a beach? Then, when Louise and Bernard returned respectively to Matchdown Park and East Mulvihill, intending to follow up the attraction which had already begun, the last thing they would have done was talk to friends or neighbours of this apparently brief holiday acquaintance. But North and Magdalene would have a knowledge of each other, a shared memory which, however casual, would make their later meetings natural.

In this case North might well have contacted Magdalene to disclose his wife's conduct, or Magdalene him to reveal Bernard's. Even Ulph, David thought, wouldn't find anything fantastic in such a supposition.

He hesitated for a moment and then he dialled Carl Heller's number. The landlady answered. Mr Heller had just come home from his sister-in-law's, he was taking off his coat at this moment. The telephone slightly distorted his voice, making it more guttural.

'There is nothing wrong, I hope, Mr Chadwick?'

'No, no,' David said. 'It was just that I thought of going to Switzerland for a few days at Easter and it occurred to me you might be able to recommend somewhere to stay.'

Carl began to reel off a list of names and places. He sounded almost animated, over-helpful, as Bernard had been when asked favours. And David recalled how this man's dead brother, when asked tentatively for the loan of a fireplace, had pressed on him not one but a dozen of the latest models. Thus Carl, instead of naming a couple of *pensions*, selected from his memory hotels and tourist centres in every Swiss canton, pausing only for David to make, or pretend to make, copious notes.

'That'll do fine,' David said when Carl drew breath. 'I suppose your brother and his wife often stayed at this one?' And he named a modest hotel at Meiringen.

'My brother never went back to Switzerland after he was married. He was trying, he told me, to become like an Englishman and he dropped all his continental ways. He and Magdalene had their holidays in England, in Devon where Magdalene comes from.'

'Really?'

'That is why I was so pleased for them, for the Zürich appointment. Wait till you see real mountains, I said to Magdalene. But then my brother does this wicked thing and . . .' Carl's heavy sigh vibrated through the earpiece. 'It is a funny thing, Mr Chadwick, it will amuse you, although in a way it is sad. Always in Devon they are staying in the same place at Bathcombe Ferrers, and the place they stay at it is a small *pension* called – what do you think? – the Swiss Chalet. Often my brother and I have laughed about this. But you are a great traveller, I know, and would not be content with such a place. No, you must go to Brunnen or maybe Lucerne. Mount Pilatus now – you have it on your list like I have told you? You have the name. . . .'

In his hand David had only the soiled envelope on which Carl had written his address and now, feeling a little ashamed of the deceit he had practised, he wrote beside it just five words.

16

A rustic sign with its name burnt on in pokerwork informed him that he had arrived. Nothing else gave a clue as to why this place had been named 'The Swiss Chalet'. It was an Edwardian house, three storeys high with scarcely any visible roof. A superabundance of drain-pipes, tangled like creeper, climbed all over its façade.

The entrance was through a conservatory full of pots of Busy Lizzie. David opened the inner glass door and found himself in a hall that in colour and decoration might have been the subject of a nineteenth-century sepia photograph. He approached a cubby-hole in the wall which reminded him of a ticket office window at an almost totally disused station. On its shelf stood a bell, a brass bell painted with edelweiss and the name Lucerne. Honour was satisfied. In the Swiss Chalet there was at least one genuinely Swiss object.

Its shrill-throated ring brought a little round woman from a door marked Private. David stuck his head through the aperture, wondering if this was how it had felt to be put in the stocks. The woman advanced aggressively upon him as if she might at any moment throw a rotten egg or a tomato.

'Chadwick,' he said hastily. 'From London. I booked a room.'

The threatening look faded but she didn't smile. He put her age at just over sixty. Her hair was dyed to the shade of coconut matting, which it also resembled in texture, and she wore a mauve knitted twinset, a miracle of cable stitch and bobbles and loops.

'Pleased to meet you,' she said. 'It's Mrs Spiller you talked to on the phone.' She wasn't a native. Retired here perhaps in the hope of making a fortune. He glanced at the pitch-pine woodwork in need of revarnishing, the lamp in its bakelite shade, the visitors' book she pushed towards him whose emptiness told of failure. 'Room number eight.' He put out his hand for the key. Outrage settled in a crease on her purplish forehead. 'We don't have no keys,' she said. 'You can bolt your door if you're particular. Breakfast's at eight sharp, dinner at one and I do a high tea at six.' David picked up his suitcase. 'Up two flights.' She bobbed out from under a hinged flap. 'The first door on your left. The lav's in the bathroom, so don't hang about washing too long. There's such a thing as consideration.'

Consideration for whom? he wondered. The season had scarcely begun and the place seemed dead. It was ten past eleven, but Mrs Spiller seemed to have forgotten her last exhortation, for as he mounted the stairs, she bellowed after him:

'You never said who recommended me.'

'A friend,' David said. 'A Mrs Heller.'

'Not little Mag?'

'Mrs Magdalene Heller. That's right.'

'Well, why didn't you say so before?'

Because he had thought he must come round to it subtly, with cunning and by degrees.

'You *are* a dark horse. I bet you'd never have said if I hadn't asked. I read all about her tragedy in the papers. It upset me properly, I can tell you. I've got the kettle on. Would you like a cuppa before you turn in? That's right. You leave them bags and I'll get my boy to take them up.'

Things were going well, far better than he had expected. There was one question he must ask. Her answer would make the difference between his staying the whole weekend or leaving in the morning. 'Of course, she was here only last year, wasn't she?'

'That's right, in July. End of July. Now you pop into the lounge and make yourself comfy.'

The room was small and shabby. It smelt of geranium leaves and fly spray. Mrs Spiller shut the door on him and went off to fetch the tea. Sitting down, he wondered how often Magdalene had sat in the same chair. Suppose the Norths had stayed here too and the first encounter between Bernard and Louise had been in this very room? He contemplated the décor with his critical designer's eye, the potted plants, the wedding group on an upright piano, the snowstorm in a glass dome. Two pictures faced him, a water colour of Plymouth Hoe and a nasty little lithograph of some central European city. There was another picture in the corner, half hidden by a mahogany plant stand. He got up to look more closely and his heart gave a little jerk. What more suited to this mid-Victorian room than Millais' *Order of Release*? Susan Townsend looked through him and beyond, her mouth tilted, her eyes cool, distant, indifferent.

Before driving down here, he had done a strange, perhaps a foolish, thing. He had sent her a dozen white roses. Would she look like that when she received them, her expression changing from cold politeness as she closed the door to disgust?

'Sugar?' said Mrs Spiller into his right ear.

He jumped, almost knocking the teacup out of her hand.

'Bit nervy, aren't you? A couple of days down here will set you up. Very bracing, Bathcombe is.'

'It always does Magdalene a world of good,' David said.

'Just as well. You need your health to face up to what she's been through. What a terrible thing, him doing himself in like that, wasn't it? I've often asked myself what was at the back of it all.' Not as often as he had, David thought, sipping the hot sweet tea. 'You being their friend, you must know what triggered it all off. You needn't mind telling me. I'm not exaggerating when I say I was more or less one of the family. Year after year Mr Chant used to bring little Mag here for their holidays and Mag always called me Auntie Vi.'

'Still does,' David said stoutly. 'She often talks about her Auntie Vi.' But who was Mr Chant? Her father, of course. In the newspaper bundling his slide projector had been the announcement of Heller's wedding, Bernard Heller to Miss Magdalene Chant.

'Yes,' said Mrs Spiller, reminiscing, 'she'd been coming here with her dad since she was so high and she knows all the locals. Ask anyone in the village if they remember little Mag Chant pushing her dad about in his wheelchair. Well, not his. They used to borrow one from old Mr Lilybeer and she'd take him down to the beach. Her and Bernard, they came here for their honeymoon and then most years after that.'

'I don't suppose that Mrs North ever stopped here?'

'North?' Mrs Spiller considered and her face reddened. 'Are you referring to that woman as was Bernard's fancy piece, by any chance?' David nodded. 'She certainly did not. Whatever gave you that idea?'

'Nothing really,' David began.

'I should think not indeed. He must have been out of his mind chasing a woman like that when he had a lovely girl of his own. All the local boys was after Mag when she was in her teens, or would have been if her father'd given them half a chance.'

'I can imagine,' David said soothingly, but he was aware that for the time being at least he had spoiled the hopeful *rapport* between himself and Mrs Spiller. She was staunchly Magdalene's ally, as if she were really her aunt, and she took his introduction of Louise North's name as criticism of this adopted niece, of her beauty, her desirability. 'I think Magdalene's exceptionally good-looking.'

But Mrs Spiller was not to be so easily mollified. 'I'm off up the wooden hill,' she said and she gave him an aggrieved frown. 'You can have the telly on if you want.'

'A bit cold for that.' The room was unheated and a vaseful of wax flowers had been placed in the grate.

'I never light no fires after April the first,' said Mrs Spiller sharply.

He had discovered one thing. The Norths had not only not stayed at the Swiss Chalet at the same time as Bernard and Magdalene. They had never stayed there at all. But they had been better off than the Hellers and perhaps they had stayed at one of the hotels in the village.

David breakfasted alone off cornflakes, eggs and bacon and very pale thick toast. He had finished and was leaving the dining-room when the only other residents appeared, a dour-looking man and a middle-aged woman in tight trousers. The woman eyed David silently while helping herself from the sideboard to four bottles of different kinds of sauce.

It was a cool cloudy morning, sunless and still. He found a path between pines which brought him within ten minutes to the top of a cliff. The sea was calm, grey and with a silver sheen. Between two headlands he saw a pointed heathy island rising out of the sea and he identified it from Turner's painting as the Mewstone. This association of nature with art again evoked Susan Townsend's face, and it was in a depressed frame of mind that he set off for the village.

At the Great Western Hotel he ordered morning coffee and was shown into a wintry lounge. The place was as yet barely prepared for visitors. Through a large curved bay window he could see a one-man manually-punted ferry that plied between the Bathcombe shore and a tiny beach on the opposite side.

'A friend of mine, a Mr North,' he said to the waitress who came for the bill, 'stayed here at the end of July last year, and when he heard I was coming down he asked me if I'd enquire about a book he left in his room.'

'He's left it a long time,' said the girl pertly.

'He wouldn't have bothered only he knew I was coming down.'

'And what would this said book be called?'

'*Sesame and Lilies*,' said David because he kept thinking of Susan Townsend who was Ruskin's wife all over again. With what he thought must be a mad smile, he left all his change from a ten shilling note on his plate.

'I will enquire,' said the girl more pleasantly.

David watched the ferryman come to the Bathcombe shore. He unloaded a cargo of empty squash bottles in a crate. Possibly the single cottage on the other side was a guesthouse. Come to that, the Norths could have rented a cottage here or a flat or stayed with friends. They might not have come in July, they might not have come to this part of Devon at all.

The girl came back, looking sour. 'Your friend didn't leave that gardening book of his here,' she said. 'He didn't even stay here. I've checked with the register. You'd better try the Palace or the Rock.'

But the Norths hadn't stayed at either place. David crossed the inlet by the ferry to find that the solitary house was a youth hostel.

Shepherd's pie and queen of puddings was served at the Swiss Chalet for luncheon. 'Well, did you meet anyone who knows Mag?' asked Mrs Spiller when she came in to serve him instant coffee and pre-sliced processed cheese.

'I hardly saw a soul.'

The coconut matting curls bounced and all the bobbles on the lilac jumper quivered. 'If it's excitement you want, I don't know why you didn't settle for Plymouth. Folks come to Bathcombe to get a bit of peace.'

Suppose the Norths had 'settled for' Plymouth? They might have come to Bathcombe just once for a day's outing. But would a passionate love affair have arisen from one isolated encounter on a beach? David couldn't picture slow, stolid Bernard, his deck-chair moved alongside Louise's, exchanging addresses surreptitiously.

'I'm not complaining,' he lied. 'It's a charming place.'

Mrs Spiller sat down and put her fat mauve elbows on the table.

'That's what Mr Chant always used to say. "It's a charming place, Mrs Spiller. You get real peace and quiet here," he'd say, and him coming from Exeter where it's not what you'd call rowdy, is it? By the way, I've been meaning to ask you, how's Auntie Agnes?'

'Auntie Agnes?'

'I'd have thought Mag would mention *her*. Not that you could blame Mag, a bit of a kid like her, but I've always thought she had a lot to thank Auntie Agnes for. But for her she never would have gone to London and got married.'

His mind wandering, David remarked that perhaps this wouldn't have been a bad thing.

'You've got something there.' Mrs Spiller passed him Marie biscuits from a packet. 'But she didn't know how it was all going to turn out, did she? I remember back in 1960 thinking to myself, that poor kid, she'll never have a proper life tied to an old man like that.'

'Mr Chant, you mean?' David said absently.

'Well, maybe I shouldn't call him old. I dare say he wasn't above fifty-five. But you know how it is with invalids. You always think of them as old, especially when they're crippled like Mr Chant was.'

'Arthritis or something, was it?'

'No, you've got it wrong there. Multiple sclerosis, that Auntie Agnes told me. She came down with them in 1960 and he was real bad then. Too much for Mag on her own.'

'I suppose so.' David wanted to get on with the hunt. He wasn't interested in diseases of the central nervous system and he was awaiting his chance to escape from Mrs Spiller.

'They're very slow in developing, them illnesses,' she was saying. 'You can have sclerosis for twenty or thirty years. Mind you, he had his good days. Sometimes he was nearly as good as you or me. But other times . . . It went right to my heart, I can tell you, watching that lovely girl pushing him about in a chair and her only in her teens.'

'Her mother was dead by then, I suppose?' David said, bored.

'That's what they used to tell people.' Mrs Spiller put her face closer to his and lowered her voice. The middle-aged couple sat some fifteen feet from them, looking out of the window, but Mrs Spiller's extreme caution implied that they were spies whose sole mission in visiting her guesthouse was to satisfy themselves as to certain unsolved mysteries in the Chants' family history. 'I got it all out of that Auntie Agnes,' she whispered. 'Mrs Chant had run off with someone when Mag was a kid. They never knew where she ended up. Saw what her life would be, I reckon, and got out when the going was good.'

'Like Magdalene.'

'A wife's one thing,' Mrs Spiller bristled. 'A daughter's quite another. When Auntie Agnes wrote and said Mag was going up to London to find herself a job I thought, that's the best thing that could happen. Let her have a bit of life while she's young enough to enjoy it, I thought. Of course, Auntie Agnes wasn't young, her being Mr Chant's own auntie really, and it's no joke looking after an invalid when you're past seventy.'

'No doubt she managed.'

'I don't reckon she looked ahead when she took it on. She wasn't to know Mag'd meet Bernard and write home she was getting engaged. Mind you, I never knew any of this till Mag and Bernard came down for their honeymoon. That was two years later and Mr Chant had passed on by then. That's why I asked if you knew what had become of Auntie Agnes. Dead and gone too, I dare say. It happens to all of us in the fullness of time, doesn't it?'

'Depends what you mean by the fullness of time,' said David and he thought of Bernard with a bullet through his head because he had loved unwisely.

Susan had begun on the last chapter of *Foetid Flesh* when Bob opened the back door and came in softly. She stopped typing at once, a little dismayed at the look on Paul's face. He had been trundling his cars between the legs of her chair, but now he squatted still and stiff and his expression would have seemed a mere blank to anyone but his mother who could read it.

'Where did the flowers come from, Susan?'

It was Paul who answered him. 'A man called David Chadwick. Roses are the most expensive thing you can send anyone in April.'

'I see.' Bob stood with his back to them, staring out of the window at the elms on which not a bud, not a vestige of green, showed. 'Chadwick . . . And daffodils are the cheapest, aren't they?'

'You picked your daffodils out of the garden.'

'All right, Paul. That's enough,' Susan said. 'It's not so long ago you said it was silly to send people flowers.' She smiled at Bob's back. 'And you were quite right,' she said firmly. 'I can see Richard outside. I expect he's wondering where you are.'

'Then why doesn't he call for me?' But Paul went, dodging the hand which Bob suddenly and pathetically put out to him. Susan took it instead and, standing beside him, again felt the physical pull he exerted over her, the attraction that emptied her mind and left her weary.

'Have you thought about what I asked you?'

For a moment her only answer was to press more tightly the hand she held. And then it came to her in a swift unpleasant revelation that this was her reply. Physical contact and then renewed, stronger physical contact was the only way she could get through to him. The closer intimacy which awaited them if they married would be just this pressure of hands on a full and complete scale, the desperate soulless coupling of two creatures in a desert.

She looked up at him. 'It's too soon, Bob.' His face was grey and drawn, no longer even handsome, and it was tenderness rather than desire that made her want to kiss him. She moved away, for suddenly her delaying answer had made kissing wrong. 'Come and sit down,' she said. 'You don't mind about the roses, do you? I don't know why he sent them.'

'Because he wants to know you better, of course. Susan, the world is full of men who'll want to know you better. That's why I have to – you have to . . . Susan, if I'd seen you as I see you now, when Louise was still alive, would you have . . .?'

'When Louise was alive?'

'If I'd fallen in love with you then, would you have come away with me?'

She was afraid without knowing the reason for her fear, 'Of course I wouldn't, Bob. Even if you'd wanted to marry me then, Louise couldn't have divorced you. She was a Catholic.'

'My God,' he shouted, 'I know that!'

'Then, don't torment yourself.' She hesitated and said, 'I suppose you could have divorced her.' And would it have been different, would there have been true companionship for them without the spectre of Louise's death and Heller's between them, their sole wearisome topic of conversation? 'Yes, you could have done that,' she said tiredly.

'But I couldn't have done that,' he said, and his eyes had darkened from blue to a frightening impenetrable black. 'It's because I couldn't have done that . . . Oh, Susan, what's the use? It's past, gone for ever. Heller loved my wife and killed her and I ought to be free . . . Susan, I'll never be free!' He quietened, shivered, and gradually his face assumed the look it wore when he explored his obsession. 'Everyone persecutes me,' he said. 'The police have been here again. Didn't you hear that dog? The whole street must have seen.'

'But why, Bob?'

'I suppose your friend Chadwick put them on to me.' There was a sneer on the fine-drawn mouth as he glanced at the white roses. 'They wanted to know if I'd known Magdalene Heller last August.' He turned to stare at her with those sombre eyes and she, meeting them, was for the first time afraid of him. 'She persecutes me, too,' he said in a dull, dead voice.

Susan said helplessly, 'I don't understand.'

'God knows, I hope you never will. Then there's your Mrs Dring.' He drew in his breath sharply. 'I gave her the sack this morning. It was bad enough having to listen to her going on about Louise, but I could have stuck that.'

'What happened, Bob?'

'I found her rooting through Louise's dressing table. I think she was looking for those letters. She must have read about them in the papers and thought she'd got the chance of a peepshow. There was a scene, I said things I shouldn't have and so did she. I'm sorry, Susan. Nothing goes right for me, does it?'

He put out his hand to her very slowly as if to pull her towards him, and she was on her feet, bewildered and uneasy, moving to clasp that outstretched hand, when the telephone rang urgently into their silence. He dropped his head into his hands with a gasp of despair.

Susan lifted the receiver and sat down heavily when she heard Julian's brittle chit-chat voice.

'I've found a buyer for the house, my dear. Our old friend Greg.'

Knowing him of old, Susan sensed that the pause had been made for her to fill with praise and congratulation. Like someone hazarding a half-learned foreign language, she felt she must speak just to prove she could. Anything she might say would do. 'Why does he want to live out here?'

'You may well ask,' Julian said, 'after that delicious little mews place of his. The fact is Dian has been playing up and he feels there are too many naughty temptations in London. So I'll send him along, shall I?'

'I hope I'll still recognise him.'

She was aware that Julian had made some sharp sarcastic reply to this, but the words were just words, meaningless, without power. At the sound of a movement from the living-room, she looked up and saw Bob framed in the doorway. His face and body were in shadow, a dark silhouette, and, poised there, his figure suggested a man on the brink of an abyss. She covered the mouthpiece with her hand.

'Bob . . .'

He made a queer little gesture with one of those shadowed hands as if staving something off. Then he moved out of her sight and she heard the door to the garden close.

'Are you still there, Susan?'

'Yes, I . . .' How different this conversation with Julian would have been if she could have used it as the opportunity to tell him she was going to be married! In that moment she knew quite certainly she could never marry Bob. 'I'll see Greg any time he likes to come,' she said calmly, and then, with the politeness of a distant business acquaintance, 'It was good of you to phone. Good-bye.'

She sat by the phone for a long time, thinking how she and Bob were separated now only by two thin walls and ten feet of air. But those barriers were as impenetrable to her as the enclosures of his mind. She shivered a little because when they kissed or sat in silence she was almost happy with a happiness quenched at once by glimpses into that hooded mind.

17

Using his story of the lost book, David spent Saturday afternoon calling at every hotel on the South Devon coast between Plymouth and Salcombe and at each he drew a blank. Plymouth itself defeated him. He counted twelve hotels and guesthouses in the A.A. guide alone and, having tried four of them, he gave up. The Norths must have rented a house or stayed inland.

Must have? The chances were that they had been to North Devon, that they had been there in May or June. And Magdalene might have been telling the truth. It was not on a beach or a seafront restaurant that Bernard had met Louise but in fact in a suburban kitchen, drinking tea.

'Had a good day?' asked Mrs Spiller, slapping a plateful of pork pie and lettuce in front of him. 'Pity it's too early in the year for you to do the boat trip to Plymouth. But they don't run till May. Mag always went on them boats. Still, I dare say you wouldn't fancy it, you being the nervy type.'

He had never thought of himself as a neurotic. Perhaps the urgency and at the same time the fruitlessness of his quest was telling on him. 'Is it a particularly perilous voyage?' he asked sarcastically.

'Safe as houses normally, only there was the *Ocean Maid*, after all, wasn't there?'

The name rang a faint bell and then he vaguely recalled distasteful headlines and remembered reading in the papers of a catastrophe, similar to the *Darlwyne* tragedy, but with a happier ending. A glance at Mrs Spiller told him she was avid for conversation and he had no one else to talk to, nothing to do. 'She was a pleasure boat,' he said. 'Didn't she go aground off the coast here?'

Mrs Spiller took a cup from a side table and filled it from David's teapot. 'She was taking folks on trips from Torquay and Plymouth, calling in here and at Newton. Due back at six she was. The next thing we knew it was on the wireless she was missing.' A few drops of tea fell on to her embossed lilac bosom. She took a paper napkin from a tumbler and scrubbed at the stain. 'Drat that tea! What was I saying? Oh, yes, well, Mag had been a bit bored and lonely, not knowing what to do with herself, so I said, Why not go on the boat trip? and she did. I got her a real nice packed lunch and I saw her off on the boat myself, never thinking they'd go and run out of fuel and get themselves stranded overnight.

'Just a pair of slacks and one of them thin tee shirts she had on. You've got a lovely figure, so why not show it off? I said. Mighty cold she must have got on that boat, though. Well, it got to six and it got to seven and still she hadn't come and then we heard about it on the news. I was in a proper state, on the point of sending a wire to Bernard. You don't know what to do in a case like that, do you? You don't know whether you're worrying them needlessly like. Especially as I'd egged Mag on to go, got her ticket and all. I blamed myself really.'

'Didn't he go on the trip, then?' David put his knife and fork down and looked up, suddenly chilled.

'Go on the trip? How could he? He was up in London.'

'But I thought you said . . .'

'You're miles away tonight, Mr Chadwick, you really are. This was *last* year, last July. Mag came down on her own. You're mixing it up in your mind with the other years when Bernard came with her. Anyway, as I said, I never wired him and it was all right and poor little Mag none the worse for what she'd been through. She didn't let it keep her in for the rest of the time she was here. Palled up with some folks she'd met on the boat, she told me, and she was off with them every day. I was glad I hadn't got Bernard down here all for nothing, I can tell you. You've gone quite white, Mr Chadwick. Not feeling queer, I hope?'

Magdalene hadn't lied. Bernard had met Louise just as she had told him. Perhaps it was true also that she had never set eyes on North until the inquest, had never plotted with him to do a murder, never handed him a gun nor sat with him in The Man in the Iron Mask. Wasn't it possible too that Sid and Charles had never seen them there together, but had concocted an amusing story to while away half an hour while they drank the drinks he had paid for?

On Sunday morning he packed his case and left the Swiss Chalet. Five miles inland he stopped for petrol in a village called Jillerton.

'Clean your windscreen, sir?'

'Thanks, and would you check the tyre pressures while you're about it?'

'Can you hang on five minutes while I see to this gentleman?'

David nodded and strolled across the village street. One day, he thought, he might look back to this weekend and laugh at himself. It had taken him a two-hundred-mile drive and surely two hundred questions besides two wasted days to find out that Bernard Heller had never been here at all.

There was only one shop in the street and, although it was Sunday, the door was open. David went inside aimlessly, eyeing the coloured car stickers, the pixie statuettes and the carved wooden stags, replicas of which he had seen for sale in Vienna, in Lacock, in Edinburgh and on the pavement by Oxford Circus underground. On a shelf behind this array of mass-produced bric-à-brac stood mugs and jugs in Devon pottery, hand-painted in cream and brown and not unattractive. He could think of no one but Susan Townsend to whom he wanted to give a present and if he bought her a souvenir she would probably send it back. The white roses might be wilting on his doorstep at this moment.

Some of the pottery was lettered with obscure proverbs and this he disregarded, but the mugs, plain and prettily shaped had a christian name written on each of them, Peter, Jeremy, Anne, Susan . . . There would have to be one for Susan, of course. What was wrong with him, what sentimental madness had seized him, that everywhere he looked he had to see her name or her face?

There was a plain one at the end of the shelf that he could buy his mother for her nightly hot chocolate. He lifted it, turned it round and saw that it wasn't plain after all. In common with the rest it had a name written in elegant brown calligraphy.

Magdalene.

Could Bernard have ordered it for Magdalene on one of those previous visits of theirs, ordered it and neglected to collect it? He was setting it down again thoughtfully when a voice behind him said, 'A very uncommon name, isn't it, sir?' David turned in the direction from which the deep Devon burr had come and saw an assistant who was perhaps his own age. 'I've often said to my wife, we'll never sell that one, not with a name like Magdalene.' And, raising his voice, he called to someone in the room behind the shop, 'I'm saying to this gentleman, we'll never sell that mug Mr North ordered.'

'*Mr North?*'

'I remember because the circumstances were a bit – well, funny,' said the assistant. 'Last August it was, right in the height of the holiday season. Still, you won't want to be troubled with that, sir. The gentleman won't come back for it now, so if you're interested . . . But no, not with a name like Magdalene.'

'I'll have it,' David said in a bemused voice.

'I call that handsome of you, sir. Ten and sixpence, if you please.'

'You said there were funny circumstances.'

Wrapping paper in hand, the young man paused. 'If you're going to have it, I reckon you're entitled to know. The gentleman was staying at the King's Arms. That's the inn on far side of the green and my uncle keeps it. Mr North ordered the mug for his wife, he said, but when he didn't come for it and he didn't come. I had a word with uncle. 'Tis a Mrs *Louise* North, he says, not Magdalene. Queer that, we thought. Looks as if 'twere for a lady friend and the gentleman not quite above board.'

'So you didn't want to embarrass him by taking the mug over to the hotel?'

'Proper embarrassing it would have been too, sir, seeing as the lady, his true wife that is, fell sick with one of these here old viruses the day after they came. 'Twould have set her back a bit to hear her husband was carrying on.'

'Is the King's Arms that smart-looking pub on the green, did you say?'

'That's it, sir.'

North had a fondness for smart little pubs. . . .

'Rather unfortunate for them, Mrs North being ill like that,' David said casually and, as he spoke, he remembered Magdalene Heller's words. When Bernard met her she had been ill. . . . So it was after this holiday, then, they had met? 'It must have spoilt their time here.'

'Mr North didn't let it get him down, sir.' The assistant shrugged, perhaps at the villainy of mankind in general or London people in particular. 'Went on that boat trip, he did, without his wife. The *Ocean Maid*, you'll have read of in the London papers. He told me the tale when he came in to order that little mug, how they'd been drifting for hours, never knowing how close they were to the rocks. 'Twould put you or me off our holiday properly, wouldn't it, sir? But that Mr North he didn't turn a hair. I said to my wife at the time, you can see it'd take a mighty big upheaval to get him down.'

Susan was almost sorry she was nearing the end of *Foetid Flesh*. In a way it had taken her mind off the tragedy next door and off Bob. Now her problems, only subconsciously present while she typed, would rush to fill the hours the finishing of the typescript must leave empty.

Page four hundred and two. The whole thing was going to run into four hundred and ten pages. Jane Willingale's hand-writing had begun to deteriorate in the last fifty sheets and even to Susan, who was used to it, some words were nearly indecipherable. She was trying to interpret something that looked like an obscure shorthand outline when Doris hammered on the back door and walked in with Richard.

'You don't mind if I leave him with you for a bit, do you, my dear? Just while we go for drinks with the O'Donnells. Bob was asked but he won't go anywhere these days. If you ask me, he's got persecution mania. Still, you'll know more about what goes on in his mind than the rest of us, no doubt. The police were here for hours in the week. Did you see?'

'Bob told me.'

'And I heard him yelling at your Mrs Dring when I was passing yesterday. He's in a very nasty nervous state. Many a time I've seen them like that in the nerve wards. I expect you know best, but if I were you I shouldn't fancy being alone with him. White roses, I see. They'll soon wilt up in this temperature. Unlike me. I could stay here all day, but I can see you want to get on. Pity it's always so perishing at the O'Donnells'.'

The outline was 'murder'. Susan typed it with a faint feeling of inexplicable distress. She heard Richard go upstairs and the sound of little cars trundled out on to the landing. Seven more pages to go. To decipher the last, almost hysterical rush, of Miss Willingale's novel was going to demand all Susan's concentration.

The children had moved their toys to the stairs now. She must be tolerant, she must control the admonition until they became really unbearable. Bump, bump, crash, whirr. . . . That was the latest tank plummeting to make a fresh dent in the hall parquet.

'You're making an awful racket,' she called. 'Can't you go outside for a bit?'

'It's raining outside,' Paul's voice came indignantly.

'You know you're not to play on the stairs, anyway.'

She waded through a long sentence and turned the page. The writing had suddenly improved.

My darling,

You are in my thoughts night and day. Indeed, I do not know where dreaming ends and . . .

It didn't make sense. But this wasn't even Jane Willingale's writing. It sloped more, the capitals were larger, the ink different.

Susan frowned and, taking a cigarette, inhaled deeply. Then, holding the sheets up to the light, she contemplated Bernard Heller's love-letters.

18

'Can we take the motorway outside?' Paul asked, adding virtuously, 'It's stopped raining, but the grass is wet and I thought I ought to ask you.'

Susan hardly heard him. 'What, darling?'

'Can we take the motorway outside?'

'The electricity won't work outside and it's too cold to leave the door open.'

Paul stuck out his lower lip. 'It's not fair. We can't play on the stairs and we can't come in here because you're working. You've got your papers in an awful mess again and you've got ash all over them. If I mess them up you just get mad.'

So she had never burnt the letters. Perhaps in her heart she had always known she hadn't, but she also knew that she had certainly not tucked them between the main body of Miss Willingale's manuscript and the penultimate page. What reason would Doris have for doing such a thing, Doris or Mrs Dring?

'Paul, you haven't been playing with my papers again, have you?'

'No, I haven't!'

'Are you quite sure?'

'I haven't touched them,' the little boy flared. 'I *swear* I haven't. Cross my heart. I haven't been at your desk since the day before you were ill, the day you had to go to the trial about Mrs North.' Self-righteous indignation turned his face a bright tear-threatening red. 'You said if I touched them again you wouldn't let me wear my watch and I didn't touch them.'

'You needn't make a big thing out of it. I believe you.'

'Except for once,' he said defiantly, 'the day you were first ill. I wanted to *help*. Your papers were in an awful mess. You'd left some of them on the coffee table so I put them back with the others, all tidy. I thought you'd be pleased!'

David was jubilant. He had been right, he hadn't wasted his time. Beyond all doubt now, Robert North and Magdalene Heller had known each other since last summer.

He was jubilant, but there was much he didn't understand. All along he had assumed that their meeting, knowledge of each other, love perhaps for each other had grown from the love affair between their marriage partners. Now it seemed that these two, the widow and the widower, had met first. North had gone alone on a boat trip and when it seemed they would be stranded at sea all night had been drawn towards Magdalene who was very likely the only other solitary passenger on that holiday voyage. David could picture her, a little frightened perhaps, but still flaunting her body in her trousers and her thin tee shirt, and he could picture North comforting her, lending her his coat.

But Bernard had been in London and Louise ill in bed.

Was it credible that on returning home North or Magdalene had brought the four of them together? Hardly, David thought. North had ordered the piece of pottery for her, had surely met her every day for the rest of his holiday. Mrs Spiller had spoken to him of her having 'palled up' with someone she met on the boat. By the end of their holiday, David was sure, they were already in love. North would never have introduced Magdalene to his wife nor she North to her husband.

How, then, had they contrived that the others should meet?

David spent Monday morning in Knightsbridge among the antique shops, hunting for Chippendale furniture to dress the set of *Mansfield Park*. His search was fruitful and at half past twelve he crossed the street to the tube entrance on the corner of Hans Crescent.

A girl whose face seemed familiar came out of Harrods at that moment and bore down on him relentlessly. Recognition came with a sickening twist. It was ironical that he should encounter the second Mrs Townsend when more than anything in the world he wanted to see the first. The absurd coincidence made him smile and she took the smile as an enthusiastic greeting.

With a violent snort, she dumped an enormous coloured paper carrier on the pavement between them. 'So you didn't buy that place, then?' she said with the loud directness he found repellent. 'Did you know Greg was after it? Only he won't cough up more than eight thou and God knows we're on our beam ends. There's wads of it going out every month to that woman in Matchdown Park and what's left all goes on nosh.' She drew breath noisily. 'You wouldn't believe what I've just had to pay for a lobster.'

David eyed her warily. She looked younger than ever this morning and particularly uncouth. The one-piece garment she wore – a dress? a coat? – was made of thick oatmeal-coloured material, striped here and there with grey and fringed at hem and wrists. It made her look like a squaw, the juvenile delinquent of the tribe.

'My husband is bonkers about food,' she said. 'Here, you might as well carry that for me. It weighs a ton.'

In fact, it must have weighed close on half a hundred weight. As David lifted the bag, a protruding bundling of wrapping paper slipped and a large red claw sprang out. Elizabeth Townsend marched to the pavement edge.

'Can I get you a taxi?'

'You're joking. I'm going on the bus.' She glared at him. 'D'you know what I'm going to have for my lunch? Yoghourt. That's what I've come down to. And I love food, I just love it.' She sighed and said crossly, 'Oh, come on, before the lights change.'

He followed her, humping the bag.

'I thought I might go to lunch with Dian,' she said petulantly. He almost asked who Dian was and then he remembered the mews house and the flaming bamboo screen.

'Why don't you? It's only just down the road.'

'Well, I don't quite like to. I'm not usually funny about these things. Julian says I rush in where angels and all that jazz. No, the point is Dian's got a man giving her a whirl. Not really like Dian, is it?'

David said heartily that indeed it was not.

'I'd have said Dian was the complete prude. Frigid, I expect. But then Minta rang up this morning and when I said I'd drop in on Dian, she said, I wouldn't because her boyfriend's there again.' Thrusting back the red claw, David said he saw what she meant. 'I don't want to burst in on them, you see. For Christ's sake, don't say a word to Dian. I know she's a mate of yours. Live and let live, after all. Dian hasn't said anything to Minta – she wouldn't, would she?'

'I shouldn't think so.'

'But with Minta living opposite she couldn't expect to get away with it. Minta told me this bloke's car's been there half a dozen times in the past fortnight and she's seen him sneaking in after Greg's gone to the studio. Of course, she dropped a hint to Greg and that's why he wants to take Dian out of harm's way.'

Every step was taking him further and further from the tube station. As Elizabeth Townsend trailed relentlessly on past bus stops, he had been searching for an excuse to dump the shopping and make his getaway. And now he did dump it, but not because he wanted to escape.

'Is that all Minta has to go on?' he asked, trying to keep the breathlessness from his voice. 'Just seeing a man's car outside Dian's?'

'She saw him go in,' said Elizabeth Townsend sharply.

'But, Mrs Townsend . . .'

'Oh, call me Elizabeth. You make me feel about ninety-six.'

'But, Elizabeth . . .' It was a relief. The other name conjured up a very different face and voice. 'He could be a salesman, a surveyor, an interior decorator, anything.'

'Yeah? I tell you he's a sexy fellow of thirty and Dian's a real dish. You know damn' well Dian and Greg haven't been having it for two years now and Dian's always off on her own. You can take it from me, she's all mixed-up over this bloke. You're green, David, that's your problem. But Minta's not and I'm not and when we hear a fellow's been sneaking round to a girl when her old man's nicely out of the way, we know what to think.'

'Faithful Dian? Frigid Dian?'

'You are rooting for her, aren't you? So she's not faithful, she's not frigid. This proves it.'

At this point the bottom fell out of the bag. He looked at the aubergines, the lemons and the tins of *fois gras* which rolled into the gutter and said happily, 'Elizabeth, I'm awfully glad I met you. Tell me, if you could choose, what's the nicest place you can think of for lunch? The place you'd most like to go to?'

'The *Écu de France*,' she said promptly, stuffing two lemons into the pocket of her Red Indian garment and eyeing him optimistically.

'I can't bear to think of you eating yoghourt,' he said. 'I never liked it.' He hailed a taxi and, opening the door, bowled vegetables and fruit and cans on to the seat. 'Jermyn Street,' he said to the driver. 'The *Écu de France*.'

He heard a chair shift and scrape from inside the office as he approached the door and when he came in the woman who was waiting for him sat a yard or two from his desk, her expression grimly virtuous. Ulph was sure she had been examining the papers which lay face-upwards on his blotter. They were a draft of the programme for the police sports gala and Ulph smiled to himself.

'Good morning,' he said. 'You wanted to see me?'

'I don't care who I see,' the woman said, 'as long as it's someone high up, someone as knows the ropes.' She patted her fuzzy red hair with a hand in a Fair Isle glove and she looked at him in truculent disappointment as if she had expected to see someone big, aggressive, authoritative. 'You'll do,' she said. 'I reckon you'd be interested in a fellow called North.'

'May I have your name, madam?'

'As long as it doesn't go no further. Mrs Dring. Mrs Leonard Dring. My first name's Iris.' She took off her gloves and laid them on the desk beside her handbag. 'I work for this North, cleaning like, or I did till he give me the push Saturday. What I wanted to tell you was, I work next door too and I was working there the morning Mrs North was done in.'

Ulph nodded, his face reserved. This was not the first time he had encountered the spite of the discarded servant. 'Go on, please.'

'There was three fellows digging up the road at the bottom of them gardens. Mrs North used to give them their tea, regular like. Well, about nine-thirty it was, I was in

Mrs Townsend's kitchenette and I heard this banging on
the back door next door. Well, I didn't think no more about
it and I was doing my windows, in the lounge that is, when
I see this chap go down the garden path, tall chap in a
duffel coat. Mrs Townsend and me, we thought it was one
of them workmen. He lets himself out of the gate and goes
off up the road.'

'Perhaps to get his tea at a café instead?'

'So we thought at the time. I reckon that's what he
wanted us to think. The point is there wasn't never more
than *three* men working on the road. I'll tell you how I
know. I said to my husband. "How many chaps was there
working on the cemetery road? And he says, Three." Never
more than three. And he's never wrong, my husband,
there's nothing that man doesn't know. I said, "You're
pally with that old fellow, the foreman that was, you ask
him." And that's what he did. Three fellows there was, all
the time, the old chap, the man and the young lad. And
what's more, when I heard the banging at the door that
dog never barked. It was out the front, laying in wait, and
it could see the side door all right. Like my husband always
says, them animals have got more sense than we have. They
don't take no account of duffel coats and folks setting
themselves up as workmen.'

'You delayed a long time before you came to me, Mrs
Dring,' Ulph said quietly. 'Could it be that you've only
come now because you have a grudge against Mr North?'

'If you don't believe me, you ask Mrs Townsend. She
knows. It was her put the idea into my head.'

Probably she supposed that her departure would be the
signal for him immediately to set the law in motion. Ulph
sat quite still, reflecting. His own construction of the murder scene, almost totally visual, had shifted and changed.
North had done it very simply, after all. Ulph saw that
there had been scarcely any premeditation at all and North,
who had acted on impulse, had merely covered his tracks
afterwards.

He had stayed at home that morning not to contrive a
false suicide but to have it all out with Heller. He would
have told Louise and let her warn her lover if she liked.

Ulph touched his forehead and felt the muscle that jumped above his eye when he was nervous. Hadn't he done just that thing, confronting his own wife and the man she loved? Hadn't he too tried to discuss matters with them rationally and calmly? His wife had shut herself in her bedroom, flinging herself on the bed in a storm of tears.

Very likely it had been that way with Louise North, and the two men had gone up to her together. But first Heller had slung his raincoat and his heavy briefcase on the kitchen table, keeping the gun in his jacket pocket. Ulph knew very well that if a man, even a peaceful, mild man, owns a gun he is liable to use it under stress. Louise had given Heller the idea, perhaps erroneous, perhaps true, that her husband was violent and tyrannical. Aware of the kind of scene which awaited him, Heller would have brought his gun. Just as a threat, of course, just as a tool of persuasion.

And North? Perhaps Heller had arrived later than expected and the husband, tired of waiting, was ready for work in coat and gloves. Thus they had entered the bedroom together. Had they struggled and the gun off? Ulph thought so. In the struggle Louise had been inadvertently shot by Heller and when, in his horror at what he had done, he had bent over her, fallen beside her on the bed, North had taken the gun and shot him as he lay. Taken it in a hand already, but perhaps not with murderous intent, protected by a strong driving glove. Then, later, the instinctive actions of self-preservation, Heller's hand to be closed for the second time round the gun – lest the glove had eradicated earlier prints – and, hideously, a third shot to be fired. It had been raining. A duffel coat with hood up, the moment's pause to knock at the back door as the workmen always knocked, and then the deliberately slow stroll, heart pounding, blood thundering, to the fence, the street, the wide unsuspecting world outside.

With a good counsel, Ulph thought, North might not get very long. He had been intolerably provoked. The woman had turned his home into a house of assignation and written foul things of him to her lover. And suddenly Ulph remembered how North had spoken of his neighbour's kindness to him, as if he thought of her as more than just a doer of good deeds. She was divorced, he recalled. Was there a chance that she would wait for North?

Ulph got up and cursed himself for a sentimental fool. There had been no woman waiting for him when at last he had found himself a free man. He glanced at his watch. North would be still at work, home in three hours or so. As he prepared the things he must say and do, he thought with a faint amusement of David Chadwick and the theories borne of a fruitful imagination. What else could you expect of a scene designer? Still, for a day or two Ulph also had believed in the possibility of collusion, of conspiracy. He felt a little ashamed of himself.

19

He looked again at the photograph of the Norths that had been taken on their holiday and this time the background to their smiling faces was familiar. The inn sign was too blurred for its name to be readable, but he recognised the half-timbering on the gables of the King's Arms and the white fence that surrounded Jillerton's village green.

David had stacked this paper with other souvenirs, depressing, a little macabre, of Bernard Heller. Here were the records of his brief and humble intrusions into the public eye, and here the announcement of his marriage to the girl who had wheeled her sick father along the Bathcombe shore. The print was faded but Bernard's handwriting not at all, the figures of his wedding date sharp and blue with the little distinctive and very continental tick across the ascender of the seven.

He looked at them all musingly for a moment and then he went to the telephone. Inspector Ulph was out and no one could tell him when he expected to return. David hesitated, pushed away inhibition and the fear of a rebuff, and dialled again. It was the child who answered.

'May I speak to your mother?'

He sounded a nice sensible boy, older than the impression David had from a fair head once seen on a pillow. 'Who shall I say?'

'David Chadwick.'

'We've got your flowers in a vase.' He could never know how much pleasure he had caused with that simple statement. 'Wait a minute and I'll fetch her.'

David would have waited all night.

'Thank you for the flowers,' she said. 'I was going to write to you, only things – well, haven't been very easy.'

He had meant to be gentle, tactful, cunning in his approach. The sound of her voice stunned him into abruptness. 'I must see you this evening. Can I come now?'

'But, why?'

'I have to see you. Oh, I know you can't stand me and, I tell you frankly, it's North I want to talk about. Don't put the receiver down. I should still come.'

'You're an extraordinary man, aren't you?' There was no laughter in her voice. 'I wouldn't be frightened this time,' she said, and then, 'Perhaps it would clear the air.'

Paul fell asleep quickly that night and Susan wondered if it was because the house was almost certainly sold now. It was still daylight, the evening soft and spring-like, and she had no need of a coat to go next door.

The Braeside windows were all tightly closed. A secret shuttered house, she thought. Hadn't someone once likened death to a secret house? And she forced her eyes not to look upwards as she made her way to the back door.

Bob had taken upon himself the right to enter her house without knocking and, although until now she had never availed herself of it, she felt that with him she must have a similar privilege. This was the first time she had entered Braeside since that Wednesday morning. The door yielded to a push and the kitchen yawned emptily at her. Did it seem bare because Heller's coat and briefcase were missing from the table?

'Bob?'

She had called his dead wife's name like that and, getting no answer, had gone upstairs. Suppose history had repeated itself? The niche where the Madonna had stood was empty now, an open mouth in the wall.

'Bob?'

The living-room was stuffy, but clean and as tidy as if no one had lived in it for a long time. For a second she didn't see him, he was sitting so still in the chair where she too had sat and talked to the police inspector. A bar of sunlight made a wavering gold band down the length of his body, passing across his eyes, but he stared through it, undazzled, like a blind man.

She went over to him, knelt at his feet and took his hands. The touch of his skin was no more exciting to her now than Paul's, and she felt for him only as she sometimes felt for Paul, pity, tenderness and above all an inability to understand. But she loved Paul. Had she ever been close enough to Bob to love him?

'Susan, I've come to the end,' he said. 'The police came to me today at work, but never mind that. Never mind that now. I went mad, I was corrupted, I suppose. I don't want to blame anyone else. If I was led into things – well, I was a grown man and I don't want to blame anyone else.' He held her hands more tightly. 'I'm glad,' he said, 'that they can't get anyone else for all this. They can't find out. You don't know what I mean, do you?'

She shook her head.

'Just as well. I don't want you to know. Tell me, did you ever think I might, well, do you an injury?'

Speechless, she looked at him.

'The suggestion was made,' he said hoarsely, 'and I – for a while I . . . It was only for a day or two, Susan. I didn't know what you knew and what you'd seen. I really love you. I love you, Susan.'

'I know,' she said. 'I know.'

'And Louise loved Heller, didn't she? You know that Everyone knows that.' He gasped and, leaning forward so that the beam of light shivered and cut across his shoulder, said fiercely, 'What I did, it was from jealousy. I couldn't stand . . . I had provocation, didn't I, Susan? And maybe I won't have to go away for very long, I'll come back to you.' He took her face in his hands. 'Do you know what I'm trying to tell you?'

'I think so,' she faltered and she stayed where she was, kneeling, because she thought that if she got up she might fall. She had come here to tell him that she still had his wife's letters, that they had never been burnt. His hands palpated her skin. She had thought of him as a blind man but now he was like someone who is deaf and who can only discern speech by feeling the subtle and tiny movements of the speaker's bones.

Perhaps he had really become deaf, for he gave no sign that he had heard the dog begin to bark, hollowly at first and then with fury as the car door slammed.

'You've been crying,' David said.

'Yes, I didn't know it showed.'

The traces of tears were not disfiguring, only the evidence of an unbearable vulnerability. The puffiness they gave to her eyes, like some beautician's exclusive treatment, served to make her look very young. 'I was boorish on the phone,' he said. 'I'm always boorish with you.'

'It doesn't matter,' she said indifferently. 'At the moment I can't feel that anything much matters. You came to talk to me about – about someone we both know. I think you're too late. I – I don't think he'll come back here.'

'Do you mean he's been arrested?'

'That's what you wanted, isn't it?' she said harshly. He couldn't tell if it was personal hatred in her eyes or despair at the world she lived in. She turned away her head and sat down as if she must, as if her legs would no longer support her. 'Oh, I don't condone it,' she said. 'It's too soon yet, I can't fully realise it.' She swept back the fair hair which had tumbled across her forehead. 'But, d'you know what jealousy is? Have you ever known it? Have you?'

David didn't answer that. 'Is that what he told you?' he asked. 'That he did it from jealousy?'

'Of course.' Her voice was hard and brittle. 'He went over the edge. It was an impulse, he wasn't sane.'

'You're so wrong, Susan.' She had let the christian name pass. From indifference, he thought bitterly. 'I want to tell you something. It might comfort you. I don't say it would make you feel differently towards North, although . . .' He sighed quickly. 'But it might make you think better of me. May I tell you?'

'If you like. I haven't anything else to do. It will pass the time.'

He had wanted very much to tell this story of his, and he would have told it to Ulph had the inspector not been otherwise occupied. It was a dreadful story and, as the truth of it had come to him by degrees during the day, he had shocked himself into a kind of horror. In a way it was as if he had invented it, as a writer of the macabre invents, and then is troubled by the sick fecundity of his own mind. But David knew that his story was true and therefore inescapable. Because it was true and it changed the whole aspect of North's conduct and North's motives, it had to be told. But this girl was the wrong audience, although to him she was right in every other respect. He already felt for her the tenderness that wants to save its object from cruel disillusionment, but it had come to him too that she might contemplate waiting for North and, during that long wait, arrive at what she now denied, condonation of an act that to her was the outcome of uncontrollable jealousy.

'North met Magdalene Heller on holiday in Devon last July,' he began. 'They fell in love. It might be better to call it a physical enslavement on North's part.' She wasn't looking at him and her face was impassive. 'When they came home,' he said, 'they began meeting, sometimes in a London pub and, no doubt, in other places as well. Magdalene wanted him because he's handsome and well-off by her standards. I've told you why he wanted her. Perhaps he also wanted children, but I don't know.' He watched her make a very faint movement of one hand. 'I think it was Magdalene who thought of the idea, who was perhaps, to put it dramatically, North's evil genius. Magdalene had a gun, you see, and in September Magdalene's husband had tried to gas himself because he knew she no longer loved him. A man who attempts suicide may attempt it again and may succeed.

'I don't know when they first began to plan it. Perhaps not until after Christmas. It would have been in January or February that Magdalene gave North one of Heller's business reply cards to hand to Louise and propose that they have central heating installed. No, it wasn't a coincidence that Heller happened to work in the Matchdown Park area.

It was because he did that Magdalene formed their plan on these particular lines.'

'What lines?' she said in a low, scarcely audible voice.

'As soon as Louise had filled in the card and signed it,' he went on, 'she began to tell her neighbours about the central heating project. Heller came along in his car to discuss it with her and every time he came that dog barked so that everyone was aware of his visits. Louise North had been looking very unhappy because she too knew that her husband was being unfaithful to her. She talked to no one of it, but she couldn't help the misery that showed in her face. She had only one thing to distract her, the plan for improving the heating of her house, and of course she told her neighbours about it. But when North was asked by them for his opinion on the scheme, he simply denied all knowledge of it. For this was the one sure way of making certain that Heller's visits would be taken as illicit.'

Now, at last, she did turn her eyes to his. 'But that is quite absurd.' Indignation had replaced all the deadening effect of shock. 'Of course people asked Bob about his central heating and of course he denied it. He told a friend of mine quite decidedly that he couldn't afford central heating. This idea of yours – I don't know what you're leading up to – this idea is ridiculous. If Bob had been lying, what do you suppose would have happened if people had asked him and Louise about it when they were together? Very probably they did ask.'

'And if they did?' David asked quietly. 'Wouldn't it have made them believe all the more firmly in Louise's guilt to hear her insist while her husband turned away and looked embarrassed? Wouldn't they have felt sorry for him as the deceived husband doing everything he could to conceal his wife's treachery?'

'Louise North was in love with Heller,' she said stubbornly. 'He came here three or four times and Bob knew very well why he was coming. Look, I know you're obsessed with these ideas of yours, but you weren't living here. You don't know the people involved. The day before she died Louise came in here in tears to tell me all about it, to beg me to go in there the next day and hear the whole story.'

For a moment he was checked. Suppose his theory was all wrong, all hot imagination? Susan Townsend would never speak to him again. 'She actually told you,' he said urgently, 'that she was in love with Heller?'

A flicker of doubt creased the skin between her eyebrows. 'No, but I . . . Of course she came for that. Why else would she have come?'

'Perhaps to tell you that her husband was being unfaithful to her and to ask your advice.'

She looked at him blankly and then she blushed, deeply and painfully. 'You mean that I would have been a good adviser because my husband had been unfaithful to me?'

It was dreadful that he, of all people, should have to wound her in this way. His throat was dry and for a moment he couldn't speak. Then he said, 'Because of that, of what you said, she wouldn't have expected you to show much sympathy to the guilty partner of a marriage, would she? And yet that is what you believed she was.'

'I still believe it,' she said with sudden passion. 'I believe in Bob's unhappiness.'

'Yes, I expect he was unhappy. There can't be much happiness in being driven to do frightful acts by a woman like Magdalene Heller. They flared at each other at the inquest, didn't they? All acting, or perhaps the rage of Lady Macbeth?'

'What are you really trying to say?'

'That Bernard Heller and Louise North weren't lovers at all. That they were never more to each other than salesman and housewife.'

20

She took a cigarette and lit it before he could. Her hands were very steady. The puffiness under her eyes had almost gone, leaving blue shadows. He noticed how thin her hands were, so thin that the wedding ring slid to the first joint when she moved her fingers.

He stammered a little. 'You've taken it very calmly. I'm glad of that.'

'Only because I know it isn't true.'

He sighed, but not with exasperation. How could he expect her to understand inconstancy, disloyalty? 'I know it's hard to take at first,' he said quietly.

'Oh, no, it isn't that.' Her face was almost serene. 'When you began I was afraid it was all going to be true, and now I know it isn't I feel, well, easier. I don't bear you any malice,' she said seriously. 'I know you meant to do the right thing. I like that.' She gave him a stiff brisk smile. 'You're a kind considerate person, really. It's true that . . .' And now she lowered her eyes. 'It's true that I let myself get fond of Bob North. We needed comfort from each other very much because . . .' Her voice had grown very matter-of-fact, 'Because we'd reached a low ebb in our lives. I'm getting over the shock of it now. I'm used to shocks,' she said. 'He did a dreadful thing and we shall never see each other again. It wasn't as if we really ever had much in common. I'm going to move away quite soon and I've always got my little boy to think of. I shall never forget Bob, how frightened he was and how haunted.' She paused and cleared her throat. 'But you want to know why I'm so sure your idea's wrong.'

'Yes,' he said tiredly, 'yes.'

'Well, then. Heller and Louise were in love, I know they were. You see, Heller was writing love-letters to Louise as far back as last November. I've got them here – Bob left them with me – and you can see them if you like.'

'Forged,' David said, as he turned them over in his hands, although he knew they couldn't be. He had remembered them now, letters which had been identified in court by Magdalene and by *Equatair's* managing director and by Bernard's own brother. 'No, I know they can't be.' He read them while she, lighting a second cigarette from the first, watched him with gentle sadness.

'You see, they're both dated 1967, last year.'

He read them again, slowly and carefully, and he looked again at the dates, November 6th, '67, and December 2nd, '67. There was no doubt when they had been written, but there was something wrong with them just the same. 'He is not an old man and may live for years. He has no rights, no hold over you that anyone would recognise these days.'

'How old is North?' he asked.

'I don't know,' she said and she stopped, distress puckering her face. 'About thirty, in his early thirties.'

'Odd,' David said. 'Strange that Heller should have described him like that.'

'But it's true, he isn't an old man.'

'No, he's so young that it was absurd of anyone who knew his age to write of him like that. That's the way you talk of someone in late middle-age, someone of, say, fifty-five. It's as if Heller were arguing with someone very young, putting the maturer, more realistic viewpoint. And what about this? "We just have to hang on and wait till he dies." Why should North have died? He's strong and healthy, isn't he, as well as young? And that about his rights, about him having no rights that anyone would recognise these days. I should think ninety per cent of the population wouldn't deny that husbands and wives have legal and moral rights over each other, and the hold is pretty strong.'

'It takes a good deal of legal machinery to break it,' she said dryly. 'But you're forgetting that Heller was in an unstable state, he was writing hysterically.'

'And yet these letters aren't hysterical. Parts of them are calm and tender. May I ask why North gave them to you?'

'He wanted them burnt. He hadn't the strength of will to do it himself.'

David almost laughed. The man had wanted them burnt all right because although on first glance, on cursory examination, they seemed genuine, a closer perusal might have shown some oddity that revealed Louise could not have been their recipient. Why had he shown them to Susan Townsend? Because he wanted to be sure of her sympathy, her pity, her recognition of himself as injured. He had succeeded, David thought bitterly.

'Do you know what I think?' She didn't, she didn't seem to want to. She was listening to him out of politeness. He went on just the same. 'I believe the man referred to wasn't a husband at all. The woman who received these letters was tied to someone, certainly, but tied only by duty.' He looked up and saw that she was very tired. 'Forgive me,' he said. 'May I take these letters away with me?'

'I don't see why you shouldn't. No one else wants them.'

She gave him her hand, passed before him into the hall. It was as if he had called to see her on some practical business, as if he and not the society photographer had bought her house.

'You shouldn't be alone,' he said impulsively. 'I wouldn't leave you, only you must loathe the sight of me.'

'Of course I don't, but I'm quite used to being alone. I was in a bad state after the inquest, but I was ill then.' She opened the front door and as soon as he appeared, framed in light, the dog began to howl. No wonder North had stroked its head, patted it, that last night David had been here, for it had been his innocent henchman. 'I wish we could have met under different circumstances,' she said.

'But we have met.' He didn't wait for her answer, for it might have quenched hope.

Until she was married Magdalene Heller had lived with her father, a victim of multiple sclerosis, aged about fifty-five. She had been a devoted nurse to him until she went to London and met Bernard. But she couldn't get married and leave her father; she had to wait for him to die. Mr Chant must have needed a great deal of care and attention that could only be provided by the daughter who understood. The chronic invalid was harsh and ungrateful, resenting the health of the girl who nursed him and sometimes violent to her. But it was her duty to stay with him and see her fiancé only occasionally, when he could come and stay near her in Exeter or she manage a day in London.

David assembled these facts in his mind and when he came to East Mulvihill he had formed a theory, subsidiary to his first, like the tiny offshoot on the body of a hydra. Carl Heller opened the door of the flat to him. Did Magdalene retain him there like a porter to do her bidding? His dull lethargic face was abject tonight, the heavy jowls as pendulous as a bloodhound's.

'You have seen the morning papers?' he asked, pausing between each guttural word. 'They have arrested Mr North for killing my brother.' Never before had David seen anyone actually wring his hands. 'Oh, my brother and his wrongdoing . . .' He seized David's arm with a quick clumsy movement. 'I can't believe it. Magdalene is sick, lying down. Yesterday when he did not come and he did not phone I thought she would go mad.' He shook his head, threw up his hands. 'She is better now, calmer. And all this misery has come upon us through my brother's wrongdoing.'

'I don't believe he did anything wrong, Mr Heller. He wrote some letters once to Mrs North, didn't he?'

'Wicked letters. I shall never forget how in the court I had to say those letters were written by my brother to that woman.'

'But he did write them to her?' David followed him into the sitting-room. The table was bare and the place tidy, but every piece of furniture was filmed with two days' dust.

Carl sat down, but jumped up again immediately and began to lumber about the room like a carthorse in a stall made for a pony. 'I don't mean he did not write them,' he said, but that I was ashamed to say he had. My brother to write of poor Mr North that he was useless and better dead!'

'Mr Heller . . .' David knew that it would be pointless to try to explain anything to this man whose slow stupidity was intensified because he was distraught. 'Will you tell me something? It may be meaningless to you, not to the point at all, but tell me, how did Bernard make his sevens?'

Astonishment, anger even, at the apparent inconsequence of the question wrinkled Carl's brow while his face – did he think David was mocking righteous chagrin? – flushed a dull brick red. But he stopped pacing and, taking the pencil David handed to him, licking the tip of it, drew a seven with a tick across the ascender.

'I thought so. He was educated in Europe, in Switzerland. Now make a one the way Bernard did.'

For a moment it seemed as if Carl wouldn't comply. The frown deepening, he stared at David, and then, shrugging, drew on the paper an outline very like an English seven. David slid the paper from under the big hand and looked at it thoughtfully. Magdalene had married Bernard in 1962, had met him in 1961. It all fitted and yet . . . Why hadn't the police seen who had access to Bernard's current notebooks, why hadn't the managing director of *Equatair* who knew Bernard's writing and style of making figures, why hadn't Carl?

'You said to me once that for the sake of getting on in his job, Bernard wanted to appear as English as possible. Did he ever alter his way of making these continental ones and sevens?'

'I think he may have.' Carl nodded, not understanding, not wanting to understand. 'Five years ago he said to me he would make himself so English no one would know.'

David said softly, 'Five years ago, then, he began to write his sevens without the tick and his ones as an upright stroke . . .' He said it softly because he had heard a door open behind him and footsteps in the narrow passage.

She was in a dressing-gown. A negligée would have been wrong for her and the thing she wore was a long stiff bell of quilted stuff, black shot through with blood red. It caught the light like armour. Her face was white and stiff and quite old-looking. She was a queen on a court card, the queen of spades.

'Back again?' she said. She was trying to be defiant but she was too frightened to manage the strong voice necessary for defiance. 'I want a drink of water,' she said to Carl. He fetched it, nodding humbly. Her nails rattled against the glass and she spilled some of the water. It trickled down her chin and on to the black quilting. Now she had a voice again, a poor travesty of a voice, as if she had really aged. 'Bob North killed them, after all. Just as well we didn't have any more to do with him. He must have been a fool, letting himself get caught like that.'

'Murderers ought to be caught,' said Carl stupidly.

'They ought to be tough,' she said, 'and see they don't.'

'I wonder if you would be tough enough,' David said, and he added conversationally as he got up, 'It would be interesting to see.' It will be interesting, he thought, tonight, or tomorrow. The green eyes, iridescent, shallow, rested on him for a long moment, and then she went back into the bedroom, the glass in her hand, her long stiff skirts rustling on the floor. He listened as he passed the door but behind it there was only a silence so deep as to be stronger and more frightening than any sound.

'I wanted to know,' David said when she answered the phone, 'if you were all right.'

'But you phoned last night to know that,' she protested, 'and again this morning.' At least, he thought, she didn't say, 'Back again?' 'I'm quite all right. Really I am. Only the police are here all the time . . .'

'I want to see them myself, but afterwards, may I come and see you?'

'If you like.' she said. 'If you like, David.' She had called him by his name and his heart turned a little. 'But no stories, no theories. I couldn't stand any more.'

'I promise,' he said. She would have to attend the trial and by then she would know him well enough to let him go with her. She would hear it all there and she would need him beside her when she heard the evidence against the two people in the dock.

So David put the phone down and went to tell Ulph what Magdalene Heller and Robert North had done. How they had invented a love affair between two mild and gentle people who had never harmed them except by existing; how they had spread upon their characters so much filth that her friends and neighbours and his twin brother had vilified them; how they had done it simply because Louise North could not divorce her husband and Heller was going to take his wife away to Switzerland.

But before he went into the station entrance, he paused for a moment and leaned against the railings of the treeless park. They had driven past this place, he and Bernard Heller, and yet it was not as he had been then that David suddenly saw him, nor as he had been when he lay dead in the arms of the dead woman he had never really known. He remembered instead the fat jovial clown and the tedious jokes and the unfailing generous kindness.

Perhaps he would tell Ulph of his last discovery first. He was not a vindictive man, but he wanted to see Ulph's face when he learned that Magdalene Heller had kept her own love-letters, the letters Bernard had sent her in 1961, and used them as the documentary evidence of an adultery that had never been. He wanted to see Ulph's expression and, ultimately that of a judge and a jury.